D1011193

Also by John Marco

THE EYES OF GOD
THE DEVIL'S ARMOR
THE SWORD OF ANGELS

THE SKYLORDS:
STARFINDER

STARFINDER

A Skylords Novel

JOHN MARCO

DAW BOOKS, INC.

DONALD A. WOLLHEIM, FOUNDER

375 Hudson Street, New York, NY 10014

ELIZABETH R. WOLLHEIM

SHEILA E. GILBERT

PUBLISHERS

http://www.dawbooks.com

Copyright © 2009 by John Marco.
All rights reserved.

Jacket art and frontspieces by Tom Kidd.

DAW Book Collectors No. 1473.

DAW Books are distributed by Penguin Group (USA).
Book designed by Elizabeth Glover.

All characters and events in this book are fictitious.
All resemblance to persons living or dead is strictly coincidental.

The scanning, uploading and distribution of this book via the Internet or via any other means without the permission of the publisher is illegal, and punishable by law. Please purchase only authorized electronic editions, and do not participate in or encourage the electronic piracy of copyrighted materials. Your support of the author's rights is appreciated.

First Printing, May 2009
1 2 3 4 5 6 7 8 9 10

DAW TRADEMARK REGISTERED
U.S. PAT. AND TM. OFF. AND FOREIGN COUNTRIES
—MARCA REGISTRADA
HECHO EN U.S.A.

PRINTED IN THE USA

For Melissa, Christopher, Victoria, Anthony, Justin, and of course, Jack, the first person ever to see a cloud horse.

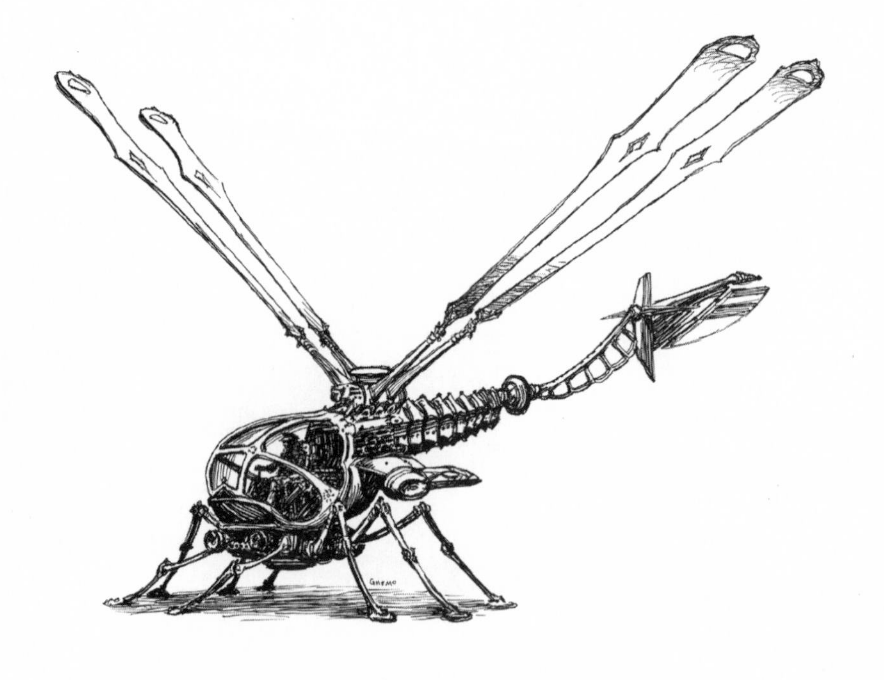

THE EDGE OF THE WORLD

MOTH WAS FLYING his kite near the aerodrome when he heard the dragonfly crash.

Just minutes before he had seen the craft overhead, its four wings rapidly beating the mountain air. Now the heat of the crash splashed against Moth's face. The kite unspooled from his hand, floating helplessly away. The wind was strongest here at the north side, blowing the dragonfly off course. The mangled wings of the vessel stuck out from the ground, drooping in the flames. Moth raced toward the wreckage, pumping his arms and looking toward the aerodrome. Others had seen the crash too and were hurrying to help. Another dragonfly buzzed loudly overhead, circling the airfield.

"Skyhigh!" Moth cried, waving at the craft, hoping frantically his friend was aboard.

Moth skidded to a stop when he reached the wreck. Flames had engulfed the long tail section and the craft had cracked in two. Behind the cloudy canopy Moth could see the pilot slumped over his controls. A helmet hid his head and his face was turned away.

"Hold on!" shouted Moth, not knowing if the man could hear him or not. He would need help to free the pilot, but help was still far away. Moth swatted at the smoke. The sting of fire pricked his face. At thirteen, Moth was a wiry, slight boy, faster than he was strong. He had grown up around the aerodrome and had seen dragonflies crash before.

"I'm coming!" he told the man. "Don't be dead. Oh, please don't be!"

Flames reached for his clothes. Moth climbed over the bent nose of the craft and, without thinking, used a hand to steady himself. He cried out as the hot metal burned his skin, making him stagger back. Men from the aerodrome were rushing forward. Not far away, the other dragonfly settled onto its landing claws, its mechanical wings shaking Moth's bones.

"I can't reach him!" yelled Moth to the unseen pilot. "Hurry before he cooks in there!"

The dragonfly's canopy popped up and out hurried Skyhigh, ripping off his helmet and pulling himself from the cockpit. Sweaty blond hair drooped into his eyes as he scrambled down from his aircraft, waving madly for Moth to move away.

"Move off!" bellowed the Skyknight. He charged forward, holding his helmet by the strap like a sling. Moth stepped aside, watching as the young man climbed across the same pile of bent metal, his gloved hands pulling him toward the canopy. "Close your eyes!" Skyhigh ordered. His arm cocked back and he let his helmet fly, swinging it like a hammer against the glass canopy. The canopy shattered. Skyhigh pulled at the shards of glass, trying frantically to reach his fellow Skyknight. Moth once again climbed atop the debris, wanting to help.

"Is he alive?"

"I told you to go!" roared Skyhigh, not even taking the time to look at Moth as he peeled back sections of glass and struts of metal. Others had finally reached the wreckage now, men like Skyhigh dressed in dark blue uniforms or brown leather jackets. A man with an axe shouldered past Moth, smashing down the twists of metal. Behind Moth, someone boomed out his name.

"Moth!"

Major Hark stood away from the smoke and flames, letting his men swarm in to help. The rock-jawed commander beckoned to Moth with a crooked finger. "Get over here *now*."

Moth jumped down from the broken fuselage. "I couldn't

get to him," he explained, frustrated. "I tried, but the fire . . . It was too hot."

Major Hark snarled, "You don't have gloves or an axe or anything! You keep away from the wrecks, you hear me? You're a *kid*."

"So what? I work at the aerodrome! I should do nothing?"

For a moment Hark forgot about the crash and his wounded man. He reached out and snatched Moth by the collar, pulling him further from the scene. "You could have been killed, boy. What if you'd fallen?" Hark snapped Moth's collar, letting him go. "You're lucky your clothes didn't catch fire."

Moth had worked in the aerodrome for nearly three years now and was used to Hark's chewings out. The Major had always been fair to him, though, and Moth wasn't really afraid of him.

"I was the first one here," Moth grumbled, looking back toward the others. They had managed to pull the pilot free of the cockpit, grabbing hold of his limp arms. Skyhigh watched with a worried expression, his face red and smudgy. A crowd started to gather from the aerodrome. Among them were some squires, boys about Moth's age who looked after the Skyknights and their airships. Moth shot them his usual look of contempt. He was as close to Skyhigh as any of the squires, but he was not a squire himself and never could be.

"It's Diggy," said Hark, sighing at the unconscious pilot. Diggy was one of the younger pilots, like Skyhigh. Friendly, too.

"Is he alive?" Moth asked.

Major Hark barked to his men, "Well? Did he make it?"

One of the rescuers pulled off Diggy's helmet and put his fingers to his neck. "He's alive!" he called back, and the other Skyknights cheered. The man kneeling over Diggy started cutting the scarf around his throat free. Another pulled up his eyelids and stared into his eyes. Skyhigh tugged off his gloves and tossed them to the ground, shaking his head.

"Come on, Diggy," he muttered.

His pain knifed at Moth. Skyhigh Coralin was more than just a friend. He was everything Moth dreamed of one day being.

He was also the best pilot Moth had ever seen. Like all the other pilots, Skyhigh had given up everything to come to Calio just so he could fly. In other cities a man could be a baker or a physician, but anyone who dreamed of flying belonged in only one place, really—Calio. The mountain city. The edge of the world.

Major Hark called to Skyhigh. "Coralin, get your ship out of here. Get back to the aerodrome."

Skyhigh finally lifted his blue eyes. "What about Diggy?"

"Nothing for you to do. Just get your ship away from the cliff."

The winds at the edge of the field could easily lift the dragonfly if they gusted just right. Calio wasn't just the end of their world; it was also the highest city ever built. To the north of Calio stretched the Reach, like a sea of fog that never ended. Flat and peaceful, the mists went on to the horizon, but over the Reach loomed Calio, standing guard against the things within it—and beyond.

Skyhigh reached for the gloves he had thrown down. "Moth, come here," he called.

Eager to get away from Hark, Moth bolted toward Skyhigh. Hark called over to him to stay clear of trouble, but Moth wasn't listening. He was glad his friend was safe, and not in the wreck that had grounded Diggy.

"You all right?" Skyhigh asked as he pulled on his gloves.

"Yeah, fine," Moth nodded. "Diggy will be all right too. You'll see."

Skyhigh turned and started back toward his own dragonfly. Among the Skyknights it was bad luck to talk about crashes. When their friend Pepper had died, Skyhigh had just shrugged and said, "Flying is dangerous," but Moth knew how broken up he'd felt. He looked that way now, too, his blue eyes full of distance.

"What were you doing out here?" asked Skyhigh.

"Flying my . . ." Moth stopped walking. "Oh, my kite!" He looked back to where he'd been flying the kite, but of course it was gone now, taken by the winds into the foggy Reach. "Leroux made it for me," he sighed. What would he tell the old man? His birthday gift was gone, and he'd only had it for an hour.

Skyhigh continued toward his waiting ship. Moth hurried after him. "No maneuvers for me tonight," said Skyhigh. "I'll be at your party."

"Great." Moth was barely listening. The gleaming metal of the dragonfly entranced him. Only Skyknights flew in the crafts, and sometimes so did their lucky squires. Moth thought the ships beautiful, long and slender like the insect they were named for, with four glassy wings. They were still a new invention, though, and only Lord Rendor—now Governor of Calio—really understood them.

"I've got something for you," said Skyhigh.

Moth broke from his trance. "Huh?"

"A present for your birthday. You listening?"

"Yeah." Moth smiled. "You know what I really want for my birthday?"

"Yup." Skyhigh glanced over at the crowd. Hark was already walking back to the aerodrome. "Get in fast. Don't let the others see you."

Excitement propelled Moth up the fuselage, Skyhigh blocking him from view as he scrambled into the cockpit. There were two seats in a dragonfly—one for the pilot and one for a passenger. The passenger seat was smaller and more cramped than the pilot's, but Moth didn't care. He ducked down into it, feeling only a little guilty.

Diggy'll be fine, he told himself.

Skyhigh climbed in after Moth, pulling the canopy down over them. Moth peered over his shoulder to watch him work the controls. He tossed some switches and the wings began to flutter. A hum went through the vessel as its strange engine warmed the cockpit.

"What about Fiona?" Skyhigh said loudly.

Why was he asking about her now? "What do you mean?" said Moth.

"Will she be there?"

"If she can." Moth hoped Fiona would come to his party, but admitting that would only make things worse. He could just make out Skyhigh's grin. "We're friends."

"Uh-huh." Skyhigh's leathered fingers wrapped around

the control sticks. The whine of the engine grew as the wings speeded up, almost disappearing. “Hold on.”

Moth held tightly to his seat. Skyhigh tugged the sticks and the dragonfly leaped skyward. It was only a league or two to the hangars, but Moth didn’t care. The ride would be short but astonishing.

THE KNIGHT AND THE KESTREL

MOTH LEFT THE AERODROME grinning with excitement. A flight in a dragonfly was the best birthday gift Skyhigh could have given him, and his ears still rang from the racket of wings and whirring engine. As he walked dizzily along the avenue to his home, his legs wobbled a bit from the ride. Skyknights got used to the sensation, he knew, but young riders like Moth usually threw up. Moth hadn't thrown up and was proud of himself for that. One day, if he was really lucky, he might be a Skyknight himself.

The apartment he shared with Leroux was far from the aerodrome, in a tall building of orange stone overlooking the city square. It was a building full of poor folks and pensioners like Leroux, crammed into the oldest section of Calio. A hundred coats of paint flaked from the building into the street, and above his head Moth could see some of the place's occupants out on their tiny balconies. After three years with Leroux, Moth knew almost all of them. He waved up at old Mrs. Jilla.

"Moth," she called down to him, happy to see him. "I made your birthday cake." She gestured with her hand. "This thick, with berry cream on top!"

Mrs. Jilla always shouted, even when she was standing next to you. "Thanks a lot," Moth hollered back. "See you later!"

He began climbing the stone steps to Leroux's apartment. Decades of wind and rain had worn the stairs dangerously smooth. Moth kept a grip on the rusty metal railing to keep from falling. The perilous trek down to the square had kept Leroux indoors lately. The old knight looked frailer than usual too, unable to shake a cough that had lodged itself in his lungs. Worried, Moth forgot about his lost kite and his ride in the dragonfly. Maybe a party wasn't a good idea.

When he reached the door to the apartment, a gas light flickered to life over the threshold. Their apartment had one of the few lights that still worked, always coming on at dusk. Moth pushed open the unlocked door and cheerfully announced himself.

"Leroux, I'm home," he called, stepping inside.

There were only two rooms in the apartment, and Leroux wasn't in the main living space. Moth supposed he might be napping in his bed, then noticed the top of his white head out on the balcony. Most of the building's apartments loomed over the square, but Leroux's had what the landlord called a "mountain view." They were in the harshest, ugliest part of the country, and having a view of the mountains wasn't something to be envied.

To Moth's delight Leroux had decorated the apartment for his party. The old knight had cleaned up Moth's usual mess of books and papers and had laid out the plates and glasses. Mrs. Jilla's cake took center stage on the table, a fluffy, pink confection with roses made of frosting.

"Flowers?" grumbled Moth. He thought of sticking a finger in the berry cream but stopped himself. Paper streamers hung from the cracked ceiling and bowls filled with Moth's favorite snacks were placed around the room. Leroux had spent money he really didn't have on the party, making Moth feel worse.

"I'll tell him about the kite tomorrow," Moth decided, then slid open the grimy glass door of the balcony. "Everything looks great, Leroux. Thanks a . . ."

Moth stopped talking at once. Old Leroux was sitting in his chair, staring out over the hills. His pet, an old kestrel he called Lady Esme, perched on the balcony's shaky railing. She had been with Leroux since anyone could remember, much longer than a bird should live, but her feathers looked as bright as an eagle's. But time had been less kind to Leroux. Gaunt from lack of appetite, his once clear eyes were misty with cataracts. His hair, snowy white, was combed lifelessly to the side.

"You're home?" said Leroux, struggling to his feet. "I didn't hear you."

Moth tried to hide his distress. "Why are you dressed like that?"

Instead of his usual clothes, Leroux had dug out his old uniform. A worn-out grey coat hung down to his knees. On it was emblazoned the crest of his old order, the long-dead Eldrin Knights. He wore the boots as well, scuffed and faded. A great buckle of tarnished silver cinched a wide belt around his pencil-like waist. Leroux stood as straight as he could.

"Like it?" he asked Moth. "It still fits—see?"

The truth was that it barely fit at all. In his younger days Leroux had been quite muscular. "Yeah, it does," Moth lied. "But why?"

"You turning thirteen put me in mind of it," said Leroux. But Moth's reaction had embarrassed him. "I won't wear it tonight, don't worry. I just wanted you to see what I looked like once."

Living with Leroux had never been dull. The old man was full of surprises, and not all of them good. He had always been strange, ever since Moth had met him. Back then he used to spend all day in the square with his kestrel, telling stories about his days as an Eldrin Knight and watching the new breed of warriors sail overhead in their airships. At ten years old, Moth had been enamored of the old man's tales. Especially the ones about the Skylords.

"Leroux, you should rest," said Moth. Now that the sun was going down the chill had picked up. "Come inside with me."

"You sit with me here," said Leroux. There was room enough for only two chairs on the balcony. The better, less rusted one was Moth's. Leroux gestured toward it. "Tell me about the kite. Did it fly well?"

"Great," said Moth as he took a seat. On the floor between their chairs sat a bowl of gumdrops. Moth watched as Leroux picked up the bowl and tossed one of the treats to Lady Esme.

"I figured she should have something special today, too," said Leroux.

Lady Esme ate every kind of food imaginable, except of course birdseed. At supper time she always sampled from both their plates.

"Who shopped for you?" asked Moth. "Mrs. Jilla?"

Leroux began coughing, answering only with a nod. To Moth the cough sounded frighteningly familiar.

"It's what happens when you're old," Dr. Trik had told Moth. "Keep him comfortable and rested. And keep him away from the candy!"

There didn't seem much sense in that, so Moth let Leroux eat as many gumdrops as he wanted. Between the old man and the bird, Moth was going to the candy shop nearly every other day. His job at the aerodrome paid only pennies, but he had everything he needed, thanks to Leroux, and didn't mind spending his money on treats.

"If your mother was here," said Leroux, popping a candy into his mouth, "she'd be proud of the way you've grown up. *I'm* proud of you, Moth. You know that, yes?"

"Yeah," Moth answered.

"I know it's not the same," said Leroux. "It's all right to miss her."

Suddenly Moth couldn't talk. His mother had been dead for three years now, taken by the same kind of coughing sickness Leroux seemed to have. Being so high up in the mountains made it easy to get sick, but remembering his mother had never gotten easier for Moth. He had no brothers and sisters, and had never known his father. He didn't even know why his mother had ever come to Calio. All he had was Leroux, a grandfatherly friend who'd taken pity on an orphan.

Far below, the train to Medona blew its mournful whistle, following the winding tracks through the mountains. Dark smoke puffed from its stack, hanging like a cloud in the air. The train was their only real link to the rest of the world, and every time it arrived was an event. Moth liked the train almost as much as the dragonflies and airships.

One day, thought Moth, *maybe I'll be on that train.*

"If I can't be a Skyknight, that's what I'll do," he said.

"Eh?"

"The train. I'll see the world, even if I can't see it from the sky."

"Don't give up on your dreams," said Leroux. "That's what old people do." He held out his arm for Lady Esme. The kestrel hopped on, her talons gently grabbing the fabric of his coat. "Now that you're thirteen you can show them you're a man." Leroux smiled. "When I was thirteen I squired for an Eldrin Knight. That's the age to do it."

"That's not how it works anymore. They save those jobs for important kids. Sons of lords and governors. Not sons of cleaning ladies."

It was an argument Leroux always refused to accept. This time, though, it saddened him. "If there was someone I could talk to for you, I would," he said. "But they're all gone. No one listens to an Eldrin Knight anymore. Only you and Esme listen to me now."

"Listen to your stories, you mean," joked Moth. He reached over and took a gumdrop for himself. "I don't mind. Never have."

Old Leroux narrowed his eyes on the mountains. "I have one more story for you, Moth."

"Really? I thought I heard them all." He sucked on the candy, hoping for one of Leroux's grand tales about the land beyond the Reach. It was forbidden for anyone to cross the Reach, and those who tried surely never made it. The Reach bewitched people, making it impossible to cross. But Leroux had done it, or so he claimed, and his stories about the world beyond their own were legendary. "So?" asked Moth. "What's it about? The Skylords?"

Leroux dodged the question. "Later. Your friends will be here soon."

"We got time," said Moth. "I told them to come after supper. Go on, tell me the story."

"This is a special story, Moth. It's a gift. To tell you now would spoil it."

"A gift?" Moth grew intrigued. "A birthday gift?"

"Of course. You think all I have for you is a kite?"

Moth grimaced. "Yeah, about the kite . . ."

"You're old enough now to hear this story, Moth." Leroux settled back in his chair, looking as if he might fall asleep. "And to have the gift."

The old man had lapsed into one of his senseless moods. "All right," said Moth softly. "You can tell me the story later. Whatever you want, okay?"

Leroux closed his eyes. "I'm tired. Let me rest a little. Wake me when your friends come."

Moth agreed, waiting with Leroux until the old man drifted to sleep. His words about stories and gifts baffled Moth, and worried him too.

He's getting worse, he realized.

Leroux's kestrel, Lady Esme, had hopped back onto the railing. Instead of eating gumdrops, though, she stared at Moth with the strangest eyes he had ever seen.

DINNER

FIONA SAT AT THE ENORMOUS TABLE, her eyes fixed in an empty stare at the gleaming silverware and crystal. Trays of food lay cold under metal lids. At the opposite side of the table, a vacant chair waited for Fiona's grandfather to arrive. An embarrassing silence hung over the dining room. Fiona blew a strand of red hair out of her eyes just to hear a noise.

Two of the mansion's servants stood near the table, beneath a gigantic painting of an old fashioned fox hunt. Their names were Jonathan and Lucie, a married couple who, like all the mansion's servants, had arrived in Calio long before Fiona and her grandfather. Jonathan and Lucie had served the last three Governors of Calio, in fact, and knew every minor fact about the grand house. They were impeccable, uncomplaining, and, to fourteen-year-old Fiona, as boring as everything else about the city.

Fiona hated Calio. Through the window of the dining room, she could see why it was called "the edge of the world." Calio was a two day train ride from Medona and four days from Capital City, where Fiona was raised. She had left behind her friends and everything familiar, falling into her grandfather's hands when her parents had suddenly died. For three months now she had been with her grandfather Rendor, yet still she hardly knew him.

Jonathan cleared his throat to break the silence. "Mistress Fiona, you've waited the proper amount of time now. I'm sure the Governor wouldn't mind you starting without him."

But Fiona wasn't hungry. These meals with her grandfather always killed her appetite. Luckily, he'd been too busy lately to bother with them more than once a week.

"It's okay," said Fiona absently. Secretly she liked her grandfather being late. It always forced him to apologize to her. Still, there was Moth's party to attend. If her grandfather didn't get here soon. . . .

Outside the sun dropped below the hills, yet she could still make out the mists of the Reach in the fading light. Growing up she had heard about the Reach and wondered what it really looked like. Now that she had seen it for herself Fiona wasn't impressed. To her it looked like a cottony blanket, bumpy and white, spreading out forever so that it covered the whole north world.

Could it really be that big, she wondered? Some folks believed faeries lived beyond the Reach. Old Leroux thought so, at least. Fiona didn't know what to believe.

"It's the land of the Skylords," her grandfather had told her. It was why they had come to Calio, and why the city had been built. "The Skylord problem," that's what her grandfather called it. And the important people back in Capital City believed him enough to make him a governor.

Looking at the Reach, Fiona simply couldn't imagine anything dangerous about it. It all seemed so peaceful to her. If the Skylords did exist, they had been quiet for hundreds of years.

At last the doors of the dining room opened and her grandfather breezed into the chamber. He straightened the tie beneath his bearded chin, dressed in his usual blue suit and grey waistcoat.

"I'm sorry," he announced. "Business."

He smoothed down his clothes, composing himself. After three months together, the old man was still uncomfortable around Fiona.

Because he doesn't want to be here, she thought blackly. *Because he'd rather be working.*

Her grandfather Rendor always kept a full schedule. He was over sixty now, yet he remained virile and quick. He was even handsome, Fiona supposed. Striking, like her mother. Fiona wasn't like either of them. With a teenager's awkward bones and her shocking red hair, she knew she would never become the beauty her mother had been. Nor would she be a genius like her grandfather.

The Governor let Jonathan pull out his chair, then smiled cordially at Lucie as she poured him a glass of wine. When he looked across the table at Fiona, he seemed ridiculously far away.

"You waited for me," he said. "You needn't have."

"You're the one who wants these dinners," Fiona replied.

Her sharp reply drew a frown from her grandfather. "Family is important, Fiona. I make what time I can for you."

Family was the one thing neither of them had anymore. Fiona was an only child, and Rendor's wife had left him years ago.

Probably because he paid no attention to her, guessed Fiona.

Her mother had been an only child, too. She had told Fiona once that her grandfather had always been secretive and ambitious. He had even been a soldier once, one of the legendary Eldrin Knights, but Fiona found it hard to picture that. He was cold and distant, and his coldness had driven Fiona's mother to marry the first man who ever showed her kindness—Fiona's father. When the airship accident had taken them away, only Rendor was left to care for Fiona.

Jonathan and Lucie went to work serving the food—a fricassee of duck, a hodgepodge of vegetables, bread that had gone stone cold and goat cheese from the farms that clung to the side of the mountain. Lucie spooned small portions of everything into Fiona's plate, even laying a napkin across her lap. Fiona watched as her grandfather tore hungrily into the food.

"So?" he said after a moment. "Tell me about your day."

It was the same question he always asked, not even bothering to look up from his food.

"I took a walk," said Fiona. "Down to the farms."

"See anything interesting?"

Fiona shrugged. "Some animals."

Rendor reached across the table for the bread, tearing off a great hunk and dipping it in his gravy. Fiona sighed, picking at her duck with her fork. Then, a wicked little idea popped into her brain.

"I heard that a dragonfly crashed today," she said.

Her grandfather's chewing slowed. "That's right." He motioned for Jonathan to serve him more duck.

"Is the pilot okay?"

"Some bruises," said Rendor. "Nothing serious."

"How many is that since we came here? Crashes, I mean. Three?"

"Bad wind," said her grandfather. "That's how it gets at the end of the day. The wind comes out of the Reach."

"Oh." Fiona pretended to be very interested. "The dragonflies don't do so good here, huh? Is that why you've been so busy lately? Working out the kinks?"

All the pleasantness left the old man's bearded face. *"Kinks?* There are no kinks in the dragonflies, Fiona. They're precision machines. It takes a better pilot than most to fly them up here, that's all."

Rendor was famously proud of his inventions. His obsession for flight had led him to create the airships, the great, teardrop-shaped vessels that floated through the countryside. There were always airships in Calio, tethered at the aerodrome or making the trek back to Medona. But the dragonfly was his greatest achievement. Fiona had been six years old when the first one took flight.

"If it's too high and windy here, why not move them away?" asked Fiona. "Build an aerodrome back in Medona, or maybe Capital City."

"You know why, Fiona. Because of the Skylords."

"But they crash here. People die when your ships crash."

As soon as she'd said it, Fiona knew she'd gone too far. Her grandfather put down his fork and gazed at her across the table.

"You think I don't care about that."

"Grandfather, I—"

"No, you do. You think I don't care when people die, that all I care about is my work. But my work is important, Fiona. You're young. You have no idea how things really are or the dangers we face. What I do protects Calio, Fiona. It protects our whole world."

Fiona felt her face growing hot. "I don't see anything to be afraid of," she said. She pointed out toward the Reach. "You know what that looks like to me? A lot of nothing. No one's even seen a Skylord. Why should we be afraid of something we can't see?"

Instead of answering her question, her grandfather returned to his meal. "Someday," he said calmly, "mankind won't have to be afraid of the Skylords. Someday we'll have enough airships and dragonflies to defend ourselves from everything across the Reach." He picked up his wine as if about to toast what he'd just said. "By the time you're my age, Fiona, airships will be everywhere. They'll replace the trains and all the horses and carts, too. Flying will be everyone's gift. And it'll be safe." He took a sip of wine, then looked seriously at Fiona. "Do you blame me for what happened to your parents?"

Fiona sat very still in her chair. She was about to lie, then said, "Yes."

Her grandfather picked up his fork and knife again. "Good. That's out of the way, then." He went back to eating. "In a few days there'll be an important meeting here. There'll be governors coming from the other provinces. I won't be able to spend any time with you, Fiona."

"Governors? Coming all the way out here? Why?"

"To talk about the Skylord problem," said Rendor. "I'll need you to stay out of the way, please."

Fiona pushed her plate forward. "Can I be excused now?"

Rendor looked up, finally noticing she hadn't eaten a bite. "Aren't you hungry?"

"I'm going to a party tonight. I'll eat there."

"What party? Not for that boy Moth, I hope."

"It's his birthday," Fiona explained. "I told him I'd be there."

"He's a cleaning boy, Fiona. I'm a Governor, for pity's sake. You running around with him makes you look like a vagabond."

"He's my friend. I don't have any other friends, Grandfather."

Rendor's expression grew thunderous. "That's my fault too, is it?"

"There are no girls my age here! Nothing but boys and old men."

"It's a big city, Fiona. You'll find other friends if you look harder."

Fiona got out of her chair, letting her napkin fall to the floor. "What do you care what I do? You don't want me here. I'm just a burden to you. You just said it yourself; I'm in the way."

"That's not what I meant. Sit down."

"I don't want to sit down," said Fiona fiercely. "I don't want to eat dinner with you anymore. Stop asking me how my day was, *please*. Stop pretending you care about me!"

Rendor put a hand up to his forehead. A pained expression came over his face. "Jonathan, some headache powder, please," he said.

Jonathan bowed and left the dining room, eager to get away. His wife Lucie gazed down awkwardly at her feet.

"Go on, go to your party," said the governor. "We'll talk about this when my meeting is done."

Fiona paused, stunned by his decision to let her go. She decided not to thank him and headed for the door. But before she could leave her grandfather called after her.

"Fiona."

She stopped and looked at him. "What?"

"That boy, Moth. He lives with an old man. Do you know him?"

"His name is Leroux," said Fiona sharply.

"I hear that he's unwell." Her grandfather reached for the wine decanter. "Find out how he's doing for me, please."

Fiona wrinkled her nose at the request. "Why?"

"Because I want to know."

It was her grandfather's way of telling her their conversation was over. It didn't matter, though—she would be late for Moth's party if she didn't hurry.

CASTLES

DOWN IN THE DARK STREETS of Calio, the unseen clock in the clock tower struck its midnight chord. A golden moon hung directly over the Governor's mansion, lighting the gardens around the house and making shadow puppets out of the blooming flowers. The mansion stood apart from the rest of the city, perched on a small hill in the newer part of town. A five-foot wall of brick circled the mansion and its gardens, covered with crawling ivy. Thick enough for a person to walk across, the wall offered stunning views of the city and the Reach, and Fiona had quickly discovered the best spots for daydreaming.

Moth enjoyed sitting on the wall. He enjoyed being alone with Fiona, hidden from the mansion's prying eyes by the tall ash trees of the garden. When he heard the clock chiming in the distance, he realized they'd been sitting and talking for hours.

"Midnight," he whispered. He looked over his shoulder back toward the mansion, peering through the garden to see if anyone was waiting there. The mansion was surprisingly quiet. The occasional echo of a voice reached them from the streets, but the city was mostly asleep. "Should you go inside now?" Moth asked Fiona.

Fiona shook her head. She'd been quiet the whole night, even at Moth's party. She stared out past the mountain, toward the Reach. The red scarf Mrs. Jilla had made Moth for his birthday clung around her shoulders. Though summer had come to Calio, nights on the mountain were always chilly. Fiona still clutched a small sack in her hands. She had held tight to the sack the entire night. Moth was starting to think it wasn't a gift for him at all.

"Good party," he said, wanting to make Fiona smile. "Good cake."

"It was," said Fiona absently. "Too bad about Leroux." Her brow drooped a little. "He'll be all right, you think?"

"He's just tired," Moth assured her. "Once he gets some sleep he'll be fine again."

The party had broken up earlier than expected. Leroux's coughing fits had forced him to bed. After that no one talked about anything else. They had tried to move the gathering onto the balcony so as not to disturb Leroux, but it was far too tiny even for Moth's small group of well-wishers, and Mrs. Jilla warned it might collapse.

So Moth walked Fiona home.

Turning thirteen wasn't the event he'd expected. Diggy's crash had marred the day, and he was worried about Leroux, but there was something else bothering Moth.

"Thirteen feels a lot like being twelve," he said suddenly. "Is that how it was for you, too?"

"I don't remember," said Fiona. "I don't remember much of anything since my parents died."

Moth didn't want her remembering that day anymore. He wanted to save her from it. "I thought I'd be a squire by now, like the other boys my age."

"There's still time," said Fiona. "You have friends at the aerodrome. They can help you."

Moth shook his head. "You have to be highborn for that. Like you."

"I'm not so highborn."

"Money, then," said Moth. "The rich boys get to be squires."

"Skyhigh's not rich," Fiona pointed out.

"Yeah he is. He must be. He just doesn't care about it. All he wants to do is fly."

"Sometimes that's the most important thing," said Fiona. "You have to want something bad enough."

Moth laughed. "That's what Leroux says."

He kicked his legs anxiously against the wall. It really was late now, and he was sure Fiona would be in trouble.

"Won't they come looking for you?" he asked.

Fiona smirked. "My grandfather? He's asleep by now. Or working. He doesn't care. He only brought me here because there was no one else to take care of me. We had a fight about it over dinner."

"Oh," said Moth, understanding. "That's why you're so quiet."

Fiona refused to look at him. "At least you have Leroux. He loves you like a real grandfather." She choked back a laugh. "Crazy old man!"

Moth chuckled. "Yeah."

"And that bird! Where'd he find that thing?"

"Lady Esme?" Moth thought for a moment. "I don't rightly know. He never said."

"I've never seen anything like that bird in all my life. Not even at the zoo. Those weird eyes, the way she looks at folks. And gumdrops? Crazy!"

"Leroux loves her. They're always together. He spends half his pension looking after Esme."

"Really?" Fiona's expression grew dreamy. "He's gentle with you both. You're lucky, Moth."

Moth had never considered himself to be lucky, especially in the shadow of Fiona's grand home. "You're right," he admitted. "I am lucky. I don't know what I'd do without Leroux."

Fiona slipped an arm around his shoulder. "You worried about him?"

"No," lied Moth. "That's not what I mean. I'm gonna have to leave here someday, try to learn flying somewhere else. Won't do me any good sticking around here if no one lets me squire. We'll both be on our own then, Leroux and me."

"This is where the real flying is, though," said Fiona. "This is where you belong." She brightened suddenly, saying, "Hey, listen. There'll be more airships coming soon, I'll bet." Her voice dipped low. "Some governors are coming here to meet with my grandfather."

"Governors? Where from?"

"From all over, I guess. They're coming to talk about the Skylords. My grandfather's already getting ready for them."

Moth was excited about the airships but perplexed about the meeting. "That doesn't make sense. What's the big danger all of a sudden? I don't get it. Why is your grandfather getting everyone so worked up? Stories about the Skylords have been around forever. Why worry about them now?"

" 'Cause he's wild in the head," declared Fiona. "He had everyone back in Capital City talking about it. That's why they sent him here—to protect us from the Skylords."

"Leroux once told me the Skylords are beautiful," said Moth, recalling the tales the old knight told him. He let his gaze linger on the Reach. "I don't think he's afraid of them."

"Did he ever tell you what they look like?"

"Once." It had been years ago, when they'd first met. "He said they look like angels."

"See? Crazy." Fiona watched the distant mists as she spoke. "He never crossed the Reach, Moth. No one has. No one can. It's too big."

"Leroux doesn't think so," said Moth. Deep down, he wanted to believe Leroux's tales. "If no one's been across the Reach, how do we know what's there? Dragons, maybe, like Leroux says."

"And unicorns and mermaids," laughed Fiona. "Right." Yet she couldn't bring herself to look away from the Reach. "Look how far it stretches," she whispered. "Sometimes . . ."

She stopped herself. Moth elbowed her to go on.

"Tell me."

In a joyless voice, Fiona said, "I don't want to be here anymore. I hate it here. Sometimes I think about just walking off into the Reach and disappearing. I'd walk and walk and just let the mists bewitch me until I was lost. No one would ever find me if they came looking."

"What good would that do?" asked Moth. "Besides, that's not how it works. The Reach doesn't go on forever, it just looks that way. Leroux says you just have to keep on going. He says if you believe it, you'll find it—the whole world on the other side."

"That's hooey," Fiona snorted. "If that was true people would be crossing through it all the time."

"Leroux says most people get lost in the Reach because they don't have faith. Or maybe they're afraid to go through. Maybe people believe like your grandfather does, that it's dangerous over there. Anyway, I don't want you to go."

Fiona's cheek turned up in a half smile. "No?"

"Not until you give me my present!"

Fiona rolled her eyes. At last she unclenched the sack from her hand. "Here," she said, placing the sack into his waiting palm. "Happy Birthday."

The velvet bag felt soft in Moth's fingers, but inside it was something hard and weighty. He reached eagerly into the sack. When he saw Fiona's gift his breath caught.

"Whoa . . ."

It wasn't just a knife, but the knife of a Skyknight, with a folding blade and a burl wood handle studded with bronze rivets. Moth held it up to the moonlight. Stamped into the handle was a likeness of a dragonfly. He had seen knives just like it on the belts of every Skyknight at the aerodrome, the only weapons the flyers carried other than the guns of their aircraft. They were precious and they were rare, and Moth couldn't believe Fiona had gotten him one.

"To get you started," she explained. "It'll remind you of your dream."

"How'd you get it?" asked Moth. He grimaced at his friend. "You didn't steal it, did you?"

"What?" Fiona erupted. "What a brainless question! Of course not!"

"All right, I'm sorry," offered Moth. "But how?"

"It belonged to one of the flyers that died. It was for sale in one of the shops down in the square. Cost me a pretty penny, too. But if you don't want it . . ."

Fiona reached for the knife but Moth whipped it away.

"I didn't say that," he said, grinning. He studied it, then bit his lip. "Whose was it? No, don't tell me! It's better I don't know."

"They didn't have a sheath for it, but maybe you can find one."

"Leroux can make me one," said Moth. He pulled open the blade, admiring its shine, then snapped it closed. He didn't know how to thank Fiona. Instead of words, he leaned over and kissed her.

"You're welcome," said Fiona softly.

Moth slipped the knife into his pocket. "It's late. I should go now, see how Leroux is doing."

Disappointed, Fiona nodded. "See you tomorrow, maybe?"

"After my job. Come around for supper if you want." Moth slipped down from the wall, landing on the side away from the mansion. He looked up at Fiona, who lingered there as if she didn't want to go. "Fiona?"

"Yeah?"

"About what you said before. It won't work, you know. You can't just run and hide. You can't just go live in a castle somewhere far away."

Fiona thought about that but didn't answer. She swung her legs over the other side of the wall. "Good night, Moth," she whispered, then dropped down out of sight.

LEROUX'S GIFT

MOTH RETURNED HOME nearly an hour past midnight, climbing the creaky steps of the building and nudging open the apartment door. Leroux remained asleep inside his bedroom, snoring comfortably. Outside on the balcony, Lady Esme rested in her makeshift nest of sticks and straw, stirring as Moth entered. He put a finger to his lips to keep her quiet as he tiptoed inside. The glass door to the balcony had been left open a crack, giving the kestrel entry to the apartment. Empty bowls and cups lay strewn across the small living space, the remnants of Moth's party. He would clean up in the morning, he decided; he was far too tired to do it now.

There had never been enough money to buy Moth a proper bed, and the apartment was too tiny for another anyway. Moth cleared the debris from the small sofa and found his pillow and blanket in the chest they used for a table. He kicked off his shoes and fell into the lumpy cushions, exhausted. With a twinge of sadness he realized his birthday was over. Closing his eyes, he remembered his flight in Skyhigh's dragonfly. If he was lucky he would dream about it . . .

Instead he dreamed of Fiona. She had run into the Reach and he was chasing her and telling her not to be afraid. He heard his name being called and thought it was Fiona's grandfather, but when his eyes fluttered open he saw Leroux looming over him.

"Moth? You awake?" asked the old man. His gray nightshirt

looked ghostly in the moonlight. His bony head hovered above Moth's face.

"Leroux . . . ?" Moth sputtered. "It's nighttime . . ."

"I have to tell you something," said Leroux. His eyes were wild, his body shaky. Moth sat up in alarm.

"What's wrong?"

"The story!"

"What?"

"The story I have for you. Remember?"

Leroux's complexion glowed a sickly white. Moth reached out to feel his clammy forehead.

"You're hot . . ."

Leroux batted his hand away. "Don't mother me, boy. It's time to tell you."

"You're sick." Moth blinked hard to clear his sleepy mind. "I should get the doctor. What time is it?"

"Are you listening to me? You have to listen, Moth."

Leroux seemed desperate, completely unlike himself. Moth studied his face, wondering if he was sleepwalking. "All right," said Moth calmly. "Just go back to sleep and tell me in the morning. You can tell me in the morning, all right?"

"Now," Leroux insisted. He came in close enough for Moth to feel his breath and whispered, *"Lady Esme isn't a kestrel."*

Moth sat up. Leroux was frightening him now. He'd never seen the old man so badly off. "I think we should both go back to sleep," he said gently.

"Listen to me!" Leroux shrieked. "It's time to tell you the story! Lady Esme isn't a kestrel. She's a person, not a bird! Do you hear?"

"A person." Moth nodded. "Okay."

"Yes." Leroux grew calmer. "A woman. Not a regular woman, Moth. She's a woman that I loved . . . from over the Reach."

A grin of relief broke over Moth's face. It really was just one of his mad tales. "So the women across the Reach are birds?"

Leroux frowned. "What? No! She's not a bird at all. She's a woman, Moth. The Skylords changed her into a bird. And you have to help me change her back."

"Who is she?" Moth asked, playing along.

"I can't tell you that." Leroux put a finger to his lips. "Secret things."

"Oh."

"If I could tell you everything, I would. How I wish I could! But now you know the truth about Esme, and that's what's most important. She needs your help, Moth, to get back."

"Uh huh." Moth turned to sit upright on the sofa. "You sit down," he urged Leroux. "Tell me."

Leroux sat beside Moth, his shoulders slumped from his mad burden. "I've tried for years to change her back, but I could never figure out how. It's the Reach, you see? It's damnable once you cross over. I'd be lost." He shook his head, looking sick with grief. "My poor Esme. I'm too old to help her now. But I tried, Moth. I did try."

His story made no sense at all, yet Moth pretended to understand. "You'll feel better in the morning. Just sleep."

"No," Leroux whispered. "It's too late." He turned, staring intensely. "Moth, I have to hand this all to you now. You have to save her. You have to take her back across the Reach. Find Merceron. He'll help you."

Afraid of the answer, Moth asked, "Who's Merceron?"

"A friend. A wizard. He knows about Esme. By now he's figured out how to help her." He licked his dried lips. "Yes, surely by now. Otherwise she'll be like this forever. . . ."

Out on the balcony, Lady Esme had fallen back asleep, paying them no attention at all. It seemed to Moth that the bird had more sense than its master.

"Esme looks fine to me, Leroux. She's happy! Why don't we just leave her the way she is? She's gets everything she needs. Gumdrops . . ."

"No! I promised her I'd save her, Moth. She's been like that so long she's probably forgotten what it's like to be real! You have to help her."

"But how? If you couldn't do it, how can I? Maybe it's better this way, really."

"But there is a way," said Leroux carefully. "My gift to you. It will help you find Merceron. I've spent my whole life trying to figure it out. Now you must try, Moth."

"I thought this story was your gift. Now there's another? Where is it?"

Leroux grimaced. "I can't tell you. But it's yours, Moth. I'm giving it to you."

Finally Moth was too frustrated to hear any more. "All right," he said firmly, "I get it. I understand. Thanks."

"Will you help Lady Esme?" asked Leroux. "Promise me you will, Moth. You must promise me."

"I will, Leroux, I promise. I'll help Lady Esme. I'll figure out the gift and I'll go find the wizard Moralon."

"*Merceron*, Moth. His name is Merceron."

"Merceron. Right. I won't forget." Moth stood up, taking Leroux's frail hand. "But I can't do this if I'm tired. It'll be a lot of work. I have to get some sleep first."

Leroux nodded. "Yes, yes. All right."

"You sleep too," said Moth, directing the old man back to his bedroom. "We'll talk all about it in the morning."

Leroux stopped at the doorway of his room. "I can't tell you any more," he said. "My story is finished now."

Moth was past caring. "Fine. I got it all anyway. I'll take care of everything." He turned away, desperate to get back to sleep. "Good night."

There was no sound as Leroux went back into his bedroom. Finally, everything was quiet.

Morning came too quickly for Moth. Bright sunlight poured in from the balcony, beckoning him awake. He turned his face away with a groan. As his brain came to life, he remembered the ridiculous conversation he'd had with Leroux just hours ago. He stirred, angry about what had happened but worried, too.

"Dr. Trik," he moaned to himself, hoping the doctor could help him. Moth doubted he could go through the whole thing again tonight. He sat up, listening for Leroux. "Leroux?"

Lady Esme flapped overhead suddenly, startling him. The kestrel landed at his feet, calling madly in her high-pitched shriek.

"Quiet!" Moth snapped, cupping his ears.

The bird's beak pulled at his pant leg. Moth shook free and

shooed her away. Esme leapt up in a storm of feathers, cawing loudly and dashing toward Leroux's bedroom. There she waited at the open door, dark eyes staring strangely at Moth.

Moth stood up slowly. Something in the kestrel's eyes told him what had happened. Without words, he simply *knew* it. His heartbeat galloped, yet he could barely move at all, forcing himself toward Leroux's bedroom. His shuffling feet brushed Esme away as he peered inside.

On the bed lay Leroux. He had stopped snoring.

GOVERNMENT MEN

OLD AGE WAS TO BLAME for Leroux's death. Moth didn't need Dr. Trik to tell him that. The years had piled onto Leroux's back until he simply couldn't bear them any longer. And it wasn't a shock to Moth either. Instead, it felt like there was a great hole inside him. He had sat at the edge of Leroux's bed for a time, watching his lifeless face before fetching the doctor. Mostly he wanted to thank Leroux.

By the time Dr. Trik had finished, the whole building knew what had happened. Mrs. Jilla arrived with her cat in her arms, instantly concerned about Moth. Moth had expected the old lady to dissolve into tears but she did not. She was strong for him instead, insisting he come back to her own apartment while Dr. Trik and his helpers took away Leroux's body.

"That's nothing you should see," she told Moth, taking his hand. Other neighbors, some of whom had been at Moth's party the night before, nodded in agreement, urging Moth to go.

Lady Esme was in her usual spot on the balcony, sulking in her nest. The bird barely acknowledged Moth as he left with Mrs. Jilla. She seemed lost in the same fog that had engulfed Moth himself, a haze of disbelief and loneliness. Up in Mrs. Jilla's apartment, Moth let the kindly lady feed him and speak gently about the cycles of life and death, but the food had no taste and the words were meaningless to him. He was afraid to go back to Leroux's apartment until the old knight's body was removed. Where would he go now that Leroux was dead?

He couldn't pay for the apartment himself. He had no family and no savings either, just the meager wages he made at the aerodrome.

Overwhelmed, he closed his eyes and lay on her sofa, not realizing how tired he was until he awoke two hours later. Eager to see what was happening back at home, he thanked Mrs. Jilla, promised he would return soon, and headed down the flights of outdoor stairs toward home.

As he reached the tiny landing outside Leroux's apartment he noticed the door swinging open on its hinges.

"Dr. Trik?" he called "You here?"

Moth took one step inside the apartment and gasped. A handful of men in dark suits swarmed through the place. With crowbars and axes they had opened the walls and ceiling, cut into the floor and the furniture, and overturned Moth's books and papers, tossing them everywhere. Noticing Moth in the doorway, they stopped and turned on him.

"What're you doing?" Moth cried.

The man nearest to Moth lowered his axe, looking like a well-dressed thug. For a moment he stared, unsure what to do. "You live here?" he asked.

"Yeah, I live here. Who are you?" Moth demanded.

The other men drew closer. The first man put up a hand to stop them. "Don't," he directed. Then he called out, "Governor? The kid's back."

Moth thought of running, then of screaming for help. The door to the balcony was wide open. Lady Esme was gone. Moth backed up a single step, but froze when he saw a man emerge from Leroux's bedroom. Unlike the others, this was a man he knew.

Governor Rendor was unmistakable with his salt and pepper beard and stately attire. The towering figure had to stoop to get through the bedroom door, then rose up high like a cobra when he saw Moth.

"Good day, boy," he pronounced.

Moth was dumbstruck. "What . . . ?"

"Don't be alarmed," said Fiona's grandfather. He glided casually across the debris-strewn floor toward Moth. "Your friend

Leroux is dead. This apartment belongs to the government now."

"But my things . . ." sputtered Moth.

"Confiscated. For now."

Moth glanced nervously around the room, trying to make sense of what was happening. "Where's Leroux? Did Dr. Trik take him?"

The Governor replied, "He'll be buried like an Eldrin Knight. I'll see to that myself. Your friend Leroux was a great man. People forget what the Eldrin Knights did for this country. Now . . ." He squatted down to get closer to Moth. "Can you tell me where the bird is?"

"Bird?" asked Moth. "What bird?"

Rendor's smile was as tight as a bowstring. "It would be a help if you told me."

"A help for who? What are you doing here? What are you looking for?"

"The bird, boy. Where is she?"

Moth inched toward the door. Governor Rendor's men closed in to stop him.

"No," Rendor snapped at them. "Leave him." He once again towered over Moth. "I suppose I have Fiona to thank for making you afraid of me. Are you afraid of me, boy? You needn't be. If you help me find the kestrel I'll reward you."

"What do you want with her?"

"Enough questions. Just help me find her."

"You won't find her in the floorboards," Moth snarled. "And you have no right to take my stuff."

The Governor examined him closely, as if trying to decipher a puzzle. Finally he turned away. "Get back to work," he told his men.

"No!"

Moth rushed at Rendor, but a henchman snagged his arm. The Governor shook his head. "Let him go."

Afraid, confused, Moth watched helplessly as the others went back to searching the apartment. Then, sure he'd be in danger if he stayed, he turned and bolted from the apartment, his feet clattering down the staircase as he raced away.

* * *

Governor Rendor went to the doorway, watching Moth speed down the stairs. When he reached the bottom, the boy ran along the street, disappearing quickly around a corner. The man who had taken Moth's arm stood next to the Governor, wondering what to do.

"I could go after him," he suggested.

Rendor thought for a moment. All he had seen on the boy's face was shock. No concealment, no obscurity. Just surprise.

"Let him go," said Rendor finally. "He doesn't know anything."

As his man rejoined the others, Rendor leaned against the door, sure that Leroux had been true to his word. Leroux had talked about the Reach but hadn't whispered a word about the Starfinder, not even to young Moth. Rendor was sure of it. He glanced into the ramshackle room. The Starfinder was his now. All he had to do was find it.

THE BLACK SHIP

BY THE TIME MOTH REACHED the aerodrome his lungs ached from running. In his mad dash to get away he raced through the streets of Calio's old section, cutting across the busy marketplace filled with vendors, and then at last to the north side of the mountain, into the flatlands where the aerodrome stood. In the shadow of a docking pylon he came to a halt, resting against the concrete structure to catch his breath. His eyes scanned for anyone who might have followed him. Overhead came the whoosh and buzz of speeding dragonflies. Two massive airships had already moored near the hangars, tied down by steel cables. The airfield was noisy with activity, but the empty stretch of land between it and the city was quiet.

Moth bent forward, putting his hands upon his knees to catch his breath. Leroux was dead. That was all he should be thinking about, and yet . . . and yet . . .

Questions zoomed through his brain. Fiona's grandfather wanted something, but what? Moth thought of Lady Esme. Where was that blasted bird? And where was Fiona? He needed to speak to her, find out what was going on.

Moth peered around the pylon. He had never seen the aerodrome so busy. On the main strip outside the hangars a contingent of Skyknights gathered near one of the airships. Passengers poured through the open doors of the ship's control car. The Skyknights looked resplendent in their blue dress uniforms, their jackets stiff with starch and studded with brightly polished buttons. Along the side of the airship draped a long, scarlet banner, the standard of Heres, a city in the far south of the country. Moth suddenly remembered what Fiona had told him about the meeting her grandfather had arranged. The governor of Heres was probably aboard that airship right now.

And yet there was no sign of Rendor or his men. Moth paused, wondering about his plan. He had no place to go, and really only one friend he could turn to for help. He scanned the group of pilots for Skyhigh.

No sign of him.

Moth took a deep breath, combed his hair with his fingers, then stepped out onto the field. Up ahead loomed the main hangar, one of a dozen such buildings lined up like soldiers on the south side of the aerodrome, all constructed of the same gleaming metal with rounded roofs to accommodate the giant airships. The main hangar was also where Skyhigh's platoon barracked.

With so much activity going on, Moth didn't expect anyone to care much that he'd arrived. He was late for work, but if he grabbed a mop or bucket no one would notice him. He hurried inside, entering the gigantic hangar through one of its gaping doors. Skyknights and their squires threaded through the dragonflies and crates of machine parts. Moth glanced around for Skyhigh. Out on the strip he could see the dignitaries milling near the airship.

"Moth!"

The shout made Moth jump. He turned to see Major Hark striding toward him, his body wrapped in a perfectly tailored uniform.

"Where you been, boy? We've got people coming. I need you to start on airstrip two."

Major Hark didn't notice Moth's rumpled clothes or sweat-stained face. His tense expression revealed the pressure he was under today. For a moment Moth stared blankly at the Major, wanting to beg his help. But he could not. He couldn't trust anyone now, only Skyhigh.

"I'm sorry," he told Hark. "I couldn't get here any sooner. Stuff at home—"

"Save the excuses and get to work, will ya? There's another ship coming in and I have to get the strip brushed down. Just get your broom and get out there, check?"

"Yes sir," Moth answered. "I'll do that. Have you seen Skyhigh anywhere, sir?"

"Skyhigh's getting ready to fly escort," snapped Hark as he turned back toward the crowd. "Don't get underfoot."

Moth gave a curt reply, then sighted Skyhigh walking out toward the airstrip. He waited until Hark was safely away before he bolted toward his friend. Unlike the others, Skyhigh was dressed for flying, his helmet nestled in the crook of his elbow. Moth came up behind him, snagging his sleeve.

"Skyhigh, wait!"

Startled, Skyhigh quickly tugged back his arm, annoyed until he noticed who had grabbed him. "Moth?"

"I have to talk to you," said Moth. He glanced around, wanting no one to overhear them.

"Can't. Not now," replied Skyhigh, and kept on walking. "The dragonfly's waiting."

Moth followed him out onto the gravel-paved field. He could see Skyhigh's craft at the end of the strip. Out to the east a big, black spot was moving against the blue sky, getting slowly closer.

"Skyhigh, hold on," Moth urged. "It's important."

"Later," Skyhigh called over his shoulder.

"Please!"

The Skyknight stopped. Turning, he saw Moth's face twisting with emotion, on the verge of tears. "Moth?" he asked. "What's wrong?"

"Leroux's dead." The words simply dropped from Moth's mouth. "And when I got back to the apartment Governor Rendor was there tearing it apart. He's taken everything. Now he's looking for Lady Esme . . ."

"Moth, go easy. Leroux? I just saw him last night."

"This morning," Moth explained. "He must have died in his sleep. When I woke up he was in bed, just laying there." Moth took hold of Skyhigh's arm again and pulled him toward the wall of the hangar, out of sight. "I went and got the doctor. After that I went up to Mrs. Jilla's. When I got back to the apartment Fiona's grandfather was there! There were men with him, and they were ripping up everything—the walls, the floors. Then Governor Rendor came out and wanted to know about Lady Esme. He said the apartment belongs to the government now. All our stuff!"

Over Skyhigh's shoulder, the black spot from the east came steadily closer. Moth could hear a distant thrumming as it approached. Skyhigh shook his head in confusion.

"Why would the Governor take your home?" he wondered aloud. Then he looked at Moth, his eyes filled with sympathy. "Leroux . . . Moth, I'm sorry."

There hadn't been time for Moth to grieve. There still wasn't. "Skyhigh, I think Fiona's grandfather might be after me. He's looking for Lady Esme. Maybe he thinks I have her."

"Do you?"

"No! She must have flown off somewhere before Rendor got there."

"He's not just looking for Esme, Moth. If he's ripping up the walls . . ."

"And the floors and the furniture!"

Skyhigh's eyes flicked toward the approaching black mass. Moth realized it was an airship, bigger then any he'd seen before, with two engines suspended from its superstructure and fins along its tail, swept back like a shark's.

"The *Avatar,*" pronounced Skyhigh.

Moth's mouth fell open. He had heard about the *Avatar,* the newest airship in the fleet. She had taken her maiden flight less than a month ago, setting a record from the yards at Kerre to Capital City. But the *Avatar* wasn't a passenger vessel. Rendor himself had designed her. With armored flanks and platforms filled with guns, she was the world's first lighter-than-air warship.

"That's why Rendor called the other Governors here—to show them the *Avatar,*" Moth guessed. "You think?"

"Don't know. But I'm supposed to be flying escort for her. I gotta get up there, Moth. Quick."

"Skyhigh, I don't know where to go," said Moth. "I have to

hide. I have to talk to Fiona, see if she knows anything. I can't let Rendor find me."

Eager to get to his dragonfly, Skyhigh puzzled over the problem. "All right," he mused. "You can't stay here. And you can't go back to the apartment."

Moth looked at him anxiously. "Where, then?"

A light flickered in Skyhigh's eyes. "I know a place." His voice dipped to a whisper. "The barn."

"That rusty old place?"

"Yeah, it's perfect," said Skyhigh. "No one goes there ever. I know, because that's where I go when I want some privacy. There's even blankets there already."

Moth's nose wrinkled at the thought. The "barn" as they called it wasn't a barn at all, but an abandoned hangar from the old days of the aerodrome. It had quickly grown obsolete, unable to house the newer, larger airships or to take the pounding of winters on the mountain. It was also set back from the rest of the aerodrome.

"Maybe," said Moth. "You're sure no one goes there?"

"Trust me, nobody's ever bothered me up there." Skyhigh gave a wink to show his meaning. Not surprisingly, he was popular with Calio's ladies. "Use the west side door," he told Moth. "It looks rusted shut but it's not. When you get inside you'll see a little loft for storing supplies. That's where the blankets are. There's some candles up there, too." Once more he glanced at the approaching *Avatar*. The ship was clearly visible now, stalking toward the city like a thunderhead. "Listen to me, Moth. You wait there in the barn for me. I'll get there as soon as I can but you wait, got it?"

Moth nodded. "Yes."

"Don't stick your head out or come looking for me. I'll find out what I can from Fiona and be there as soon as I'm able. I'll bring you some food, too."

"All right," Moth agreed, but his stomach pitched with apprehension. "I'll wait for you."

Skyhigh smiled, putting his hand on Moth's slight shoulder. "We'll fix this. Just stay safe until I get there."

IN THE DARK

MOTH WAITED UNTIL the sun was down before lighting his first candle. The supplies Skyhigh had promised him were exactly as described, tucked into a small loft overlooking the floor of the hangar. Moth struck the wooden match against the wall, then touched the flame to the candle wick. The soft light illuminated the countless motes of dust floating around him. From his place in the loft he could see crates of unused parts and the cobwebby skeletons of broken-down aircraft. Outside, a breeze flexed the metal walls of the hangar.

Reaching the barn had been easy. No one had seen Moth leave the aerodrome, crossing over the south side of the field to where the old hangar stood apart like a lonely, rusted farmhouse. Once inside, he had discovered the loft with ease.

Then, he waited.

An unseen draft made the flame on his candle dance. Moth's stomach rumbled with hunger. In the echoing space of the hangar the noise sounded ridiculously loud. It had been hours since he'd eaten, but his mind wasn't on food. Skyhigh would bring food, but no one could bring back Leroux. Without wanting to, Moth realized that his life had suddenly collapsed.

"All alone . . ."

Unable to bear his own thoughts, Moth retrieved the candle and descended the wooden ladder down to the hangar's floor. Every manner of discarded junk surrounded him. Dusty boxes lined the walls and unused piles of aircraft parts tottered in rusty heaps. Most of it wasn't worthy of attention, until he discovered a particular mound pushed into a corner and covered by a sooty white tarp. Moth held up his candle for a better look. The bent nose of the thing stuck out from its covering.

"A dragonfly . . . ?"

Eagerly he pulled off the tarp, revealing the broken-down craft beneath. Only three of its four wings were still attached, all of them cracked. The engine was gone completely, and the front landing claws had collapsed so that the whole ship sloped forward. There was no canopy either, just a cramped cockpit of worn-out fabric, but the control sticks and instruments remained.

"Beautiful," Moth whispered, running his hand over the craft. She was younger than she looked, but the damp air of the hangar hadn't been kind to her, nor had the dozens of pilots that had probably trained in her. She was first generation, too, and Rendor's designs had improved a lot over the years.

Moth leaned over the cockpit, about to climb in, when he heard a noise at the other end of the hangar. He held his breath. Finally, the sweet sound of his own name lilted across the darkness.

"Moth? Where are you?"

"I'm here," Moth called, moving toward the voice with his outstretched candle. The light from the flame reached across the hangar, falling on the worried faces of Skyhigh and Fiona.

"Moth!" Fiona cried. She ran to him with arms out wide, nearly toppling his candle. Melted wax burned his fingers, but he was too happy to care.

"You're here," he sighed.

She held on to him. "Poor Leroux. Oh, Moth . . ."

A knot tied itself in Moth's throat. "Yeah," he croaked. He didn't want to cry, not in front of Skyhigh. "I can't believe it."

Skyhigh came out of the darkness with a box in his hands. "We brought food," he said, holding it out for Moth's inspection. "You all right so far? Any trouble?"

"No, nothing," said Moth. "It's been quiet." He looked at them both. "What about you? You hear anything?"

"Let's go up to the loft," said Skyhigh. "You can eat while we talk."

He stepped past Moth and headed for the ladder. Fiona looked at Moth helplessly.

"Moth," she said, "Skyhigh told me what happened. I want to help."

"It's your grandfather, Fiona. Did he say anything to you?"

Fiona blanched. "He's already looking for me."

Skyhigh was already halfway up the ladder. "C'mon!"

Moth and Fiona followed him, climbing the wooden rungs up to the dusty loft. The candle in Moth's grip nearly went out as he climbed, one-handed, before giving it over to Fiona. As Skyhigh spread out the blanket, Fiona tipped the melted wax out of the candle and onto the ledge. Gently she set the candle into the wax, blowing on it until it hardened.

"There's some meat pies, some apples, some cheese . . ." Skyhigh announced each item as he unpacked the box. "And water. Here . . ."

He handed a battered canteen to Moth, who quickly unscrewed the cap. The one thing he really wanted was a drink. He took a long, thirsty pull of the water, wiping his mouth on his sleeve. Together they sat cross-legged on the blanket, staring at each other in the candlelight.

"Thanks," said Moth, but he felt embarrassed suddenly, like one of those vagabonds that sometimes crawled off the train from Medona. The pity in Fiona's face made it even worse. "Are they looking for me?" he asked flatly.

Skyhigh hesitated, as though he didn't want to answer. "Some of Rendor's men came to the aerodrome. They're asking questions about you, Moth. Hark pointed them in my direction. Idiot."

Moth's stomach somersaulted. "What'd you tell them?"

"What do you think I told them? I said I haven't seen you and I don't know where you'd run off to. Made it sound like I was real worried about you, too."

Fiona nodded. "I told my grandfather the same thing. He came looking for me at dinnertime. I don't think he believed me, though."

"He'll be keeping an eye on Fiona, you can bet on that," said Skyhigh.

"You sure you weren't followed?" asked Moth.

"I snuck out of the mansion. No way anyone saw me," Fiona said confidently.

"Fiona, you shouldn't have come," Moth told her, annoyed at the risk she had taken. "Once your grandfather knows you're gone he'll be looking for you, too."

Skyhigh shot a glare at Fiona. "Yeah, that's what I told her, but she wouldn't listen."

"Doesn't matter. I'm not going back anyway."

Moth reared back in surprise. Skyhigh just rolled his eyes.

"Fiona, you have to go back," said Moth. "You can't stay here with me."

"Yes I can," insisted Fiona. Her face hardened like candy brittle. "My grandfather's putrid and I'm not going back to him, not after what he's done."

"Stop," said Skyhigh, putting up his hands. "First we have to figure out what's been going on."

Fiona smouldered at the interruption. "He took Moth's home, Skyhigh."

"But why?" Skyhigh countered. "That's what really matters here."

"Fiona, don't you have some idea why?" Moth asked pleadingly. "Why would your grandfather be searching our place? Why's he taking everything?"

"He doesn't want *everything* you have, Moth," said Skyhigh. "Just something in particular."

"But we don't have anything! You've seen our place. All Leroux had was that stupid bird, and now she's gone too."

Skyhigh took one of the meat pies and broke it in half, handing part of it to Moth. He chomped down on the other half, saying, "And what about that bird, huh? Why's he looking for her?"

Moth had asked himself the same question a thousand times. "I don't know. Maybe . . ." He stopped himself.

Skyhigh kept on chewing. "What?"

"It's stupid. Just something Leroux told me last night. But it's crazy."

"Go on and say it," urged Fiona.

"It was just one of his stories. And it was the middle of the night. He woke me up to tell me that Lady Esme isn't really a bird. He said she's really a woman from across the Reach."

Skyhigh took a hard swallow of pie. "That really is a story!"

"See? It's dumb." Moth finally bit into his food. "He was feverish. I should have run out to get the doctor but I didn't. Maybe if I had he'd still be alive."

"Forget that," said Skyhigh sharply. "Leroux was old. No one could have helped him. Go on with what you were saying—Lady Esme?"

"Leroux said he had a gift for me. I thought his silly story was the gift, but now I'm not sure what he meant. He wanted me to help Lady Esme get back to normal." Retelling the tale frustrated Moth. "He said he met her over in the Reach and that they fell in love, but then she got turned into a bird."

"Sounds to me like he knew he was going to die," said Fiona. "See, Moth? You couldn't have saved him."

Skyhigh steered the conversation back again. "What else did he say? What else about the gift?"

"Nothing! That's the worst part. He said it was all some secret that he couldn't tell me."

Skyhigh smirked. "I've heard Leroux tell stories. He was never shy about giving details. That was one long-winded old man. If he said he couldn't tell you something, he probably meant it."

"But none of it makes sense," said Moth.

Fiona's face scrunched up as she recalled, "Last night when I had dinner with my grandfather, he asked about Leroux. He must have heard he was sick. He wanted to know how he was feeling."

"He asked you that?" said Moth. "Why?"

"It's all the same thing," Skyhigh surmised. "He wants something. That gift, whatever it is. The kestrel, too. It's all tied up together. Fiona, did Rendor ever ask you about Leroux before last night? Did he ever mention him?"

"I don't think so," said Fiona. She twirled her red hair around a finger as she thought. "But my grandfather was an Eldrin Knight. Maybe they knew each other."

Moth gasped. "When your grandfather was at my house—he

said that! He told me that Leroux was a great man. I forgot that until now."

"And Leroux never mentioned Rendor to you?" asked Skyhigh. "Ever talk about him coming to Calio, becoming Governor, anything like that?"

Moth's mind was a jumble, difficult to untangle. "He talked so much it's hard to remember. He might have said something about Rendor once, I dunno."

"We can sneak back to your apartment," said Fiona. "See what's left there. Maybe Lady Esme came back."

"Too risky," said Skyhigh. "If he really wants the bird he'll have thought of that. He'll have someone waiting there already. Besides, Moth has to stay put."

"What, here? I can't live here forever, Skyhigh . . ."

"Not forever. Just until I figure out this mess." The Skyknight rubbed his hands together, partly in thought, partly to warm himself. "We need to know what Rendor's looking for."

"If he found it, it'll be back at the mansion," said Fiona. Her pale face darkened. "Maybe I should have stayed there," she admitted.

"It doesn't matter," said Skyhigh gently. "If he found what he was looking for then he's got it hidden somewhere safe. You wouldn't be able to find it, Fiona."

"But it belongs to Moth," Fiona fumed. "My grandfather stole it!"

"We don't even know he has it!" grumbled Skyhigh.

Moth decided to get between them. "Fiona, I lost the knife you gave me," he confessed. "It was at the apartment."

"Sure, they probably stole that, too!" hissed Fiona.

Skyhigh took a drink from the canteen. Moth could tell he was worried.

"Skyhigh? Are you gonna be in trouble for all this?" asked Moth. " 'Cause if so . . ."

"Hey, forget that," said Skyhigh. He reached out and playfully tapped Moth's cheek. "Skyhigh Coralin's not afraid of anything. What can they do, bust me down to dishwasher? Their best pilot?" He turned back to Fiona. "That meeting tomorrow—you know anything about it?"

"Just what my grandfather told me. He says it's to talk about the Skylord problem."

Skyhigh laughed. "Might as well be talking about the weather," he scoffed. "Skylords! Your grandfather just wants to make trouble. He's become a big man by making everyone afraid. Now he wants to show off that monstrosity he's built, the *Avatar*."

"That's not it," said Fiona. "He believes what he says about the Skylords. A lot of old people like him do."

Moth nodded. "Leroux did."

There was silence for a moment. The grin melted from Skyhigh's face. "I don't know what's beyond the Reach. Maybe it's *full* of women that turn into birds. Or maybe there's just nothing there. And you know what? It doesn't really matter. It's just nice and quiet in the Reach, the way things ought to be. People like Rendor just stir the pot." He gave Fiona a sideways glance. "No disrespect."

Fiona grimaced. "I don't care about him. All I want is to help Moth." She folded her arms across her chest. "And I'm not going back."

Moth gave her a sad smile. "It doesn't matter, Fiona. Now that Leroux's gone I need to think about getting on the train, getting away from here."

"Not yet," said Skyhigh. "Give me a couple of days first. Maybe things'll blow over by then. If not . . . well, just stay put, all right?"

The thought of being alone was dreadful to Moth. Suddenly he was grateful Fiona had come. "I'll stay put. Can't really show my face around here anyway."

"Good." Skyhigh stood up and brushed the crumbs from his uniform. "I'll be back as soon as I can get away. Might not be until tomorrow night. You think you'll be okay until then?"

"Sure," said Moth, though he really wasn't. "I'll be fine."

Skyhigh smiled as he looked between Moth and Fiona, sitting together in the candlelight. "Kind of romantic here," he joked. "Like I said, stay out of trouble."

THE STAR-THINGY

MOTH HAD FORGOTTEN about the wizard until that night, when he dreamed of Leroux.

In the silence of the old hangar, he lay asleep in the loft near Fiona. Too exhausted to force himself awake, he looked upon Leroux's face in the dream and was happy. They were together on a train, then suddenly in an airship, and Leroux seemed young again. He spoke clearly, without his cough, his eyes bright and free of cataracts. Until that point Moth hadn't remembered what Leroux had said about Merceron.

"Are you embarrassed to tell them?" Leroux asked. "Do I embarrass you, Moth?"

"No!" Moth insisted. Now they were no longer in the sky, but had somehow dropped into a thick, merciless fog. "I don't care what people say, Leroux. They can laugh; it's okay."

When he looked again, Leroux was dressed as an Eldrin Knight. "Merceron," he said.

Moth felt lost in the mists. "I don't want to talk about this. I want to go home, Leroux. With you."

He sat up, breathing hard, relieved the dream was over. But he wasn't at home or in the mists or on a train. He was in the darkness of the hangar. Fiona remained asleep beside him. At first he thought the dream had woken him, but then he heard an interminable scratching on the metal roof, like an animal trying to claw its way inside. Moth sat very still, listening for voices that never came. He heard the wind, smelled the must of the hangar. The scratching continued.

Long hours had passed since he'd last been outside. In the cover of night he was sure he wouldn't be seen. The nub of a candle still burned on the ledge. As he reached for it, Fiona stirred.

"Moth?" Her voice was soft, half asleep. She blinked uncertainly. "What's wrong?"

"Probably nothing," Moth said gently. "I heard something, that's all."

The scratching came again. Fiona sat up and looked at the roof. "That?"

Moth started backing down the ladder. "I'll check it out. Go back to sleep."

"How can I?" Fiona scrambled out of her blanket. "I'm coming too."

Moth didn't argue. Together they climbed down the ladder, then tiptoed across the hard floor of the hangar, Moth leading the way toward the west side doors.

"Hold this," he said, handing the candle to Fiona.

Encrusted with rust, the doors rattled as he jerked them apart.

"Shh!" hushed Fiona. "Not so loud."

"It's not me," Moth argued. "They're old."

He slid the doors apart as quietly as he could, just wide enough for them to squeeze through. Cool mountain air struck their faces, blowing out Fiona's candle. A full moon gazed down brightly on the city.

Moth realized quickly that the noise had stopped. Fiona noticed, too.

"Maybe we scared it away," she suggested. "Whatever it was."

Moth stepped out to look around the building, careful to stay within the shadows. "I don't see any—"

Something came rushing from the sky. Moth leaped back. A flutter of outstretched wings brushed against him. In the light of the moon Moth saw the bird fluttering toward him.

"Esme!"

Lady Esme landed at his feet. Astonished, Moth and Fiona both knelt to greet her.

"How'd she find you?" asked Fiona.

"She must have been watching me!" said Moth. "She probably followed me all day!"

The bird called insistently, then leaped skyward and flew off. Moth jumped up to stop her.

"No!"

She winged her way over the hangar and out of sight. Moth and Fiona dashed around the building. Frustrated, Moth gazed up at the stars, wanting to scream.

"She's gone!"

"Moth, quiet . . ."

Moth scanned the sky, desperate to find her. Then, as quickly as she had flown off, Lady Esme reappeared. This time, something large and silvery glinted in her talons. With effort the kestrel carried the object toward them, beating her wings and setting it on the grass.

"What is it?" asked Fiona, bending down to look.

Moth knelt and picked it up. "Some kind of instrument. Like for a ship."

It looked like a sextant, a tool seamen used to navigate the oceans. At the top of the thing was a long tube with glass lenses, like a small telescope, attached to a wheel with pinpoint markings along its side. There were all manner of levers on the thing, engraved with symbols Moth didn't understand. Near the bottom of the device a spotless mirror shined. As Moth lifted the object to look at it more closely, the mirror reflected his curious face. Fiona leaned over him, studying the thing. She reached out and pointed at the pinpoints on the wheel.

"They look like stars," she observed.

"They do," Moth agreed. "Like constellations."

He pointed the instrument skyward and peered through the scope. A crystal clear image of stars exploded into view. "Whoa, powerful . . ."

There was no distortion at all, as though he could just reach up and touch the heavens. He handed the strange object to Fiona, who did the same—and with the same awestruck reaction.

"Amazing. I've never seen anything so clear before!" She put her face close to the mirror, watching the reflection of her own, huge eyeball. "What's this part for?"

Moth shrugged. "I don't know. Sextants don't have mirrors. And that writing on it—that's not normal either."

Lady Esme waited on the grass beside them. Moth's eyes met Fiona's, sharing the same impossible thought.

"This is Leroux's gift," Moth whispered. Suddenly he felt the chill of the mountain air. Lady Esme stared at them, her strange eyes full of intelligence. "Either you're a very smart bird," said Moth, "or you're not a bird at all."

Fiona kept her voice low. "That's the thing my grandfather's looking for," she said. "It must be."

"It's from across the Reach," said Moth. "That's why he wants it. It's probably something powerful. Magical, even."

"But why would Leroux have it? And how would my grandfather know about it?"

There were too many questions and not enough answers. "This thing, whatever it's called—this is what Leroux wanted me to use to help Lady Esme." He leaned forward, studying the kestrel, looking for something—anything—to reveal the truth inside her. "Fiona, your grandfather wanted Esme because he knew she might have this thing. He probably knows she's not really a bird."

Fiona grimaced. "Moth, I don't know . . ."

"I do know," Moth insisted. "I believe it, Fiona. Before he died Leroux made me promise I'd help Esme. I told him I would. I didn't believe it then, but now I do. It's all true."

Fiona struggled to believe it, too. "Maybe. But what can you do about it?"

"Keep my promise," said Moth. He stood up and cradled the strange object in his hands. The silvery metal glowed in the moonlight. "I have to go."

"What? Cross the *Reach*?"

"Yes," said Moth without flinching. "There's nothing here for me now, Fiona. All I ever wanted was to be a Skyknight, but that can't happen anymore. And I can't let your grandfather take this away from me." He paused, gazing thoughtfully at the quiet city. "They're already looking for me. If I stay they'll find me. I have to go *now*."

"But Skyhigh said to wait . . ."

Moth was already moving. "You can tell him what happened," he said, heading back toward the doors. Lady Esme followed, half hopping, half flying behind him. When he reached the doors he said to the bird, "Esme, fly off somewhere and hide. Wait for me, all right? I won't be long."

As if she understood every word, Lady Esme once again took flight, shooting into the night. Confident she would return, Moth squeezed back into the hangar. Fiona hurried after him.

"You can't go now," she protested. "It's dark."

"I have the moonlight. I'll be okay."

"But you won't be able to see anything in the Reach, Moth."

Moth made his way through the hangar, but not back to their loft. "I'll wait at the bottom of the mountain until morning," he said. "I'll head for the Reach when the sun comes up."

"And then what? How will you find your way through the mists?"

"I'll walk straight and keep going," said Moth. "I'll *believe*, just like Leroux told me. He said there's someone across the Reach who would help me. A wizard."

"A wizard," scoffed Fiona. "And maybe some talking frogs with funny little hats."

Moth stopped at a pile of cartons overflowing with discarded clothing. Musty coats, undergarments, boots were all shoved unlovingly into a corner of the hangar. "This'll help me," he said. He set the silver instrument safely on a barrel and started rummaging through the containers, looking for a coat small enough to fit him, tossing out clothing as he searched. "Too big," he said, again and again. Finally, he fished up a coat he thought might suit him. "Here," he pronounced, turning toward Fiona as he slipped it on. "This should keep me warm out—"

He stopped, shocked to see Fiona already buttoning up a coat of her own. "What are you doing?"

"I'm going with you," she announced. She stretched out her arms, spinning to show off the coat. The long, blue garment flared out like a skirt around her ankles.

"You can't," said Moth. "You have to go back."

"No. I can't ever go back there. I *can't,* Moth."

Moth knew she was just acting brave. Or maybe she really was afraid, but not of the Reach. "Fiona, you think you have nothing to lose but you're wrong. You have everything."

"Like what?" said Fiona tartly. "My parents are dead. My grandfather's a criminal who doesn't want me around. I have nothing, Moth. The only thing I have is you." She shoved her fists into the coat's floppy pockets. "These pockets are plenty deep. We can stuff 'em full of food." She peered into a crate packed with boots and started picking through them. "We'll need these, too," she said. "For the mountain."

Moth slid closer. "Fiona?"

"Come on, help me look. Start trying them on."

"You can't just run away, Fiona. He'll come looking for you."

Fiona was careful to keep her face turned away. "No he won't, Moth," she said, her voice breaking. "He'll just come looking for that star-thingy."

MISSING

SKYHIGH CORALIN STALKED across the misty airfield, sneaking past the silent hangars with an unlit lantern and his pockets stuffed with food and matches. Dawn was less than an hour away, and Skyhigh hurried to reach the barn before the sun came up. After a long and sleepless night spent patrolling Calio in his dragonfly he had managed to scrounge up a few more supplies for Moth and Fiona, but the day ahead promised to be another busy one, and Skyhigh knew he wouldn't have much time to spend with the kids. By now Governor Rendor was looking for Fiona, he was sure. He glanced about as he made his way to the old hangar, afraid he might be followed. Taking supplies to Moth and Fiona was a risk. If he was discovered . . .

"Don't think about it," he whispered, crossing into the shadow of the barn. He would check on them quickly, he decided, give them the things he had brought, and then be off. If he was lucky he'd be back to work by the time the cooks started slopping out breakfast.

As he rounded the west side of the building, Skyhigh put the lantern handle between his teeth, letting it swing from his jaw to free up his hands so he could open the doors. But the doors, he discovered, had already been opened. He bit down miserably on the handle of the lantern.

"Oh, no . . ."

At once he peered inside, listening carefully, The vast interior of the place stood silent. He stepped into the dark hangar.

"Moth?" he chanced. "Fiona?"

No answer. Skyhigh pushed on deeper, his mind racing with awful possibilities. His eyes scanned the blackness as he made his way toward the loft, but when he came to a disheveled pile of clothing and boots, he paused. The coats had been picked through, thrown aside in a hurry. The barrel of boots was the same.

"No!" he shouted. Angrily he tossed the lantern to the ground. The glass enclosure shattered to bits. "Moth!" he growled. "Don't you ever listen?"

He thought of going after them, but doubted he'd find them. Calio was a small city but full of good hiding places. All they had to do was wait long enough to hop on the train.

"I don't have time for this," groaned Skyhigh.

He went back toward the doors, slipping outside again into the cool air. He'd have to look for them later, he decided. Right now there were escorts to fly.

As he headed for the barracks, Skyhigh's gaze fell upon the distant Reach. He paused, staring at the endless sea of fog, sickened by a sudden sense of alarm.

"No," he whispered. "They couldn't have . . ."

Yet in his heart he knew the truth. Moth. Fiona. Bullheaded teenagers, both of them.

"Oh, you stupid, harebrained kids!"

Skyhigh made it back to his barracks just as the sun peeked over the city. His fellow Skyknights were already out of their bunks and making their way to the dining house for breakfast. Skyhigh, who had already dressed for duty, hoped to melt quietly into the group. Young squires dashed through the throngs, carrying messages or machine parts for the dragonflies. Two airships remained moored at the docking platforms, while the big, black *Avatar* stood apart from the rest, tied down with metal cables and surrounded by guards. Skyhigh avoided everyone as he slipped into the crowd.

Until he saw Major Hark.

A trio of men in dark suits were with him, listening as he spoke with wild, angry gestures. Skyhigh cursed his bad luck and turned away, heading toward the barracks instead.

Please don't see me . . .

"Coralin!"

Skyhigh froze, afraid to look back. *Rotten, bloody. . . .*

When he turned around again Major Hark was coming toward him. The dark suited men fanned out around him. Skyhigh ran through his story in his head, just the way he'd practiced. He hadn't seen Moth in days, he told himself. And Fiona? No idea.

"Something wrong, Major?" Skyhigh asked. An awkward smile swam on his face.

Major Hark looked him over. "Where you been?"

"Just going to get something to eat . . ."

"Skyhigh, these men work for the Governor," said Hark. "They've been looking for you."

"Yeah?" Skyhigh considered the men. Each had the air of Capital City about them, a kind of well-bred, well-dressed corruption. They were the men who'd searched Leroux's apartment, he was sure.

"Captain Coralin, you need to come with us," said one of them, stepping forward. He was a tall, serious fellow, brawny beneath his tailored suit. His eyes locked on Skyhigh like manacles.

"Skyhigh, it's about the Governor's granddaughter," said Hark. "She's gone missing. These men seem to think you know something about that."

Skyhigh made his decision in an instant. "Well that's just fine," he drawled. "I've got a few things to say to the Governor myself." Without a word to Hark, Skyhigh spun toward the center of the city, gesturing for the men to follow. "Hurry up. Let's not keep the old man waiting."

BLUEBELLS

FOR TWO HOURS MOTH and Fiona camped at the bottom of the mountain, huddled in their oversized coats and nibbling at the meat pies in their pockets as they waited for the sunrise. The trek from Calio had exhausted them both, slogging down a seldom traveled road to the foot of the mountain where the Reach lapped at the world like a giant ocean. There, in the shelter of an old oak tree, they rested and tried to keep warm, watching Lady Esme as she hopped along the rocks.

Then, like fireworks on a holiday, fingers of sunlight crawled through the Reach. Moth and Fiona gave their city one last look before entering the churning wall of fog.

Instantly, they vanished.

After barely three paces, Calio and the rest of the world disappeared behind them. Moth and Fiona gazed at their surroundings, wide-eyed at the white cloak that descended over them. Moth stretched out his hand, trying to catch a sparkling pinpoint of light. Like fireflies they swirled in the mists, blinking out of existence at the touch of his fingers. Lady Esme jumped up onto Moth's shoulder.

Fiona raised her face to the sky, but the sky was gone. The canteens at her belt clanged like cowbells. They had taken everything they could carry with them, filling their pockets with matches and candles and food. Their long, rumpled coats trailed along the ground. Each wore a pair of boots too large for their feet.

"Which way?" asked Fiona, her head swiveling. "I can't see anything at all."

Moth searched the landscape, unable to see even a few yards ahead. Already he felt lost. "Just keep going," he said, trying to sound confident. "As long as we keep heading straight we'll make it through."

He pictured the Reach as it looked from Calio, stretching on forever and ever, all the way to the horizon. But the Reach was a trickster, Leroux had told him.

"You just keep on walking," he whispered, "right into another world."

"I can't even tell where I'm going," said Fiona.

Moth summoned a picture of Leroux in his mind. *Just keep walking . . .*

Lady Esme was silent on his shoulder, ruffling her feathers against the dewy fog. Her sharp eyes strayed upward, searching for the sky. Fiona was right—it was hard to walk even a straight line. Moth's heart began to pound. Already he felt lost.

"Moth?" said Fiona. "What about that star-thingy?"

Moth tried to remember exactly what Leroux had told him. "Leroux said it would help me find the wizard."

"Take it out," said Fiona. "Let's try."

They paused while Moth fished the strange gift from his pocket. He had wrapped the instrument carefully in a soft, brown cloth he'd found in the hangar, the kind used for polishing aircraft. Gingerly he unwrapped it, pleased to see it intact. There were no scratches, no fingerprints, not even a smudge on its flawless mirror.

"What now?" asked Fiona. She looked at Moth as if she actually expected an answer.

Just as he had done back in Calio, Moth held the instrument to his eye and peered through the scope. Through the lens he saw the fog and the bright, mysterious lights, but nothing more. He lowered the instrument and saw Fiona's disappointed face in its mirror.

"Nothing."

Fiona reached out. "Let me try." She held the object high above her head and loudly commanded, "Show us Merceron!"

"Fiona, that's not going to work."

"Why not? If it's really magical it should work that way."

Moth snatched the thing back from her. "C'mon! This isn't a fairy tale. We have to figure out how it *really* works. No magic words, no three wishes, none of that applesauce."

"How do you know? I mean, Leroux didn't tell you how to use it, right?"

Moth grimaced, toying with the thing's mysterious levers.

"Right?"

"Okay, right. But I'm not gonna talk to it. Maybe we just have to get out of here, wait for the stars to come back. Then maybe it'll work."

Fiona glanced around. "Moth?"

"Yeah?"

"Which way were we heading?"

"Huh? This way . . ." Moth spun about, realizing that everything looked the same. "I think."

"Oh . . ."

"No, don't panic," said Moth. His chest tightened, but he refused to look afraid. He looked down at his feet and the way his boots had disturbed the ground. "That way," he pointed.

"You sure?"

Moth wasn't sure. "No," he admitted, but when he looked at Esme he noticed her sharp eyes looking straight ahead. "Look at her," he said. "Esme knows the way!"

The kestrel's gaze was full of certainty. Moth wrapped the instrument carefully in its cloth and settled it back in his pocket.

"Go on, Esme," he told the bird. "Lead us through."

Without a moment's hesitation Esme started out, hopping confidently through the fog.

"Stay close," Moth warned Fiona. He put out his hand for her. "Let's keep together."

Fiona took his hand. "Just don't let go, okay?"

They continued for an hour, hand in hand, neither of them speaking. Moth held faithfully to what Leroux had told him—the Reach simply didn't go on forever. All they had to do was keep on walking.

Soon, he told himself. *In ten more steps we'll see the end.*

But ten steps later, the fog only seemed thicker. Moth expected Fiona to start complaining, but she didn't. Instead, she began whispering to herself, her voice so low Moth could barely hear it. When he turned to look at her, her eyes were closed.

"What are you doing?" Moth asked.

Fiona's fingers tightened around his hand. "Thinking about good things," she said, and kept on walking, eyes shut, lips whispering.

"Huh?"

"It's a game my mother taught me," Fiona explained. "Whenever you're scared you just close your eyes and try to remember the best times of your life. You call up the memories real clear, and it's just like you're there again."

"Don't be scared," said Moth. "We're not lost. We just gotta keep on walking."

"Hush up," said Fiona. Quickly she fell back into her trance, rifling through her treasure chest of memories. Moth led her on through the fog.

"What are you thinking about right now?" he asked.

A smile lit Fiona's face. "Once when my parents were alive they took me on a train ride to Rivena. There was a man on the train doing card tricks with a monkey, and when we got to Rivena we all went on a balloon ride over the river." Fiona gave a tiny moan, like she was tasting something delicious. "I was eight years old. I remember 'cause it was my birthday." Fiona opened her eyes. "Now you try."

"Fiona, I'm not scared," Moth lied.

"Go on, toughie," she goaded. "Close your eyes. What was the very best time of your life?"

Moth didn't want to play her game. "Orphans don't have memories like that."

"Don't be stupid. Everyone has good memories. You'll see 'em when you close your eyes."

So Moth did as Fiona asked, holding her hand and letting her guide him through the mists. Instantly his mother's face popped up. Sometimes it was hard to remember her face, but not today. Today she came alive, so real Moth could smell her perfume.

"What are you remembering?" Fiona asked him.

Moth didn't answer right away. To play the game right, he needed a *great* memory. He searched his brain, recalling the first time he'd seen an airship and the day he discovered a tree-house some of the squires had built. He'd spent the whole day in that tree pretending to be a Skyknight until the older boys chased him away.

"I remember one time a few years ago," he began, "back when my mother was sick. We were in our old house on the square. I had just gotten my job at the aerodrome . . ." Moth took a deep breath, remembering the smell of that morning. "It was early and I was still in bed, and then I smelled my mother cooking breakfast. She'd gone out and bought us bacon from one of the farms. She walked all the way down there even though she was sick. When I asked her why, she said . . ."

Suddenly Moth opened his eyes. Fiona looked at him, eager for the rest of his story.

"Well?" she pressed. "What'd she say to you?"

The memory had taken Moth to a place he didn't want to go. "She said it was because I had gotten a job," he told her. "She said it was because she was proud of me. I guess that was the best time of my life."

Fiona squeezed his hand. "You win."

For hours they followed Lady Esme deeper and deeper into the mists, sometimes barely able to detect her in the thick fog. Moth's feet hurt badly, roughed up by the oversized boots. He held Fiona's hand tighter than ever. After a while they had both stopped speaking, until Fiona spoke the truly dreadful words.

"We're lost," she whispered. "We're really lost."

"No we're not," Moth insisted. "Esme knows where she's going."

"She's a bird, Moth!"

"She's not a bird! She's a person! And we're not lost!"

Fiona let go of his hand. "Stop. Just stop."

Moth and Esme both halted, turning to look at her. "Fiona, listen, we have to keep going . . ."

"It's getting dark," said Fiona. She looked up where the sky belonged. "It's almost night! We've been walking all day."

"I know," Moth admitted. "But we have to keep going. We have to *believe*, Fiona."

She nodded desperately. "I want to believe. I . . ." She dropped to her haunches. "I want to rest." Her eyes looked up hopefully. "Please can we rest?"

"Okay, yeah," Moth relented. "Let's rest."

He called Esme back onto his shoulder, sitting down next to Fiona. All they could see was each other. Moth held back his panic, glad he wasn't alone, because if he was he would have broken into tears.

"I'm hungry," he said, anxious to keep talking. "You hungry?"

Fiona shook her head. "No."

"We should eat. We'll eat, and we'll rest, and then we'll find our way out of here. Believe it, Fiona, okay? You got to believe it."

"Why's that going to help, Moth?" She looked at him, really wanting to know. "Wishing doesn't make things happen."

"Believing ain't wishing. Believing is knowing, and I know Leroux didn't lie to me. I know it, see? That's trust. You trust me, don't you?"

Fiona nodded. "Yes."

"Good. Believe that, then."

Moth dug out the meat pie he'd nibbled at the morning before. He took another small bite, offering the rest to Fiona. When she refused, he put it gently to her lips.

"Just a bite," he told her.

She did as he asked, swallowed, and then announced, "I'm cold."

"Me too," said Moth. He put his arm around Fiona, and at once they both stopped shaking. "Close your eyes," he whispered. "I'll keep watch."

Fiona was too tired to argue. She closed her eyes and put her head against his slight shoulder, sharing his warmth. He listened to her breathing, first quick and anxious, then slower, more relaxed. He smiled, realizing she was falling asleep. It spread over him like a contagion. Before he realized it, he was sleeping too.

Too exhausted to dream, Moth did not awaken until he felt something tickling his nose. For that first, blissful moment, he forgot about his trek through the fog, thinking he was waking up in Leroux's apartment on his own, soft sofa. But when he opened his eyes he saw Lady Esme staring back at him, standing right beside his head, and he knew exactly where he was.

His eyes opened wider. He saw sunlight. The smell of flowers filled his nostrils. He lifted his head, and to his great astonishment saw them all around him.

"Bluebells . . ."

His mother had grown them, and now he was in a valley full of them. Sunlight poured down from the purest sky Moth had ever seen. Lady Esme screeched in delight, bounding off Moth's shoulder and shooting toward the clouds. And there in the flowers was Fiona, spinning in a joyous pirouette, her red hair flying out around her, her belt of canteens banging.

"We made it!" she cried. "Ha! Leroux was right!"

In the carpet of bluebells, a chorus of hummingbirds flew out from their feeding. Lady Esme soared over the woodland, klee-klee-kleeing as she wheeled through a long, lazy spiral. Moth put a hand to his chest. His heart was thumping wildly again, but not with fear this time. This time, all he felt was gladness.

"He *was* right," Moth whispered. He gazed into the sky, up to where Lady Esme soared, and knew Leroux hadn't lied to him. "All of it's true." Laughing, he dashed out into the bluebells. "Hey Fiona! Still think Leroux was crazy?"

PICTURES IN THE SKY

THE HEADY SMELL OF FLOWERS filled Moth's nose as he stared up at the sky. Fiona lay beside him in the bed of bluebells, her fingers knitted behind her head and a mysterious smile on her face. They had eaten out of their pockets, drunk from their canteens, then reclined in the sunny field, sleepily enjoying the warmth of a summer that shouldn't exist. Amid the hummingbirds and bees they marveled at the world they had entered, watching Lady Esme sail high above them. There were no mountains; no mechanical dragonflies disturbed the tranquility. Like the grey season that chilled the other side of the Reach, they had left Calio and their troubles behind.

"Look how free she is here," said Moth. His voice was easy as he watched the spiraling kestrel.

"She knows she's home," said Fiona. "She's happy."

Moth felt happy, too. But also worried. "Do you think they'll come after us?"

"Maybe." Fiona shrugged. "If my grandfather wants that starthing bad enough." She got a puzzled look on her face suddenly. "Why don't others come?" she wondered. "Why don't more people try and cross the Reach?"

"Some probably do," said Moth. "They probably get lost. We almost got lost."

"But why is it forbidden to try?"

"It's always been that way," said Moth.

"I know but why? Why can't people come here? It's not dangerous. We sure haven't seen anything like a Skylord yet!"

Moth wasn't sure how to answer. "It's just forbidden, that's all. That's why folks don't know how good it is here."

Fiona went back to sky-gazing. "It *is* good here. Good and free." Together their eyes tracked Lady Esme through the air. Fiona gave a pensive sigh. "I wonder who she is," she said. "Is Esme her real name, do you think?"

"That's what Leroux called her, so yeah, I guess so."

"I bet she was a beautiful woman. I bet she had all sorts of men in love with her."

Moth tried to imagine what Esme might look like as a woman. She'd have golden hair, probably. Long, like a girl in a storybook. And a proper voice, too, instead of an annoying screech. It would be a pretty voice, good for singing, because Leroux liked music.

"How much he must have loved her," Fiona continued. "He spent his whole life trying to help her get back here."

That part of the puzzle remained a mystery to Moth. "Why didn't he?" he wondered. "He could have just walked on through the Reach like we did. Don't you think that's weird?"

When Fiona didn't answer Moth rolled his head to look at her. She was still staring up at Esme, but seemed a hundred miles away. "Fiona? You okay?"

She whispered, "I think she's lucky."

"Who?"

"Lady Esme. She's lucky. I don't think anyone will ever love me as much as Leroux loved her."

"Go on. Why would you say a fool thing like that?"

"Because people love beautiful things. They don't like awkward things, things that are too tall or too boney." She tugged a strand of hair out of her head. "Too red."

"What's beauty got to do with anything?" said Moth as he sat up. "Everyone's got a different opinion on that anyway."

"That's 'cause you lived your whole life in Calio," Fiona argued. "The ugliest place in the whole world. Back in Capital City people know what's beautiful and what's not. And I'm not."

Moth scoffed, "Who put all that flapdoodle in your head? It doesn't matter what some high-up Capital City snob thinks of you, Fiona. My mother taught me all that matters is what we think of ourselves. You keep going around thinking bad of yourself and it's just gonna follow you everywhere."

He stood up, stretching his arms to the sky to end the conversation. He looked around, spotted the place where they'd left their coats in the flowers, and knew it was time for them to go.

"We should move on now," he said. "We'll need to find water soon as we can, maybe locate someone who can help us around here. Someone who knows Merceron."

Fiona sat up, wrapping her arms around her legs. "Try the star machine again. Maybe it'll work now."

So far Moth had hesitated trying the thing again. If it didn't work, they'd be stuck wandering, bumbling around their newfound world. But he agreed reluctantly, rummaging through the pocket of his coat. Unwrapping the instrument's cloth, he headed back to Fiona. "I was gonna wait till nighttime."

There were no stars in the sky, only the sun and a few puffy clouds. Moth cradled the instrument in his hands, still unable to decipher its mysterious markings. Fiona sat beside him, smirking.

"Don't wait," she said. "It'll either work or it won't."

Expecting nothing, Moth raised the thing with both hands and peered through the scope. A sharp, magnified view of the flowers and trees burst into his eye. The thing was obviously a powerful telescope, but it had to be more . . . didn't it?

At last Moth tilted it skyward—into an explosion of stars.

"Whoa!"

Fiona jumped to her feet. "Is it working?"

Moth was too dumbstruck to answer. The machine had somehow peeled back the sunlight, exposing a heaven of bright, living stars. Slowly he tracked the scope across the sky, realizing that the stars were shifting. Bunched together like constellations, the star clusters *moved*.

"C'mon, Moth. What do you see?"

"I see . . . pictures!"

There was no other word for it. Moth knew constellations

were pictures, but these seemed alive to him, moving together, tumbling, running. And not just one big mess of stars, either. They were separate from each other, moving in their own particular dance.

"They look alive," he gasped. "The stars are alive!"

He could feel Fiona tugging his arm. "Let me!" she exclaimed, but he couldn't look away. Back in Calio, he'd spent hours at night stargazing with Leroux. He knew every constellation in the sky, by name and by story. Anxiously he searched for one he recognized.

"Moth," Fiona begged. "Please!"

"All right," said Moth, handing her the instrument. He grinned excitedly as she put her eye to the scope and pointed it upward. "Isn't that amazing?"

Fiona's frown crowded the lens. "I don't see anything. What's wrong?"

"Huh?" Moth put his head next to Fiona's, their two eyes sharing the scope. "Look, right there!"

"What? There's nothing . . ."

"Fiona, what are you talking about? The *pictures*."

"I don't see pictures, Moth. I don't see anything. It's just all sky."

"No, that's wrong," said Moth. He looked again, plainly seeing the array of constellations. "Can't you see them moving?"

Disappointed, Fiona handed the instrument back to Moth. "It doesn't work for me." Her brows shot up in surprise. "It only works for you! That's why Leroux couldn't help Esme. He probably couldn't work it either."

"But why?" asked Moth. Once again he pointed the thing up to the sky, unable to resist the magical parade of constellations. "I'm nothing special. Why does it work for me but no one else?"

"I don't know," said Fiona, sounding a little sad. "Moth, tell me what you see."

"Oh, Fiona, it's fantastic." Moth felt himself pulled into the sky. "All the stars. They're not like stars back home. The constellations . . . they're *real*."

"Real?"

"Yeah, like alive."

"Can you tell what they are? The pictures, I mean?"

Moth swept the machine across the star field, stopping on a particular cluster. "It's hard to tell," he said. Like all constellations, this one was tough to interpret. "This one might be a horse. Or maybe a train."

"A train *or* a horse?" snorted Fiona. "Some picture."

"I wish you could see it, Fiona." Moth lowered the machine. "I'm sorry you can't."

"It doesn't matter," said Fiona with a wave. "As long as you can use it to find the wizard. Do you see any wizards up there?"

"How can I tell? What's a wizard look like?"

"Probably like an old man," said Fiona. "With a hat. Ooh, and a spell book! And maybe a cat."

"Fiona . . ."

Fiona laughed as she made another suggestion. "Talk to it! Like I showed you back in Calio."

"Be serious," groused Moth. "Help me figure this out."

"I am serious." Fiona jabbed Moth with her elbow. "Go on. It likes you."

"You're a pain," said Moth, but knew he had nothing to lose. Just as Fiona had done the night before, he held the strange machine above his head and said, "Show me Merceron. Please."

In his hands the thing began to move.

"It's alive!" screeched Fiona.

Moth held on, watching as the scope turned skyward on its own. Each time he moved the object, the scope tracked back to the same exact spot. Moth looked through the lens. Against the field of stars he saw a single constellation emerge. He held his breath as the picture took shape. The pinpoints of starlight formed a rectangular shape, followed by a long, trailing tail. To Moth, the constellation looked like a kite.

"Uh, Moth?"

"Fiona, I wish you could see this! I've never seen this constellation before . . ."

"Moth, look," Fiona insisted, tugging at his sleeve. "The mirror . . ."

So far, they'd never seen anything in the mirror except themselves. But now the gleaming surface swirled and churned, distorting the world around them. When it finally cleared, they saw the image of a creature in the glass, something they had never seen before, not in their entire lives.

Something impossible.

THE WOMAN ON THE ROCK

MOTH REMEMBERED ALL of Leroux's tales vividly. The old knight had always loved telling stories about the Reach and the strange beings he had met in this world. He had once told Moth that the Skylords themselves were angelic beings, so beautiful that any man who looked at one too long would be blinded. The rivers were filled with water sprites, said Leroux, and on moonlit nights unicorns ran through the fields. But Leroux had never once mentioned dragons. Dragons didn't exist. Even if they did, dragons didn't smoke pipes. And yet that was exactly what Moth and Fiona had seen in the mirror, clearly and precisely.

It was hard to tell how big the creature was, the mirror being so small. It sat alone in a darkened room, paging through a book with its taloned fingers. Rings of smoke spiraled from its pipe, clenched between pointed teeth. Amazingly, the thing wore spectacles. They were the kind of glasses old people wore, perched on the edge of its nose. Occasionally the dragon ran a tongue across its lips as it turned the page, sipping from a tea cup.

For a long while Moth and Fiona gazed into the mirror, marveling at the dragon's long tail and yellow reptilian eyes. Then, Fiona had a terrible thought.

"What if it can see us, too?" she said. "What if it knows we're watching it?"

Moth quickly covered the star machine in its cloth. Suddenly, all he wanted to do was move. The instrument had pointed them toward a range of tall, tree-covered hills. Presuming they would find Merceron there, the pair headed off. But neither could shake the image they had seen from their minds.

"Why did that thing show us a dragon?" asked Fiona sourly. She bent down to pick up a stick, swishing it back and forth as she spoke. "Leroux never said Merceron was a dragon! He said for you to find a wizard."

"Maybe Merceron is like Lady Esme," ventured Moth. "Maybe he's a real person, but he's been turned into a dragon somehow."

"Oh, great. Then how's he supposed to help us? If he can't even get himself back to normal . . ."

"I'm just saying, that's all. If a kestrel can really be a woman, why can't a wizard be a dragon?"

Fiona stopped walking. "Maybe we should turn back."

"What? No, we can't . . ."

"C'mon, Moth. A dragon? You know what dragons eat, don't you?" Fiona poked him with her stick. "People."

"Leroux said the star machine would help us," argued Moth. "If it wants us to find the dragon, then that's what I'm gonna do." He snapped one of the canteens off his belt, but before taking a drink asked Fiona, "You want to go back home?"

" 'Course not," said Fiona without hesitation. "But I don't want to be a dragon's dinner either."

"I guess I just trust Leroux more than you do," said Moth, then took a long drink of water. After a moment Fiona gently pulled the canteen from his mouth.

"Go slow with the water," she said. "Until we find some more we need to conserve it."

Moth could tell Fiona was getting tired, because when she was tired she got bossy, too. "Here." He handed her his canteen. "You better drink some yourself. The sun's getting hotter."

Fiona nodded. Even under the trees the day was growing warmer. They'd have to find water soon.

"We need to keep going," said Moth. "Get to those hills as soon as we can."

"We won't make it before dark," said Fiona as she trudged after Moth. "It's too far."

"Then we'll get as far as we can."

* * *

By noon it was too hot for them to wear their coats. They were knee-deep in wildflowers again, with a clear view of the hills that never seemed to get any closer.

Of the trio, only Lady Esme seemed tireless. She kept a watchful eye on Moth and Fiona as she wheeled overhead, scouting out the landscape. Moth glanced into the perfectly blue sky, wishing for rain.

"How come there's no birds up there?" he wondered.

"Probably too hot for them."

"No, really," said Moth. "There were birds back there in the trees and those hummingbirds we saw, but none in the sky."

"Maybe Esme scared them off. Kestrels eat other birds, don't they?"

Moth wasn't sure about that. Esme had been too spoiled, eating off Leroux's plate, to bother with anything like hunting. "Weird though, don't you think?"

Fiona trudged on, already bored with the conversation. "I'm thirsty," she said. She stopped to take one of the canteens from her coat. "Just a little drink, okay?"

An hour later, they could go no further. A lazy breeze crawled through the valley. The din of crickets and wildlife sounded in the trees. Moth spotted a nook in one of the hillsides, the perfect place for them to rest.

Their stomachs rumbled and their feet ached from walking in their heavy boots. "Let's stop for a good while, okay?" pleaded Fiona. "Maybe spend the night here."

Suddenly, Lady Esme called down from the sky. She was flying directly above them now, her loud cries echoing through the valley.

"Is she talking to us?" asked Fiona.

Moth watched as Esme broke her spiral and flew out over the trees. "She wants us to follow," he said. Together he and Fiona dashed after the bird, clambering over rocks and pushing through the trees. Moth broke through a thicket onto a gravelly slope, losing his footing and falling on his backside. Suddenly he was sliding down, down . . .

Face first, he tumbled into the water. He rolled himself upright, sputtering, up to his waist in an emerald-green lagoon.

"You all right?" asked Fiona frantically. She came down the slope after him, sending gravel spilling into the lake. Lady Esme dropped down onto Moth's shoulder.

"Look at this place," gasped Moth. In Calio, where all their water came from rain, there were no lakes. Moth had never seen one before, but he was pretty sure they weren't supposed to be green. "Look at that color . . ."

"Come out," warned Fiona. "I can't even see your feet."

Moth cupped up some water. In his hands it was perfectly clear. Yet the half of his body submerged in it was invisible. He put the water to his lips and tasted.

"It's fine," he decided. "Better than fine!"

Fiona knelt down at the edge of the lake and fished out his coat. "You forgetting something?"

"The star machine!"

Moth watched as Fiona took it from his pocket, unwrapping it. Her eyes shot up in amazement. "It's not even wet."

"You see? Magic!" Moth spun through the water, heading out where it was deeper. "Maybe this isn't water at all! Maybe it's all melted emeralds."

"Or maybe you're just swimming in slime."

"It's not!" Moth shot back. Lady Esme flew from him to land beside Fiona. Moth laughed and fell back into the water, floating on his back. "Come on in, Fiona. Cool off with me!"

Fiona answered, "At least have the sense to take your boots off. You probably can't even swim."

"Nope, can't swim a lick," said Moth.

Fiona pulled off her boots, tossing them onto the slope with their coats. Moth sloshed toward Fiona, pulled off his boots and threw them into the pile, then put out his hand.

"Ooh," exclaimed Fiona as she drifted into the lake. "It's not cold at all."

"Not too cold, not too warm. Everything about this world is perfect."

They led each other deeper into the lake, around outcroppings and into the crannies where the water rose to their shoulders. Loons and other water fowls nestled in the overhanging branches. From the shore Lady Esme called to them. Moth held tight to Fiona's hand.

"That way," he said, guiding her further around the bend. Fiona kept hold of him.

"Don't go drowning on me," she warned.

The lagoon extended long past the rocks. They could see now how it twisted into a river that headed toward the hills. Moth ventured out a little further, until the water was around his shoulders.

"We can follow the river all the way to Merceron," he said. "All we have to do is make our food last."

"You like soggy meat pies?" Fiona asked. "Yours were in your coat. Remember?" She pulled on Moth, wanting to go back. "We shouldn't have left our things," she said. "It's too deep here anyway."

Moth took one last look at the winding lagoon, until a flash of golden hair snagged his attention.

"Come on," urged Fiona, dragging him away.

"Shh!" Moth ducked down until the water was up to his chin. "Fiona, look . . ."

There, lying against a giant rock, was a woman, her bare back soaking up the sun, her entire lower body submerged in the emerald water. Her head rested on her arms, turned to one side. Her face held an expression of utter contentment, her eyes closed.

"She's . . . *naked*," Fiona whispered.

Moth tried to hide his grin. "Yeah . . ."

She was like the storybook princess Moth had imagined Lady Esme to be, her hair so impossibly golden it rivaled the sun. Her peaceful, porcelain face showed no trace of fear or shame. Like everything they had found so far in this world, she was perfect.

"Go on, put your eyeballs back in your head," scolded Fiona. "Haven't you ever seen a woman before?"

Moth shook his head. "Uh-uh."

Fiona frowned, not getting his meaning. "Just don't stare like that, okay? Maybe she can help us."

To Moth's surprise Fiona trudged toward the rock, pulling him along. "Excuse me," she called out. "Hello?"

Moth felt like a little brother being dragged around. He snatched back his hand, taking his chances in the deeper water, trying to look older than his thirteen years.

"I think she's sleeping," said Moth. "Maybe we should just leave her alone."

"She's the first person we've seen here," said Fiona. Louder this time, she shouted, "Ma'am? Excuse me, ma'am? Can you help us?"

At last the woman's eyes fluttered open. They were close enough now for Moth to see how green her eyes were, the same jewel color as the water. She rolled onto her side to watch them.

"Oh . . .," gasped Moth, stunned by her nakedness.

"I'll do the talking," said Fiona. She smiled like a politician as they approached the woman. "We're sorry to bother you," she said, "but we're sort of lost. My name's Fiona . . ."

"I'm Moth," Moth interjected. He put up a hand in greeting. "Hi."

The woman returned a dazzling smile. Once more she turned, sinking a little in the water to recline against the smooth rock. "Where are you from, young ones? I don't know you." She studied Fiona in particular, seeming perplexed. "What a color your hair is! And your wrappings—why?"

"You mean our clothes?" asked Fiona. "It's what we wear. We wear clothes where we come from."

Clearly the woman was confused. She leaned closer, eyeing Moth. "These waters are Shelian," she said. She pointed to where the waters wound toward the mountains. "Where is your clan? In the Tiger Teeth?"

"Clan? No, ma'am, we don't have a clan," said Moth. "We're looking for someone."

"A Shelian?" asked the woman.

"Uh, we're not sure," mused Fiona. "We're from—"

"From somewhere else," Moth said quickly. "Someplace far away from here."

The woman tried to be accommodating. "These are Shelian waters. Do you know that?"

As the woman waited for their answer, she pulled herself onto the rock, up out of the water. Moth braced to see the rest of her, shocked by what he saw. Next to him, Fiona's jaw fell open.

The woman's lovely human flesh disappeared beneath her torso, changing into the glistening and scaly body of a fish. The enormous tail undulated as it helped her onto the rock, its multicolored fins shining like a rainbow. Casually she tucked her tail beneath herself.

"Younglings?" she queried.

Moth couldn't speak. The woman—the *mermaid*—blinked in puzzlement.

"You are lost?" she asked them. She patted the rock beside her. "Come sit with me. The sun is good today."

Moth shuffled closer to Fiona, realizing that the woman thought they were just like her. "Uh, Fiona . . ."

"You're a mermaid!" Fiona blurted.

Moth took Fiona's arm. "That's right," he chirped. "A mermaid. Nothing unusual about that, right? Let's just go now . . ."

"Moth, look at her!" Fiona sputtered.

Moth turned toward the woman and said, "We're sorry we bothered you . . ."

But the woman looked alarmed now. She squinted down into the water. Her eyes widened in something like horror as she realized there weren't tails beneath the strangers, but legs.

"Who are you?" she asked. "Where are you from?"

"Look, we don't know anything about your people," said Moth, knowing he couldn't lie. "We're from across the Reach. We're looking for a wizard named Merceron."

The mermaid slipped back into the water. "You're humans!" she gasped. "Humans can't be here. It's forbidden!"

"But we had to come," said Fiona. "We have to find Merceron."

"We're not here to hurt anyone," added Moth quickly. "Really, we just need some help. Do you know Merceron? Does he live in those hills?"

The mermaid seemed genuinely frightened now. "I cannot speak to you," she told them. "Go and forget this place. Go now, *please*."

Like a porpoise she dove into the water, speeding away into the emerald lagoon. Moth and Fiona watched her go, stupefied.

"She was afraid of us," said Fiona. "Why?"

Suddenly, their perfect world didn't seem so perfect anymore.

"My heart's thumping in my chest again," said Moth.

Fiona took hold of his hand. "Mine too."

A DIFFERENT SKY

EVEN AFTER A LONG DAY of walking, Fiona doubted she could ever fall asleep. With their long coats for sleeping bags, she and Moth lay beneath a carpet of stars, gazing up in wonder. Fiona had seen stars at home, of course, but the gray skies of Capital City had never looked like this, and she knew that counting them all would take the rest of her life. In this world—whatever this new world was called—the stars actually *twinkled*. Some even streaked across the night, leaving a dusty, fading trail. Wide-eyed, too excited to sleep, Fiona imagined she and Moth were in a safe place, where none of the strange creatures of this world could find them.

In truth, they were not very far from the place where they had seen the mermaid. After that odd encounter, they had somehow found the strength to hike an hour more, but with little progress. Feet aching, legs aching, they found another solitary nook along the bank of the sparkling river, spreading out their coats and settling down for the night. Lady Esme stayed close to them, descending from the sky as darkness fell. Moth used a single, precious match to start a fire, just big enough to warm a meat pie for the three of them to share.

But of course it was not enough, and as he lay next to her, Fiona could hear the pleading rumbling of Moth's stomach.

"Sorry," he said, putting a hand over his belly.

Fiona tried not to think about food. Their supplies, which seemed so ample the day before, had dwindled quickly. "Pretend you had a big meal. Pretend you're so full you'd get sick if you ate another bite."

"How am I supposed to make myself believe that?" said Moth. "We'll find some food along the way tomorrow, don't worry. We just haven't been looking for it, that's all. This place is bound to be loaded with good stuff to eat. Maybe we'll catch some fish."

"Don't mention fish, please," said Fiona. A picture of the mermaid bloomed in her mind. Why had it frightened her so much?

"I hope we see her again," said Moth. His voice was almost dreamy.

Fiona didn't turn her head, afraid to see that look in his eyes, the kind of look that said he'd never seen anything so beautiful in his life as that mermaid. "We won't," she told him. "She's afraid of us. She's probably told her whole family about us by now. We'll be lucky if they don't crawl up on shore and strangle us while we're sleeping."

"Mermaids don't do that," Moth scolded. "Really, Fiona, sometimes . . ."

But he didn't finish his sentence. He just grumbled and went back to looking at the stars. They were altogether different here in this world, and not just because they were brighter. They were mixed up and jumbled, like someone had shaken them in a box and strewn them across the sky. Fiona had given up trying to locate the few constellations she knew back home. Suddenly, everything perplexed her.

"When I was little," she whispered, "my mother used to take me outside at night and show me the stars. I used to want to touch them, so my mother would pick me up and lift me as high as she could. She'd tell me to stretch out my hand. 'Stretch, Fiona!'"

Moth asked with a chuckle, "Is that how you got so tall?"

"I really thought I could catch a star. She used to tell me that someday I'd be big enough to reach up and grab them for myself." Fiona's smile faded. It should have been a happy memory, but it wasn't. "Why do parents lie to their kids like that?" she wondered.

"They didn't lie, Fiona. Parents don't lie."

"Yes, they do. Mine told me they'd come back. But they went up in that airship and died." Finally, she turned to face Moth. "What did your mother tell you when she was sick? Did she tell you she was going to die?"

Moth's face puckered. "No. She told me she'd be all right."

"See?" Fiona went back to stargazing. Then, another thought came to her. "Why do you think he's up there?" she asked.

"Who?"

"Merceron. Why does he have a constellation? Only dead people have constellations named after them. Fake people."

"Hmm, I've been thinking about that myself," said Moth. He shifted his body as if uncomfortable. "We can ask him when we meet him."

"When do you think we'll meet him?" asked Fiona.

"Tomorrow, probably." Moth nodded at his own prediction. "Yeah. Tomorrow definitely."

Fiona blinked up at the sky. "All right," she said, trying to sound courageous. "Tomorrow, then."

THE FACE OF GOD

FROM THE WINDOW of Governor Rendor's office, Skyhigh enjoyed an impressive, peaceful view of Calio. Now that night had fallen he could see the lights of the city blinking over the garden wall. The white buildings of the newer section glowed softly, standing like distant statues against the greenery. A row of ash trees blocked the older portions of the city from sight, a tactic Skyhigh knew was deliberate. The mansion was far too beautiful to be marred by the sight of poor folks.

Skyhigh moved away from the window, anxious for his meeting with Rendor. He'd been held in the mansion all day, kept from leaving or speaking to anyone beyond the servants. He'd even been given his own comfortable bedroom—a luxury for a Skyknight used to bunking with so many others. He'd been fed and given clean clothes, too, but to his great surprise he hadn't been questioned about Fiona's disappearance.

Finally, after Skyhigh had been entertaining himself as best he could and was on the verge of maddening boredom, the manservant named Jonathan had come to escort him to Rendor's office.

"The Governor will be with you shortly," Jonathan had assured him.

That was nearly an hour ago.

Near the full-length window sat Rendor's enormous desk, turned out to face anyone coming into the room. Behind the desk sat a big chair of lime-colored leather. Knowing he shouldn't, Skyhigh plopped down into the chair. With his hands gripping the big armrests, he surveyed the office like a king. All manner of books and bric-a-brac lined the wooden shelves. Tiny sundials, time pieces, and devices of dubious scientific value caught Skyhigh's eye. On the desk sat an orrery, a small, moving model simulating the movement of the planets, each of them represented by silver balls. The toy fascinated Skyhigh. He flicked his finger at one of the balls, sending it spinning around the sun.

"Comfortable?" boomed a sudden voice.

Skyhigh looked up into the face of Governor Rendor, standing in the doorway.

"Yes," he replied without a trace of embarrassment.

The air between them was charged with tension. Skyhigh rose from the chair to face his captor. He had seen the governor before, but only from a distance. Rendor was a notorious recluse, but he was also a genius, the father of the flying age. Skyhigh couldn't help but admire him. Rendor was dressed impeccably in a black frock coat and trousers, the silver chain of a pocket watch drooped across his belly. A salt-and-pepper beard hid his unexpressive lips. When he spoke his voice was toneless.

"My granddaughter is gone," he said.

Skyhigh stepped around the vast desk. "If you're so worried about her, maybe you should have talked to me sooner."

Rendor stalked into the chamber, toward a sideboard where his liquors were kept. "Please don't be offended, Captain, but my time has been devoted to men of greater stature than your own." He popped the top from a crystal decanter of brandy, pouring himself a glass. "The other governors have gone now, thank heavens. Now I can touch on this matter of my granddaughter. Would you like a drink, Captain?"

"No," said Skyhigh. "Just some answers."

"We all want answers, Captain," said Rendor with a grin. "Life is full of mysteries." Glass in hand, he walked over to a pair of chairs by the unlit hearth. Between the chairs was a small table of varnished wood, on top of which sat a cigar box. "For instance, I'm wondering why my granddaughter would run off with a cleaning boy."

"Governor, I had nothing to do with Fiona's leaving," said Skyhigh.

Rendor sat down and sniffed at his brandy "I already know where Fiona's gone, Captain. She and that boy Moth . . ." He looked up from his drink. "A friend of yours, isn't he?"

"Yes," declared Skyhigh. "He is."

"That boy is a thief." Rendor gestured to the vacant chair. "Sit."

Skyhigh bristled at the order. "If you know where they are, why don't you go after them?

"Because they've gone through the Reach."

"Have they?"

"You know they have," said Rendor. "But that's not why I brought you here. Now . . ." Once again he motioned to the chair. "Will you please sit down?"

This time Skyhigh did as requested. He couldn't help but feel intrigued. For two days he had puzzled over Leroux's mystery gift. Now at last he might get some answers.

"Before you start questioning me," he said, "you should know that I won't betray the children. All I care about is helping them."

Rendor suddenly laughed. "That girl! She paints me as quite a monster, doesn't she? Go on, then—protect her from me, Captain. Keep your secrets. Whatever my granddaughter and the boy have told you is meaningless anyway. Neither of them have any idea what's going on."

The old man opened the mahogany box and chose a cigar. From the pocket of his waistcoat he produced an exquisite gold lighter, lit the cigar, and drew in a puff of sweet smelling smoke. His eyes closed with enjoyment; his brow wrinkled with thought.

"Have you seen the *Avatar*?" he asked.

Skyhigh nodded. "Yes," he replied. "I've seen her. Why?"

"What do you think of her? The truth, Captain. What do you really think of her?"

"She's marvelous," Skyhigh admitted. "Is that why you brought the other governors here? To show them the *Avatar*?"

"Partially. But there was something else I wanted to show them as well. Something that once belonged to your friend Leroux." Rendor held the cigar smoke in his mouth, tasting it. "Do you know to what I'm referring?"

"No, I don't," said Skyhigh, because he truly had no idea what Leroux's gift had been. Now, it seemed, Moth had found it.

"The boy didn't speak to you about it?" Rendor pressed.

Skyhigh didn't blink. "No. Never."

Rendor smiled. "I don't believe you, Captain Coralin. Whatever you think of me, it will go better for both of them if you tell me what you know. It might make it easier to find them."

"Find them?"

"Of course. The boy has taken something that belongs to me. Now I have to get it back." Behind the veil of cigar smoke, Rendor's eyes were searching. "Skyhigh," he said, testing the name. "Maybe we're not so different. Both of us dream of flying with the birds. Only I'm too old to pilot a dragonfly. It's airships for me, but it's not the same."

For a moment the tension between them disappeared. Rendor actually looked sad.

"But you've been up there with the birds, the clouds," said Skyhigh. "You know what it's like. It can't really be described."

"Truly, the world's a different place from up there," agreed Rendor. "It is mankind's birthright to fly. I've always believed that. I tell you, Captain, we are born to it, like the birds themselves. Why else would God put such a desire in the hearts of men? Children look up at the sky and they want wings. They want to touch the face of God."

"Yes," Skyhigh sighed. "That's how it was for me. I was fifteen when I saw my first dragonfly at an exhibition. You used to run those, remember?"

Rendor's face lit up. "There were always lots of children at those shows."

"That's the first time I ever saw you," Skyhigh confessed. "I thought *you* were God then. Nothing else mattered to me after that. All I wanted to do was fly."

"Major Hark says you're his best pilot," said Rendor. "Brash, he told me, but a natural talent. It takes a natural talent to control a dragonfly. Not everyone can master it."

"I have," said Skyhigh. "There aren't many things I do well, but I can fly the hell out of a dragonfly."

"Good," Rendor observed. "Now you're being honest with me. I think this will work."

"What?" asked Skyhigh. "What will work?"

Rendor put down his cigar on the edge of the table, so that the ashes were just about to fall on the carpet. "Moth and my granddaughter have gone through the Reach. I wonder—have you any comprehension of what that means?"

"Not really. I know that it's forbidden . . ."

"Forbidden, yes, and for good reason. By going through the Reach they risk the ire of the Skylords."

Skyhigh held back a laugh. "The Skylords again? Governor, that fairy tale might frighten people back in Capital City, but not me."

With a face like thunder, Rendor said, "I didn't bring you here for your opinions, Captain. Your opinion of the Skylords is as dust to me."

"Why *did* you bring me here?" snapped Skyhigh. "You kept me waiting for two days while you wined and dined your friends. And now you're gushing on about flying while Moth and Fiona are in trouble. I would have thought you'd show a little more interest in your granddaughter, instead of complaining about what you say Moth stole from you."

"And you claim to know nothing about what he stole! Do you expect me to believe that?"

"Governor, it doesn't matter to me what you believe." Skyhigh stood up, determined to leave. "All I care about is those kids, even if you don't. Now, either charge me with a crime or let me get out of here."

Rendor rose from his chair, picked up his cigar, and walked over to the window. "Captain, I need your help."

"My help? You're kidding, right?"

"We're going after them," said Rendor. "You, me, and the crew of the *Avatar*. We're going through the Reach. We're taking a scout ship, too. And the best pilot I can find." The old man puffed on his cigar. "That's you, isn't it?"

"Yes, but . . ." Skyhigh groped for an explanation. "Why?"

"Captain, haven't you been listening?" asked Rendor. He turned from the window with a frown. "To get back what's mine."

A STRANGER

THEIR TINY FIRE HAD LONG died out by the time Moth and Fiona fell asleep. In the nook by the river, Moth felt safe enough to dream. They were good dreams, mostly, about his birthday and Leroux, and how he'd never cared about the Reach before his troubles started. He awoke briefly to find Fiona sleeping next to him. Lady Esme had tucked herself against Fiona to keep both of them warm. Seeing them put a tired smile on Moth's face as he drifted back to sleep.

It might have been a minute later or an hour—Moth couldn't tell—when he awoke to the sound of crunching branches. Supposing it an animal, he opened his eyes expecting to see a looming tiger or bear. He held his breath, his eyes adjusting to the darkness, and saw the outline of a man standing over him.

Moth gasped and scrambled back, startling Fiona awake. Her scream sent Esme flying.

"No!" hushed the man. A finger shot to his lips. "Quiet!"

Moth and Fiona staggered to their feet. Head swimming, Moth peered through the darkness as he grabbed Fiona's hand. "Who are you?" he demanded. "We're not alone. If you harm us . . ."

The man squatted down and held up his hands. Moth's sleepy eyes could barely make him out. "No harm, no harm," he said quickly. "Don't be afraid."

"What do you want?" hissed Fiona. "We don't have anything to take."

Moth saw a grin open on the stranger's face. "I'm not here to rob you, girl. No, no. I'm a friend, here to help . . ."

He spoke quickly, too quickly for Moth's drowsy brain. All Moth knew was that he looked unsavory. "Go on!" Moth ordered. "Leave us alone! The others will be back soon. If they catch you here . . ."

The man cackled. "Am I an idiot, boy? I didn't know that!" He stood up, the moonlight catching his weathered hat, its wide brim shadowing his grizzled face. "You're alone. I know you are because I've been watching you."

Fiona let go of Moth's hand and stepped toward the stranger. "Watching us? Why? I'm the granddaughter of Governor Rendor. If anything happens to me you'll—"

"No!" said the man, covering his ears. "No names! The less I hear the better for us all."

"Who are you?" Moth asked again. He was less afraid now, but growing wildly curious. "Why were you watching us?"

"To help you," said the man. A tall, lanky fellow, he stooped down to face them, his long, threadbare coat brushing the grass. "You need help, don't you? You're lost."

"We're not lost," said Fiona hotly. "We know exactly where we're going. We have—"

"A map," Moth jumped in, hoping Fiona wouldn't mention the star machine. "Besides, it's not your business where we're going. How'd you get here anyway?" Moth squinted for a better look him. "You're a human, aren't you?"

Once more the man laughed, an unsettling, mad giggle that made Moth cringe. "Oh, yes. As human as the day I stepped through the Reach! And proud of that I am, too. But we talk too much . . ." He scrunched his head on his shoulders and listened to the night. "We should go now."

"Go? With you?" Fiona folded her arms. "We're not going anywhere."

For the first time the man seemed genuinely annoyed. "I know where you're going," he said in a dangerous whisper. "You're looking for Merceron."

"Who told you that?" said Moth. He slid toward his coat to protect the star machine, then saw Lady Esme already guarding it.

The man shook his head. "No names, no questions."

"Moth, we only spoke to that mermaid," said Fiona. "She must have told him." She glared at the stranger. "Is that right? Did she tell you about us?"

"We're running out of time," said the man. His voice was almost pleading. "In a few more hours the sun will be up. Walking to the hills will take too long." He hoisted a thumb over his shoulder. "I have a boat ready to go. I'll row you there, but we have to leave now."

"Why?" asked Moth. "What are you afraid of?"

The man's face twisted under his wide hat, as if considering how best to answer. "No," he said finally. "We can't talk about it."

"What do you mean, can't?" said Fiona.

"Can't! Can't!" raved the man. "As in *cannot!* We can't speak of any of this. I wouldn't even be here if Serana hadn't begged me. The more we talk the more time we give them to sniff us out."

"Who are you talking about?" asked Moth. "Please, you're not making any sense."

"No, that's it," snapped the man. "Close your mouth and move your legs. Do it now or I'll leave without you. I'm risking too much helping you."

He turned his back and started walking toward the river. Moth and Fiona glanced at each other, stunned by what was happening. They were in danger, probably, but Moth had no idea what kind. Or maybe the man was just a lunatic.

"That mermaid told him to help us," said Moth. "But why?"

"He's leaving," said Fiona. "Should we call him back?"

Moth couldn't think straight. They hadn't expected to see another human here, and it was still a long, exhausting walk to the hills. A boat ride would make that a lot easier. And if the man knew Merceron . . .

"Wait!" Moth called after him. "We're coming!"

RAPHAEL'S RIVER

THE FIRST HINTS OF DAWN greeted Moth as his eyes fluttered open He was in the little boat, and didn't even remember falling asleep. Lady Esme clung to the prow like a figurehead. Near her, Fiona remained blissfully asleep. And there was the stranger in the middle of the boat, positioned between Moth at the bow and Fiona at the stern, rowing slowly and tirelessly toward the hills.

Moth lifted his head and rubbed his forehead. "How long have I been sleeping?" he asked groggily.

"Couple of hours," the nameless man replied. "You and your friend must be dog tired. You both dropped off talking to each other."

Moth glanced past him toward Fiona and Esme. Both seemed safe and content. Hadn't he expected them to be? Moth wasn't sure. He was grateful for the stranger's help, but he still had no answers. Remembering the star machine, Moth groped in a panic for his coat. It was right where he'd left it, in the bottom of the boat.

"I told you," said the man softly, careful not to wake the others. "I'm not a thief." Then he grinned, adding, "Well, not anymore."

He had taken off his hat and laid it in the boat, freeing his face of shadows, yet he remained a mystery. He'd simply taken them aboard and shoved off down the river, which wasn't green anymore but a typical, boring shade of blue. There wasn't anything magical about the man, either. No tail, no wings; just a man, thin and ragged, like the vagrants that sometimes got off the train in Calio. A wiry brown beard covered his chin and his hair hung limply down his forehead.

"Look there," whispered the man, craning his neck toward the hills. They'd made good progress while Moth was sleeping. "Another hour or two," he guessed.

"You're sure we'll find Merceron there?" asked Moth.

"Maybe. It don't really matter. What you'll find is the sunken forest. That'll keep you hid."

He was still talking in riddles. "So you don't know where Merceron is?"

"Just rumors. That's all anyone knows. Me, I never seen a dragon in my life. Don't care to, either."

Moth slumped. "Great. So what's so important about this forest?"

The man went on rowing. "Let's just get you there, all right? I told you—too many questions."

Moth felt uneasy again. What did he mean, he wasn't a thief *anymore*? "Why are you helping us? It makes no sense. Who are you? How'd you get here?"

"If I tell you," the man whispered, "then you can't tell another living soul about me. Do you hear? And don't tell me about yourself either. That would be even worse."

"I won't," said Moth. "I promise."

"My name is Raphael Ciroyan," said the man. "From Outer Berne." His brow crinkled. "Feels good to say it. Been a long time. This boat—made it myself. Didn't know the first thing about boat making when I got here. Learned it all on my own."

From the look of the boat that was easy to believe. "Raphael . . . I never heard that name before."

"It was my father's name," declared the man proudly. "He's dead now. My mother too. I had a brother when I left the world, but never had much use for him anyway."

"And you live here? Through the Reach, I mean? By yourself?"

"Not quite by myself," said the man. A grin stretched across his face. "You know anything about mermaids, boy?"

Moth shook his head. "I didn't even know they existed till yesterday."

"And I bet you nearly lost your mind when you saw her, eh? That's their magic, to turn our heads the way they do. They're crazy about human men. Whenever one comes through the Reach they try and keep him for themselves. Beautiful creatures, but lonely. Forget what you're thinking about mermen; there's no such thing. Just maids. Makes them real hungry for companionship."

Moth imagined what that was like, loving the idea of living with the mermaids. "So that's why you came here? For the mermaids?"

"Nah. I didn't even know they were here. I came across the Reach because I had to. Wasn't anything left for me in the world. Had folks chasing after me, too. Law types."

"Oh," said Moth darkly. "So you are a thief."

The accusation made Raphael bristle. "You ever been to Outer Berne?"

"No," Moth admitted. "I've never been anywhere but Calio."

"Calio? Calio's as soft as the queen's garters compared to Berne. Real hardscrabble there. Nothing but dead industries, hopelessness. Would you blame a man for stealing to feed himself? That's all I did." Raphael's smile was roguish. "More than once, I admit."

"So you ran," said Moth. Raphael's story wasn't so different from his own. "When was that?"

"Oh, a long time ago. So long I can't even remember. Mermaids make a man forget a lot of things. I ran from the noose right into those tender arms. Didn't make much sense to think about going back."

"She's the one that told you about us, right? That mermaid we saw?"

"Serana's her name," said Raphael. "Yeah, she told me. Humans aren't supposed to come through the Reach. Been a long time since the last one. And there's never been children come across."

"So there's others? Where are they?"

Raphael's face darkened. "It's not safe for humans here, and it's not safe for you. That's why I'm helping you, because you're just kids. And because you know Merceron's name." Seeing Moth about to speak, he put up a hand. "No, don't tell me how you know it. Don't tell me anything. Let's just get you to that forest."

Frustrated, Moth leaned forward. "Raphael, what are you scared of? What are we hiding from?"

Raphael shook his head, rowing deliberately. "Find Merceron. He'll be able to answer your questions." At the front of the boat, Fiona started to stir. Raphael smiled. "She's the one with the temper, eh? Not you, though. You're easygoing."

"She's my friend," said Moth.

"Older than you, I'm guessing. Tall girl."

"Careful," warned Moth. "Don't let her hear you say that."

"Too late," groaned Fiona. She sat up, blinking and scratching her red head, searching the river. "We almost there?"

"Hold tight, little gal," said Raphael. "We'll be there soon."

The sun was over the top of the trees when the little boat coasted into the bay. Raphael stored his oars, letting the craft drift toward shore as his passengers marveled at the forest. Sugar-white sand pushed up against the trees, forming a gleaming beach, but the trees themselves were like nothing Moth had ever seen. He and Fiona crowded the prow for a better look.

"The sunken forest," Raphael announced. "The end."

In fact the river did seem to end here, spilling out into a broad lagoon that broke past the sand in spots to flood the forest. Enormous tangles of roots erupted out of the sand like the gnarled hands of giants. There were places where the sand had gathered in ribbons through the forest, making little pathways. In other spots the roots were submerged. The sight of it made Moth shrink.

"How are we supposed to get through that?" he groaned. Lady Esme hopped onto his shoulder with a cry of distress.

The boat drifted to shore, beaching itself on the brilliant sand.

"Is Merceron far?" asked Fiona.

"Don't know," said Raphael. "Maybe."

With little comfort from their guide, Moth and Fiona glanced at each other.

"I can take you back, if you want," said Raphael. "But you can't stay with the mermaids. You'll have to head home through the Reach."

"No," said Fiona. Determined, she hopped over the gunwale to splash ashore. "We've come too far. We'll find Merceron. I know we will."

Moth made to follow her, pausing to consider his strange new friend. "Is there anything else you can tell us?"

Raphael smiled sadly. "Yeah," he said. "Move fast." He pointed to the top of the forest, which was so thick it formed a roof of leaves and branches. "That'll hide you," he said. "Just keep your mind clear. Forget about me. Don't even think about me. Don't think of home, don't think of anything. Just keep on moving."

Moth nodded, as confused as ever. "Thanks," he said, and reached out to shake Raphael's hand. "And don't worry—I'll keep my promise. I won't tell anyone about you."

"Does that go for you too, little gal?" Raphael asked Fiona.

"Promise," said Fiona. She added wistfully, "I wish you could stay with us."

"Can't," said Raphael. "But you don't need me. You got each other, and you got each other this far. Just remember what I told you—keep moving and don't think about anything."

Moth grabbed his coat, felt the bulge of the star machine in its pocket, and leaped out of the boat. Together he and Fiona trudged to shore with Lady Esme, then watched as Raphael Ciroyan shoved off with his oars, heading back to his mermaids.

THE BLACK HERON

SERANA RETURNED TO HER ROCK the next day, happy to be alone once again. She was worried about Raphael but not *too* worried; he would find his way back to the lagoon, she was sure. And they had done the right thing, helping the human children. Serana was sure of that, too. She reclined lazily on her rock, her tail gently swishing the water, and closed her eyes against the hot sun. The warmth felt good on her skin and scales. Her family's waters extended only a few miles, but they were wonderfully quiet waters, and except for Raphael Ciroyan no other humans had ever disturbed them until the children arrived.

Forget them, Serana told herself.

It wasn't helpful to think about them. Thoughts like that could only bring trouble. And it was such a beautiful day . . .

Serana wasn't like her sisters, who preferred the deep waters of their caves and never went exploring. They were musical, while she was quiet. They were sound, but she was dreamy. Someday, she would even explore the sunken forest itself.

"Someday," she vowed softly.

A group of egrets floated nearby, picking at insects with their long beaks. Serana watched them with mild interest, until she noticed another bird near them, wading close to shore. Her lips pursed with surprise. Slowly, silently, she slid down the rock into the water.

The black heron was the first she'd seen all season. A rare

bird for Shelian waters, they were omens of good fortune—particularly to the first maid who saw one. Serana moved toward the creature, her finned tail turning slowly, propelling her forward. Sharklike, her eyes just above the surface, she watched the bird track the marshy shore. Black herons were easily startled, she knew, and impossible to catch. Her sister Danre had tried to catch one once, bounding after it like a seal and coming home with her hair in tangles. Serana didn't want to catch it, though. All she wanted was a really close look. Close, so that she could remember it.

But it was easy to get too close. In a sudden, feathery splash, the heron leaped and flew over Serana's head.

"Oh, wait!" she cried, darting up from the water and watching the heron flap down on the other side of the lagoon, where it floated near a shallow tributary filled with cattails. Determined, Serana swam for it, pushing swiftly through the emerald water. The sandy bottom of the lagoon brushed her belly. When she peeked up her head, the heron was just a few yards away.

"Beautiful bird," she crooned. "Look at you—a treasure."

The bird ignored her, as if it knew a mermaid could never catch a heron. Floating away, it followed the narrow rivulet into the grass and disappeared. Serana smiled, suddenly enjoying the chase. The powerful muscles of her tail could propel her easily in the shallow waters. Arms outstretched, she swam after the heron, pushing aside the reeds to reveal the long, thin waterway snaking through the forest.

"Where are you?" she asked sweetly. "Just let Serana see you."

She spied the trees as she swam, watching them for movement. The water continued to get more shallow, forcing her to use her arms more.

"Treasure?" she called.

She went a few more yards, but all she saw were another pair of egrets. Dragonflies buzzed through the reeds. The sun burning her naked skin, Serana decided to turn back.

"Looking for this?"

Serena spun at the voice. A figure stood in the stream, its boots covered in mud and bits of grass, its body concealed within a dark, dragging cloak. A shadowy hood hid its unseen face. Serana froze, amazed and terrified. Despite its shape, the thing wasn't human. It held the heron in its bone-white hands, spidery fingers clutched around the bird's neck.

Serana stared at the thing. She had never seen one before, but knew what it was. She wanted to flee, but the figure blocked her way. She sank as far as she could into the water, exposed and vulnerable.

"It's good luck to catch a black heron," said the thing, its voice sugary sweet. "Or should I just eat it? It looks delicious!"

The appalling question sickened Serana. "Let it go. Please. . . ."

She could sense the creature's smile beneath its inky hood. Invisible eyes moved over Serana covetously. "Mermaid, mermaid, with hair of grass," the creature sang. "Mermaid, mermaid, sad little lass."

The voice chilled Serana. A woman's voice?

"Silly song!" it crowed. "From a place I once knew. Why do I remember it?" It paused, cocking its cowled head. "Your hair isn't grass."

It watched Serana, the dying heron completely forgotten. Serana knew it hadn't come just for the bird. Why did it stare so?

"Are you lost?" she asked, trying not to sound afraid. "Maybe I can help you."

"Yesss," replied the figure, drawing out the word like the hiss of a snake. "You can help me, child. We have heard a rumor of humans here." It lifted its head, sniffing deeply in a great inhalation, revealing hints of its hideous face. "We smell them!"

"Humans?" gasped Serana. "No, not here," she lied. "Not ever here . . ."

The thing splashed forward, frightening her. "They come! Have you seen them?"

"No," said Serana, clasping her hands to her breast. "Never a human!"

The figure mocked her alarm. "Oh!" it mimicked, laughing again. "Why are you afraid? The loyal should never be afraid. Are you loyal to the Skylords, child?"

"Yes, always," said Serana. "But we are quiet maids here. There's never trouble here, no reason for you to come."

"Quiet maids," the thing repeated. "Pretty maids."

It came closer still, bending down to look at Serana, its breath thick. Its features were slight, womanly. With a jerk of its wrist it killed the half-dead heron, then extended it out toward Serana.

"A gift, pretty one."

Tamping down her revulsion, Serana reached out her shaking hand, refusing to look directly at the creature. Instead she looked at the silver chain around its waist, the stout, unbreakable symbol of its bondage. The cold brush of its fingers against her own shocked Serana.

"Will you eat it?"

Serana shook her head. Again the thing laughed.

"What do mermaids eat?" it asked. "Seaweed and cockles!" It stood, clapping loudly. "Seaweed and cockles and hair of grass! Sirens who make men breathe their last!"

At last it turned to go, singing its horrible song as it left her. For a long time Serana was unable to move. She held the dead bird—her beautiful heron. The touch of the creature had sickened her.

But she was alive. Even after lying to the creature. Now, Serana knew, she had to flee.

Dropping the heron, she raced from the shallows toward her green lagoon, diving for the deep, deep waters of home.

THE DOOR IN THE HILLSIDE

RAPHAEL CIROYAN HAD NOT known where to find Merceron, but he had given Moth and Fiona one important piece of advice—there was nothing in the sunken forest that was poisonous. They could eat whatever fruit they found.

For Moth and Fiona, both famished from walking, the news was a gift. They had run out of meat pies and neither of them knew how to hunt, so they gorged themselves on citrus and berries, finding the forest abundant with both. But more amazing still was the darkness that shrouded the sunken world. The pale, ancient trees twisted ever upward, spreading out their widest arms at the very top, making a canopy that even sunlight struggled to penetrate. As Moth trudged along, he peered up at the roof of interwoven limbs, sucking the juice from a sweet, purple fruit.

"How can fruit grow without sunlight?" he mulled. "How can anything grow without light?"

Fiona cradled a handful of blueberries, delighting in their sweetness. Lady Esme, perched on her shoulder, plucked them from her palm. The berries had moist, shining skin, the kind of bright, impossible blue more suited to a bird. A while back they had found a vine full of them. After one taste, Fiona had picked the vine clean.

"Who cares how it got here?" Fiona retorted. "We have food now. And it's dry here." She glanced down at her boots, still wet from the bogs. "My toes are cold."

"They'll dry overnight," said Moth, pausing to look around. The forest was mostly quiet, with small mammals and birds moving in the shadows but nothing to threaten them. The trees reminded Moth of corpses, their white bark like bone, white like Leroux's skin on his deathbed. Near the water the trees had been almost normal. But not anymore. Not here. "It's because there's no sun," he realized.

Fiona kept popping berries into her mouth. "I gotta eat," she said, disinterested.

"What's wrong?" Moth asked. "You've been like this all day."

"Like what?"

"I dunno. Snappy."

"Look around, Moth. You see anything to be smiling about? We're lost."

"We're not lost. We're following the star machine. This is where Merceron lives . . ." Moth stopped. "Oh . . ."

"What?" snorted Fiona.

Moth smiled softly. "You're not mad," he said. "You're scared. That's why you don't want me to use the star machine again. You don't want to see Merceron."

Fiona gave Esme one more berry, then tossed the others away. "So? He's a dragon, Moth. What do you think he'll do when he sees us?"

"If he was dangerous, Leroux wouldn't have told me about him. Raphael wouldn't have taken us here if—"

"Raphael was a criminal. Maybe he just wanted to get rid of us. Did you ever think of that?"

Moth tossed aside his own fruit, then rummaged through his big pocket for the star machine. So far they had only looked at Merceron once, mostly because Moth knew how frightened the dragon made Fiona. But they were getting closer now. Moth could feel it. There wasn't time for her to be afraid.

"Look," he told her, kneeling in the sand. He unwrapped the instrument and laid it down carefully. As if it knew what he wanted, the scope began to turn, pointing in the direction they'd been traveling all day. "Show me Merceron," ordered Moth.

Fiona gave a sigh of dread. Moth watched, eager to see the

dragon-wizard again. The mirror swirled with smoke. Moth bent lower. He saw movement in the mirror, crowded by darkness.

"There," said Moth, his heart pounding. "I see him."

A glimpse of tail, a glint of tooth, and all around them trees, bone-white like the ones around them now. Merceron was moving. No longer inside his lair, he stalked the dark forest, almost impossible to see. Long talons cut through stringy vines. The spectacled eyes flashed and disappeared.

"What's he doing?" Moth wondered. Fiona inched toward him, peering over his shoulder.

"I can barely see him," she whispered.

Was he hunting? Looking for them? Moth glanced at Lady Esme, hoping for a hint of recognition, but the bird was looking skyward instead, longing to take flight. Suddenly Fiona pointed at the mirror.

"Look at those trees." She glanced around. "They're the same ones."

Moth picked up the star machine. "We're really close now." He licked his lips, annoyed that he was feeling afraid too. "We can't stop now, Fiona."

Fiona looked like a tall glass of milk. "We came this far," she agreed. She turned to the kestrel on her shoulder and said, "Lady Esme, stay with me, all right?"

As Moth moved, the star machine turned with him, pointing through the trees. The image of Merceron began to fade.

"If he's nearby we'll hear him," whispered Moth. "I hope."

He tucked the thing back into his pocket, stalking forward, leading Fiona and Lady Esme. Their feet crunched against the roots and fallen branches. Moth ducked low, watching the trees grow ever whiter, the sunlight ever more dim. Sweat dripped down his face, but his mouth was cottony dry.

Then, a noise.

Moth and Fiona peered hard through the forest. A glimpse of movement flashed up ahead, just like in the mirror. Fiona froze, her eyes widening to saucers. Moth tried hard to see, but the trees blocked his way. He put a finger to his lips, then took Fiona's hand. Together they tiptoed closer, closer, until at last they saw it.

There in the shadows it hunched among the trees, its claws scraping a tree branch it held. To Moth it looked like the dragon was . . . *whittling?*

"What now?" whispered Fiona. Her mouth was right up against Moth's ear, yet he could barely hear her. He sucked his lower lip.

"We can't just hide," he decided. "We have to face him." He looked into Fiona's eyes for strength. "Okay?"

Fiona hesitated. "What? Just walk over and say hi?"

"Yeah."

He stood up, surprising even himself, and readied to face the dragon. Fiona managed to stand as well, and with Lady Esme on her shoulder, remained at Moth's side as they took their first bold step.

"Hello!" Moth called. "Merceron?"

Utter silence. The world just froze. Moth and Fiona continued one more step, then another. Then . . .

Trees cracked and vines snapped. Movement exploded before them. Moth and Fiona jumped back. The shadowy mass ripped through the forest. Moth held up his hands, his mouth opening to shout, then realized the thing was not coming toward them at all.

"What . . . ?"

"He's running!" cried Fiona. "Moth, he's running away!"

Moth shook off his terror and bolted after him.

"Hurry!"

Fiona followed, Lady Esme leaping from her shoulder to take the lead. Moth didn't need the star machine anymore—Merceron left a gaping trail to follow. Even in the dark they could see his massive outline, but the dragon moved so quickly it was like chasing a leopard through the trees. Trees collapsed as the creature muscled them aside, his four thick limbs speeding him through the forest. Moth and Fiona kept up as best they could, vaulting over the fallen trees. Already they were losing sight of Merceron.

"No!" cried Moth. "Merceron, wait!"

The darkness swallowed the dragon whole. A ground-shaking noise followed, like the gate of a castle slamming shut. Moth stopped running, putting his hands on his knees and panting.

"Where's Esme?" asked Fiona as she skidded up beside him.

From somewhere up ahead, the kestrel answered her call.

"She's all right," gasped Moth.

"But Merceron's gone! We lost him!"

Again Lady Esme gave her throaty cry, this time sounding farther away. They rushed after her, over the trampled grass and past cracked, dangling branches, finally coming to an enormous hillside. Rows of white trees surrounded the hill; mud-colored moss clung to its rocks. At its foot was Esme, hopping impatiently in front of a gigantic slab of metal nearly invisible in the gloom, its surface grimy and drooping with vines.

"Merceron's lair," Moth whispered. "This door—that's what we heard. He's inside."

Lady Esme flew back to him, landing on his shoulder while he pondered the door.

"He's hiding?" erupted Fiona suddenly. "From us? That's ridiculous!"

Moth couldn't remember ever seeing her so exasperated. "We can wait," he suggested. "Maybe he'll come back out."

"What? Uh-uh." Fiona pulled off her coat and tossed it to the ground. "I didn't come all this way to have him slam a door in my face."

"Fiona . . ."

"I'm sick of waiting!" she fumed. Her eyes flashed as she turned toward the door. "And I'm sick of running. No more!"

Red hair askew, Fiona marched, rolling up her shirt sleeves as if spoiling for a fight. The door in the hillside loomed above her, and when she pounded against it her fist made no sound at all.

"Hey, dragon!" she bellowed. "You're running away? Are you kidding me? We're just kids!" She pounded again. "Do you have any idea how far we've come? Huh? You don't even know who we are!"

Moth slipped from the tree cover, glimpsing Fiona's desperate face. It wasn't anger he saw anymore, but anguish.

"Please," she cried. "I know you're listening to me. We need your help. Lady Esme needs your help."

Fiona put her head against the giant portal as if listening for something. Her whole body seemed to collapse. The hillside was silent. Fiona peeled herself away, her eyes rimmed with frustration. She looked at Moth hopelessly.

"It's all right," Moth told her. "We'll find another way."

Behind Fiona the door creaked open, revealing a sliver of perfect darkness. From inside the hill issued a resonant, velvety voice.

"Esme."

THE PACT

ONCE THE DOOR CLOSED behind them, all was darkness. Moth could feel Merceron in the giant chamber, the dragon's breathing swelling like some great machine.

"Merceron?" called Moth. "We're here. We have Lady Esme." He paused, holding on to Fiona. "We know you're here. Please speak to us."

A slithering noise echoed through the room. Moth squinted, wondering how something so large could stay invisible.

"Don't try to scare us," said Fiona. "We're not afraid of you."

"Please, Merceron. We can't see you."

"Oh," came the resonant voice again, "but I can see *you*."

Moth blinked, and there before his face was a massive, devil-horned head. He jumped back, nearly falling over.

"Moth!" cried Fiona, her arms shooting out for him.

From a dark corner of the chamber came a sudden glow of light, the soft flicker of a newly lit lamp. The light crept through the chamber, slowly revealing their reptilian host.

Merceron reclined on a bed of old, lumpy cushions, a pair of wings tucked beneath him. His spectacled eyes stared adoringly at Lady Esme, perched in his upturned palm. The thin ridges of his long jaws curved in a smile.

"Esme," he crooned. "My beautiful friend."

Next to Moth, Fiona stood pale with astonishment. Merceron was just as they had seen in the mirror, both humanlike and mythical, as big as an elephant and refined as a scholar, his eyes twinkling behind his glasses, his body cloaked in a red velvet jacket. Greenish scales covered his hide and a crest of horns ran down his back and along his spiky tail.

"You do know Esme," said Moth. "Leroux was right."

"Leroux?" Merceron examined Moth, then Fiona. "Neither of you have the features of his family." His head coiled forward, sniffing the air. "But you, girl, have the blood of Rendor in you."

"That's right," said Fiona. "How'd you—?"

"Let me see you better," said the dragon, bringing fire to his free hand with a snap of his claws. His tail came around and plucked the flames from his talons, then bounced like a tentacle around the chamber, lighting a trio of lamps. "Better?"

"Yes," nodded Moth. The place was gigantic, its smooth walls lined with messy, overstuffed bookcases. Near a cavernous fireplace rested a cupboard and a big, lumpy chair. Merceron's pipe, the one they'd seen him smoking in the mirror, lay on a rickety table. The dragon stretched his sinewy neck toward the children as Lady Esme hopped to the top of his wrinkled head.

"Esme, come here," called Fiona.

Merceron laughed. "Don't be afraid for her. Esme and I have known each other since before you were born, girl."

"I'm not afraid," countered Fiona. "I'm not the one who ran away, remember?"

"Hmm, you're a Rendor, all right," snorted Merceron. His eyes flicked to Moth. "What are you called?"

"My name's Moth." Not knowing how to explain things, Moth reached into his pocket and pulled out the star machine. "Leroux gave me this."

With a sudden roar the dragon swatted the device from Moth's hand. A crashing foot ground the thing into the floor.

"Hey!" cried Fiona.

The dragon lifted his foot and peered down at the star machine with a groan of disappointment. Moth scrambled to retrieve it, worried it would be in pieces. Amazingly, not even its mirror was damaged.

"I can't harm it, boy," grumbled Merceron, collapsing into his chair. "No one can."

"What it is?" asked Moth. "Do you know?"

"Of course I do," said Merceron in an irritated voice. "Everyone in this world knows what is it. Everyone bears its curse."

Lady Esme hopped down to the arm of his chair, brushing her wing against him. To Moth, she seemed to be comforting him.

"So?" pressed Fiona. "What is it?"

"The Starfinder," the dragon grumbled. "The indestructible, all-enslaving Starfinder."

Moth ran his fingertips over the device. "Starfinder . . ." At least now it had a name. "It brought us to you, Merceron. Just like Leroux said it would."

"What?" The dragon rose, towering over Moth. "You used it?"

"Yes," said Moth. "It took us right to you."

Merceron boomed with laughter. "Ha! Leroux did it! He figured it out!"

"Well, no," said Moth. "Not really."

Merceron turned to Fiona. "So Rendor helped him?"

"My grandfather?" scoffed Fiona. "Please. He never helped anyone in his life."

"Grandfather? Ah . . ." Merceron's grin displayed a mouthful of teeth. "You're one to be careful of, then—Rendor's offspring."

"My name's Fiona," she shot back. "And I'm nothing like my grandfather."

"It's true, Merceron," said Moth. "Nobody helped us. I used the Starfinder on my own."

"That's impossible," said Merceron. "You're just a boy!"

His disbelief annoyed Moth. "We're not lying to you. All Leroux said was that he couldn't get back here to help Esme. Do you know what he meant?"

All the joy left Merceron's face. "I do. It means we both failed Esme."

Moth wrapped his hands around his oversized teacup, watching Merceron puff lightly on his pipe. On the table next to them sat the Starfinder. Fiona sipped suspiciously at her tea, considering the dragon over the rim of her cup. Merceron leaned back in his chair, blowing smoke rings from his nostrils.

They had explained everything to Merceron—about Leroux and their journey through the Reach, and how Fiona's grandfather was searching for the Starfinder. They left out nothing, and while they spoke Merceron listened attentively, never interrupting, not even when they told him about Leroux's death. Finally, when their tale was done, the dragon grew contemplative.

"Leroux was a good friend," he said sadly. Scaly lids closed halfway over his eyes. "Such a shame. Your people live such short lives."

Fiona set down her teacup. "Did you give Leroux the Starfinder?"

"Can it help make Esme human again?" asked Moth.

Merceron exhaled a plume of tobacco smoke. "Leroux kept his secrets, and secrets aren't easy for humans. Your grandfather, Fiona—now there's a man of secrets. I bet he never even told you he came here with Leroux."

"Huh?" choked Fiona. "He came *here*?"

"Rendor?" gasped Moth.

"Rendor," nodded Merceron. "Leroux didn't come here on his own. They came together. Eldrin Knights, they called themselves."

"Yes," said Moth, "but Leroux never said anything about Rendor."

Merceron chuckled. "You see? Secrets! They came through the Reach to see what was here and to spy on the Skylords. They were lucky to get back to your world."

"So then it's true about Esme?" asked Moth. "Leroux said she's not really a bird."

"Did they love each other?" asked Fiona.

The dragon extended a bony finger, coaxing Esme onto it. "Oh yes," he sighed, holding the kestrel up to his face. "She was brave and beautiful. It was easy to fall in love with her."

"Who was she?" asked Moth. "Who did this to her?"

Merceron's face clouded with shadows. "I suppose Leroux couldn't tell you the truth. Your grandfather either, Fiona."

"What truth?" pushed Moth. He'd waited so long for the story he thought he'd burst if he didn't hear it right now. "Please, Merceron, tell us."

Merceron's voice dipped low. "This is the realm of the Skylords. Only they have the power to transform creatures. They're the ones who made the Starfinder. And until you, Moth, they were the only ones ever able to use it."

"I tried it myself," said Fiona. "But I can't make it work."

"As did I," said Merceron. "Leroux, too. Only you can use its powers, Moth, and that's a mystery to me." The dragon's massive shoulders shrugged. "But it's back now, and it's a curse to us."

"Why?" Moth asked. "What's it do?"

"You've already seen what it can do." Merceron lifted the Starfinder off the table. "It strips away all privacy, all freedom. It gave the Skylords command of the sky."

Moth felt lost. "All I did was hold it up to the stars. It showed me the constellations like they were alive."

"Precisely," said Merceron. "They are alive. In your world the stars just make pictures, but here every constellation is a real being. Like me."

"That's impossible," scoffed Fiona. "How can that be?"

"Because the Skylords made it that way. They weren't always as they are now. Once they were like you. Afraid. Ignorant. The sky helped them make sense of the world. Imagine seeing a dragon for the first time! Or a centaur! We were like gods to them. So they drew their star maps and put us in the sky. And when they grew up, they gave their constellations different names. It wasn't just a dragon anymore. It became Merceron."

"You must be a real important dragon to get your own constellation," said Fiona.

"I used to be," replied Merceron. His smile faded. "Not anymore."

"So the Skylords made the Starfinder to control the rest of you?" asked Moth. "Their enemies?"

"We were all their enemies once they took to the sky," said Merceron. He laid his pipe down on the table. "Skylords are a jealous people. They think the sky belongs to them. The whole sky, mind you, in every world, and if they knew your grandfather had made machines for humans to fly . . ."

"Even the birds," whispered Moth. "That's why they don't fly here, isn't it? They're scared of the Skylords."

Merceron lowered himself from his chair, almost kneeling. "Come here," he said. As Moth and Fiona left their seats, he wrapped his tail around them gently. "When Leroux and Rendor came across the Reach," he told them, "dragons were at war with the Skylords. We battled them for our right to the sky. Then they created the Starfinder. The gryphons, the eagles . . . all were forced to bow to them. That's what the Skylords did to my dragons."

"But you got away," said Fiona. "Did you run?"

"Not at first. At first I tried to rally my kin, but they were weary of fighting. Eventually they turned on me. But I still plotted. And I wasn't completely alone. I still had friends willing to help me."

"Leroux?" asked Moth excitedly.

"Yes. And someone else." The great eyes of the dragon fell again on Esme. "She was the one who stole the Starfinder. By then she and Leroux were already in love. I hid them here, in this hideaway. But the Skylords knew what Esme had done. They punished her, did . . . *that* to her."

Moth was beginning to understand. "That's when you gave Leroux the Starfinder."

Merceron nodded. "We made a pact. We knew the Skylords would never enter the human world. I promised Leroux I'd find a way to return Esme to normal. And Leroux made a vow to return here one day with Esme. But he never did, because he never figured out how to use the Starfinder."

"What about my grandfather?" asked Fiona. "Was he part of the pact too?"

"Your grandfather knew what we'd found, Fiona, but he couldn't speak of it. It was forbidden for him to come across the Reach, and even though he wanted the Starfinder it wasn't his to claim. He and Leroux both promised never to speak of it to anyone. Leroux would try to unlock its secrets, but if he died before doing so . . ."

"The Starfinder would be Rendor's," said Moth.

"No!" Fiona protested. "We can't let him have it. He hates the Skylords. If he has the Starfinder he'll just use it to invade here."

"Merceron, all I want is to help Esme," said Moth. "Can the Starfinder change her back? After that . . . well, I don't know. But Esme needs our help."

Merceron's eyes swelled with sympathy. "Only the Skylords can change her back. The Starfinder can't help you with that."

"So what do we do?" asked Fiona.

"Nothing." Merceron dropped back into his chair. "I'm afraid you've wasted your time coming here."

"What do you mean?" asked Moth.

"I've told you my story. That's all I can do."

"What? No! You have to help us. Leroux said you would."

"He was wrong. I told you, there's no way to save Esme. It's impossible." Merceron picked up his pipe again. "I've done all that I can."

Fiona stepped forward, her face thunderous. "You told us you owe Esme. Is this how you're going to repay her? She'll be a bird forever if you don't help us!"

Merceron ground his teeth. "I'm stuck here, don't you see? An outcast! If the Skylords find me they'll kill me for sure."

"But we can't go home," said Moth. "If we do, Rendor will get the Starfinder."

The dragon lit his pipe with a flick of his claws. "You may stay here for a day. *Only* for a day. The Skylords will find you if you remain any longer."

"You mean they'll find *you*," sneered Fiona. "Some dragon you turned out to be! I thought dragons were supposed to be fierce. But you know what? You're just a coward."

"Fiona, stop . . ."

Merceron wouldn't look at either of them. Bristling at his disregard, Fiona stormed off into a connecting chamber.

"She's like her grandfather," sniffed the dragon. "He had a head like granite, too."

Unsure what to do or say, Moth took Lady Esme onto his shoulder, then started after Fiona.

"Moth?"

Moth paused. "Yeah?"

"Have you figured it out yet?"

"What?"

"About Esme. Have you figured it out yet?"

Moth bit his lip. "Uhm, I don't think so . . ."

"Oh, you must have," said Merceron. "Think! Why didn't the Skylords kill Esme? She stole the Starfinder, conspired against them. She even fell in love with a human. Why do you think they'd ever let someone like that go free?" Before Moth could answer, the dragon swung his big head around. "Because she's one of them, Moth. Lady Esme is a Skylord."

TINKERING

INSIDE MERCERON'S LAIR, night and day felt precisely the same. There were no windows to the outside world, and no clocks among the clutter lining the shelves. Moth only knew it was bedtime because he was so tired, yet sleep somehow evaded him. Beneath his threadbare blanket he gazed into the crackling hearth, remembering how the dragon had lit it for them with a snort of fiery breath. Fiona lay beside him, staring up at the dark ceiling, a roof so high it was almost like being outside.

Throughout the night she had barely said a word. Even the news about Lady Esme garnered only a cynical shake of her head. She had gone off to explore the lair alone, finding a treasure trove of handmade objects, including an enormous piano-like instrument carved from a giant tree trunk.

Moth rolled onto his back to gaze up at the ceiling with Fiona. The way the firelight twinkled on the stone made him think of the Starfinder, and then about Esme. He stole a sideways glance at Fiona, trying to think of something—anything—to wrest her from her mood.

"I've never been swimming," he whispered. "My mother told me she used to swim in a lake at night when she was a little girl back in—"

"Why are you telling me this?" Fiona interrupted.

"Just thinking." Moth's eyes scanned the walls, picking out the shadowy knickknacks on the shelves. "Look at all these things he's made. Must help him pass the time."

"Sure. He's got nothing better to do."

"Look, I know you're angry," said Moth, "but we'll figure this out. Remember what Raphael said? We got each other, and we got each other this far."

"Yeah, he was a big help," grumbled Fiona. "Just like Merceron. Just another person willing to walk out on us." Her face bunched up in a grimace. "Just like everyone else."

Moth sat up and leaned on his elbow. "I've been thinking. Maybe the Starfinder can locate someone else who can help Esme. Maybe there's another wizard we can ask."

"We don't even know what the constellations are here, Moth. We only found Merceron 'cause Leroux told you to."

"Yeah, but Merceron would know. He could tell us that, at least."

"Fine," said Fiona. "You go ask him."

She rolled onto her side, turning her back on him. Undeterred, Moth tossed off his blanket and quietly left the chamber. He hadn't seen Merceron since going to bed, but he supposed the dragon was sleeping, too. But when he reached the main chamber it was empty, with only a puny fire sputtering in the gigantic hearth. Across the cavern a sliver of light crept in from the big metal door.

"Merceron?"

Moth went to the door and peered outside. Just beyond the threshold he caught a glimpse of Merceron in the strangled moonlight. The dragon was down on his haunches, concentrating on a long ribbon that looked like leather or bark, pulling it tightly in his claws and stripping it down with his teeth. Around him was scattered all manner of bric-a-brac—huge squares of animal skins, bent metal rods, tree branches, shavings of wood. There were tools, too, punches and chisels and needles, but mostly Merceron worked with his teeth and claws. All alone beneath the protective canopy, he stripped down the supple ribbon, bending it occasionally to test it.

"Come closer if you want to see," said Merceron suddenly. "Your staring makes me nervous."

"Sorry," said Moth, stepping closer. "What are you doing?"

"Keeping busy. Where's your friend? Sleeping?"

"Kind of," said Moth, running his eyes over the dragon's pile of material. "She's kind of upset."

Merceron kept on working, punching holes in the long ribbon with his pinky claw. "And Esme?"

"She's all right. She's with Fiona. One thing about old Esme, she could sleep through anything. Even Leroux's snoring."

Merceron laughed. "Oh, I will miss him." His voice trailed off with a kind of shrug. "I always thought I'd see him again."

It was still hard for Moth to think of Leroux. He blew into his cheeks, wanting to change the subject. "So what's all this stuff? You making something?"

"Tinkering helps me think." Merceron picked up a rod of metal, poked it through one of the holes he'd made, and bent it effortlessly into a ring.

"Whew," whistled Moth. "What's it going to be?"

Merceron sighed in annoyance. "If you can't sleep, just watch quietly, all right?"

"All right," Moth agreed, but knew he couldn't. After a minute he said, "We'll be going tomorrow. Can you tell us anything more to help us? I was hoping you could maybe tell us about some other wizard. You know, point us in the right direction."

"A wizard?"

"Yeah. Even just a name, so I can use the Starfinder. Someone whose picture's in the sky, like you."

"You have to be a scholar of the sky to use the Starfinder properly, boy." The dragon dropped down onto his tail with a huff. "Like the Skylords." He lifted his face, his view obscured by the trees. "Even if I gave you a name it wouldn't help."

"But I have to try," Moth argued. "Leroux would want me to."

"Is he the one who told you I was a wizard?"

"Aren't you?"

Merceron smiled faintly. "I suppose I must have seemed like one to him. All dragons can do things that look magical, but I'm no wizard. More of a sage, really. A keeper of knowledge."

"What? Like a librarian?" Moth recalled the hundreds of books in the lair. "Leroux must have thought a lot of you, or else he wouldn't have sent me to you."

"He must have thought a lot of you too, Moth." The dragon

set aside his work. "If only you could have seen Esme the way she used to be. She was like a goddess once. And she wasn't like the other Skylords, either. Esme knew the difference between right and wrong."

"Leroux told me the Skylords are like angels," said Moth. "But you make them sound like monsters."

Merceron smiled. "To Leroux, Esme really was an angel."

"Why didn't they just kill her? I mean, after what you say she did to them."

"The Skylords would never kill one of their own. That's their idea of being civilized, I suppose. Besides, what they did to her was far worse. Imagine being stuck as a mindless bird."

"A bird." Moth thought about that, about all the times he'd looked up at birds and wished he were one of them. "At least she can fly. That's more than most of us ever get to do." He took notice of Merceron's wings, neatly tucked close to his velvet jacket. "You could fly too, if you wanted. If you weren't so afraid."

"Flying . . ." Merceron's expression filled with longing. "It's been a very long time."

"I have a friend back in Calio named Skyhigh," said Moth. "He flies all the time. He's a Skyknight."

"Skyknight?" puffed Merceron. "What's that?"

"They're like regular knights, only they fly dragonflies and airships. The ones Governor Rendor invented."

"What about the Eldrin Knights?"

"Oh, they've been gone for years," said Moth. "Leroux was probably the last of them. Besides Rendor, I guess. Fiona says her grandfather always wanted to fly. She says that's why he hates the Skylords, because they don't want humans polluting the sky. He thinks it's man's destiny."

"Rendor's a grand thinker," said Merceron. "Brave, though. And smart like a dragon." He turned to Moth curiously. "Have you ever been up in one of his machines?"

"Skyhigh took me up a few times," said Moth, breaking into a smile. "I love thinking about it, daydreaming. It's amazing being up there."

"Someday maybe you'll be a Skyknight too, eh?"

"Maybe." Moth kicked at the dirt. "Probably not."

Merceron brought his tail around and lightly poked Moth with it. "Why not? You seem like a bright boy. Can't you get yourself one of those dragonfly things?"

"It doesn't work like that," said Moth. "They're not for sale, and even if they were I wouldn't have the money. But I'll fly one day. I might never be a Skyknight, but I'll fly." He looked up, wanting to see the sky, his view blocked by the canopy. "These trees hide you from the Skylords. That's it, isn't it? Why you don't fly anymore, I mean."

"The Skylords, yes," the dragon drawled. "And . . . others." Immediately he went back to work, this time grabbing up a wide, fat piece of animal hide. "Got to keep at it."

"Uh, Merceron?"

"Uhm?"

"Will the Skylords come after us? Raphael Ciroyan was hiding from them, I think, but he wouldn't tell us why. What will happen to us if they find us?"

Merceron's fingers worked without any obvious purpose. "It's the Starfinder they want, not you," he said, but his tone was unconvincing. "You just make sure you take care of each other, you hear? Youngsters! Running around, always getting hurt." He tore a great rent in the hide, then cursed his imprecision. "Got to watch what I'm doing. Why don't you go inside? Make sure your friend's all right."

"I told you, she's fine . . ."

"She's not fine!" bawled Merceron. "Someone who loses her loved ones is never fine! You're not fine, are you? If you were fine you'd have had the sense to stay home!"

Moth stumbled back, stunned. Merceron lowered the piece of hide with an exasperated breath.

"You know, I've been thinking," he said in a halting voice. "Maybe you're right. Maybe you can get help somewhere else."

"Yeah?" said Moth cautiously.

Merceron nodded. "There are other dragons who might be able to help you," he said. "It's been decades since the war ended. Maybe they've learned something since then about Skylord magic."

"You mean how to turn Esme back to normal?"

"I said maybe. I don't know. It's just a thought."

"Where are they?" asked Moth. "Are they far?"

"In Taurnoken," said Merceron. "And yes, it's far. You won't have the cover of the forest, either." The ridges over his eyes came down in a fretful frown. "There's a lot of open terrain between here and there."

Moth felt a spark of hope. "Can you tell us how to get there?"

Merceron lifted the piece of hide he'd been working on. "How's this look to you?"

"I don't know. What is it?"

"Nothing yet. When I'm done it'll be a saddle."

"A saddle?" chuckled Moth. "For the biggest horse in the world, maybe!"

Merceron looked right at Moth, his expression dreary. "Do I look like a horse?"

Moth's mouth dropped open. "Merceron . . . you?"

"You want to fly, don't you?" The dragon glanced around at the materials scattered at his feet. "There's not much time. You should probably give me a hand."

UNDERWAY

SKYHIGH STOOD ON THE *Avatar*'s carriage deck, last in a line of forty crewmen. Chest out, his helmet tucked under his arm, he kept his eyes fixed on his commander at the window, and upon the Reach dead ahead.

Promptly at dawn, the *Avatar* had risen five hundred feet above Calio. Untethered from her giant mooring post, she had levitated soundlessly into the air, so gently that Skyhigh would never have known they were moving if he hadn't been looking out a window. Now he could see dragonflies flapping noisily around the city, patrolling the skies.

Throughout the night Skyhigh had waited aboard the airship, watching workmen load her holds with crates marked DANGER and fill her billowing envelope with lifting gas. They fueled her engines, oiled her guns, polished her brass, and tightened the millions of bolts in her superstructure, yet her mission remained a mystery.

Commander Erich Donnar stood before his crew, outlined by the morning light against the window. He held his hands clasped behind him, slapping his gloves together as he paced, his blue eyes as calm as the sea. The first man ever to captain an airship, Donnar was more than just Rendor's friend; he was the perfect choice to command the *Avatar*. With one eyebrow cocked higher than the other, he searched the sky until Rendor strode across the deck.

"Attention!" he called, bringing the crew back to life.

Skyhigh stared straight ahead, watching Rendor from the corner of his eye.

"The *Avatar* stands ready, sir," Donnar reported. "Prepared to depart on your order."

Rendor nodded at the news. "At ease, everyone."

At last Skyhigh looked directly at him. In his dark coat, his silver hair slicked back, he was much the same as he'd been in his office—determined and supremely confident. The chain of his watch dangled across his belly. He had even placed a snow-white flower in his lapel.

"Good morning," he said to the men. "We're about to embark on the mission of a lifetime. Most men never get a chance like this, so consider yourselves lucky. We're going to do something that's been forbidden to humanity since the start of time. We're going *there* . . ." He pointed toward the misty horizon. "Through the Reach."

A murmur stirred through the crew. Skyhigh's stomach did a somersault.

"The *Avatar* is the greatest, most powerful airship ever built," Rendor continued. "You've all had time to study her; you all know what she can do. But the things on the other side of that fog out there are going to put her and you to the test!" The Governor glowered at the men, then broke into a mysterious grin. "And if you're thinking I'm just some crazy old man, just you wait."

Some of the crew glanced at Donnar for reassurance. Donnar just nodded.

"Now," said Rendor, "here's what you need to know . . ."

Skyhigh leaned in.

"Three days ago, a thirteen-year-old boy named Moth left Calio and crossed through the Reach. He has an object of great value with him. Our mission is to get it back. We're going to find him and the object, and we're not coming home until we do."

Rendor gestured to Donnar to speak. "Commander."

"We'll be traveling low and slow," Donnar told the crew. "We've taken on as much hidrenium as we can carry, but once it's gone we'll be stuck. That means no high speed climbs and no wasting fuel. We'll be traveling in daylight only—no night flying. And there'll be no friendlies to help us, either."

Skyhigh couldn't believe no one had mentioned Fiona yet. He raised his hand.

"Yes?"

"Question," said Skyhigh. "We're looking for a girl, too, aren't we?" His eyes landed on Rendor. "Aren't we, Governor?"

"Yes," replied Rendor. His jaw tightened. "My granddaughter Fiona is with the boy. You all know that already."

Again Skyhigh put up his hand.

"What?" snapped Donnar.

"I'm wondering, sir—just what exactly are we going up against?"

The crew waited anxiously for an answer.

"Things that fly, Captain Coralin," said Rendor. "Now, all of you—do your job."

Commander Donnar barked an order for the *Avatar* to depart. Up ahead, the Reach loomed and rolled, looking like it went on forever.

Like it would swallow the *Avatar* alive.

FOLLOWING THE RIVER

NEEDLES OF WIND PRICKED Moth's face as he peered down into the valley far below. Fiona huddled next to him, so close that a blade of grass couldn't grow between them. Strapped down in Merceron's makeshift saddle, their bodies hunched forward against the dragon's neck, they scanned the wonderland beneath them, struggling against the onslaught of wind. Moth's hands ached from clutching the rope looped around Merceron's chest. The buckles pressing against his legs had torn tiny rents in his pants. His dark coat flew out behind him like the tail of a comet.

The world below raced by in blurs of green and gold. The river they were following snaked through the forests and along flower-strewn hills. Low flying clouds smashed harmlessly against them. Moth could see forever.

He nudged Fiona with his elbow. She turned, and her eyes were bloodshot. All morning and afternoon she'd been talking to herself while they flew, chattering under her breath things that sounded like prayers.

"Look there!" Moth shouted. "How's that look?"

Fiona looked down. Merceron's head tilted to see what Moth had found. Throughout the day they'd stopped so the dragon could rest, always in places where no one could see them.

"Yes," said Fiona, anxious to be on land again. The clearing was close to the river and surrounded by hills. "Down, Merceron, please!"

Merceron tilted his wings, slowing them as they wheeled downward. He had tied his spectacles around his ears to keep them from falling off. His velvet jacket snapped underneath the saddle he'd strapped across his back. Moth heard the dragon sigh with relief.

"We'll rest now, Merceron," Moth told him, patting his scaly neck. "You can catch your breath a while."

Beside them soared Lady Esme, spiraling down, chasing the dragon to the ground. Moth called to her and Esme answered back. They were all tired and in pain, yet Moth couldn't help but feel delighted. Fiona turned green again.

"Oh, I hate this," she groaned. "You hear me, Moth? I hate flying!"

Moth's own head swam as they corkscrewed down. Merceron's wings shot out as the ground rose up. Moth and Fiona held on as the dragon bounced to earth, the shock of their landing jerking them in the saddle.

"I'm gonna be sick," croaked Fiona. She began fumbling with her straps. "Moth, help me . . ."

Instead of undoing his own buckles, Moth reached over and undid the one pinning Fiona's waist to the saddle. Merceron hunched low to the ground, looking over his shoulder.

"As soon as you're ready, I could use a break."

"I'm trying!" fumed Fiona.

She managed the final buckle, nearly falling off his back, walking away with a wobbly gait. Moth carefully unbuckled his own straps, holding onto the rope as he lowered himself down. Merceron stood up and stretched with a roar of pleasure.

"Thank the stars! You little trolls are heavier than you look."

Fiona bent over, hands on her knees over a patch of daisies. "Can't you fly any better then that?"

Moth stood between them. "I thought it was amazing!"

Fiona parted her hair to glare at him. "Flying is crazy. It's irrational!" She put her hand over her mouth. Moth looked away.

"Uh, let's camp over there," he suggested, pointing to a spot far from Fiona's mess.

Merceron winced as he reached back to rub his aching muscles. "And what was that you were muttering the whole time, girl? It was like a cricket crawled into my ear."

Fiona was too busy retching to answer.

"That's a game she plays," said Moth. "When she's scared, she thinks about all the best times in her life. It works, too. I tried it."

Merceron seemed intrigued. "I like that. I will try it, too."

"Why?" asked Moth. "Are you scared, Merceron?"

Throughout the day Merceron had told them almost nothing, not about the Skylords or Taurnoken or about whatever dangers lay ahead.

"Water," Merceron sighed. His wings drooped behind him. "I'm going to the river. Look after her, Moth, will you?"

Moth watched him go, slipping quietly through the trees toward the riverbank.

"He's hiding something," Moth whispered. Fiona stumbled past him, her skin a little less green now. "You all right?"

"I'm great, Moth," she groaned. She dropped into the grass, scrunching up and using her hands for a pillow. "Just great . . ."

Moth sat down cross-legged next to her. Lady Esme hopped closer to him. He checked nervously for the Starfinder, feeling it in his coat pocket.

"Is this something or what?" he chuckled. "We were really flying!"

"I feel like I'm going to die."

"That'll pass. Happens to Skyknights all the time. You're airsick."

Through the trees, he could just make out Merceron by the river. The dragon looked repeatedly over his shoulder as he drank from the running water. His body dragged against the ground, about to collapse.

"Look at him," said Moth. "He can't go on anymore. Not today. We should stop here for the night."

Fiona barely nodded. "Excellent idea."

"We can start clearing away some of these branches."

"I need a minute."

Moth smiled. Despite her complaining, he was proud of Fiona. Not many people could fly a dragon all day. They were probably the only two ever to do so.

"He's not telling us much, huh?" said Moth.

Fiona finally managed to lift herself onto an elbow. She studied Merceron through the trees. "He's afraid of the Skylords."

"I guess so," said Moth, but they hadn't seen even a hint of the Skylords yet.

"I don't trust him." Fiona's eyes narrowed. "Maybe we should go on by ourselves."

"That's stupid. We don't even know where to go."

"We've got the Starfinder."

"What, walk?" Moth shook his head "Stupid."

"How do we know where he's taking us? Just where is Taurnoken anyway?"

Moth couldn't answer. Only Merceron had answers. He got up and brushed the dirt from his backside. "Stay here with Esme, all right?"

Fiona waved as he headed for Merceron. The river bubbled musically over the rocks. He found Merceron laying on its pebbly shore, his long snout partially in the water. The dragon could barely lift his head. He rolled an eye toward Moth.

"Just a little longer," he said. "We'll get going again soon."

When he was up in the air, Merceron looked masterful. But down on the ground he just looked old.

"I think we'll stay here for the night," said Moth. "Look at you—you can't go any further. And Fiona . . ." He turned to see up through the trees, where Fiona was sprawled on the ground. "She's not much good for anything right now."

"She doesn't like me much, does she?" remarked Merceron.

Moth didn't want to lie or hurt the dragon's feelings. "She just doesn't know you, that's all."

"She doesn't trust me. That's what happens when children are abandoned. They stop trusting."

"I trust you," said Moth.

"Why?"

"Because Leroux told me to."

The answer made the dragon smile. "What about Rendor? Was he cruel to Fiona?"

"No, not really," said Moth honestly. "He just kind of ignores her. That's what hurts her most. He just doesn't care about her."

"Wrong. All parents love their children, and their children's children."

Moth examined the dragon. "Why don't you come away from the water? We'll make a place for the night."

"I can't," groaned Merceron. "Not yet. I ache, boy. My bones . . ."

"Just like Leroux. He used to get all achy that way, too. That's rheumatism. Everyone gets it when they're old. You gotta keep moving, keep the joints from grinding to a halt."

"I've been moving all day," sneered Merceron. "What else you got?"

Moth climbed up the dragon's side. "I used to give Leroux rubdowns when he was achy. Where does it hurt? Here?"

Gently he dug his palms against the scaly flesh, running them along the muscles of the creature's wing.

"Oh!" Merceron cried. "Oh . . ."

Merceron's whole body deflated. He moaned contentedly.

"Yeah, this'll help you," said Moth, remembering all the times he'd done the same for Leroux. A flood of memories came at him suddenly. He'd been there for Leroux when he could, hadn't he?

"You know, you could help Fiona trust you if you talked a bit more," Moth suggested. "We hardly know anything about you. And what about Taurnoken? You never tell us anything about your home."

"You can't tell a human about Taurnoken. It's too beautiful for words."

"Will we be there soon?"

"We'll follow the river from here," said Merceron. "That feels wonderful, Moth. Don't stop . . ."

Moth's hands moved along the dragon's spine. "I'm sure the other dragons will help us when we get there," he said. "They'll remember you and want to help."

"They'll remember me, all right."

"They'll probably celebrate! Didn't you talk to anyone while you were hiding?"

"Not dragons," said Merceron.

"No family? No one?"

Merceron tensed. "Are you hungry? Maybe we should eat."

"You don't want to talk about this, do you?"

"Bright boy."

Moth worked quietly, asking no more questions. He rubbed and rubbed the dragon's aching muscles. Within minutes, Merceron was sleeping.

STARGAZING

AS THE SUN WENT DOWN in the valley, so did the temperature. Moth and Fiona cleared a place amid the grass, using the sticks and branches they'd gathered to build what looked like a nest around them. Merceron lit a fire with his fingers, then surprised the others by making the flames dance into the forms of animals. Soon the moon came out, and then the stars. Moth fed Lady Esme from the supplies they'd brought from Merceron's lair. Together they huddled in the light of the fire, munching on strips of dried meat while the dragon entertained them. Each of them had napped, and now, as midnight came, they were all wide awake.

Fiona remained quiet, but managed to smile at the bird Merceron made from the fire. Using his claws, he drew in the air to let the bird take flight before disappearing. Lady Esme watched the thing, fascinated. Moth gently scratched her feathered head.

The Starfinder sat on the grass in front of him, its mirror blank, its levers and scope unmoving. Moth gazed up as he bit into an apple, marveling at a sky absolutely pregnant with stars. Being on the run had given him precious little time for stargazing. He picked up the Starfinder, noting the patterns etched into its gleaming metal, trying to match them to the ones twinkling overhead.

"Merceron," he said softly, "do you know all the constellations?"

Merceron took his pipe from his pocket. "Most of them," he said as he emptied the dottle onto the ground. Moth liked watching Merceron light his pipe, because he always made a show of it. Carefully the dragon packed the bowl with fresh tobacco, then produced a flame at the tip of a long fingernail. He moved the flame in a circular motion around the bowl, puffing gently. Then he let out a long, relaxed breath and leaned back. "Point one out to me," he said. "I'll tell you what it's called."

Moth had already chosen one, a constellation he had seen engraved on the Starfinder. "There," he said. "That one looks like an airship to me."

"Close. That's the Gothrol, the ship of dreams." Smoke drifted lazily out of Merceron's nose. "A ship that can travel anywhere—seas, mountaintops, deserts. They say if you fall asleep aboard Gothrol, you'll wake up in whatever place you dreamed of going."

"Come on," squawked Fiona. She put her palms up to the fire. "There's a lot of crazy things here, I know, but who could make something like that?"

"The seafolk of Lorn. They're all dead now, but once they traveled all over the world, probably when the Skylords were young."

"Does the Gothrol still exist?" asked Moth.

"Of course," said Merceron. "I told you—every constellation is something or someone that exists in the Realm. The Starfinder can find all of them. Go on, pick another." Merceron nudged Fiona with his tail. "You try this time."

Fiona looked up without much interest. Her eyes moved over the stars, stopping suddenly on a group right above their heads. "There," she pointed. "With that bright star."

"The red one?"

Fiona nodded.

"I know that one. What does it look like to you?"

"Like a horse," said Fiona instantly.

Merceron looked astonished. "That's Jorion, the centaur. Do you know what a centaur is?"

"Yeah, like half a man and half a horse stuck together."

Moth laughed. Merceron just smirked.

"Ugly beasts, centaurs. Jorion is their chieftain." Merceron took the pipe from his mouth and used it to point toward the constellation. "That red star represents his eye. Centaurs are great hunters. They can see almost as well as Esme."

"Are there many centaurs?" asked Moth.

"Oh, yes. They live in a valley not far from Taurnoken. No one sees much of them, though."

Fiona studied her constellation. "What are they like?"

"Arrogant," snorted Merceron. "Hard to abide. Even the Skylords leave them alone. They don't think much of dragons, either."

"Why not?" asked Moth.

"Jealous, probably. Centaurs don't live the way dragons do. They think with their fists instead of their heads. When the war with the Skylords ended, they called us cowards. They thought we should have kept on fighting. Maybe that's true, but how would they know? They didn't lose anything. They can't fly."

It was strange seeing Merceron angry. He bit down hard on his pipe. Moth could tell he was thinking about more than just centaurs.

"Will we see any centaurs when we get to Taurnoken?" asked Fiona.

Merceron shook his head. "Taurnoken's a dragon city, Fiona. Centaurs aren't welcome. They're not welcome anywhere."

"Why? Because they're ugly?"

"I told you why," said Merceron.

"You told me you don't like them."

"No one likes them, Fiona. That's why they stay in their valley." Merceron tilted his head back to exhale a stream of smoke. "But they're brave, at least. Not much brains but a whole lot of heart."

"Merceron, can we see Jorion with the Starfinder?" asked Moth.

Fiona sat up. "Yeah!"

"No," said Merceron.

"Why not?" Moth reached for the Starfinder. "All I have to do is call his name, right?"

Merceron glared at him. "If you want to be like a Skylord, go ahead. Speak Jorion's name. Invade his privacy. Spy on him."

Moth set down the Starfinder. "Oh."

The dragon's tail came around his shoulders. "Don't forget why the Skylords made the Starfinder," he said gently. "Think what it would be like to be a slave."

Moth felt his face getting hot. "Sorry."

Merceron extended his tail toward Fiona, tugging her closer. "Listen to me now, both of you," he said, his voice dropping to a whisper. "There's something I want to tell you."

Moth and Fiona pressed together in his embrace. Merceron struggled with his words.

"I left a mate in Taurnoken," he said. "Her name is Dreojen."

"A mate," said Moth. "You mean a wife?"

"A brood mate is more than a wife," said Merceron. "Humans take wives. They live together for a blink of an eye and call that love. They watch the sunrise together. Dragons watch rivers being born. We watch volcanoes live and die. Do you see?"

"I think so," said Moth. It was hard for him to imagine such stretches of time. "You spend all your lives together."

"But you left her," Fiona blurted. "You just left her?"

"Where I was going, she couldn't follow," said Merceron. "There was no life for her living in a hole in the ground, hiding from the Skylords. I was too dangerous for her to be around."

"So you left her," snorted Fiona. "Typical."

"C'mon, Fiona. He had to!"

"Don't argue about it," said Merceron. "You were wondering about me, so I told you." His eyes glazed over with memories. "But it's been a long time . . ."

"You must be dying to see her again," said Moth excitedly. "What will you say?"

"Yeah, that should be good," quipped Fiona.

Merceron let Lady Esme climb onto his shoulder. The stars and firelight shined in his reptilian eyes.

"I will tell her that I've missed her," he said. "That I missed our togetherness. That I miss everything that we once had. And I'll be afraid when I see her, and I'll shake like a child." Then, Merceron looked right at Fiona and said, "And I'll hope that she forgives me for leaving her."

THE DECOY

SKYHIGH EASED BACK ON the sticks of his dragonfly, bringing the craft level with the horizon. Now that the sun was down, there was only moonlight to guide him. He watched the distant mountains, guiding the dragonfly into another long, lazy turn. The whine of the engine and the beating of glass wings shattered the peace of the forest below. Somewhere behind him floated the *Avatar*. The moon and stars shone down through the dragonfly's canopy, projecting a wavy reflection of Skyhigh's smiling face.

It felt good to be in the air again, away from the crowded *Avatar*. Since breaking through the Reach they'd been running low and slow, leaning over observation platforms to locate Moth and Fiona. So far, they'd found nothing.

Except for the mermaids.

Skyhigh nearly fell overboard when he saw them.

At first the mermaids had stared back up at them, amazed and horrified by the airship's arrival. Skyhigh and his crewmates had crowded the rails, waving and hooting at the beautiful creatures until the mermaids dived away, disappearing into their shining green lagoon.

After that, the day fell into tedium. Commander Donnar paced the deck while the *Avatar* crawled through the sky. Rendor kept to his quarters, not appearing until the sun went down. As the *Avatar* floated stationary above the ground, Skyhigh took his dragonfly for his first patrol.

No one had ordered him to be quiet or subtle. Both those things were impossible for a dragonfly anyway. He fired up the engine, looked out into the dark void, then rocketed from the *Avatar*'s hangar. He felt the moonlight on his face, the thick air of the forest rising against his wings, and the glorious sense of freedom he only got when flying.

For almost an hour the sky remained perfect. Each time Skyhigh wheeled the craft around for another orbit he saw the *Avatar*'s yellow beacon flashing in the distance. He wasn't sure why he was on patrol or what Rendor expected him to find, but the dragonfly's guns were loaded. Skyhigh's mind drifted as he flew over the moonlit forest. The engine sang to him like a lullaby.

Completing his turn, he spotted the *Avatar*'s beacon. He leveled the wings, pointed the craft for another orbit, then noticed its position in the sky. The darkness made it hard to be certain, but the airship seemed lower to him now.

His first thought was that the *Avatar* was in trouble. He throttled up the power just as something struck the canopy. Instantly the glass spider-webbed.

"Great," he fumed, jerking the ship to the right, away from whatever had hit him. Probably a bird, he supposed. The canopy shook, threatening to shatter. Skyhigh settled the ship by reducing power. Just as he got it back under control, another blow came.

"Hey!"

The dragonfly lurched left on a damaged wing. Skyhigh glanced for a look, but the wings were still moving too quickly to see. He wrapped his fingers tightly around the sticks, but when he saw the black form sweep across the moonlight he knew he hadn't hit a bird.

The thing flashed by too quickly to describe. Its batlike wings swooped down toward the dragonfly. Skyhigh banked into a corkscrew. Through the twisting, broken canopy he could see the yellow beacon still descending.

"What are they doing?" he cried, slamming the dragonfly upright again. From somewhere behind him the thing caught up, pounding on the fuselage.

"That's it!" spat Skyhigh. He jerked back the gun lever and hooked it around his finger. "You're a fighter? Then let's fight!"

He pushed in the throttle, jerked back the sticks, and rolled the dragonfly into a loop. As the craft screamed out of its roll, he squinted through the canopy. When a hint of wing caught the moonlight, Skyhigh squeezed the trigger.

A rat-a-tat of bullets sailed across the sky. The bat-thing dove and weaved. It raced headlong for Skyhigh, crashing again against his ship. The canopy shattered. A storm of glass and rushing wind pounded Skyhigh's helmet. His dragonfly plummeted.

Skyhigh didn't shout or panic. His hands worked the sticks, his feet pumped the pedals. The broken wings of his craft strained to bite the air. Wind pulled tears from his eyes as the ground rushed toward him. He listened to the whine of his engine and the telltale wail of his wings, while he was wrestling the controls. Slowly at first, the spin corrected. As the wind got under the craft again, the dragonfly's nose started to lift. Skyhigh held his breath when he saw the trees.

"Hurry," he whispered. "Now now now . . ."

He rammed the sticks back hard, willing the dragonfly skyward. The tallest of the trees scraped the bottom of the craft as it tore overhead, splintering branches. Skyhigh punched the throttle one more time. He was still a good way from the *Avatar*, but when he sighted her again she was already grounded, settled in a clearing. Men swarmed out of her hull.

"Rendor . . ."

The dragonfly screamed over the treetops. A minute passed, then another. The trees thinned out below him; Skyhigh had the clearing in sight. The *Avatar*'s beacon grew brighter and brighter, calling him home.

"Come on," he told his broken craft. "Just hold together . . ."

Too late, he saw a glimmer of the thing barreling toward him. Too late, he tried to turn. Another crash, another broken wing, and the dragonfly was falling.

"No!"

Skyhigh held the nose as level as he could, bracing himself for the crash. Pilots died in crashes. Friends died.

"Not me, boys," he yelled. "Not me!"

He cleared the trees, streaking down like a meteor. Up ahead he saw the *Avatar*. Grass and rocks rushed past him. He pumped the pedals, twisting what was left of the wings to catch the wind and bleed off speed.

He'd crashed before, he told himself.

Just let me walk away from it. Just let me walk away . . .

It was the last thought he had as he buried the dragonfly in the dirt.

He was only unconscious for a moment. When he opened his eyes, the engine was screaming. Stubs of glass wings beat the empty air. He saw blood on the console, then tasted it on his lips. Breathing through his broken nose felt like fire in his nostrils.

"Fire . . ."

He had to get out of the dragonfly. He found his wits, tore off his helmet, and somehow managed to free himself from the cockpit. As he staggered from the vessel, he remembered that what happened wasn't just an accident—something had attacked him.

He drew his dagger and ran for the *Avatar*.

"Hey!" he shouted. "I'm here!"

A whoosh of air swept overhead. Skyhigh didn't look up, and he didn't look back. He simply ran as fast as he could, shouting, hoping someone would hear him.

"Here! I'm here!"

Behind him, the bat-thing dropped from the sky. Skyhigh heard its footfalls shuffling nearer. He scrambled toward the *Avatar*, saw figures stirring in dark hiding spots, then heard the unmistakable voice of Rendor.

"Now!"

A tidal wave of light seared Skyhigh's eyes. An inhuman screech echoed behind him. A gunshot fired amid the shouts. Blinded, Skyhigh turned his face away, stumbling over. He hit the ground, then felt hands grabbing him up again. He opened his eyes to yellow spots and the blurred sight of crewmen swarming the clearing. Ahead of him, something was fighting to free itself from a tangle of nets and ropes.

"Get off me!" roared Skyhigh, shaking off the crewmen. He couldn't even see their faces. As they fought to drag him back to the *Avatar*, Skyhigh heard Rendor again.

"Let him go."

At once the men backed off. Slowly, Skyhigh's vision began to clear. Rendor was smiling. Behind him, the captured creature wailed and cursed.

"You all right?"

Skyhigh was breathing too hard to answer. He nodded, pointing at the thing. "What is *that*?"

"Well done," said Rendor. "That was excellent work. Just excellent!"

"What?" sputtered Skyhigh. "You mean you sent me out here to lure that thing?"

The thing's violent cries made it impossible for Rendor to answer. From out of his coat he pulled a hidden pistol. He strode over to the tangled creature, kicked it onto its back, and put the weapon to its head.

"Quiet!"

The fanged mouth snapped shut. The thing rolled its eyes nervously toward the gun. Skyhigh strained for a better look. A mass of yellow hair sprouted from the creature's head. Two veiny wings folded against its back, protruding from its dark robes. Around its waist hung a fat silver chain. Rendor squatted down beside it and cocked the hammer of his pistol.

"I can put you out of your misery, monster," he said. "Or you can help me. You have three seconds. Decide."

ALISAUNDRA

IT TOOK NEARLY AN HOUR for Skyhigh's nose to stop bleeding. While the *Avatar*'s surgeon sewed up his torn lip, Commander Donnar peppered him with questions. The *Avatar* had lifted off again, and Rendor and his bizarre captive had disappeared soon after coming aboard. Skyhigh's dragonfly had been badly damaged, but Donnar assured him it would be repaired.

"Wing damage, mostly," said the commander. "She won't look like much but we'll get her back in the air."

At the moment Skyhigh didn't care about his craft or his broken nose. Just as the surgeon trimmed his last suture, Rendor came onto the bridge.

"Coralin?"

Skyhigh rose unsteadily out of his chair. "You used me," he spat. "You dangled me out there like a piece of meat just so you could catch that . . . *thing*."

Rendor turned without apology and started back the way he'd come. "Follow me."

"Hey!" barked Skyhigh. He hurried after Rendor, catching up to him in a narrow corridor and grabbing hold of his shoulder. "I almost died out there!"

Rendor reached up and forcefully removed Skyhigh's hand. "Captain Coralin, any one of us could die out here," he said. "If you want an explanation, keep your mouth shut and come with me."

The Governor strode off quickly, his polished shoes clacking against the metallic floor. Skyhigh shadowed Rendor to the aft cargo area, sighting a pair of men with rifles at the end of the corridor. The bays were the most secure area of the airship, where the weaponry was usually stored.

"Open it," Rendor ordered.

One crewmen lifted the door. The other trained his rifle inside.

"This," said Rendor, "is a Redeemer."

The little chamber was completely empty except for a figure secured in chains, kneeling against a steel wall. The guards moved in, pointing their weapons. A head of long blond hair lifted to stare directly at Skyhigh. A fanged maw smiled grotesquely.

"Beautiful man . . ."

The voice was human, and yet it wasn't. Just like the eyes. A dark robe hid most of the creature's body, belted around the waist by a gleaming silver chain. Scales instead of skin gave the thing a grey-green pallor. Clawlike hands ended in twisting, crusty fingernails. A gargoyle's face masked what might have once been a woman. But most amazing of all were the wings. They sprouted from its back, poking out of its robe, twitching in the chains that bound them.

Rendor took a cigar from his vest. "Ugly as a mud fence, isn't it?" He lit his cigar with his fancy lighter. "I figured you should see it for yourself."

Skyhigh moved in closer. "What is it?"

"A priest of the Skylords," said Rendor. "A Redeemer. Go on, take a good look. I think it likes you."

"Beautiful flying man," repeated the creature. Its pink tongue darted out, making Skyhigh jump. "So scared!" it laughed. "Run, run. Fly away home!"

"She's going to help us," said Rendor. He went right up to the creature and blew his cigar smoke in its face. "Aren't you?"

"The children have to pay," said the creature. "They broke the forbidden law!"

"What law?" squawked Skyhigh.

"Crossing the Reach," said Rendor. "For coming into their world."

"The Masters' world!"

"The Skylords?" puzzled Skyhigh. "Rendor, what is this thing? Not its name. I mean what *is* it?"

Rendor pointed at his captive with his cigar. "Look at it, Captain. Can't you tell?"

"It looks . . . human."

"It was human," said Rendor. "This is what happens to humans who get caught by the Skylords. Take a good look at Skylord mercy, Coralin."

The creature proudly tilted up its face. "I serve the Skylords!"

Rendor shook his head in disgust. "Still think I've been telling fairy tales?"

Skyhigh didn't know what to believe. "Why are they called Redeemers?"

"You heard her—they serve the Skylords." Rendor's expression was contemptuous. "Bloody slaves. They come through the Reach hoping to find something better. Poor folks mostly. And criminals. Get used to it, Coralin. You're going to see a lot of strange things over here."

"Let me out now," purred the creature.

Rendor flicked his ashes on the floor. "Your friend Moth's been lucky so far. These things roam in territories. Moth and my granddaughter had to have come this way, but somehow they managed to slip past it."

"How do you know?" asked Skyhigh. "How can we be sure they're all right?"

"Because this thing wouldn't be here if she'd found them. She'd have taken them to the Skylords by now."

Skyhigh felt sick.

Rendor puffed on the cigar until the tip glowed ruby red. "That's right, isn't it, monster? You just let two humans walk right past you. Kids! What would your masters think of that, I wonder?"

The creature struggled in its chains. A crewman nudged it with his rifle barrel.

"I have to take you," it told Skyhigh.

"What?"

"To the Skylords," said Rendor. "To be turned into one of them. They'll do it to all of us if they get the chance."

"I was human once," claimed the Redeemer. "Beautiful once. Like a mermaid." Suddenly it broke into song. "Mermaid, mermaid, hair of grass! Mermaid, mermaid, pretty young lass!"

Skyhigh turned away. "How's this thing supposed to help us, Rendor? It's insane!"

"Oh, she'll help us," said Rendor. He leaned forward, coming face to face with the thing. "Because if she doesn't, someone else will find Moth and Fiona. And if that happens the Skylords aren't going to be too happy."

For the first time the creature looked afraid. "Help you." It nodded.

"But how?" wondered Skyhigh. "You can't just let it go. How's it going to find them?"

"Like a dog on a leash, Coralin," said Rendor. "Ever seen a bloodhound?"

He reached beneath his coat, this time pulling out a length of flowered fabric. Skyhigh was sure he'd seen the pattern before, then realized it was from a dress Fiona had worn.

"Redeemers read thoughts. They can feel the presence of humans better than the Skylords because they were human themselves once." Rendor hovered over the pathetic creature. "You've felt them by now. You must have. Have you been looking for them?"

The creature smirked and looked away.

"You won't be smiling when your masters find those children," Rendor taunted. "But if you help me find them first I'll let you go free. The Skylords won't even know they were here."

"I serve the Skylords," said the Redeemer.

"Do you know where they are?" pressed Rendor. "Or Merceron?"

The creature spied the strip of fabric in Rendor's hand. "Give it to me."

"Who's Merceron?" asked Skyhigh.

Rendor held the piece of Fiona's dress under the creature's

nose. Skyhigh watched as it sniffed the fabric, its expression melting with longing. He actually thought the creature might weep.

"Young girl," it whispered.

"She's been here?" asked Rendor. "You've felt her?"

The Redeemer closed its eyes and nodded. "Mermaids lie. But they will be punished too."

"What's it talking about?" asked Skyhigh.

Rendor asked the creature, "Can you feel her now? Is she near? Is she with the dragon?"

"Dragon?" blurted Skyhigh. "Huh?"

"Shut up, Captain, please," snapped Rendor. He leaned toward his captive. "Can you feel her? Do you feel anything with her?"

"A boy," said the Redeemer. "And something else." It opened its yellow eyes. "What are you looking for?"

Skyhigh wanted to know the same thing. "What is it, Rendor? What was it Moth stole from you?"

Suddenly the Redeemer gasped. "The Starfinder!"

Rendor jerked back. "Get out of my mind!"

Frustrated, Skyhigh demanded, "Rendor, tell me what's going on. What's this thing talking about?"

"The Starfinder!" crowed the Redeemer. "It's strong! I can feel it!"

Skyhigh felt like screaming. "What Starfinder? What dragon?"

"Later," said Rendor, brushing Skyhigh aside. Without any malice he asked his prisoner, "What's your name?"

"I am the Twelfth Priestess."

"No," said Rendor. "That's your slave name, the name the Skylords gave you. What was it before they did this to you? What was the name your parents gave you?"

Her expression made Skyhigh shudder. She seemed to be thinking back to a long ago dream.

"Do you remember your parents?" asked Rendor.

"Alisaundra," she whispered. "My name."

"Alisaundra." Rendor dropped his cigar to the floor and crushed it out with the toe of his shoe. "I'm not sure what else the Skylords could do to you, Alisaundra, but I'm sure they'd think of something. What would they do if they knew you let that boy and girl get away? Would they destroy you?"

The creature cast her yellow eyes to the floor, slumping in her chains. Rendor hovered over her.

"Help me and I'll let you go free," he promised. "Forget the Starfinder. Forget you ever saw us. All you have to do is take me to those children."

FIRE AND CLAWS

FOR A FULL DAY MORE Merceron carried the children north, following the river. After so long in the air, even Moth was tired of flying. He was sick of the river that seemed to lead nowhere. Laying flat against the saddle, pinned with Fiona between the ever-beating wings, Moth turned his face against the wind and saw the sun starting to go down. Fiona's hands clutching the straps around Merceron's neck were white-knuckled. Her red hair blew straight back from her head.

Merceron had promised them Taurnoken, but Moth's hopes faded with the falling sun. How long could he hold on? How long could Lady Esme fly alongside them? He wanted to talk but couldn't find the strength. He wanted to reach out and touch Fiona and tell her it would all be okay.

Four days, he realized.

That's how long they'd been here. Less than a week ago since Leroux died. Why did it seem so long ago? Why did it take forever for a dragon to fly back home? Moth closed his eyes, willing something—something good—to happen. That's what they needed now.

"I see something." Fiona lifted her face to peer past Merceron's head. "Merceron, I see something!" she said again. "Is that it?"

Merceron's giant wings fanned out into a glide. His body slackened with relief.

"Taurnoken," he sighed.

Lemon-yellow spires reached into the clouds, splashed by the last of the sunlight. Moth saw aeries and balconies, giant stages big enough for airships. There were no streets, nothing at ground level but the river. There were only the towers, all of them dragon-sized, stitched together by gleaming bridges. Jutting platforms clung to their sides, the way thorns climbed up a rose bush. Great, open gaps lay between them for the dragons to soar.

But the sky was empty.

Fiona's face scrunched. Underneath them, they felt Merceron's body tighten. His wings beat with urgency again, speeding them faster. Lady Esme quickly fell behind.

"Merceron, wait for Esme!" shouted Moth.

Merceron paid no attention. The river splayed out beneath them, meandering past the towers, pooling in blue lakes. Merceron threaded past the first tower, then wheeled toward the heart of the city.

"Gone!"

His panicked tone made Moth shrivel.

"Merceron, slow down!" Fiona cried. "Esme can't keep up!"

Merceron glided back toward Esme, gathering her close to his wings as he surveyed the city. Shadows grew over the darkening towers. Lifeless, abandoned homes gaped at them.

"Dreojen," shuddered Merceron. "Dreojen!"

"Where is she, Merceron?" asked Moth. "Hiding?"

Overcome by the sight of his vacant city, Merceron pointed himself toward an enormous tower near the center of Taurnoken, a broad, silvery spire with bridges spreading out from it like branches, connecting it to all the smaller towers around it. A massive platform protruded from its entrance, overhanging the river a thousand feet below. Merceron nearly tackled the platform in his zeal to get down, spilling across its smooth surface. Lady Esme landed next to him, soft as a butterfly.

By now Fiona had become expert at undoing her buckles and hurried off Merceron's back. Moth dropped down after her, amazed at the size of the tower. The platform led to a colossal archway, big enough for a dozen dragons to enter side by side. Beyond the archway waited a dim, canyon-sized hallway.

"Merceron, was this your home?" Fiona asked.

"In a way." Merceron's eyes widened with emotion. "This is my library."

The wind whistled as it swam between the towers, but not another voice reached them, not a single blinking eye. The ebbing sunlight touched the arch, spilling into the empty hall.

Merceron didn't ask the others to follow. He moved in a trance, awash in memories. Moth felt himself growing smaller as they passed under the arch. The bone-white ceiling soared overhead. Blades of sunlight pierced the crystal windows. Moth's shuffling boots echoed through the emptiness, a hallway that spread out into endless other halls.

"This is the library?" asked Fiona. "Where are all the books?"

Merceron scanned the looming shelves in disbelief. "It's all gone. Everything I ever learned, all our histories." He pointed at a vacant bookcase. "Our poetries were there! Our maps, our kin books . . ."

Lady Esme fluttered up into the bare shelves, looking around with her sharp eyes. She gave a mournful call.

"Dreojen was here. They were all here when I left!" Merceron swept his tail around. "This whole place was alive!"

"The war," said Fiona. "It must have been."

"It was over!"

"Maybe it wasn't over for the Skylords," said Moth.

Merceron's nostrils flared. "It's Taurnoken," he said. "They always hated Taurnoken. Too tall for them, too beautiful. Too much like their own city."

"Like Calio," said Fiona. "That's what my grandfather says. He told me the Skylords would hate Calio if they ever saw how high it is."

"It's jealousy," fumed Merceron. "Wicked, vile jealousy."

He slumped, heartbroken. Moth remembered the Starfinder in his pocket. He looked up at Lady Esme, wondering what to do next.

"If they left here we can find them," he said. "Right, Merceron? We can still find Dreojen and the other dragons."

"Yes, maybe," said Merceron. He nodded but wasn't really listening. "I don't know."

He walked off, deeper into the hall. Moth headed after him, but Fiona grabbed his coat.

"No," she whispered. "Leave him alone."

The hall grew silent. Moth and Fiona explored the empty shelves. They watched the sun slip down the horizon. They tossed treats in the air for Esme to catch. They worried.

After an hour, they went looking for Merceron. The crystal windows beamed moonlight into shafts, lighting their way. Moth listened for Merceron, but all he could hear was the constant wind around and through the towers. The library yawned, gloomy and haunted. Moth peered back and realized they were lost.

"Where's the archway?" he asked. "Did we turn?"

Fiona looked about, puzzled by the darkness and look-alike shelves. Esme sat obliviously on her shoulder, waiting for another treat.

"We'll go back," she said. "Merceron will find us."

They turned to retrace their steps, then saw movement at the end of the hall. A flash of wings made Moth grin.

"There you are!"

A ray of moonlight struck the figure as it stepped out from the shelves. Small, man-shaped, its black wings fluttered from its shoulders.

"Hello, little ones," it called, its mouth shining with fangs.

Moth and Fiona backpedaled. Another creature stepped from the shelves.

"Pretty bird!" it hissed. "Delicious bird!"

Fiona snatched Esme into her arms. "Moth, what are they?"

Moth spun her around. "Run!"

A third beast dropped down in front of them. "Don't go!" it laughed. "Let us see you!"

A dark robe, a silver chain—Moth noticed little else. The one before him hunched down, stalking toward Fiona. "I will take her hair!" it cackled. "Red hair for me!"

"I will have their coats and boots!" said another.

Fiona tossed Esme into the sky. "Esme, fly!" she shouted. Then, with all her lung-filled might she cried, "Merceron!"

The creatures chittered and laughed and made a ring around them. Moth balled up his fists.

"Get away!"

His bluster delighted the creatures. Moth searched for an opening. Black wings spread out to trap them. Moth drew back, hoping for at least one good shot. The closest creature hovered just out of range.

"Child," it taunted, "soon you will be one of us."

Moth held his breath, pushed Fiona behind him, then felt a rush of wind. A sudden howl rattled the crystal windows. Teeth bared, mouth aflame, Merceron came like a battering ram down the hall. Fiona cheered, Moth struck the creature hard in the face—and they ran.

Fire and claws raked the hall. Orange light blinded them. A fireball engulfed the creatures, incinerating two of them. The third leaped into the air. A reptilian arm hooked around it, slamming it to the ground. Merceron pinned it, his smoking snout pressing down upon its chest.

"Stop!" the creature pleaded. "Mighty dragon, mercy! Mercy!"

Flames lit the hall. The burnt remains of the creatures smoldered. Moth and Fiona got to their feet, huddling against the pillar. Merceron's body shook with rage. The scales along his back glowed red. His massive jaws snapped open.

"No!" screamed the creature.

Moth couldn't watch. Before he turned away, Merceron hissed, "Where are they?"

The winged creature trembled beneath him. "Gone!" it stammered. "Everyone!"

"Why?" demanded Merceron. "The Skylords?"

"No more Taurnoken. My Masters have said so!"

Merceron snorted fire. "Where have they gone?"

"I don't know! I swear, Mighty One! We came for the children!" The thing twisted its head, looking straight at Moth. "That one has the Starfinder! We feel it!"

Merceron lifted the creature and dashed it hard against the wall. "The children are mine! Tell your masters!"

The thing spun back to its feet, spread wide its monstrous wings, and darted from the hall.

"Tell them!" Merceron roared after it. "Tell your masters Merceron is back!"

Moth looked breathlessly at Merceron. Until now, he'd never feared the dragon. He held Fiona, afraid to let go. Fiona clutched her chest, staring through the smoke and fire.

"Merceron?"

The dragon's wrathful eyes scowled. "Redeemers," he said. "They've found us."

THE WAY THINGS HAVE TO BE

THE NEXT MORNING, MOTH and Fiona awoke with the sun. Merceron stood nearby, guarding them from a platform on the library tower. His drooping expression told Moth he'd been awake the whole night. He nudged Moth with his tail, trying to smile but failing to manage it.

"No time for breakfast," he said softly. "We need to get moving."

He turned away, his look distracted as he scanned the sky. So far, things had been quiet. If they were lucky, the Redeemers would leave them alone until nightfall.

"They never fly during the day," Merceron had explained. "The Skylords won't allow it."

That single, curious statement remained with Moth all night. He dreamed about it, his sleep filled with fitful nightmares of being chased and captured, of becoming one of them. Even then—even with his own wings—the Skylords would keep him from flying.

He and Fiona gathered their things and climbed once more onto Merceron's back. Merceron hadn't told them where they'd be going, only that he might know where his beloved Dreojen was hiding. In the early days of the war, he explained, he and Dreojen had scouted out aeries in the cliffs where they could hide. Finding her was a terrible long shot, but with the dragons gone and the Redeemers chasing them, it was the only chance they had.

With the children on his back and Lady Esme at his tail,

Merceron leaped from the tower with a sickening lurch. The sun felt warm on Moth's face, but he knew he'd soon be shivering from the wind. He tucked himself down against Merceron's powerful body, wishing desperately for sleep.

They flew on northward, following the river again, the river that never ended. And then they were falling, gliding down gently to the earth, and Moth didn't know why. Merceron flared his wings and landed by the river, his claws alighting on the soft, loamy bank.

"Nice!" joked Fiona. "We're there already?"

Merceron smiled but didn't laugh. "Unbuckle yourselves," he said.

They did as he asked, sliding off his back and looking up at him inquisitively. Lady Esme circled overhead, as surprised as they were by the abrupt landing. Merceron's enormous head sank on his shoulders.

"Moth, Fiona . . ." His voice broke. "I need you to give me the Starfinder now."

Confused, Moth reached into his coat. "Okay. Why?"

He handed the device off to Merceron, who cradled it in his giant claw.

"What's going on?" asked Fiona. "What's wrong?"

"*You're* going on," said Merceron. "Without me." He sneered at the Starfinder. "Without this."

Moth was incredulous. "What? We can't go on by ourselves, Merceron. How are we supposed to find the other dragons?"

"You can't," said Merceron. "I'm going to find them alone. You're going to Pandera. The Valley of the Centaurs."

"By ourselves?" Moth's head was really spinning now. "How?"

"It's a two-day walk from here," said Merceron. "Just follow the river. Pandera is surrounded by mountains. Once you clear these trees you'll see them. The river flows right underneath the mountain. It's a tight squeeze, but you can make it."

"That's crazy!" said Fiona. "You're going to just leave us out here? What about those creatures?"

Merceron hefted the Starfinder. "If I don't take this away they'll find you for sure," he said. "It's the Starfinder they really want. They'll be coming for it now."

"Oh my god," sighed Fiona. "That's why you told them your name! That's why you want the Skylords to know you're back—so they'll chase you instead of us."

"You'll be safe with the centaurs," said Merceron. His words fumbled with emotion. "The Skylords won't bother you there, and the centaurs won't give you up easily. They're arrogant, but they're brave. Remember I told you that?"

"What about you?" asked Moth. He could feel himself starting to panic. "Where will you go?"

"To find Dreojen, if I can. Esme will come with me. This is still about getting her back to normal, Moth. It's what I owe her." The dragon lowered himself to look right into Moth's face. "I'll be back for you when I can. Stay with the centaurs until then."

"Merceron, I can't," choked Moth. "I can't be alone anymore. There's so much I still want to tell you. About Leroux. About *me*!"

"You'll not be alone, boy! You'll have Fiona. And I'm not abandoning you. I'll be back, I swear it."

Fiona's face hardened. "Oh, it's so easy for you. It's so bloody simple for all of you to just walk away."

Merceron shook his head. "No, it's not. It's just the way things have to be."

"Merceron, no," pleaded Moth.

"If the Redeemers find you they'll take you back to the Skylords," said Merceron. "And the Skylords won't hesitate because you're children. They'll enslave you both. And they'll get the Starfinder."

"But they'll kill you!" Moth cried.

"They will try," admitted Merceron. "But I'm not easily killed, boy. I am a dragon!" He smiled at Fiona. "And you, girl—you're the older one. You take care of him, hear me? And if you feel afraid, play that game you taught me. The one where you remember the best things in life."

"I'll take care of him," said Fiona coldly. "I'm not going to leave like everybody else."

Merceron's long tail came around them both. Moth could feel it trembling as it hugged them. "Dragons live a very long time," he said, "so they choose their friends carefully. They never forget them. Or leave them behind."

Fiona bit her lip, then reached out to touch his face. "Crazy old dragon," she said.

Moth felt empty. "Follow the river," he whispered. He just couldn't say good-bye.

"Follow the river," echoed the dragon. "And remember—you are my friends."

THE CASTLE

IN THEIR LONG COATS AND oversized boots, Moth and Fiona trundled along the riverbank, keeping close to the trees and doing their best to stay out of the open. It felt strange to be alone again, without Esme for company or Merceron to tell them where they were going. At first, they welcomed the chance to walk again. But walking was so much slower than flying, and as the hours wore on even Fiona wished they were back in Merceron's homemade saddle, gliding toward Pandera.

Moth himself said little as they traveled. He watched the treetops for Redeemers, worried that Merceron was wrong about the creatures only flying at night. So far, they had yet to sight the promised mountains, and they knew they wouldn't be reaching the centaur valley for at least another day. That meant a night spent by themselves—out in the open, without a dragon to protect them.

Usually it was Moth who kept the conversations going, but this time that duty fell to Fiona. With a game smile she kept her tone jolly, embarrassing Moth with her efforts to cheer him. In fact, Moth didn't want to be cheered. He was afraid, and he'd never felt so alone since the day his mother died. Being happy now seemed somehow disrespectful.

". . . and we had a big house," Fiona said as they plodded along. She had been talking about her life back in Capital City for almost an hour. It was something she rarely did, but now she didn't seem to know how to stop. "So many rooms. There was always one more light to turn out before going to bed!"

"We just had the apartment," said Moth. "All we had to do was blow out a candle."

"Well, you had Leroux at least."

"You had your parents. Both of them."

"Oh."

Moth didn't want her trying so hard. Mostly, he just wanted quiet. And to reach Pandera in one piece.

"I wonder what they'll be like," said Fiona.

"Who?"

"Jorion and his centaurs," said Fiona. "I wonder if they'll be like they are in books."

"I doubt it. I've seen plenty of dragons in books, and none of them were like Merceron. Smoking a pipe, tinkering . . ." Moth laughed. "The centaurs here probably all play chess and talk in rhymes."

"And wear spectacles," said Fiona.

"And dresses!"

"No," said Fiona sharply. "Merceron said they were brave fighters. I bet they're not afraid of the Redeemers."

"Merceron wasn't afraid of them, either," said Moth. "He just wanted to protect us."

Fiona nodded but didn't say anything.

When afternoon came they rested, finding a shady spot to share some of the food they had left and fill their canteens from the river. The river tumbled with clear water. Moth had heard of sparkling rivers, but this one actually *did* sparkle, and the fish inside it sparkled too, darting through the rocks, the sun making rainbows on their bellies. The river was wider here than it had been before, the current just a little faster. The farther north they traveled, the bigger and faster it got.

Fiona knew she couldn't tell Moth she was afraid. He was only a year younger then her, but it was an important year and he was a boy. Admit it or not, he needed her. For Fiona, that meant keeping a stupid smile plastered on her face and talking when she didn't feel like it. She surprised herself by telling Moth about the friends she'd left behind in Capital City, her pet parakeets, the trips she had taken to museums, and the day her mother and father died. She even told him about the day her grandfather came to collect her. She remembered his face, so stormy and grave at the death of his daughter, and so unhappy to have to raise another child when he was already so busy.

Moth listened to every word and barely spoke at all. Fiona could tell he was rapt. He trailed behind her, occasionally nodding when she said something important. Finally, they followed a bend in the river and came out of the forest, emerging into a rolling expanse of fields and meadows filled with wildflowers. The river chugged eastward, slicing toward a distant range of mountains. The sight stopped Fiona short.

One little curve in the river, and the mountains Merceron had promised them appeared, a sheer wall of rock across the horizon. Their staggering height stole Fiona's breath. Her eyes traced them up, up, to where their peaks disappeared in the clouds.

"It looks like a castle," she whispered.

Moth came to a halt beside her. "I don't even think Merceron could get over those mountains. No wonder the Skylords leave the centaurs alone."

For the first time in days, a sense of hope touched Fiona. They'd be safe beyond the mountains, she was sure of it. Safe with the centaurs. Safe inside their impregnable castle.

"Merceron said there'd be a way through," she remembered. "He said the river runs under the mountains."

"There's probably secret trails all over the mountains," said Moth. "Probably paths only the centaurs know about." He looked up into the sky. "We're out in the open here. It'll be getting dark soon."

Fiona started right out toward the mountains "If we move fast we can make it by tomorrow night," she said. She was buoyant suddenly, her smile genuine. "It's our castle, Moth," she said. "You told me there wasn't one, but there it is!"

"Huh?"

"Back in Calio at my grandfather's house. When we were sitting on the wall."

"Fiona, I don't remember. That was the night Leroux died."

Fiona glanced back at him. "Sorry," she said. "Let's just hurry, all right?"

She took his hand and pulled him forward, urging him faster along the riverbank. It didn't matter if he remembered or not. He'd told her that there were no faraway castles for her, no place for her to run.

He was wrong.

When night finally arrived, they found a place beneath some fruit trees to hide. Using leaves and branches for blankets, they buried themselves from the eyes of the Redeemers, leaving just enough of the sky visible to see what might be stalking them. The long walk had exhausted Moth. Although the mountains did seem closer now, he knew there were still miles to go tomorrow. He said good night to Fiona and closed his eyes, letting sleep take him away.

But soon he dreamed. Of Merceron, mostly, but also of Leroux and the Redeemers. In his dream Moth asked Leroux why he'd never mentioned the Redeemers or the terribleness of the Skylords. Leroux smiled in his dream and said, "Because I was in love."

The answer bothered Moth enough to wake him. When his eyes opened he noticed Fiona next to him, staring up at the sky through the hole in the trees.

"What are you looking at?" he asked groggily.

"Nothing," said Fiona. "Go back to sleep."

So Moth did.

Fiona searched the sky for Jorian. She could only see a little patch of stars through the trees, but they were directly above her, the same place she had seen the centaur chieftain before. She imagined him in his valley beyond the mountains, defying the Skylords, ready to protect her, and she wondered why Merceron and the dragons could ever dislike such brave creatures. If centaurs were like horses, then they were noble. Fiona knew horses. She had ridden them when her parents were alive.

She caught a glimpse of a single bright star burning hot above her.

"Jorian's eye," she whispered.

The star twinkled as it watched her.

DREAMS

THROUGH THE MILES AND the dark of night, Alisaundra could taste the children's dreams. Moth, Fiona. Asleep in a field of wildflowers, they served up a feast for her. Alisaundra leaned forward in her chains as if smelling a confection.

Night was when her senses came alive. Her hawklike eyes—a gift from her Masters—easily scanned the dark landscape below. Nearby, the man called Donnar watched the same black horizon with a squint. The noise of the airship hummed in Alisaundra's bones. She smelled the powder of the rifle at her back. She clutched the strip of the girl's dress, picturing Fiona's orange hair, her pale and freckled face.

A single chain tethered Alisaundra to the platform. Looped around her waist, it was just long enough for her to gaze through the airship's window. For two days now she had tracked the children, directing the craft along the river. Her captor, Rendor, watched her keenly most of the time, and there was always a rifle nearby to kill her if she broke her promise. Tonight, though, Rendor was gone. Only Donnar strode the platform. Only one guard threatened her.

Hunting the children had been easy. Alisaundra was sure she would find them tomorrow. She had already told Rendor where they were—all they needed to do now was follow the river.

Still, Alisaundra had her secrets.

Her eyes moved across the chamber, scanning the instruments and dials, marveling at the things the humans had built.

Did her Masters know about the airships? She didn't think so. They'd never have let the humans go so far.

Alisaundra had always thought her human memories gone for good, but somehow, being around her kind again had coaxed them back to life. When she was alive, humans crawled on the earth like beetles. Now they could fly! The miracle of what they'd done still startled her.

And then there were the dreams.

Her dreams weren't like the delicious dreams of children. They were echoes in her mind, voices she hadn't heard in eons. Familiar voices she couldn't quite remember. A father's voice. A sister's. A husband's?

Alisaundra wanted desperately to be away. Once she was gone from the airship, her bad dreams would stop. First though, she had a bargain to fulfill. She would find the children for Rendor—even though they no longer had the Starfinder.

THE RIVERBANK

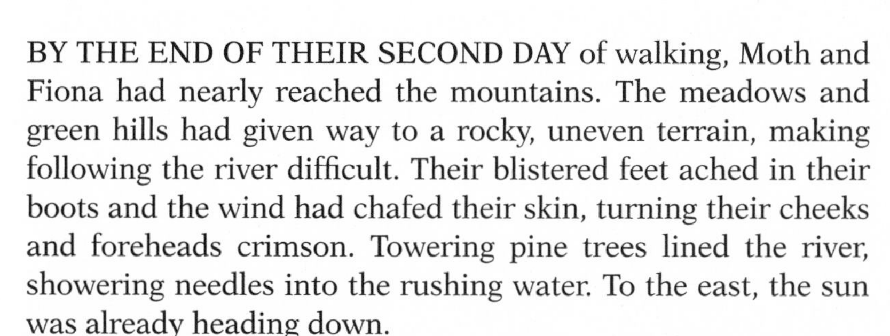

BY THE END OF THEIR SECOND DAY of walking, Moth and Fiona had nearly reached the mountains. The meadows and green hills had given way to a rocky, uneven terrain, making following the river difficult. Their blistered feet ached in their boots and the wind had chafed their skin, turning their cheeks and foreheads crimson. Towering pine trees lined the river, showering needles into the rushing water. To the east, the sun was already heading down.

Before them loomed the enormous mountains, the ramparts of Fiona's imaginary castle. Moth's eyes crept skyward as he walked, trying to see the peaks in the darkening sky and grey, growing mists. Throughout the day a storm had dogged them, threatening a downpour. So far, the rains had held off, but the wind was picking up again and Moth knew their luck was waning.

"If we don't find shelter soon we'll be drowned," he called to Fiona. "Might as well just sleep in the river!"

Fiona waved at him to keep up. "We'll make it," she promised—the same promise she'd been making all day. She walked quickly along the stones, sometimes balancing herself with outstretched arms.

"Slow down," Moth cautioned again.

"Can't," said Fiona.

"You're gonna fall!"

"Moth, we need to hurry. *You* need to hurry."

Moth considered the distance ahead. It was hard to tell just how far away the mountains still were. He looked up just as a raindrop plopped onto his nose.

"Uh-oh."

Fiona turned around. "What?"

Moth put out a hand to feel for rain. The gesture made Fiona groan.

"We should look for a place to stop," said Moth. "Some trees, at least."

"It'll be dark soon," said Fiona. "Those things will be looking for us. It's not that much farther . . ."

"Fiona, we can't make it, not when it's dark. We can't even see where we're going! We could break a leg if it starts raining!"

Fiona pointed toward the mountains. "They're right *there*!" she said. "Maybe a mile away. Just a few more minutes . . ."

"How can you tell that? You've been saying that for an hour."

A thunderclap went off over their heads. Moth glanced around for shelter.

"There," he said, spotting a clutch of nearby pine trees. "We can wait till the storm passes."

"It'll be too dark," said Fiona. "It's just rain, Moth."

She was getting desperate. Moth was getting annoyed. "We can wait," he insisted.

Fiona shook her head. "I'm going on," she said, and started off again along the river.

Moth hurried after her. "Okay, so you're testing me, is that it? You want to see if I'll follow you? You told Merceron you wouldn't leave me, Fiona!"

She whirled on him. "Moth, are you crazy? Merceron's the one who left us! And you know what? He's not coming back. He just said that so we'd leave him alone."

"That's not true!"

"It is!" Fiona railed. "Only you're so trusting you can't even see it! Nobody ever comes back, Moth. They just leave."

A patter of rain struck her face. Fiona wiped it away.

"They just leave, Moth," she said.

Moth jammed his hands into his pockets. He wanted to

touch her, but all he could manage was a smile. "Hey listen," he said. "I never thanked you for coming here with me."

Fiona had to swallow to keep from crying. "Yeah."

"And I never said I was sorry for talking about how pretty that mermaid was."

"Okay, yeah," Fiona nodded. She took a shaky breath. "I gotta go now, though. I gotta get there."

The rain came harder. Moth pulled up his collar. "Come on."

This time he took the lead, trudging carefully along the riverbank with Fiona right behind him. He could get soaked for her, he decided. She needed him. They'd find the path together. They'd find the centaurs, too. And then Merceron would come back for them. Moth was sure of it.

"What's that sound?" said Fiona suddenly.

Moth's heart jumped. "What?"

Fiona cocked her head. "That. You hear that?"

Moth heard the wind—and something else. It was such a familiar sound, so much a part of his memory that at first he didn't notice it. A hum and clang. A sound he'd always loved.

"Redeemers?"

Moth pointed across the sky. "There!"

It appeared like a ghost, the last bit of sunlight playing on its wings.

"A dragonfly . . ."

The craft buzzed out of the clouds. Behind it, blocking out the rising moon, floated a massive, black airship. Moth knew instantly it was the *Avatar*.

"That's my grandfather," cried Fiona. "He found us!"

They stood together, frozen by shock, watching the dragonfly bear down on them.

"This isn't possible," Moth sputtered. "They couldn't have. How?"

Fiona regained her senses. "We've gotta run," she clamored, pulling Moth along. "Run, now!"

"Fiona, wait!"

"Run, Moth!" cried Fiona. "I'm not going back with him!"

She was gone before he could answer, her booted feet slipping and sliding across the slimy rocks. Moth bolted after her. Behind them the dragonfly was gaining fast.

"Get away from the river!" he shouted. "Hide in the trees!"

"No! Don't lose the way! We're almost—"

Her voice disappeared. In a flash she was falling, tumbling headlong down the riverbank.

"Fiona!"

Moth slid down the bank to reach her. The current snatched her, dragging her fast. She screamed, gurgling his name, her red hair whipped by the swirling water.

"Fiona!"

He caught a glimpse of her thrashing arm. The wind swallowed her screams.

Moth ran. He fell, got up again, and stumbled over the rocks. The dragonfly closed in on him, the racket of its wings drowning his cries. He was trapped now but didn't care.

"Help!" he cried. He waved his arms to signal the pilot. The dragonfly roared overhead, then jerked back around again. "Stop!"

Rain pelted Moth's face as he stared skyward. The dragonfly descended loudly, beating the storm into a froth. There wasn't time to explain anything. All Moth wanted was to find Fiona. The craft came down hard, nearly crashing. Moth didn't recognize the pilot until the canopy popped open.

"Moth!"

Skyhigh vaulted from the cockpit.

"Skyhigh . . ."

Out of breath, too horrified to speak, Moth nearly collapsed. Skyhigh dashed over to him, grabbing his shoulders.

"Where's Fiona?" he demanded. Moth pointed toward the river. Skyhigh's eyes went wide when he realized what had happened. He shook Moth in a rage. "Why the hell did you run? I was coming to *help*!"

Moth couldn't answer. All the emotions he'd pent up for days burst like a dam. "She's gone!" he sobbed. Hot tears streaked his ruddy face. "Skyhigh . . . Fiona's gone!"

TWO THINGS

MOTH STARED BLANKLY through the dragonfly's canopy, watching the rain smash against the glass as Skyhigh piloted the vessel through the storm. The dragonfly pitched in the winds, straining to stay aloft. Ahead of them glowed the spotlight of the *Avatar*, the only visible cue they could see through the clouds. Below them the world had vanished, and Fiona with it.

They'd searched for her as long as possible, flying low over the rocks until the rain and darkness overwhelmed them. Finally, with the *Avatar* circling impatiently overhead, Skyhigh called off their search.

"Skyhigh?"

Skyhigh kept his eyes on the *Avatar*'s beacon. "Yeah?"

"I'm sorry we ran," said Moth. "I'm sorry for everything."

Skyhigh worked the controls as though ignoring him. "Yeah," he said finally. "I know. It's not your fault, Moth."

It was the kind of thing adults tell little children after they'd spilled some milk or broken a window.

"Fiona crossed the Reach because of me," said Moth. "It is my fault. None of this would have happened if—"

"Stop," said Skyhigh. "I know what you're thinking, but maybe she's okay. If she's a good swimmer she might still be alive. In the morning we'll look for her again."

Moth tried to remember if Fiona had ever mentioned swimming in Capital City. Her pastimes were horses mostly. And museums.

"Skyhigh?"

"Yeah?"

"What are you gonna tell Rendor?"

"I'm not sure. The truth, I guess. Fiona saw us coming, so she ran."

"She ran because she didn't want to go back to him."

"Was that a good decision or a stupid one?"

Moth leaned back, feeling woozy. "He doesn't care about her. All he cares about is the Starfinder."

"What is that thing anyway?" asked Skyhigh. "I still don't know."

"It's the gift Leroux wanted to give me," said Moth. "Esme brought it to me before we left."

"Esme! Where is she?"

Moth hesitated. How much should he really tell Skyhigh?

"She's safe."

Skyhigh's head turned a little. "What's that supposed to mean?"

"It's private, Skyhigh. I can't tell you."

"For crying sakes, Moth . . ."

"I'm sorry," said Moth. "I can't tell you because I can't let Rendor get the Starfinder!"

"Starfinder, Starfinder! What's the big deal? Let me see it."

"I can't," said Moth. "I don't have it anymore."

"You mean you lost it?"

Moth shook his head. "No."

"Fiona has it?"

"No."

"Who then? Merceron? He's a dragon, right?"

"Huh?" Moth sat up. "Who told you about Merceron?"

"No one. No one tells me anything! It's just something I overheard. Does he have the Starfinder?"

"Skyhigh . . ."

"I know, you can't tell me! Listen, Moth—I don't care about the Starfinder. All I want is to get you home safe. Fiona, too. If you think I'm in cahoots with Rendor, then you just go ahead and believe that. I'm still your friend, no matter what you think."

Moth leaned his head against the glass. "Everything's gotten so messed up. But I have to protect them—Esme, Fiona, everyone. I can't tell you any more."

"You have to," said Skyhigh. "If we're going to find Fiona we need to know where you were heading."

Moth looked away.

"Moth, c'mon . . ."

"Fiona doesn't want him to find her," said Moth.

"He's her grandfather! He's got a right to know what's happened to her!"

"If she's alive, she's safe," said Moth, hoping Fiona had somehow made it to the centaurs.

"That's all you're going to tell me?" Skyhigh shook his head in annoyance. "That won't cut it with Rendor."

Up ahead, the *Avatar* hung in the sky like a big, black moon.

An hour later Moth found himself in Rendor's quarters, staring out a small, round porthole. The rain had stopped, and the wind had blown away most of the clouds. In the moonlight he could see the mountains again. The *Avatar* floated somewhere between the towering peaks and the rushing river far below.

Crewmen had brought Moth new clothes. Like the coat he'd stolen back in Calio, the plain shirt and trousers were too big for him, swimming on him like mismatched sheets. There was food, too, laid out on a table bolted to the floor. Otherwise the chamber was bare, the walls little more than metal struts and panels. A cot waited in the corner, fitted with clean, crisp linen.

Moth wasn't hungry and he didn't want to sleep. He just wanted morning to come, so they could look for Fiona again.

"Even if we had wings, some of us would be pigeons."

Moth turned abruptly, startled to see Rendor stepping through the narrow doorway.

"Huh?"

The governor closed the door behind him. "It's a joke someone told me once. Looking at you made me think of it." He took a step closer, raising an eyebrow when he noticed the untouched food. "Not hungry?"

Moth shook his head. Rendor glanced at the cot.

"Did you rest at least?"

"This is all just a bribe," said Moth. "It's not gonna work. I won't help you."

Rendor hovered over the table. "Your friend Coralin warned me you'd be tart," he said. He selected a piece of cheese, considering Moth while he chewed. "Leroux didn't do you any favors. Did he at least warn you that I'd be coming after you?"

Moth crossed his arms. "You're wasting your time asking questions."

"Fine. Then just listen. You've made a right mess of things. You stole the Starfinder, made me come looking for you, and now my granddaughter is missing. She might even be dead."

"I didn't steal the Starfinder," sneered Moth. "Leroux wanted me to have it."

"Leroux was my friend long before you ever met him, boy. He was a good man but a great fool. All he ever cared about was getting Esme back to normal. And you've lost her too, haven't you?" Rendor's smile was caustic. "Like I said—a right mess you've made."

He pulled out the chair next to the table, sitting down and studying Moth with his crazy blue eyes.

"The moment the sun comes up we'll start searching for Fiona. It would help if we knew where to look."

"She fell into the river," said Moth.

"Only a fish can swim in that river, boy. By now it's carried her into the rocks. Why were you heading for the mountains? What's there?"

"Nothing," said Moth. "We were just following the river."

"You're a terrible liar, you know that?"

Instead of looking at Rendor, Moth stared out the window.

"Keeping your mouth shut isn't going to help Fiona. What about the Starfinder? Does Fiona have it? Or did you give it back to Merceron?"

Moth struggled to hold his tongue.

"All right," sighed Rendor, slapping his hands against his lap. "You ask the questions." He leaned back, tilted up his chin. "Go on. Leroux obviously kept you in the dark. Merceron, too."

"They told me enough," said Moth. "Especially Merceron."

"Did he tell you how we helped him fight his war? That Leroux and I were the ones that smuggled the Starfinder out of here? That old beast owes me that at least."

"All right," said Moth. "I do have a question for you. Why'd you ever come here? Why'd you and Leroux cross the Reach together?"

"Leroux never explained it to you?"

"He never told me anything," said Moth. "All he ever did was tell stories. I thought he made them up. He was old. He really didn't have anyone. I always thought he told those stories just so folks would listen to him."

Rendor actually looked sad. "Don't blame him for that, boy. We were Eldrin Knights. We swore to keep our mission secret."

"Mission?"

"To spy on the Skylords," said Rendor. "To find out if they really existed and what they were like. But Leroux forgot the things we saw over here. I never did. Now tell me about the Starfinder."

"Forget it," scoffed Moth.

"You must have figured out how to use it. Otherwise you'd never have found Merceron."

"You don't know that. You don't know anything."

"Not even the Skylords knew where Merceron was hiding. Only the Starfinder could have found him."

Moth turned back to the porthole. "I'm tired."

"Then sit down! I'm not going anywhere and neither are you." Rendor gestured to the cot. "There's something you need to know."

Curious, Moth sat down at the edge of the bed.

"Two things," said Rendor. "First, Merceron didn't tell you everything about the Starfinder. Second, I think I know why you're able to make it work." Rendor grinned. "You do want to know why the Starfinder works for you, don't you?"

Moth couldn't help himself from nodding. "Yes," he said. "Tell me."

"I spent my whole life trying to figure it out. So did Leroux.

So did Merceron." Rendor laughed and clapped his hands together. "I can't believe that old reptile hasn't figured it out yet!"

"Figured out what?"

Rendor smiled and said, "That you're a *child*."

"What? I'm not a child," Moth protested. "I'm thirteen."

"It's not about your age," said Rendor. "Not precisely. It's about what's up *here*." He tapped his head with his fingertip. "Your friend Skyhigh's been telling me about you. He says you're a dreamer. That you want to be a Skyknight, that you're always looking up, head in the clouds."

His accusation made Moth squirm. "I am going to fly one day, Governor. Even you can't stop me from that."

Rendor waved off his words. "Being a dreamer isn't an insult, boy. But when you get older things will be different. You won't see possibilities anymore, just obstacles."

Moth looked at him blankly. "Uh-huh . . ."

"You're confused. All right. You like stories, so I'll tell you one." Rendor poured himself a cup of tea. "I had a brother named Conrad. He was four years older than me. I loved him. I trusted him. Anything he told me, I believed. When I was growing up, all I ever wanted was to fly. Conny knew that, so when I was six or seven he told me he was going to build me a pair of wings."

"Wings?" laughed Moth. "I guess you weren't a very smart kid, huh?"

Rendor set down his cup without taking a sip. "I was a genius, but that's not the point. I did Conny's chores for him, gave him my toys, kept his secrets—anything to get those wings. I *believed*. And because nobody told me I couldn't fly, I just assumed that I could."

"I get it," said Moth. "Because I'm a dreamer I can use the Starfinder, right?"

"Maybe," said Rendor. He shrugged. "It's hard to be sure. But I bet Fiona couldn't make it work, could she?"

Moth hesitated. He promised himself he wouldn't answer any of Rendor's questions. "Why not?"

"You know Fiona better than I do. You can answer that yourself."

"Because she's not a dreamer?"

"Because she has no faith. Because she doesn't believe in anything." Rendor pulled the watch from his pocket to check the time. Only he didn't seem interested in the time. He just sort of gazed at it.

"What's the other thing?"

Rendor blinked. "Eh?"

"You said there were two things you wanted to tell me about the Starfinder."

The old man nodded. "Yes." He slid his watch back into his pocket. "The Starfinder isn't just a way of finding the creatures of this world. It doesn't just spy on them. It controls them."

"Controls them?" Moth shook his head. "No, that's not what Merceron told me."

"Merceron couldn't tell you the truth," said Rendor. "Not once he realized what you could do. The Starfinder lets the Skylords command the beings of the constellations. It's like a leash around their necks. They can't escape it." Rendor's voice got deep and serious. "I don't know how it works," he admitted. "All I know is what Esme told us. The Skylords use the Starfinder to force others to do their bidding. That's what makes it so dangerous. Think about it, Moth. The Starfinder makes you as powerful as a Skylord."

"I feel sick," Moth groaned. He remembered what Fiona had said about Merceron. Maybe she was right. Maybe all he'd ever wanted was the Starfinder. "Now I understand why you want the Starfinder so bad."

Rendor rose from his chair. "The Starfinder is the ultimate protection against the Skylords, Moth. Ever since I discovered what they truly are, I've spent my life preparing for them."

"Sure," muttered Moth. "You knew the Skylords didn't want people flying. You knew building your airships would make them mad, but you stuck your finger in their eyes anyway."

Suddenly Rendor reached down and grabbed hold of Moth's collar.

"Hey!"

The old man dragged him off the cot and shoved him toward the porthole. "Look out there!"

Moth wriggled in his grasp. "What?"

"Look at those mountains! We are two thousand feet in the sky." Rendor released him. "We have every right to be up here," he said. "Who are the Skylords to tell an eagle not to soar?" He jabbed a finger into Moth's chest. "Do you want the Skylords to tell you what dreams to have?"

Moth shook his head. "No . . ."

"No," echoed Rendor. "Because we are free. That's what the Eldrin Knights fought for—freedom. That's what it means to be human. And that's why I want the Starfinder—to stop the Skylords from doing to us what they did to the dragons."

He took a breath, smoothed down his waistcoat, then turned back toward the door.

"Wait," said Moth.

Rendor paused as he reached for the door handle.

"I was wondering—how'd you know where to find us?"

"Just think about what I told you," replied Rendor. "In the morning we'll look for Fiona."

Ignoring Moth's question, he closed the door behind him.

GONE

WHEN RENDOR RETURNED TO THE HANGAR, Alisaundra the Redeemer was waiting for him. Still in chains, she stood impatiently near the hangar's open doors, her blonde hair askew in the breeze. Four crewmen trained rifles on her, sweating despite the chill. Commander Donnar's hands were clasped behind his back. He turned expectantly to Rendor as the Governor approached.

"Anything?"

Rendor shook his head. "He's not talking. What about this one?"

"Nothing more," said Donnar.

Alisaundra hissed, "Waiting!"

Rendor stuck his face directly into hers.

"Where's Fiona?"

"Gone," said the Redeemer. "I cannot feel her."

"Have you tried? You have to try."

The creature turned toward the dark mountains. "She has gone."

Rendor's insides clenched. "You mean dead?"

Alisaundra concentrated, her snakelike eyes drawing to slits as she scanned the night. "The smell of her . . . it doesn't remain. I see her no more. Red hair . . . no more."

"Maybe she's hurt? Unconscious?"

The Redeemer gazed fiercely at Rendor. "I have given you the boy. The other is gone. Our bargain . . ."

"What about the Starfinder? Why didn't you tell me Moth didn't have it?"

"We bargained for the children. Only the children."

"Now you're playing games!" thundered Rendor.

"Shoot her," urged Donnar. "She'll just bring others if you let her go."

The Redeemer raised her chin. "Yes, shoot me," she taunted. "For the glory of the Skylords!"

"Where's the Starfinder?" demanded Rendor. "Tell me!"

"Never!" raged Alisaundra. She writhed against her chains, teeth clacking, muscles bulging in the metal restraints. "I have delivered my bargain!"

"Don't release her," pleaded Donnar. "She'll go to the Skylords, tell them where we are."

Rendor could hardly think. The Redeemer's wails, Fiona's death . . . it was all too much for him.

"Let me go!" Alisaundra howled. "Or kill me! I cannot be here! I cannot bear it!"

She was pitiful. She disgusted Rendor. Just being with humans tortured her. In her last life she might have had a lover, children of her own. She might have had a beautiful life. Now she was one of *them*.

"Give me the key," said Rendor, holding out his hand.

Donnar was aghast. "Governor . . ."

"It doesn't matter, Erich. The Skylords already know we're here. And she'll never help us find the Starfinder. For God's sake, look at her."

Alisaundra stopped her raving. Threads of spittle hung from her chin. Donnar placed the key in Rendor's palm.

"Back up," Rendor told the riflemen, "and be ready. If she does anything but head for those doors, shoot her." He twirled his finger at the creature. "Turn around."

Three stout padlocks dangled between her wings. Rendor unlocked the first one, then the second. As he stuck the key into the third he whispered, "You're wrong, monster. Fiona's not dead. Maybe you can't feel her, but I can."

He turned the key and stepped back. Alisaundra flexed, and the chains and locks fell clanging to the floor. Her wings shot out; a crewman gasped. Rendor wasn't afraid. He didn't feel anything at all.

"Go," he ordered.

Alisaundra didn't turn or say a word. She walked toward the open doors, paused like a diver at the edge of the hangar, then flung herself into the night.

Moth lay quietly in Rendor's cot, studying the darkened room. A single gaslight glowed over the door, giving the chamber a ghostly bluish hue. The food still sat untouched on the table.

Sleep evaded Moth. Every time he closed his eyes he heard Fiona's voice. No matter how long he lived—even if he lived forever—he'd always remember the way she sounded, calling to him as she plunged into the river.

"Hold on till the morning," he whispered. "We'll find you."

Maybe Fiona could hear his prayer. Or maybe it was just a lie, and they'd never find her. It made Moth feel better to think she was out there, waiting for him. Most of all, he wanted desperately to do something.

He thought about Skyhigh, and how he'd hurt his friend. He needed to apologize. *Yes,* he'd tell Skyhigh, *I was stupid. Yes, we shouldn't have run. Yes, I killed Fiona.*

"Stupid . . ."

He sat up, his heart galloping in his chest. Why was he keeping secrets? Was Fiona really better off with the centaurs? He shouldn't have let her come. They'd have to wait until morning to search for her, but there was something he could do right now.

He tossed his feet over the side of the cot and headed for the door. He didn't know the airship's layout, but he supposed Rendor was on the bridge.

Two thousand feet below, Alisaundra gazed up at the *Avatar* from a forest of oak trees. The great airship hung motionless in the sky, somehow defying the winds. It was easy to admire the ship, but not so easy for Alisaundra to understand it. How did it float like a boat on water? How had humans made so much progress? She had questions but no answers, and no one in her world to help her figure out these things.

Alisaundra felt the boy named Moth aboard the ship. After trying to sleep, he was moving again. The sense of him was strong, easy to follow.

The old man Rendor was right. Others would find the airship soon. They would wonder how humans had entered their realm, and how Alisaundra had let them get so far. There were no secrets from the Skylords. Alisaundra knew she had to save herself.

She glanced around. There were many fallen trees to choose from, some of them rotted, some of them still leaning against other, living trees. After a moment she spotted the perfect choice, a young oak with a ball of upturned roots and small, broken branches.

The Masters had given Alisaundra many gifts. Eyes like an eagle, a nose like a cat, claws for tearing and a mouth full of pointed teeth for frightening prey. And one thing more—the strength of a furious bull. Alisaundra squatted down next to the fallen oak. She slipped her hands beneath it, cradling it like a baby. With a flurry of her powerful wings, she carried the tree into the sky.

Moth expected the *Avatar* to be crowded with crewmen, but instead found himself alone in the corridor, making his way toward the front of the ship. He'd already descended two ladders, because he knew the bridge hung low on the superstructure. The gentle thrum of the airship's engines made the metal floor and walls vibrant with a peculiar music. He wondered if Skyhigh had gone to bed yet.

Voices echoed up ahead. Moth followed the corridor, halting when he saw the bridge. A panoramic window looked out over what seemed like the entire world. Rendor stood in front of the glass, studying the moonlit mountains. Crews manned control consoles, keeping watch over the dials and levers. A man dressed in a dark uniform paced across the bridge, his hands behind his back. He caught a glimpse of Moth from the corner of his eye.

"You?" The man cleared his throat. "Governor? Someone's here to see you."

Surprised, Rendor turned from the window. Moth stepped onto the bridge.

"I need to talk to you," said Moth. "It's important . . ."

A sudden crash rocked the airship, knocking Moth to the floor. Outside the window the world began to spin.

"Engine out!" someone cried. Rendor shouted. The *Avatar* lurched sideways, spilling Moth across the deck.

"Port engine!"

"Shut it down!"

"Leveling out . . ."

Moth struggled to rise. He saw Rendor holding onto a rail. The men at the consoles threw switches and cursed. Slowly, Moth felt the giant airship righting itself, but the engine noise was different now, and he had no idea what had happened.

"Moth!" yelled Rendor. "Get hold of something!"

Moth scrambled for a nearby steam pipe. The floor had leveled, yet the *Avatar* kept spinning. Just as Moth pulled himself up, the giant window burst. Glass and metal showered the bridge. Wind howled through the gaping cavity. Moth wrapped his arms around the pipe, shocked to see something coming through the window. The screeching shadow fell on him in a frenzy of beating wings. Scaly, powerful arms swept him from the bridge.

Moth screamed. He felt the rush of wind, saw the blur of horrified faces. A second later he was weightless with the stars above his head. In disbelief he watched the *Avatar* drifting away.

"Get us down!" Donnar cried. His voice cracked over the wind. Rendor held tight to the rail, staring at the blown-open window. Around him the crew worked to steady the *Avatar*.

Alisaundra had vanished. Rendor searched the sky but knew they'd never catch her. His ship was going down. Somehow Alisaundra had knocked out an engine, but Rendor almost didn't care. His blue eyes softened, sick at the fate that awaited the boy.

Just like Fiona, Moth was gone.

ALIVE

DROWNING.

First there was panic. The clutching for the sky, lungs burning, throat filled with frigid water. She remembered tumbling and the rocks beating her. The bottomless river pulling at her coat. Feet kicking, mouth screaming without sound. Bobbing up for precious gulps of air.

Dying.

How long did it take to die?

Fiona's head lay on the rocks. Was it night? She couldn't tell. Maybe she was blind.

She heard the water, very nearby. She had swum to the rocks. Or maybe the river had spit her out. Her cold legs were still, useless. She shivered and couldn't stop herself. If her eyes were open, she saw nothing. But there were things she remembered, a jumble of things that didn't belong together yet somehow held hands through her brain. She saw Moth with her mother and father, together on an airship sailing to Medona. She saw the great blackness of the *Avatar* chasing her. She smelled cinnamon. She was a little girl again.

Seeing herself made Fiona happy.

Pain stabbed her skull. Fiona thought about crying but couldn't find the strength, so the little girl in her mind began to weep.

Sleep, Fiona told herself. *Or just die. Whichever.*

* * *

The sun shone brightly on her face. Fiona hadn't seen it rise. Its gentle warmth baked her body.

I am a ghost now. In heaven.

Fiona didn't move. Her mind floated as she gazed up. The sun was a yellow flower in the sky. Her fingernails scraped the sand beneath her. When her head began to throb, she knew she wasn't dead.

Soon . . .

An animal might come and eat her. She might starve. Or she might just sleep forever. Fearlessly, Fiona closed her eyes. Her parents were in heaven, waiting there for her. Sunlight burst with colors on her eyelids. Her body felt like it was falling.

A shadow dropped across her face, blocking the sun. Annoyed, Fiona willed her eyes open. A hazy face hovered over her. Long, brown hair fell from the head and down its back like the mane of a lion. Its enormous, muscular body bent down on its two front legs to examine her. Fiona nearly smiled. She had seen this beast before.

"Are you Jorian?"

A hand came down to touch her forehead. It swept gently over her eyes, closing them. Immediately Fiona felt sleep tugging at her. And something else lifting her. Her body felt limp and out of her control. Fiona surrendered, drooping in the arms that carried her and drifting off to sleep.

SITTING DUCKS

JUST FOUR THIN LINES TETHERED the gigantic *Avatar* to the earth. Every time the wind blew, the ropes groaned and pulled at their spikes. Crews manned the guns jutting from the airship's envelope and atop her observation deck, scanning the horizon for trouble. The thousand bits of glass had been swept from her bridge, but the gaping hole left by the shattered window remained.

Rendor watched as Bottling descended a metal ladder hanging from the airship's superstructure. The engineer had spent nearly an hour inspecting the damaged engine. Amazingly, Alisaundra had managed to break off one of the engine's four propeller blades, unbalancing the *Avatar* and forcing an emergency landing. The crew had spent the night staking the airship down and cleaning up what damage they could. While they worked, Skyhigh began searching for Fiona. The Skyknight had returned a short time ago—empty-handed.

"Well?" Rendor called.

Bottling shook his head. "Not good." He jumped from the ladder, landing close to the Governor. "All the other blades have fractures."

Rendor took a handkerchief from his vest and handed it to Bottling. "How big?"

"Big enough," said Bottling as he wiped his grimy hands. "We could push it, but there's a good chance they'll snap off at speed."

Commander Donnar, who'd been directing the repair efforts, overheard Bottling's assessment. "The prop is useless that way anyway," he said. "Three blades? We're better off shutting it down."

"One engine," groaned Rendor.

"She can fly with one," Donnar pointed out.

"Sure," said Bottling. "Or we could walk home. Be just as quick."

None of them smiled at the joke.

"Balance it out," said Rendor. "Saw off the middle blade. We'll adjust the thrust from the bridge."

Bottling nodded as if he already knew Rendor's decision. "Can do." His face went into an unhappy smirk. "Speaking about the bridge . . ."

"I know."

The three men moved toward the front of the *Avatar*, where the real damage waited. Creating such a large span of glass had taken scientific wizardry, and there was no way they could replace the glass without returning home. Although the *Avatar* could fly with an open bridge, it would make steering her vastly more difficult in strong winds, and high altitudes would require heavy clothing. And of course, there was foul weather to consider.

"Ideas?" asked Rendor.

"A tarp," said Donnar. "That's all we can do for now."

"We need to be able to see where we're going," said Rendor.

"We'll use netting," Bottling suggested. "Instead of just cutting holes in the tarp, we'll sew it with squares of netting. Not too big—just enough to see through."

"Nets," groaned Rendor. "Thank god the weather here is warm." He looked up at the sky, blessing the bright sun. "All right, Bottling, get started on the prop. And form a detail to start on the tarp. I'll start thinking about how to mount it."

The engineer handed Rendor his now-filthy handkerchief back and went to work. When he'd gone, Rendor said softly, "Erich, let's post some patrols around the ship. Until we're aloft again, we're sitting ducks."

Donnar checked the sky. "How long before they come, do you think?"

Rendor shrugged. "A few days. Maybe less. First they'll watch us for a while, try to figure out how strong we are."

"We should get Skyhigh into the air, too," suggested Donnar. "Have him run some patrols to the south."

"Find him for me, will you, Erich? I want to talk to him."

As the commander departed, Rendor allowed himself an unguarded moment. Since the attack, there hadn't been time to think about Fiona or Moth. Rendor liked being busy. It kept him from feeling afraid. Now that it was quiet, all his fears rushed at him.

Across the field, Skyhigh's dragonfly glistened in the sun. Rendor smiled, remembering the thrill of seeing his invention take flight for the first time. He crossed the tall grass and went to the craft, sad to see its battered fuselage and hastily repaired wings. Still, it was beautiful to Rendor. He ran his hands over it as though it were his child.

"Governor?"

Skyhigh's voice carried across the field. The young man, handsome and blond, wore a scarf around his neck, his leather flight jacket as beat-up as his dragonfly. He pulled on his gloves as though readying for takeoff.

"Commander Donnar told me you wanted to see me," he said. "If it's about Fiona, I promise—I'll do my best to find her."

Rendor had to force himself to say his next words.

"No more searching for Fiona, Captain."

Skyhigh blinked in disbelief. "No?"

Rendor reached into his pocket and took out his watch. He ran his thumb over its embossed surface before popping it open.

"The Skylords aren't going to let us out of here," he said without looking up. "They'll try to keep us from going home, pin us here against these mountains. Until we can get the *Avatar* airborne again, we're vulnerable."

"All right, but . . ."

"We need your dragonfly. You'll be our eyes while we're grounded. I need you to run patrols back the way we came, see if the Skylords or their Redeemers are starting to gather. Daylight flights only."

"Sir?"

"Hmm?"

"When the *Avatar*'s repaired, are we going home?"

Rendor snapped the watch closed. "We haven't gotten any of the things we came here for," he said. "Not Fiona, not Moth, and not the Starfinder. No, Captain. We're not going home."

Skyhigh beamed at the news. "Good." He glanced down at the watch. "Nice watch. Real gold?"

"A gift," sighed Rendor. "From my daughter." He patted the tail of Skyhigh's dragonfly. "She gave it to me the day I first got one of these contraptions to fly. I suppose she was proud of me."

"Fiona talked about her a lot," said Skyhigh. "She loved her very much."

Rendor put the watch back in his pocket. Talking about his daughter was something he rarely did. It was easier just to look at the watch.

"Fiona's a lot like her," he said. "Strong. Beautiful."

Skyhigh looked at him strangely. "Beautiful?"

"Yes. Fiona's very beautiful. Don't you think so?"

"It's not that, sir," said Skyhigh. "It's just . . . have you ever told her that, Governor?"

"Why would I?" asked Rendor. "She hates me. She doesn't believe a thing I say."

THURMWOOD

MERCERON DESCENDED ALONG the coast, the choppy sea spraying his spectacles. Lady Esme glided alongside him, her sharp eyes searching the cliffs for an opening.

Even over the ocean's briny scent, Merceron could smell his fellow dragons. He remembered the fold in the cliffs, a crack just large enough for him to squeeze through. The tangled vines clinging to the salt-covered rocks pointed the way. Lady Esme followed Merceron as he swooped lower, the waves licking at his belly. A tiny, sugar-white beach skimmed the bottom of the cliffs.

"There!"

With a flurry of his wings, Merceron landed on the sand. Esme alighted on his shoulder. Together they stared into the dark crevice. Merceron's long snout tasted the air.

"A dozen of them," he determined. "Maybe more."

The smell of fish and seaweed mingled in his nostrils, masking the lingering note of his beloved Dreojen. For a moment, Merceron couldn't move. The tide rolled in, splashing against his back and driving Esme from his shoulder.

"Wait!"

Inhaling deeply, Merceron pushed his big body sideways into the crevice. The sunlight vanished instantly. The rocks scraped his wings. Slowly, the crevice opened into a tall, dripping cavern. Overhead, stalactites hung like daggers.

"Esme?" Merceron whispered. "Come here."

He put out his arm. The gesture called the kestrel back to him. Just as her claws grasped his coat, something moved in the shadows. Merceron scraped his talons together, summoning a fiery spark. He blew on it until it lit the chamber. On the far side of the cavern, a familiar face stared back at him.

"Thurmwood."

The dragon peeled himself from the shadows. His yellow, catlike eyes frowned. A single, upturned fang protruded from his lower jaw. Fifty years had barely changed him.

"Still alive," groaned Thurmwood as he hunched his way across the cavern. "The mermaids said so, but I didn't believe it."

Merceron held up his fiery claw. "The others, too," he said. He glanced around the cavern. "Ganomyrn, Varsilius—show yourselves."

Two more dragons slipped from the shadows. Old Ganomyrn led the younger, small-boned Varsilius into the light. In the years before the war, Ganomyrn had been a close friend, an architect who'd designed some of Taurnoken's grandest buildings. Varsilius, his son, was to follow in his work.

"Ganomyrn, where's Dreojen?" Merceron asked. "I know she's here."

Before Ganomyrn could answer, Thurmwood stepped forward. "Of course she's here," he snapped. "She's the one who led us here. She doesn't want to see you, Merceron."

Merceron frowned. "Is that true, Ganomyrn?"

Ganomyrn nodded. "I'm sorry, Merceron. Dreojen asked us to speak for her."

"Why are you here?" asked Thurmwood. Before the war, he'd been Merceron's assistant. A very able librarian, but prickly.

"Look closely," said Merceron. He gestured to Esme. "Don't you recognize her?"

Young Varsilius cried out, "Esme!"

Thurmwood put out his arm quickly, stopping Varsilius. "The humans brought her back here," he snorted. "They must have."

Merceron looked at him, surprised. "You know about the humans?"

"We hear things," said Thurmwood. "The mermaids and fey have seen their airship."

"Airship?" gasped Merceron. "What airship?"

"The black ship, near Pandera." Thurmwood's eyes narrowed on Merceron. "You didn't know?"

Merceron shook his head. An airship could only mean one thing—Rendor had come.

"The Skylords have seen the humans, Merceron," said Ganomyrn. "They're massing to stop them."

"Already?" sputtered Merceron. He was quickly running out of time. "Thurmwood, I need to see Dreojen. I have to speak to her."

"Are you deaf? I told you—she doesn't want to see you." A bit of sympathy flickered in Thurmwood's eyes. "Really, Merceron, can you blame her?"

Blame. The word made Merceron wince.

"There are others here with you," said Merceron. "How many?"

"Fifteen," said Varsilius quickly.

"What about everyone else? What happened at Taurnoken?"

Thurmwood replied, "The war, Merceron. You remember the war, don't you?"

"But I left to end the war!"

"Well, I guess that wasn't good enough for the Skylords."

Old Ganomyrn said sadly, "We fled to save ourselves."

"We don't have to explain anything to him," sniffed Thurmwood.

Merceron forced himself to stay calm. "Fine. If Dreojen won't see me, then I'll speak to you. I need your help, Thurmwood."

"My help?" Thurmwood chortled, his one, overgrown tooth making a whistling noise. "With what?"

Merceron unbuttoned a pocket on his coat and reached inside. "With this."

He pulled out the Starfinder, holding it out in his upturned claw. The other dragons fell dumbstruck.

"Are you mad?" hissed Thurmwood. "Are you *stone*? Do you care nothing for what might happen to us?"

"I had to bring it," said Merceron. "I had nowhere else to turn."

"That's why the humans have come!" said Varsilius. "For the Starfinder! Are they after you, Merceron?"

"Did you steal it from them?" asked Thurmwood. "Is that why they're here?"

"Just shut up and listen, will you?" Merceron stepped forward. "A boy gave me the Starfinder. A human, yes, but he's on the run, too . . . from Rendor, Thurmwood. That ship you told me about is his."

"Rendor?" Thurmwood put up his claws. "Enough. I don't want to know anything more."

Ganomyrn grimaced. "Merceron, if the Redeemers know you have the Starfinder . . ."

"They'll follow you here!" spat Thurmwood. "You've led them right to us!"

"Where else was I to go?" asked Merceron. "Would you rather I gave Rendor the Starfinder? Thurmwood, we were friends long before the war. I need your help! You're right—the Redeemers are after me. They know I have the Starfinder. I need to figure out a way to destroy it."

Thurmwood shook his head. "Impossible. We've been through this already. We searched the library. No spells—"

"But since then," Merceron interrupted. "Surely you must have considered it."

"Merceron, we were too busy trying to stay alive." Thurmwood waved his arm about the cavern. "Look around. Does this look like Taurnoken to you?"

"What about Esme?" asked Merceron. "Have you thought of a way to help her, at least? While you were sitting around here in the dark . . ."

"Esme and the Starfinder were gone!" cried Thurmwood. "We were rid of them, and we were glad for it! Now you bring them back to us? And humans too?" With a sweep of his wings, Thurmwood turned to go. "Leave, Merceron, please. Go back to wherever you were hiding. No one wants you here."

He slipped back into the darkness. Ganomyrn and Varsilius hesitated.

"I'm sorry, Merceron," said Ganomyrn. He put his hand on his son's shoulder. "For everything. For . . . your loss. But Thurmwood's right. We can't help you this time."

As he and Varsilius followed after Thurmwood, the little flame in Merceron's hand flickered.

"Wait!" Merceron cried. "What about the Starfinder? What about Esme? Please, Thurmwood! There's no one else who can help me!"

Thurmwood paused in the shadows. Merceron seized his chance.

"Thurmwood, if the Skylords get the Starfinder they'll come after you," he said. "You can't hide. If they get it no one will be safe."

From out of the darkness, Thurmwood replied, "Then we will wait here for them. And when they get here, we'll know who to thank for it."

Merceron slumped. "I came all this way . . ."

"Then rest. You can stay until sunset. But be gone before the night comes."

Merceron watched Thurmwood's tail disappear. On his shoulder, Lady Esme dipped her head in defeat.

THE TREASURE

EXHAUSTED FROM HIS LONG FLIGHT to the cliffs, Merceron slept. While he slept, he dreamed . . .

He was back in Taurnoken. He stood on a ledge of a tall, grand tower, overlooking the city. Ganomyrn and his son Varsilius were with him. The two were laying bricks, building the tower higher and higher.

Merceron knew Ganomyrn was an architect, not a builder. In his whole long life he had never seen Ganomryn lay bricks. Yet there he was, working with his son and cursing the Skylords.

"We'll build it as high as we want," declared Ganomyrn. "We'll build until we reach the moon!"

Merceron stood on the ledge, afraid to fall.

But I have wings, *he told himself.* Why am I afraid?

As so often happens in dreams, his mind gave Varsilius a push. The young dragon screamed as he plummeted from the ledge, falling down, down toward the earth.

Why doesn't he fly? *wondered Merceron. He looked at Ganomyrn.*

"Help him!" said Merceron. "Fly down and save him!"

Ganomyrn watched calmly as his son disappeared into the abyss. He smiled at Merceron, then went back to work.

Startled, Merceron awoke. But it wasn't his dream that roused him. An unmistakable scent had roused his sleeping brain.

He opened his eyes, lifted his head. In the corner of the cavern, she was waiting. He watched her, eager for her to come out of the shadows but afraid to frighten her away.

"Thurmwood said you wouldn't come," he whispered.

"I didn't think you'd wake up," said Dreojen softly.

Merceron hoped she was lying. "Will you come closer?"

Dreojen lingered in the shadows. Merceron put out his claw to make a fire. When the light struck his face, Dreojen grimaced.

"You've changed," she said, and dared to move a little closer.

"Have I? I don't think so. It's only been fifty years."

Dreojen spied Esme perched on a nearby rock. "*She* hasn't changed," she said. "Skylord magic. Horrible."

Merceron was barely listening. Dreojen remained beautiful, her bronze scales shimmering, her feathered mane unfaded by time. He had always thought himself lucky to have such a magnificent mate. He pushed his spectacles against his face, struck stupid with adoration.

"What about the others?" he asked. "Have they changed their minds about helping me?"

Dreojen answered coolly, "Thurmwood wanted me to remind you there's only an hour left until sundown."

"Coward," Merceron snorted. The flame in his hand crackled. He made it flare to see her better. Around her shoulders and wings was draped a velvet cape. A silver necklace sparkled at her neck—a gift he had given her long ago. "We are mates, still," he said gently. "If there's anything you can tell me, anything that will help me destroy the Starfinder . . ."

"Thurmwood wasn't lying to you, Merceron," said Dreojen. "After Taurnoken was abandoned, we all stopped trying to figure it out."

"Ah, so that you could live here," rumbled Merceron. "In a hole, instead of the city of our ancestors. Instead of fighting for what belongs to you."

Dreojen turned away with chagrin. "Stop. I won't have this argument again."

"Thurmwood is a coward, Dreojen. He just ran off like the rest of them!"

"You mean like you?" said Dreojen.

"That was different," sniffed Merceron. "I had the Starfinder. I had to leave."

"And now you're on the run again!" Dreojen chuckled mirthlessly. "I'm not heartless, Merceron. I came because I'm worried. Thurmwood told me the Redeemers are after you. They'll find you this time."

"Which is why I wasted my time coming here," growled Merceron. "I was stupid enough to think you'd all forgiven me by now. You especially, Dreojen." He turned from her and went to Lady Esme, coaxing the bird onto his shoulder. "Since you all want me gone, let me oblige."

"Where, Merceron? Where can you go that the Skylords won't find you?"

"I don't know!"

"So you'll just keep on running?"

Merceron slumped. "If you could at least tell me something about the airship . . ."

"Thurmwood says you think it's Rendor."

"He told me it's near Pandera," said Merceron. "The children are in Pandera, the ones who stole the Starfinder from him."

Dreojen looked shocked. "You sent them to the centaurs?"

"Why shouldn't I have?" said Merceron. "Jorian and his people are braver than any of your lot here. They'll take care of the children until I can get there."

"Oh, really?" Dreojen's feathered mane bristled at his insult. "Before you go, there's something you need to see."

The caverns were larger than Merceron remembered. As Dreojen led him through the torch-lit catacombs, Merceron recalled the time fifty years ago when they had first discovered them together. Still, he was unprepared for Dreojen's surprise as she made him close his eyes.

"Now?" he asked eagerly.

She took him a few more paces, then released him. "All right," she said. "Open them."

Merceron glanced around the chamber. Smoky candles glowed in iron holders in the rocks. A few rickety, dragon-sized chairs sat along the stone floor. A slant of waning sunlight struggled through a crack in the cavern, pointing like a finger to a wall stuffed full of . . .

"Books!"

Hundreds of them—maybe a thousand—lined the shelves dug from the rock. Merceron ran his claws over their spines, reciting their names. Books of poetry and history, tales once penned by mighty storytellers, ancient tomes and hand-stitched diaries—dog-eared and yellow, yet lovingly preserved.

"You rescued them," said Merceron. "How?"

"Thurmwood," Dreojen explained. "He's the one that saved them."

Merceron pulled a volume from the shelf. "Thurmwood? You're joking."

"When he knew we'd have to abandon Taurnoken, he took whatever books he could. He asked me to take him to a place where they'd be safe. Look at them, Merceron—these are the most precious books we had in our library."

Merceron scanned the manuscripts. The very book in his hand had been penned by Jorjungen, a great dragon scholar.

"You may think Thurmwood is a coward," said Dreojen. "But he's risked his life to protect these books. The Skylords took everything else in the library. Burned them, probably. You're looking at all that's left of our history."

"Thanks to Thurmwood," sighed Merceron. He shelved the book. "I've been a fool."

"A small one, perhaps." For the first time, Dreojen smiled. "There's something else you should know. After you left, the Skylords demanded we leave Taurnoken. All of us. But no one would help them find you, Merceron. Maybe you won't believe this, but most of us understood why you had to leave . . . after what happened."

Merceron steeled himself. "Do you still blame me for it?"

Dreojen moved to stand beside a chair. "I did," she said, propping herself up. "For a very long time I blamed you."

"And now?" Merceron searched her eyes. "What about now?"

"Elaniel wasn't a child. I think of him as a child, but he was grown enough to know what he was doing."

Merceron lowered his horned head. Why did parents always remember their offspring as children? Whenever he dreamed of Elaniel, it was always as a youngling, barely able to fly.

"Dreojen, you didn't answer my question. I need to know—do you still blame me for what happened to him?"

Dreojen moved around the chair but would not look at him. "Sons follow their fathers. Elaniel followed you because he loved you."

"And because our cause was just," said Merceron. "Even you must see that now."

"No one loves the Skylords," said Dreojen. "But I still wonder why we sacrificed so much." She studied his coat and bulging pockets. "The Starfinder?"

Merceron removed the Starfinder from his pocket. Its silvery surface gleamed in the candlelight. The object mesmerized Dreojen, but not because of its beauty. To her, the Starfinder was a symbol for everything she'd lost.

"The others won't change their minds," she said. "Whatever you do, you'll have to do alone."

"Is there a chance you'll come with me?" asked Merceron hopefully. "It's been so long."

Dreojen's golden eyes swelled. "This is my home now. This time, I'm not leaving."

Merceron wanted to argue, but couldn't. A wall remained between them. Brick by brick, the years since Elaniel's death had made the wall strong. He realized Dreojen still hadn't answered his question, then realized she didn't have to. She would always blame him for his death, at least a little.

The sunlight through the crack began to fade. Night was coming fast. Night might bring Redeemers. Merceron summoned Esme to his shoulder again.

"It's time," he told his mate.

They embraced without a word. Merceron held Dreojen, wanting to tell her he'd return someday, but knowing he could never make such a promise. In his heart, he knew he'd never see Dreojen again.

* * *

Merceron and Esme emerged from the crevice into the last rays of sunlight. The tide had risen, splashing over Merceron's clawed feet. Overhead the stars were emerging. Merceron fondly scratched Esme's feathered neck. Things had gone from bad to worse. They were out of options.

"I'm sorry, my Lady," he told Esme. "There's only one person who can help us now."

EGG

THE BLACK TOWER REMINDED MOTH of a lighthouse. From what he could tell from his tiny cell, it was the only structure on the island, jutting up from the barren earth like an outstretched arm. Sluggish water surrounded the island, licking at its gray shores. Moth stared through the barred window, watching the sun go down. There were no candles in his prison, and no torches or lamps, either. Once the sun was gone, all he'd have was the light of the moon.

The Redeemer had carried him for hours, flying off with him into the cold night, her powerful arms wrapped around his chest like snakes. At first Moth had screamed and screamed, afraid she would drop him. He imagined himself falling, tumbling helplessly to the ground, his body breaking against trees and rocks. Then, when his voice gave out and he could no longer scream, he lay limp in the creature's grasp, carried away like a half-dead squirrel.

And she had done it all without saying a word.

A chill wind rolled off the water. Moth put his nose through the window bars. The lower the sun fell in the sky, the faster it seemed to drop. Darkness gathered above the tower, and Moth could see stars popping out one by one, like freckles on a face. The freckles reminded him of Fiona. He wondered if she could see the stars, too. He wondered if she was even alive.

His empty stomach rumbled. He scanned the sky, waiting

for a rescue that probably wasn't coming. Once, he thought he heard the engine of a dragonfly, but it was only the wind.

Moth's cold fingers slipped from the bars. Looking out the window took too much effort. He had to stand on tiptoe just to see. When he turned away, he glimpsed a single bloodshot eye blinking through the peephole of the door.

"Hey!"

The eye disappeared. Moth ran to the door.

"Get back here!"

He put his own eye up to the square. The hall was nothing but shadows. He strained to see, finally catching a glimpse of his jailor pressed against the wall. Her wings lay flat against her back. Yellow, straggly hair tangled on her shoulders.

"I see you!" said Moth. "Why are you spying on me?"

The Redeemer skulked a little closer. Around her waist hung a thick silver chain.

"Why are you keeping me here?" asked Moth. He banged on the door. "Let me out!"

The creature watched him, infuriatingly silent.

"I need food, water!" Moth demanded. "You gonna starve me? Say something!"

"You're small," said the Redeemer. She cupped her hands over her ears. "But loud. Softly, speak."

"Huh?" Moth took a breath. "Okay, listen. I want to get out of here. Do you understand?" He opened his mouth wide to make the "O" sound. *"Out . . ."*

"Noooo," mimicked the creature.

"Why?" cried Moth. "I'm nothing! You can let me go, I won't tell anyone. The Skylords won't even know I was here."

"The Masters know already," said the Redeemer. "You are the Starfinder boy."

Moth's heart sank. If the Skylords knew that, they'd be coming for him.

"Is that why you snatched me? For the Starfinder?" Quickly he turned out the pockets of his coat. "Look! I don't have it, see? I don't know where it is."

"The dragon Merceron has the Starfinder." The Redeemer's smile frightened Moth. "I can feel it."

"Merceron? Do you know where he is?"

"He is with the feathered Master. They run. But soon we'll find them."

"And then what? You're just gonna hand the Starfinder back to the Skylords? Let them make slaves of everyone?" Moth sneered, "Slave. That's you!"

The Redeemer brushed her filthy fingernails over her silver chain. "Soon you will have one of these, too," she said. "Then you will serve the Skylords. Or, if you wish, you will die. The Masters are generous."

"C'mon, you were human once," said Moth desperately. "You're still human, I bet, right? You can let me go. You can just open the door and—"

The Redeemer turned and began walking away.

"Wait!" cried Moth. "If the Skylords come they'll kill me!"

She paused.

"Please," said Moth. "If you let me go, maybe I can help you. Maybe Merceron can figure out a way to change you back to normal."

The Redeemer hesitated. Moth could see her struggling. If he could just nudge her a little more . . .

"You're a *person*," he said. He pressed himself against the door, making that little square of his face look as sincere as possible. "No matter what the Skylords did to you, you're still human. Just do the right thing. All you have to do is make a choice."

For just a second, Moth thought he had her. For just a flash, her face seemed human again. But too soon it vanished.

"I made a choice, a long, long time ago," she said. "I belong to the Skylords now."

As the Redeemer walked off into the shadows, Moth sank from the door. Outside his window he heard the wind again. He imagined the sound was a dragonfly, coming to rescue him.

Moth guessed it was midnight by the way the moon hung in the sky. He had passed the hours by counting the bricks in the wall, watching a spider weave a web, picking at a scab, and tossing pebbles out the window. His stomach ached with hunger. Once he'd read a book about a prisoner who'd gone mad thinking about food. He slumped against the wall beneath the window, wondering which would kill him first—lack of food or the Skylords.

His eyes had grown accustomed to the dark, adjusting to the little bit of moonlight slanting through the bars. His mind wandered to his warm bed in Leroux's apartment. Suddenly, the moonlight faded. Moth stood and peered through the window, guessing a storm was coming. Instead he saw what looked like an enormous silver cloud passing overhead. He craned his neck for a better look, astonished to see wisps of fire breaking off the cloud, flashing as they died away. A noise like the braying of some giant beast rumbled from the sky.

It wasn't an airship or a storm cloud, but whatever it was stopped somewhere above the tower. Moth twisted for a better look, finally stopping when he heard the door to his cell creaking open.

"Come," said the Redeemer. She entered quickly, pulling Moth away from the window.

"Huh . . . ?"

The Redeemer shoved him toward the door. "Hurry. He's waiting."

Moth spun on her. "Who's waiting?" He pointed toward the roof. "That thing up there?"

The Redeemer grabbed his wrist and pulled him from the cell. Moth stumbled after her, trying to keep from falling. "What is it?" he asked. "A Skylord?"

Out in the dark hallway, the creature released him. "Artaios," she said. She pointed toward the winding stairwell. "It's time now. Move."

Moth couldn't make himself obey. "No," he refused. "I won't go."

"It's time," she repeated.

"No!"

"Artaios is waiting!" Her claws snapped out and grabbed Moth's coat. "Go or I will drag you!"

Moth knew she could do it—she had flown with him all the way to the island. He decided not to plead or beg. Inside he was panicking, but outside he put on his bravest face.

"Fine," he snapped. "I'll finally get to see one of these monsters for myself!"

The Redeemer followed him up the dark staircase, urging him to hurry. Up and up the steps spiraled, the slimy walls the only way for Moth to keep his balance. The higher he climbed, the louder the noise grew from above, something like the crackling of fire.

Light crept over the top of the stairs, a silver light that popped and glistened, hissed and brayed, flooding down upon the tower. Moth stepped out onto the roof. He stared up at the enormous cloud-thing in bewilderment. The Redeemer's cold claw gripped his shoulder.

"Look!" she said, her voice dripping with awe. "Artaios comes!"

Finally, Moth could see the whole thing clearly. The clouds were creatures, horselike things with vapors for tails and long, smoky limbs that pawed at the air. Sparks shot from their nostrils and fire from their hooves, yet they looked so insubstantial that a strong wind might blow them away. There were four of the beasts, and behind them a vessel, tethered to the horses by golden ropes.

A chariot, realized Moth, peering through the haze. The translucent carriage had no wheels—at least none that Moth could see. Smoke swirled around it, revealing hints of bronze and inlaid jewels. Slowly the thing floated down toward the roof. The horses—if they were horses—appeared and disappeared in the mists. The chariot hovered at the edge of the roof, wrapping the tower in vaporous tendrils.

"Down," the Redeemer commanded. She fell to her knees, pulling Moth with her. "Do not look at him," she said, "not until he speaks to you."

Moth still didn't know who or what had come for him, and keeping his eyes down was impossible. He lifted his chin just as a figure stepped from the mists.

It was a man, and yet not a man, dressed in white linen with one bare shoulder and naked, muscular arms. Gold piping trimmed his tunic and the lacings of his sandals snaked around his calves. Light surrounded him, pouring from his chariot—or was it he himself that gave the light? His hair was a golden waterfall, his skin like polished bronze. A blade gleamed at his side, a long sword of pulsing metal.

The being stepped from the mists, pausing a few feet from where Moth knelt with the Redeemer. As if to explain what he really was, two gigantic wings fanned out behind him. The wings folded gently forward, encasing the man in downy feathers. His sparkling eyes beguiled Moth.

This is what Esme must look like, he thought. But he refused to cower. Defying the Redeemer's order, he stood up.

"Great Artaios," stammered the Redeemer. "Here is the boy I promised you. A stupid boy! He hasn't even the sense to kneel!"

"Artaios," said Moth. "That's your name?"

"Silence!" shrieked the Redeemer. "Don't you dare speak!"

Moth ignored her. If he was going to die, he'd do it like a man. "You're a Skylord, huh? I heard Skylords were beautiful. Someone I once knew told me that." He put out his chin. "I'm not afraid of you."

Artaios the Skylord looked Moth up and down. He studied his face, then his old, wrinkled coat. He sniffed at his dirty hair and grimaced at his fingernails. Finally, he looked down at the Redeemer.

"*This* is the one who commands the Starfinder?"

The Redeemer nodded quickly without raising her head. "Yes, great Master. He's the one!"

Artaios' bright eyes widened. He looked young to Moth, though Moth knew he must be impossibly old. "I have never seen a human child before," he said. "And never a living thing but a Skylord who could command the Starfinder."

"I can," countered Moth. "And I'm not a boy. I'm thirteen."

"Thir . . . ?" Artaios laughed. "Thirteen *years*?" His white wings fluttered. "You're right. You're not even a boy yet. You're an egg! But I've never seen an egg command the Starfinder either, so that makes you remarkable." Artaios kicked at the Redeemer. "Get up."

The Redeemer flew to her feet. "I serve you, Master."

"This boy is in rags. He looks starved. Have you fed him?"

"No, Master, no," said the Redeemer. "We waited, is all."

Moth couldn't help staring at Artaios. His youth and golden hair reminded him of Skyhigh, but his voice was more like thunder, and his skin like mirrored bronze.

"Are you hungry, Egg?" asked the Skylord.

"Yes," answered Moth hotly. "And my name's not Egg. It's Moth."

"Moth? Like an insect?" Again Artaios laughed. "If you're hungry, you will feast."

Moth hesitated. He expected an execution, not an invitation. "Where are we going?"

"To the Palace of the Moon," said Artaios. He gestured to his chariot. "I've seen your wretched airships. Floating junk. Come with me, Egg, and I will show you what it means to fly."

THE HOUSE OF JORIAN

FIONA AWOKE WITH A SHOUT. The dream she'd been having fled from her mind. She lifted her head from the pillow of grass, heart pounding, and tried to recognize her strange surroundings. The fabric walls, the smell of clean air, the unfamiliar scene through an unshuttered window—all these things bewildered her. Then like a knife came the one thing she remembered.

Pain.

It throbbed in her skull, driving her down to the pillow again. She squeezed her eyes tightly shut and sobbed, hoping someone would hear her.

"Hello?" she called, but it was a kitten's voice that spoke, and no one answered.

Fiona turned her head, spotting a giant archway with a curtain for a door. The fabric was left open, but she couldn't see what was on the other side. When her fingers clawed her bedding, she realized she wasn't in a bed at all, but sprawled out on clean, soft straw and tucked into a blanket.

Heaven had beds, or maybe even clouds, so Fiona knew she wasn't dead. She remembered the river. And drowning, too. She remembered . . .

"Moth!"

Her cry startled someone in the other room. The sound of heavy footfalls came closer. Fiona pulled her blanket to her chin as a big shadow darkened the doorway. A face peered around the corner, first puzzled, then lighting with pleasure as it noticed Fiona.

"You're awake!"

Fiona squinted her blurry eyes. The face was pretty, with the complexion of cream and gemstone eyes. A woman's face. A tall woman, Fiona decided, until she rounded the doorway on the four legs of a horse. Instead of hair, a white mane rippled down her shoulders. Pointed ears twitched with excitement. Her hooves clopped closer. She smiled at Fiona in the bed of straw, bending as if to coo at a baby.

"Look at you!" chirped the woman. "Now don't be afraid. Just lay still and catch your breath."

Fiona forgot her many pains. She sat up, gaping in disbelief. She knew horses and she knew humans, but the thing staring at her was both. From its withers on up was the body of the most stunning woman Fiona had ever seen, with skin as soft as a teardrop and long, snowy hair that touched its equine shoulders. Her coat was white as well, looking like velvet to Fiona, her back draped with scarlet fabric tied to her tail with a golden braid.

"Nessa," said the woman softly. She pointed to herself, repeating the word. "Nessa."

When Fiona didn't answer, the creature frowned. "Poor thing." She knelt down on her forelegs, running human fingers through Fiona's tangled hair. "Don't worry. I'll teach you to speak."

At last Fiona said, "You're a centaur!"

Startled, the creature jerked back. Then she laughed and said, "You understand me! Oh, I knew I was right about you! I knew you would speak!"

"Yeah, I can speak," said Fiona. "I'm a person. I . . ." She put a hand to her aching head. "Where am I?" She glanced down and noticed her clothes had changed, replaced by a soft, baggy tunic that looked like a nightshirt, tied around her waist by a belt of fabric. "What happened to my clothes?"

The centaur pinched her nose. "Phew! They were rags."

Fiona looked under the blanket. Her legs and feet were naked. "My boots! My stockings . . ."

"Mended," said the centaur. "And dry now. Sit back . . ."

Fiona's head was spinning. She felt like a mess and knew she looked it too. She lay down again, staring up into the creature's remarkable eyes. "Tell me what happened. Where am I?"

"Pandera." The creature lightly touched Fiona's bruised head. "How does that feel?"

"Hurts." Fiona winced. She felt the bruise again, this time detecting bumpy threads. "Oh my god, stitches?"

"You were in the water with the rocks," said the centaur. "You're lucky to be alive."

"I was with somebody . . . a boy . . . my friend Moth."

The odd face grew gentle. "Only you made it through the mountains."

Fiona thought hard, yanking memories from the darkness. "Pandera," she said. "I saw you," she remembered. "On the sand. You saved me."

"Tyrin found you," the creature corrected. "He was hunting when he saw you on the bank. The river must have carried you under the mountain."

"Tyrin. Okay. And you're Nessa?"

"Yes." The centaur smiled.

"And this is Pandera. I remember now. We were running. I fell into the river. Someone was chasing us."

"Who?"

Fiona glanced away. A dragonfly had chased them. Her grandfather. If Moth wasn't dead, then surely they'd caught him.

"Moth," she whispered, trying not to cry.

She felt sick. Her dry throat threatened to retch. Nessa saw this and hurried a nearby bowl to her lips, but Fiona pushed it away.

"I have to go," she groaned. "Maybe he's out there somewhere. Maybe he needs me."

"You have to rest," Nessa insisted. "A few more days at least."

"A few more? How long have I been here? What is this place anyway?"

"You're in the house of Jorian," said Nessa. "You've been here three days."

Fiona felt panicked again. Merceron had sent her and Moth here, she remembered, so they'd be safe. But three days?

"I have to see him," said Fiona. "I have to see Jorian."

"You will," promised Nessa. "When you're well enough."

"No," said Fiona. "I have to see him right now!"

Nessa shook her mane. "Child, Jorian keeps his own time. Jumping up and down won't make a difference." She patted Fiona's chin. "I should know. I'm his wife."

When Fiona woke again, the sunshine through her window was gone, replaced by pearly moonlight. Her head was clearer, too. It still ached, but she could remember things better now. She rolled over, comfortable in her bed of straw, expecting to see Nessa watching over her, but the room was empty. Peaceful, too.

Fiona relaxed, unafraid this time. She listened and heard noises coming from outside the home. A sniff brought the scent of cooking fires.

She sat up, combing fingers through her knotted hair and wondering what to do. She needed to find Jorian. She needed to find Moth, too, and hoped the centaurs would help her. But her side ached and her head still throbbed, and she doubted she could get very far.

"Lucky to be alive," she whispered, remembering Nessa's words. She tossed aside the blanket, hoisting her long shirt to study the bruises on her legs. The rocks had beaten her up. The river had almost drowned her. "But they didn't," she said defiantly. "I beat *them*."

Carefully she got to her feet, testing her wobbly legs. The straw and cool stone tickled her naked toes. Nessa had taken her stockings and boots, but Fiona couldn't spot them anywhere. The noise outside grew to a commotion.

"Nessa?" Fiona called. "Hello?"

The noise and the smell of food lured Fiona toward the doorway. She peered into the connecting chamber. This one was similar to her own, with walls made of fabric and mortared stones. Heavy shelves with tools and cooking utensils stood near a wooden table, where a candle burned in a dish.

Fiona saw no chairs, though, supposing that centaurs had no need of them. More importantly, she saw another doorway, this one leading outside. Fiona tiptoed toward it, not wanting to hide but not really wanting to be discovered either. When she reached the threshold she peeked out into the night.

Her eyes grew wide at the sight before her.

A hundred centaurs had gathered in the center of a village, laughing and running, laying and eating around an enormous well of fire. Moonlight flooded the valley, revealing their colorful coats and fine, brocaded clothing. Some had weapons, some were naked, and some were as small as ponies, with little chirping voices that sang out as they played. Some were white like Nessa, others every shade imaginable, from shining onyx to honey gold, all with dancing manes and long, swishing tails. Around the flaming well burned smaller fires used for cooking, where spits of fowl and joints of meat turned slowly and greasily. A big, bare-chested male chugged wine from a jug, splashing it across his bearded chin.

Awestruck, Fiona stepped out into the warm night. In the distance she saw the mountains, towering around the valley. Trees and green hills spotted the landscape. Supple grass yielded beneath her toes. She put a hand to her chest, feeling her racing heart.

Fiona slipped closer to the centaurs, ducking first behind a thatched fence, then a short stone silo. A thunder of hooves suddenly clamored through the village. Two centaurs galloped furiously toward each other, their shoulders tucked like battering rams. Around the flaming well the other centaurs watched, cheering the combatants. Fiona strained for a better look. An enormous crack echoed out as the centaurs collided. The smaller, brownish centaur tumbled backward. The victor, his charcoal skin glistening, beat his chest and howled.

Fiona stepped out from her hiding place. The dark centaur was Jorian. Somehow, she was sure of it.

"Males," scoffed a voice from behind. "Such show-offs."

Fiona jumped. There was Nessa, shaking her head with mock disapproval.

"You move quietly for someone so big," said Fiona. "You following me?"

"I saw you leave the house," said Nessa. "You needn't hide. I told you—you're safe here." She looked Fiona up and down with a motherly eye. "Your color's better than before. You're well enough to skulk around at least."

Fiona could tell she wasn't really mad. She turned back toward the center of the village. "That's Jorian, right?"

"My husband," said Nessa with a grin. The younger centaur had gotten up again, grappling with Jorian. The bigger centaur tossed him aside.

"Why are they fighting?" asked Fiona.

"Because there are females around," joked Nessa. "Don't human males show off?"

Fiona had to laugh. "Yes!"

Nessa put her hand on Fiona's shoulder. "Come on," she said. "He'll want to see you."

The moment they stepped out of the shadows together, the other centaurs fell silent. Jorian turned from his opponent, rearing back like a stallion when he noticed Fiona.

"The child!" he bellowed.

The centaur chieftain galloped toward them, stopping short of Fiona, towering over her with the moon behind his wild outline. His human skin was the color of ash, his animal coat a lustrous charcoal. He wore no shirt, only silver bands around his upper arms and the remnant of scars across his downy chest. His eyes were like Nessa's eyes, as sparkly as diamonds, and a long jet mane ran down his back like the fin of a sea monster. With the grace of a savage king, he bowed.

"I am Jorian."

All Fiona wanted was to touch him. She could barely stay her hand. Jorian was the dream she'd had, the very vision of the constellation twinkling now above her head. Like Merceron he seemed godlike, as though he'd lived forever, as though nothing could harm him, not sword, nor arrow, nor Skylord.

"Fiona's my name," replied Fiona. "From Capital City. I . . . we . . . my friend Moth and me. We came to find you."

Nessa said to her husband, "The one I told you about. The one that was with her."

The Chieftain nodded. "Your friend is gone," he said, not unkindly.

"What?"

"Jorian knows what you told me about the boy, Fiona," said Nessa. "He sent scouts looking for him past the mountains."

"Your friend. The one named Moth," explained Jorian. "My scouts searched the river where Tyrin found you. The shoals too. There was no one else."

Fiona couldn't breathe. "Then they got him."

Nessa's hand remained on her shoulder. "Who, child? Tell us who was chasing you."

"Tell us all," said Jorian. He moved aside so that Fiona could join the rest of them. "You have a story everyone wants to hear."

LITTLE QUEEN

FIONA SAT ON A SMALL WOODEN box near the fire, seeing the awe she felt reflected back in the eyes of the centaurs. Jorian gathered his people around the well, calling to the smaller ones who were playing to come and see the human child. A female hurried a plate of food into Fiona's lap, and a gigantic mug of wine was set at her feet. Nessa stood beside Fiona, hovering in her maternal way while the other centaurs made a circle around them. The younger, honey-skinned centaur who'd been wrestling Jorian muscled his way to the front.

"This is Tyrin," announced Jorian. "The one who found you."

Tyrin might have been a teenager, or he might have been a hundred years old. It was impossible for Fiona to know. His sharp features beamed as he lowered to face Fiona.

"Nessa said you would be all right," he said. "I'm glad to see you, Fiona of Capital City."

A few chortled good-naturedly at her name. Fiona grinned, feeling stupid.

"Uhm, thank you," she said. "Thank you for saving me."

"Eat," said Jorian. "And tell us your story."

"She can't eat that," said Nessa, taking away Fiona's plate. "She's been sick." The plate was piled high with meat, and Fiona was glad to have it gone. "I can bring you bread. Would you like bread?"

Fiona shook her head. "No, ma'am, not now," she said politely, wanting only to be back in her bed of straw. A small female centaur went from staring intensely to finally reaching out her hand. Fiona grimaced as the creature fingered her hair.

"Look!" declared the girl centaur. "Such a color!"

The others nodded, and for the first time Fiona noticed that none of them—despite their rainbow of colors—were red-haired. She blushed as the centaur combed her fingers through her tangled locks. The girl, whose own hair was wonderfully golden, sighed.

"So pretty," she chirped. "Like summer."

"Thanks," said Fiona stiffly.

"Tell us your story now," said Jorian. "We're listening."

They were more than just listening. They were rapt. Fiona shifted as the centaur girl continued combing her hair. How could she begin, when there was so much she didn't understand?

"Go on," Nessa urged her gently.

Jorian knelt down on one of his forelegs. "Who was chasing you? The Redeemers?"

"Yes," said Fiona. "And others, too. I was with my friend, Moth. We came through the Reach together."

"Why?" asked Jorian. He seemed genuinely perplexed, as if the news of the Starfinder hadn't reached Pandera.

"Moth brought something important with him," said Fiona. "Something some other people wanted." She bit her lip, then asked, "Lord Jorian, do you know about the Starfinder?"

The centaurs gave a collective gasp. The girl stopped combing Fiona's hair.

"The boy—your friend—he has the *Starfinder*?" asked Jorian.

"No," said Fiona. "Not anymore. He did, but . . . Oh, it's hard to explain!" she snorted. "He had the Starfinder when we left Calio. That's the city across the Reach where we come from. The Starfinder was there. A man named Leroux gave it to Moth. He—"

"Leroux," rumbled Jorian, glancing darkly at his fellow centaurs. "We know Leroux, girl. The dragon lover."

"Huh?"

"He came during the Skylords' war with the dragons. The dragons gladly took the help of a human, but wouldn't dirty their hands making friends with a centaur." Jorian's chest puffed out. "You know this man Leroux? Was he chasing you as well?"

"Leroux's dead," said Fiona. "And he was a good man. He gave Moth the Starfinder so that he could help Lady Esme."

"Esme? The Skylord?" thundered Jorian.

"Let her finish," scolded Nessa. "You're scaring her."

"I'm not scared," said Fiona. She hopped off her little box to face Jorian. "Your pardon, Lord Jorian, but you don't know what you're talking about. Leroux loved Esme. All either of them wanted was to help the dragons."

"Don't tell us our history, girl," Jorian warned.

"Someone has to, 'cause you got it all wrong. I know you hate the Skylords, but Lady Esme isn't like the rest of them. She's the one that stole the Starfinder, just so everyone could be free." Fiona stood her ground. "Centaurs, too."

The gathered faces looked on, waiting for Jorian to erupt. The Chieftain bristled as he spoke.

"Before Lady Esme ever stole the Starfinder, before your friend Leroux even set foot here, we centaurs offered our help," he said. "But we weren't good enough for the dragons. We couldn't fly. We weren't as pure or beautiful or wise as them, they said. And do you know what happened to them?"

"Yes," said Fiona sadly.

"They were driven from their city. But not us, girl. We're still safe here in our valley."

The circle of centaurs nodded. Jorian himself grew pensive. He gestured to the makeshift chair.

"Sit," he told Fiona.

Fiona did as he asked. In the light of the moon and the crackling fire, she looked at the proud faces of her hosts. Merceron had said the centaurs were brave. He didn't much like them, but he'd spoken the truth about them. Fiona decided to tell the truth too.

"Me and Moth came here because a dragon told us to," she said. "A dragon named Merceron. He said we'd be safe here. He's the one who has the Starfinder now."

"You gave the Starfinder to Merceron?" asked Nessa.

"He's still alive?" chimed Tyrin. "He must be older than time by now!"

"Merceron was Leroux's friend," grumbled Jorian. "And a friend to that other one, too."

Fiona blanched. "Other one?"

Nessa thought for a moment. "Rendor!" she recalled.

"Rendor," Jorian muttered.

"My grandfather," said Fiona.

All the centaurs gaped at her.

"I guess you know him," said Fiona sheepishly.

Jorian looked astonished. "Rendor is your grandfather?" he asked. "Rendor is the one who came here with Leroux to help the dragons fight the Skylords."

"No," said Fiona. "That's not true. They came to spy on the Skylords, that's all. They came because they wanted to know what was here on the other side of the Reach. They didn't mean to get caught up in the war. It just happened."

Jorian scoffed. "It doesn't matter. Your grandfather, your friend Leroux—they were outlaws. If the Skylords had found them, they would now be Redeemers."

"Lord Jorian, it's my grandfather who's chasing us," said Fiona. "It's not just the Redeemers. My grandfather wants the Starfinder too. He's come with an airship. I think he has my friend Moth."

"Why?" asked Jorian. "And why did you give the Starfinder to Merceron?"

"Moth knows how to use the Starfinder," said Fiona. "Nobody else can make it work, just Moth and the Skylords. If my grandfather finds that out . . ."

Jorian swished his tail in agitation. "And Merceron?"

"A friend," said Fiona. "The Redeemers were after us. He led them away. He told Moth and me that you'd protect us from them."

The big centaur sniffed at the compliment, but Fiona could tell he was pleased. "Dragons are cowards, and if the Skylords catch that old bone-bag Merceron they'll blow him out of the sky. But . . ." Jorian sighed. "He did the right thing sending you to us."

"What about the Starfinder?" asked another of the centaurs, a dignified male with a greenish-white mane and a chain of office around his neck. "Why does Merceron have it? Did he steal it?"

"No," disagreed Fiona. "He took it so that he could find a way to destroy it. He took it to find the other dragons."

"There is no way to destroy the Starfinder," said Jorian. He looked pensive as he rubbed a clenched fist. "Merceron is wasting his time. And if the Skylords find him first . . ."

His voice trailed off. The centaur with the greenish-white mane took the hint and shooed the others away.

"Go," he told them. "Let us think."

After some grumbling the centaurs broke their circle, leaving only Jorian, Nessa, and their strange green advisor around the fire well. The girl who'd been toying with Fiona's hair giggled a good-bye into her ear, and young Tyrin smiled as he trotted off, winking at Fiona before going. Weak and exhausted, Fiona rose from her seat.

"I think I should rest some more," she said wearily. "I don't feel too good."

Nessa's hand went to her shoulder again. "Wait."

Fiona looked at each of them. "What's wrong?"

Jorian's brow thickened into a ridge. He turned to the other male. "Kyros?"

"They'll come for her," said Kyros without hesitation. "First they'll take Merceron and the Starfinder, then the boy, then her."

"The Skylords?" asked Fiona.

"Don't worry," said Jorian. "We'll protect you."

"What about my grandfather?"

"Rendor?" Jorian frowned. "What of him? The Skylords will deal with him, too."

Fiona almost laughed. "You don't know him, Lord Jorian. He's smart. And he's got a ship with him, a flying ship with guns, weapons. He won't give up. He's a powerful man where I came from, a Governor."

"What's a Governor?" asked Nessa. "Some sort of ruler?"

"Like a king?" asked Kyros.

"Well . . ."

"That would make you a princess," said Jorian with a smile. "You look like a princess."

"I do?"

"Like a queen," said Nessa. "A little queen."

Fiona was baffled. With stitches in her head and her hair in tangles, she felt more like a beggar than a queen. "I'm just a girl," she told them. "And I don't think you understand what I'm saying. My grandfather will find me. Maybe before the Skylords do, maybe not, but either way there's gonna be trouble for you all."

"Child, we do understand," said Kyros calmly.

"But we are centaurs!" said Jorian. "The Skylords have more sense than to come attack us, and if your grandfather is dumb enough to try, we will fight him." The Chieftain of Pandera folded his arms over his battle-scarred chest. "No one will take you, Little Queen. As long as you are our guest, you are safe."

THE PALACE OF THE MOON

THROUGHOUT THE NIGHT and all the next day, Artaios' chariot carried Moth north. Aided by some unseen magic and pulled by the team of ethereal horses, the craft moved swiftly across the sky, never buffeted by the wind or troubled by cold. The mist and fire of the strange horses made an envelope around the chariot, protecting its angelic driver and his small human captive. They had flown higher than any airship had ever gone, higher than Moth's imagination, the world below them was a blur of green forests and rivers. The Redeemer named Alisaundra flew alongside them, never tiring or complaining as she kept up with the chariot, her wings beating with unending strength.

Artaios held the golden reins of his team, guiding them across the sky. They were called "cloud horses," the Skylord had explained, creatures made of both air and flesh that somehow existed in both realms. Only Skylords could command them, Artaios boasted, for the beasts were far too noble to serve lesser beings. Moth spent hours watching the cloud horses, fascinated by the fire sparking from their hooves, the way their limbs dissipated into vapor. He wondered what would happen if he touched one, if his hand would pass right through it or if his skin would burn.

Most of all, Moth marveled at the thrill of flight. Being in Artaios' chariot wasn't like flying a dragonfly or looking down at the world from an airship. Those things were wonderful too, but they were unnatural. The chariot was like the air itself. It flew the way a bird flew, riding the wind.

Born to it, thought Moth. *Like Artaios.*

In that first night of flying, Artaios said almost nothing to Moth. Instead, he let Moth gape in confusion at all the things he was seeing, occasionally smiling or tossing off a comment that made no sense. Moth knew Artaios was showing off. He remembered what he'd learned about Skylords, about how arrogant they were, and how they thought humans were inferior. And yet Moth appreciated Artaios' gift. No other human had ever flown like he was flying now. Not Skyhigh. Not even Rendor.

Moth forgot his hunger, and almost forgot his fears, too, until he caught a glimpse of Alisaundra grinning at him through the clouds.

That's what they'll do to me, he reminded himself, and he backed away from the rail of the chariot, refusing to enjoy the flight any further.

Exhausted from all that had happened, Moth fell asleep in a corner of the chariot near Artaios' feet. When he awoke the Skylord was looking down at him. Artaios held the golden reins of the vessel in his hands. Night had fallen and the moon glowed behind his head, giving him a ghostly hue. Moth rubbed his eyes, feeling like a dog at its master's heel. Artaios' expression was peculiar.

"Stand up now," he said.

"Huh?"

Half the Skylord's mouth turned up in a grin. "You'll want to see this," he said, then reached down and took Moth's arm, lifting him to his feet. Moth steadied himself, blinking the sleep away. Orange flares leaped from the cloud horses. Warm wind tugged at Moth's coat. Darkness blanketed the world below, but up ahead rose a crown of peaks, gleaming in the moonlight. Moth leaned over the rail.

A city!

Spires reached from the top of the mountains, breaking from the rocks. Domed towers and balconies poked skyward.

Archways disappeared into dark tunnels. Fluted columns supported floating gardens, and trestled walkways weaved along the hillsides. Moonlight set the city ablaze, giving off an eerie, almost blinding light, illuminating the creatures flying between the structures.

"The Palace of the Moon," said Artaios proudly.

The city rose up to swallow them, and the beings threading through the night revealed themselves.

"Skylords," Moth whispered.

They were everywhere, hundreds of them, walking along the avenues and taking flight from balconies on dove-white wings. Moth held tight as Artaios directed the chariot down, into the city's lustrous heart. The winged beings flocked like geese to greet them, coming alongside the chariot and calling greetings. Moth looked around, stunned by the gathering, then realized Alisaundra was gone.

"Where's the Redeemer?" he asked.

"Sent ahead," replied Artaios. His grin widened. "He's expecting us now, Egg."

Moth sneered at the nickname. "Who?" he shot back.

"Korace," said Artaios.

"Who's—"

"Enough!" Artaios guided the chariot over the tops of the first towers. "Stop chattering like a wood nymph and behold!"

The Skylords escorted them over the moon-painted city. The ghostly horses dove lower, fading in and out of their own fiery mist. Up ahead loomed a ridge of ashen rock, projecting out from a mountainside like the horn of a rhino. Along the ridge rode a series of towers connected by an ancient bridge, each tower larger than the one before it. The final tower, perched at the very tip of the horn, hung out over the mountain in a shroud of vapor, held aloft by fragile fingers of stone.

"What's that?" asked Moth as the chariot made its way to the tower. He could see other Skylords already gathered on its roof, along with a handful of Redeemers. "Who's Korace?" he pressed.

Artaios held the reins lightly now. The cloud horses slowed as they pulled closer to the tower. A breeze stirred the Skylord's hair. Moth looked down again, saw puddles at the base of the mountains, and realized they were lakes.

"This is impossible," he said. "It should be freezing up here! I shouldn't be able to breathe . . ."

Artaios delighted in his wonder. "You're about to see something no other of your kind has ever seen, Egg. This is a great gift I give you."

Moth was too dazzled to think straight. "What?" he asked. "You mean this place? It is amazing . . ."

"Wait," said Artaios.

He put his hand on Moth's shoulder as the chariot slid across the enormous roof. Skylords parted to make way, jerking on the chains of their Redeemers, pulling them along like pets. The tower was so large Moth could barely see the end of it. The chariot touched down on the rooftop. The cloud horses floated to a stop, as insubstantial as air.

Moth did his best to mask his fear. He looked out over the gathered Skylords, amazed by their luminous beauty and sickened by their cruelty. The leashed Redeemers chattered, falling to their knees. Except for one.

"Great Artaios!" called Alisaundra. She hopped to the front of the gathering, dropping down before the chariot and lowering her face to the ground. "Korace awaits you!"

Moth looked up at Artaios and asked one more time, "Who's Korace?"

"My father," Artaios answered. "Ruler of us all."

THE FLIGHTLESS BIRD

MOTH STOOD SILENTLY in the center of the arena, a tiny speck in a massive, moonlit bowl. Next to him stood Artaios, smiling, occasionally waving at the Skylords flying through the galleries. Trees jutted from the ancient walls, curving skyward as their roots clung to the rocks. Colorful birds danced between the balconies, stacked hundreds of feet high. Overhead, the moon shined directly into the arena, drawing an eerie luminance from the stone. A breeze touched Moth's face, but he did not shiver. Whatever magic made the air breathable somehow made it mild, too.

Artaios had called the place a "convocation." Moth had expected a council chamber or a briefing room like the ones the Skyknights used in Calio, something small where they could meet Artaios' father. Instead they were in a giant stadium. Moth looked nervously at the gathering Skylords, marveling at the way they appeared from the sky, dropping out of the darkness.

Like throwing bread to pigeons, he thought, remembering walking with his mother once along an avenue in Calio. They'd brought a bag of stale crusts with them to feed the birds, and the pigeons nearly drowned them.

The memory made Moth ache. Calio was home. He knew that now, and knew he'd never see it again. Soon he'd be like Alisaundra. Head bowed, the Redeemer stood behind him, her inhuman gaze watching him unceasingly.

"What are we waiting for?" demanded Moth. "Where's Korace?"

Artaios glanced down in annoyance. "Eggs do not summon gods," he said.

"My name's Moth, all right? Not Egg."

Artaios laughed. "You're a child. You've seen nothing. You know nothing. So you are Egg."

Ahead of them stood an empty silver throne, its tall back adorned with folded metal wings. Behind the throne stood a line of white columns spouting fire. Behind the columns was the nothingness of empty sky. Moth imagined Korace arriving out of the air just like all the others, alighting on his giant throne. He'd be like Artaios, Moth envisioned, only bigger, carrying a pulsing sword just like his son. As a hush fell over the convocation, Moth braced himself.

"He comes," whispered Artaios. He dropped down to one knee, his white wings brushing the stone floor. "Kneel."

Moth whispered back, "I won't."

A sudden slap cracked against the back of his head. "Kneel!" hissed Alisaundra.

Moth whirled around. "Keep your dirty hands off me!"

Then he was flying suddenly, lifted by his coat and kicking in the air as Artaios dragged him upward. The gathered Skylords laughed and hollered. Before Moth could struggle free, Artaios fluttered down again and tossed him across the floor.

"On your knees!" cried Artaios. His wings spread out as he landed next to Moth. Stunned, aching, Moth didn't bother to rise. As he glanced up he saw a figure walking slowly toward the throne, walking with a cane in his gnarled hand.

Walking.

Moth lifted himself to his knees, refusing to bow his head. The giant he'd been expecting was instead a wizened creature, the mere shadow of a Skylord. White robes drooped from his shriveled body. He had two brawny escorts ready to catch him should he fall. He dragged himself toward his throne, his cane clicking slowly against the stones, his useless wings flat upon his back. When at last he reached the throne, the escorts lifted him into the silver chair. As Korace caught his breath, a puff of feathers fell from his wings.

"Father," Artaios greeted.

Korace nocked his cane into the arm of his throne. He bid them closer with a skeletal finger. Artaios took Moth by the collar and stood up.

"Speak clearly and with respect," he warned, then shoved Moth forward.

Korace seemed to disappear in his enormous chair. Unlike the other Skylords, there was no twinkle in his eyes, the light having faded long ago. His skin reminded Moth of an old book, the kind with paper so dry and yellow you couldn't touch it anymore without tearing it. Thin hair lay flat against his emaciated skull, a sickly shade of bluish white. His head bobbed with a tremor.

"Here he is, Father," said Artaios. "The one who commands the Starfinder."

Moth waited for a response but Korace's face was blank. Was he deaf?

"The dragon Merceron has the Starfinder now," Artaios continued. "The Redeemers have felt it."

Korace's eyes squinted to see Moth better. His expression was something like disgust.

"The boy has told me nothing, but denies nothing either," Artaios went on. "His silence is his confession."

"Confession? Of what?" cried Moth.

"For crossing the Reach," said Artaios. "For breaking the ancient pact. For hiding what belongs to us, and for consorting with dragons."

"So this is a trial?" Moth pointed at Alisaundra. "Is that my punishment, to be turned into one of those things?"

Before Artaios could answer, Korace made a whispering sound. Moth listened very hard but couldn't understand a word.

"What's he saying?" Moth asked.

Artaios went to his father's side, kneeling down beside the silver throne and taking the old creature's hand. Artaios nodded as Korace spoke.

"Come forward, Egg," said Artaios after a moment. "Let my father look at you."

Moth stepped up reluctantly. Korace spoke again into Artaios' ear.

"My father says you're tiny," explained Artaios. "Like an insect. He says you are well named."

Moth shrugged off the insult. "Maybe. But sometimes it's the little bugs that are hardest to catch."

"There's no place for you to run, Egg," Artaios assured him.

"Artaios, you don't have what you really want. You don't care about me. You just want the Starfinder. And you know what? I'm glad I gave the Starfinder to Merceron. Tell your father that."

Korace held up his hand before Artaios could speak. With a great effort he said, *"You bring us war."*

His gravelly voice startled Moth. The whispers from the convocation stopped. Korace struggled to his feet, managing to flex his withered wings, revealing bare patches of skin where feathers had been.

"We had peace with the Starfinder," he rasped. "And we had peace when it was gone. Now we have war again."

"That's not my fault," said Moth. "The Skylords started the war."

Enraged, Korace began to shake. Artaios steadied him.

"We will find Merceron, Father," Artaios promised.

"No." Korace managed a frightful smile. "Merceron will find us."

"Oh," said Moth, "so I'm your hostage." He looked accusingly at Artaios. "Is that why you brought me here?"

Artaios replied, "If Merceron wants to save you, he'll return what is ours."

"Why? So you can enslave everyone again? Merceron won't let that happen. If you think so you're crazy."

Korace collapsed back into his throne with a fit of coughing. Artaios rubbed his shoulder until the spell subsided. "Humans," Korace spat. "The worst of them all."

Moth stepped closer. "You're no better than us, Korace. We're just like you, except we don't have wings. We can even fly."

Korace looked up as if he'd been struck. "Yes," he hissed.

Artaios flashed a warning look. Finally, Moth understood.

"Now I get it," said Moth. "That's why you hate us."

"Egg . . ."

"Because we can fly and you can't!"

Up in the galleries, the Skylords hooted slurs, swirling madly over the arena. Korace hung his head in embarrassment.

"You wretched little beast," snapped Artaios. His hand went to his sword. "I should kill you where you stand."

Moth raised his chin. "Sure, go on and do it! See how long it takes you to get back the Starfinder when I'm dead!"

Artaios jerked the blade halfway from its scabbard, releasing a burst of orange light. "Child, beware me . . ."

"Your father started the war, didn't he?" Moth pushed. "He couldn't stand the thought of other creatures flying, not if he couldn't fly anymore. That's why he hates the dragons. That's why he hates humans, because we're just like you!"

Artaios' sword leaped out in a streak of fire.

"Master, no!"

Something jerked Moth backwards. Stumbling, he saw Alisaundra throw herself between them, sprawling before Artaios.

"My lord mustn't!" she begged. "Remember the Starfinder!"

Artaios kicked her, rolling her over. Miraculously she crawled back to him, stroking his feet. "Great one, don't kill him. He is the answer!"

Moth couldn't speak. Deliberate or not, the Redeemer had saved him. He stood up again as Artaios shook Alisaundra off his sandaled foot. The blade glowed furiously in the Skylord's fist.

"You see this creature?" said Artaios. He spat down at Alisaundra. "Look at her. Look what we can do!"

Moth pitied Alisaundra. He wished she would rise up, just once, and claw Artaios' arrogant face.

"I see what you can do, Artaios," said Moth. "You think you're gods, but you're not. You're just bullies."

Artaios sheathed his flaming sword and stepped over Alisaundra. "Did I not tell you to hold your tongue? To respect my father and this place? Truly, you must wish to die."

"You're wrong," said Moth. "And you're wrong if you think Merceron is going to give you back the Starfinder. He doesn't care about me."

Artaios' smile was terrible. He kicked at Alisaundra. "Get up," he growled.

The Redeemer rose, averting her eyes.

"Speak the words," Artaios commanded.

Alisaundra hesitated. "Dragons live a very long time," she said. "They never forget their friends or leave them behind."

"What?" gasped Moth. It was as if the words had been ripped from his brain. But the words weren't his—they were Merceron's.

"Your friend Fiona is alive," said Artaios. "She made it to Pandera."

"How do you know that?" asked Moth desperately. "How'd you know what Merceron said?"

Artaios sighed as he gestured at Alisaundra. "These things are grotesque but gifted. Alisaundra has been close enough to you to know all your thoughts, Egg. There's nothing you can hide from her."

"Fiona . . . ?"

"Sent with you to the centaurs by Merceron. Don't worry. She lives. For now."

Moth could barely breathe. "Fiona doesn't have the Starfinder. All she wants is to get away from her grandfather. If you're in my head then you know that's true!"

"Rendor."

Spoken like a curse, the word came from Korace. The ancient ruler gripped the arms of his throne with withered fingers. His dead eyes fixed hatefully on Moth.

"Rendor seeks the Starfinder," said Artaios, "but it's of no use to him. He's not a child, nor is his granddaughter. You are the only human in all the Realm that can work the Starfinder. And we'll never allow the Starfinder to cross the Reach again."

"You mean you're going to kill them?"

"There's no escape for them, Egg. They're already surrounded."

"But Fiona's innocent! And Rendor can't even use the Starfinder! You said so yourself!"

"If he escapes he'll find another child, one young enough to work the Starfinder. One like you."

"Artaios, no . . ."

"You may go wherever you wish in the palace," said Artaios

dismissively, "but Alisaundra will be watching you. If you try to run, she will find you."

He turned his back on Moth, returning to his father's side and taking the ruler's frail hand. A veil of sorrow darkened his face. Korace closed his eyes and whispered to his son. Though Moth couldn't understand his words, it was obvious Korace wanted to go.

"Come," said Alisaundra, taking Moth's arm and leading him away.

"Wait," Moth protested. "Artaios, don't you dare harm Fiona, you hear me?"

"Stop!" Alisaundra hissed into his ear.

"Do you hear me, Artaios? If you hurt her, I'll—"

Alisaundra covered his mouth with her powerful hand. Quickly, she dragged him away.

MORNING PATROL

SKYHIGH SCANNED THE HORIZON as the warm sun of dawn struck the side of his face. He had taken flight less than twenty minutes ago, but already he was many miles away from the safety of the *Avatar*, streaking southward over hills and forests. He watched with awe as sunlight peeled back the darkness, marveling at the world it uncovered. Since the grounding of the *Avatar*, Skyhigh had made this same patrol a dozen times. So far, he'd seen a handful of Redeemers and some distant, flashing clouds that looked oddly like horses, but he hadn't seen a single Skylord yet. They would come soon enough, he supposed, because Rendor was sure of it. But for now, for this one brief morning, they were safe.

Wind buffeted the dragonfly's glass wings. Skyhigh fought the craft for control. She hadn't flown the same since her fight with Alisaundra. Though Bottling and his crew had patched her up, she handled more like a donkey cart now than a precision machine. Still, her guns were working and she was airborne, and for that Skyhigh was grateful. In a day or two more the *Avatar* would be airworthy too, and they could finally get moving again. Skyhigh hoped Rendor would keep his promise and not leave the Reach, but there were men like Donnar onboard who wanted to head home—without Moth and Fiona.

Skyhigh leveled the craft and stretched his vision as far as he could. Twenty minutes south, in daylight hours only. Those were his orders, and as he watched the chronometer on his console tick down the seconds, he prayed he'd see nothing more than a bird up ahead. Once the Skylords came they'd be trapped. And once they were trapped, no one would be in the mood to search for the children. Skyhigh still didn't know if Rendor wanted Fiona back or just the Starfinder, but it didn't really matter. If they fled home to Calio, the kids would be doomed.

"Ten . . . nine . . . eight . . . seven . . ."

Finally the chronometer clicked down to zero. Relieved, Skyhigh banked the dragonfly westward, toward the rising sun.

"Sorry, Skylords," he sang. "Not today!"

He could report a clear sky, at least for one more patrol. Skyhigh settled back, letting out the breath he'd been holding. He narrowed his eyes against the sunlight, estimated a flight time, and dialed up a new time on the chronometer. In less than an hour he'd be back at camp. He'd breakfast quick, catch a nap while the crew checked and fueled the dragonfly, then head back out for his late morning loop. If things stayed quiet . . .

A sudden mass eclipsed the sun, heading straight for the dragonfly.

"Holy . . . !"

Skyhigh jerked back the sticks, shooting the craft upward and back. The engine shrieked in the riptide of air. Up came the thing, racing toward him, the biggest, darkest Redeemer Skyhigh could imagine. He made to turn, but the creature was already on him, beating its gigantic wings as it hovered in midair. Skyhigh's finger curled around the gun trigger. If he could just draw a bead . . .

The outline of the thing against the sun seemed wrong somehow. Finally, a great horned head shot fearlessly toward the tiny craft. Through the clouded glass blinked massive yellow eyes. A fanged mouth opened wide, revealing a reptilian tongue.

"Rendor!" roared the creature.

Skyhigh's hand slipped from the trigger. It wasn't a Redeemer's voice that shook his craft, but a dragon's. Its scaly face filled the canopy, frowning in annoyance at Skyhigh's silence.

"Are you hard of hearing, human?" it bellowed. "Take me to Rendor!"

THE PROMISE

MERCERON REMOVED HIS PIPE from his coat, sighing as he stuck it between his teeth. He was out of tobacco, out of patience, and grateful just to be on the ground again. Lady Esme rested on his shoulders, slumping in the very same way, both of them exhausted from days of flying.

"I told you," the dragon growled, "My name's Merceron. Just tell that to Rendor—he'll remember me."

A dozen humans with rifles had swarmed out of the tethered airship the moment he and Esme landed. His arrival caused the expected commotion, but none of the men dared come any closer than twenty-odd yards. Nearby, the noisy contraption he'd faced in the sky landed hastily in the shadow of the airship. Its buzzing wings came to a stop, the glass top popped out, and out came the man he'd terrified in the air. Merceron raised a curious eyebrow at the machine.

"It *does* look like a dragonfly."

The young man tossed his helmet to the ground as he rushed forward, his expression incredulous. Lady Esme gave a call when she noticed him.

"Esme?" he exclaimed.

Merceron took the pipe from his mouth. "You'd be Skyhigh Coralin. Right?"

"How'd you—?"

"We have a mutual friend." Merceron waved his tail in annoyance at the others. "Tell your buddies to back away, would you? I'm tired and cranky, and if anyone shoots me, I might accidentally incinerate them."

"You must be Merceron!"

"So I've been saying," sighed the dragon. He looked over the airship, impressed by its size. "Is Rendor inside that thing?"

The young flier searched the camp. "He must be. Why are you looking for him?"

Suddenly another man appeared, stepping out from a curtain of rifles. "Coralin, move away from that thing!"

"Thing?" harrumphed Merceron.

The flier gave a surprising smile. "Commander Donnar, this is Merceron," he said with a flourish. "The dragon who helped Moth and Fiona. That bird on his shoulder is Lady Esme."

Hearing her name, Esme flew from Merceron's shoulder toward the Skyknight. The man stretched out his arm, where she landed with a delighted screech.

"You *must* be a friend," Merceron observed. "Lady Esme was always rather prickly."

The older man—Donnar—stood before his soldiers. "What do you want, dragon? You're not the only one here with firepower."

Merceron tilted his horned head. So far, every human he'd ever met had been audacious. Then, another figure came rushing through the throng, buttoning up a long frock coat.

"My god!" exclaimed Rendor. "Fifty years and you look exactly the same." He shouldered confidently past his men. "All of you, put your guns down," he ordered.

The one called Donnar started. "Governor?"

"Forget it, Erich. This old beast is harmless." Rendor walked right up to Merceron and crossed his arms. "Aren't you?"

Merceron looked over the rim of his glasses. "You've gotten chubby."

Rendor didn't laugh. He turned toward the others, waving them away. "Hey, work to do, remember? I want to get airborne by nightfall."

Slowly the crowd dispersed. Rendor told Donnar to stay, then turned to Skyhigh. His words fell away when he noticed Esme on the young man's arm.

"Esme . . ."

His voice was whisper soft. He moved toward the kestrel, reaching out his hand, then pulling it back. "Merceron, does she know what happened to Leroux?"

Merceron shrugged his enormous shoulders. "She's heard the talk, but it's hard to know how much she understands. She's more bird than Skylord now."

Skyhigh studied Esme sadly. "She doesn't know about Moth either."

"Uh, Coralin . . ."

Merceron frowned. "What about Moth?" He looked between the humans. "Rendor, what's happened?"

Rendor blanched. "I'm sorry, Merceron. I know why you've come, but we don't have the boy any longer. Whoever told you that—"

"What?" Merceron's voice boomed through the camp. "You had Moth? He was *here*?"

Rendor gestured toward the airship. "Before the attack. Our ship . . ."

"Rendor, I didn't come here looking for Moth! What happened?"

"He's gone, Merceron. Like I said, we were attacked. A Redeemer—"

Merceron's head roared forward. "Tell me where he is!"

Rendor stood firm, even as the others backed away. "The boy is gone," he said calmly. "My granddaughter, too. We tracked them with the help of a Redeemer named Alisaundra. When they saw us, they ran. Fiona fell into the river by the mountains. Captain Coralin picked up Moth."

"Gone? No! Not dead!"

"We don't know," said Rendor. "Maybe Moth's still alive. Fiona . . ." He paused. "Maybe not."

"Merceron, I was the one that chased them," said Skyhigh. "They ran when they saw my dragonfly. We tried to find Fiona, but . . ." His voice trailed off. "We just don't know."

"What about this Redeemer?" pressed Merceron. "She did that?" He pointed a claw at the obvious hole in the airship, now covered by mismatched fabric. "She's the one that took Moth?"

"The night we found them," said Rendor. "She didn't take anything else. Just Moth."

Merceron tried to think. "Then he's still alive," he mused. "The Skylords know he can use the Starfinder. They know everything by now."

"How?" wondered Rendor.

"Because you let a Redeemer get close to him, you fool! They can pick a human brain like a lock. Everything he knows, she knows now. And that means the Skylords know it, too."

"But he's alive?" asked Skyhigh. "You're sure?"

"The Skylords don't care about Moth. All they want is the Starfinder." Merceron glared at Rendor. "Sound familiar?"

Rendor brushed the insult aside. "Do you have it?"

"Fiona, Rendor," Merceron reminded him. "Where did you look for her?"

"Along the river bank," answered Skyhigh. "It was raining the night she disappeared. I flew out the next morning but didn't find anything."

"What about the mountains? Did you search over the mountains?"

"How could we, Merceron?" countered Rendor. "They're too high. Look at our ship!"

Already Merceron was regretting the reunion. "Look past the mountains for her," he said. "If Fiona's alive, that's where she'll be."

Rendor squinted at him. "How do you know that? Did you send them there?"

"Moth didn't tell us where they were heading," said Skyhigh. "Why were they following the river?"

"There's a narrow gorge in the mountains, like a tunnel. The river flows under the mountains there. You may not be able to fly over the mountains, but you can swim there."

"Where?" asked Rendor.

"Pandera." Merceron stuck the pipe back in his mouth. "That's where I sent the children."

"To the centaurs?" Rendor exclaimed. "Why?"

"To keep them safe, both from you and from the Skylords."

"Oh, brilliant," scoffed Rendor. "Now Moth's been kidnapped

and Fiona is drowned. If you wanted to keep them safe you should have kept them with you!"

Merceron snapped back, "Don't pretend to care so much about your granddaughter. You're only here for one reason, Rendor."

"You have the Starfinder," accused Rendor. "I know Moth gave it to you. You're lucky the Skylords haven't found you yet!"

"Whoa!" said Skyhigh, stepping between them. "Merceron, where is Moth? Do you know?"

"The Palace of the Moon," said Merceron. "Most likely."

"Great," grumbled Rendor.

"Palace of the Moon?" Commander Donnar looked at each of them. "What's that?"

"The city of the Skylords." Merceron glowered at Rendor. "All these men and you couldn't even keep a boy safe. And look at your ship!"

"Stop!" cried Skyhigh. "Merceron, why would they take Moth there?"

"It's obvious," said Rendor. "They want the Starfinder and they think we'll trade for it." He looked expectantly at Merceron. "Well? Do you have it?"

Merceron had almost changed his mind. He'd flown all this way, flown to the very edge of exhaustion, just to face this inscrutable man. He reached into his pocket. He thought about Moth. He thought about Elaniel, his long-dead son. Then he pulled out the Starfinder.

"You want this?" enticed Merceron, holding the Starfinder just beyond Rendor's reach.

Rendor smirked. "You know I do. And you know why."

"Here, then." Merceron placed the Starfinder into Rendor's hands. Donnar and Skyhigh Coralin leaned in to see it.

"That's it?" remarked Skyhigh. "It doesn't look like much. And it sure doesn't look worth all this trouble."

"That's because you have no idea what the Starfinder can do," said Rendor. "Anyone who masters the Starfinder masters all the creatures of this realm." He looked up with a wink. "Isn't that right, Merceron?"

"Is that what you told Moth?" Merceron asked.

"I told him the truth, which is more than you or Leroux ever did. Now tell me— Why did you come here, Merceron? If not for Moth and Fiona, why?"

"Because I am defeated," admitted Merceron. "Because I'm trapped and have nowhere else to turn. The Skylords know I have the Starfinder. They won't rest until they find me."

"And kill you," Rendor pointed out. "So you're giving it to me?"

"Yes," nodded Merceron. "*If* you agree to take it back across the Reach. The Starfinder can't be destroyed, and the dragons won't help me hide it. You're the only one who can get it out of here, Rendor. You must take it back to your own world before the Skylords come for you."

"Take it back?" cried Donnar. "To Calio?"

"The Skylords won't follow you through the Reach," said Merceron. "At least not yet, not until they're ready to fight you for it." He looked intently at Rendor, who was vexingly silent. "I see you thinking, Rendor. Stop it. No schemes this time. Promise me you'll take the Starfinder away from here."

Rendor turned toward his damaged airship. "It'll take time to get underway again," he said, troubled. "Tomorrow morning at the earliest."

"Be as quick as you can," Merceron insisted. "Redeemers are already gathering to stop you from leaving. Soon there will be Skylords too."

Skyhigh nodded gravely. "I've seen some Redeemers out on my patrol. Mostly in the south."

"Blocking the way home," said Donnar.

Rendor asked, "What about Fiona? If she's alive . . ."

"There's no time for you to get her," said Merceron. "If she is alive I'll find her. I'll get her back across the Reach, but for now she'll be safe with the centaurs. The Skylords won't bother her there."

"And Moth?" asked Skyhigh. "We can't just leave him with the Skylords."

Merceron smiled at the young pilot. "I'm glad to hear you say that, because we're not going to leave him. We're going after him. You, me, and Esme."

Skyhigh didn't hesitate. "Tell me how."

"That contraption of yours," said Merceron, pointing at the dragonfly. "How fast can it go?"

"Fast enough," said Rendor. "I designed it, after all."

"You designed it? And it actually flies?"

"Probably faster than you, you winged frog."

"Even so, it's a long way to the Palace of the Moon. Can she make a three-day flight?"

"Of course not. Maybe four days at worst. If you fly carefully and carry extra tanks. And glide a lot."

Merceron groaned. "Then I'll have to carry it there myself. You too, Skyknight."

"Why?" asked Skyhigh eagerly. "What's your plan?"

"I will tell you," said Merceron. "But first . . ." He rocked back on his hind legs. "I want to hear you swear it, Rendor. Swear to me that you'll take the Starfinder home with you. And I don't want a politician's promise. Swear it to me as an Eldrin Knight."

"Fine," grumbled Rendor. "I give you my word as an Eldrin Knight, Merceron. I'll get the Starfinder out of here."

THE WORD OF AN ELDRIN KNIGHT

RENDOR SAT BACK AGAINST the nobbly trunk of a pine tree, far enough from the *Avatar* to be alone with his thoughts. Dusk was falling, and his men were still hard at work. After stripping everything imaginable out of Skyhigh's dragonfly, Rendor had managed to cram it full of extra fuel, leaving barely enough room for Skyhigh and Esme to squeeze themselves inside. Merceron had spent the day getting much-needed sleep. He and Rendor hadn't bothered speaking again, and that was fine with Rendor, because he had nothing to say, not even good-bye. He watched with the rest of them as Merceron lifted the dragonfly into the air, disappearing north as the sun slipped down the horizon. Then, wanting desperately to get away, Rendor wandered out of camp.

His pistol lay ready in his lap. The Starfinder remained aboard the *Avatar* under heavy guard. Riflemen stood lookout atop the airship, searching the sky. Rendor took a cigar from his breast pocket. He'd been craving one all day but only had a handful of them left. He snapped open his lighter, flamed the tip, and drew his first, pleasure-filled puff.

It was a long, dangerous way north to the Skylords. And Merceron was old. Rendor wondered at his chances, but he knew why the old beast was so willing to try. He'd already lost one boy.

Rendor stared at the mountains through the cigar smoke.

Minutes passed. The sun crept lower, nearly gone now. Rendor heard a noise behind him but didn't bother reaching for his pistol.

"Governor?" Donnar appeared from behind the tree. "Bottling's finished securing the tarp. He wants you to look it over, make sure of it."

"Fine," Rendor nodded. Patching the hole in the *Avatar*'s carriage had been harder than he'd guessed. He was glad the job was finally done. "Still working on the engines?"

"Port side's still a little wobbly," said Donnar. "No worries. One engine will get us home."

"Home." Rendor took another cigar from his pocket and offered it to Donnar. "Take a minute with me, Erich."

Donnar, who never smoked, was immediately suspicious. "What are you doing out here, sir?"

Rendor tilted his chin at the mountains. "How high would you say they are?"

"Oh, no . . ."

"Can we make it over them?"

"Sir, we need to leave. We've got the Starfinder. Remember what Merceron said—there's just no time."

"Not much air up there. Cold too."

"Impossible," said Donnar. "With one engine?"

"One and a half," Rendor reminded him. "We'll strip her down, make her real light. Just like the dragonfly. We'll overpump the envelope."

"Are you asking for my permission or my advice?"

"She's my granddaughter, Erich."

"Yes sir, but you gave the dragon your word."

"I gave him the word of an Eldrin Knight. The Eldrin Knights are dead. Extinct. I don't think anyone's going to throw me in jail for that, do you?"

Donnar sighed as he considered the formidable mountains. "I think, sir, that I'd like that cigar now."

THE CLOUD HORSE

TRUE TO ARTAIOS' WORD, Moth had his run of the Skylords' amazing palace. With Alisaundra as his chaperon, he explored the many towers and theaters, the galleries where the Skylords made art and the libraries where they sat in quiet contemplation. He marveled at their hallways filled with sculptures and the way the spires clung to the hillsides, seemingly defying gravity, and he watched as the Skylords—young and old—sprang from place to place the way birds do, without even thinking about the miracle of flight. He stared at the stars, spit over the edge of balconies, and lost himself in the gigantic murals that graced the palace walls. And for a while, he was contented.

Artaios let his servants see to every whim a human boy might have, giving Moth his own room with a peculiar round bed and sheets so soft Moth thought they'd been spun from magical silk. Strange, delicious foods were brought to him at mealtimes, carried on gleaming platters by eager young Skylords. Moth ate them all with abandon, seeing no real harm in making his captivity bearable. Fiona was alive, at least according to Artaios, and Moth knew he would see her again. He forced himself to believe it. They'd laugh and hug and tell each other how they'd managed to survive, and then they would go home again.

As for Alisaundra, she spent every waking moment with Moth, sometimes watching him from a distance but never quite leaving him alone. She rarely spoke, showed no interest in his predicament, and yet Moth could tell he fascinated her. He had seen a spark of humanity in the Redeemer that night in the prison tower, and again when she had saved him from Artaios. Instead of calling her a monster, Moth simply called her "Alis" now.

Finally, the time came for Moth to see Artaios again. He had been spying on a pair of beautiful Skylord girls, watching them from a balcony as they gossiped, when Alis put a hand on his shoulder.

"Do not stare," she said.

Moth jumped at the intrusion. "I wasn't!"

"You were listening. Come with me. The Master wants you."

"Artaios?" asked Moth. "Why?"

Alis turned away. Curious, a little frightened, Moth followed her off the balcony, through the tower, and across a stone bridge. The Redeemer said nothing, not even bothering to acknowledge Moth as he peppered her with questions. The bridge led them to a colonnade of rounded archways, and then at last to a quiet building apart from all the others, a huge domed structure. As he walked with Alis through the open gate, Moth suspected another tribunal.

"What is this place?" he asked, his voice echoing in the stone corridor.

"Artaios is waiting for you," replied Alis. She pointed forward. "There."

Up ahead the hallway ended, spilling out into the enormous space beneath the dome. As Moth approached he saw Artaios standing in the center of the chamber, beneath a fretted roof of glass and gold. Sunlight poured down upon the Skylord like sparkling water. In his hand rested the golden reins of a cloud horse.

"Do you remember," said Artaios, "that night when I found you? I told you I would teach you what it means to fly."

Moth stepped forward, spellbound by the cloud horse. A twinkling mist shrouded the creature, lit by its flashing orange eyes. It clopped its insubstantial hooves when it noticed Moth, making no sound against the polished floor.

"What's this for?" Moth asked, unable to take his eyes off the cloud horse. "It's so small! Like a pony."

"A young one," explained Artaios. He reached into the mists and rubbed the creature's nose. "Small like you, Egg."

"But why?" asked Moth. "I don't understand."

Artaios replied, "Those machines your people make—you think that is how flying is done. They're abominations. To fly you need wings . . . or a cloud horse. Now I will teach you, as I promised."

"Artaios, I can't fly a cloud horse. What if I fall?"

"This is where all Skylords train with the cloud horses." Artaios pointed at the roof. "There's nowhere for the creature to go."

"Are you kidding? If I fall from up there I'll kill myself!"

"Am I not here to catch you?" said Artaios crossly. "Come here now. The horse will obey me."

Moth couldn't help himself, drawn forward by the amazing creature, its mist gathering at his feet, its sweet effervescence tickling his nose. With a tug of the reins, Artaios guided the horse down for Moth.

"I've never even ridden a real horse," Moth said. "What do I do?"

"Just climb on its back," said Artaios. "He'll keep steady for me."

Wanting desperately to ride the thing, Moth managed to trust Artaios. He reached into the mists, finding a solidness he didn't expect. When his fingers brushed the luminous skin, the cloud horse simply materialized.

"It knows what to do," Artaios reassured him. "Go on."

Moth struggled to lift himself over the creature's back. Its flesh yielded magically beneath him. Moth held its white mane for balance, feeling electricity coursing through the snowy hair. As if it knew Moth was ready, the cloud horse rose up again, this time leaving the ground.

"What now?" Moth cried.

Artaios let go of the reins. "Now you fly."

"Huh? No . . . !"

The horse headed steadily upward, its shifting mists turning a dazzling orange, its head and limbs almost invisible. Moth crouched to keep from falling, one hand gathering up the dangling reins. The polished floor dropped away. Beside him, Artaios was smiling, his powerful wings carrying him aloft.

"I'm gonna fall!" shouted Moth.

"You won't."

"But—"

"Calm yourself! Let the horse feel your will."

The cloud horse turned gently, pirouetting ever higher. Moth at last took up the reins and settled tightly on its back. Slowly, he felt the creature respond.

"Ah, you are doing it!" said Artaios. "Now you are flying, Egg!"

"I thought you said only Skylords could fly these things!"

"It obeys you because I am here. If I were not . . ." Artaios suddenly laughed. "I do not know!"

Suddenly Moth wished there was no roof at all, that he and the cloud horse could rise up forever. He glanced over and saw Artaios beaming proudly. Moth felt himself smiling back at the Skylord, then caught a glimpse of Alis far below.

The Redeemer's joyless expression left Moth bewildered.

That night, Moth washed away all his aches and pains in a pool of steaming water. He leaned his head against the edge of the pool, letting the warmth relax his knotted muscles as he marveled at the underground bath chamber, running like a catacomb beneath the tower of Korace. At the far end of the chamber a gentle waterfall trickled down the rocky wall, feeding the bath. Like everything in the Palace of the Moon, the chamber was enormous, yet Moth had it entirely to himself. He floated, naked, his body obscured by the minerals clouding the water.

No one had seen him naked in years, not even his mother. At first he'd been afraid, but he wasn't anymore. The hot bath melted his shyness away. Esculor, the young Skylord assigned to Moth, had explained that all the Skylords bathed this way. Young and old, male and female, they shared the baths without shame, something unimaginable in the world Moth came from.

"You have everything I have," Esculor had joked, "except wings. No one cares enough to stare."

Sure that Esculor would return for him soon, Moth stretched out his arms along the side of the pool, dunking himself quickly, then lifting himself up with a mouthful of water, squirting it like a fountain. Tomorrow, if he was lucky, Artaios would teach him more about flying. He closed his eyes, daydreaming about the cloud horse as the warm water lulled him to sleep.

Moth listened to the waterfall over his own contented breathing. Then another sound reached his ears, very softy. He opened his eyes, expecting to see Esculor. A glimpse of yellow hair appeared behind a column.

"Alis?"

Discovered, Alisaundra stepped from her hiding spot.

"Uh, Alis, I'm naked in here," said Moth, suddenly self-conscious. "Could you stay back a little?"

The Redeemer looked bemused and grossly overdressed in her heavy cloak and silver chain.

"Something on your mind?" asked Moth.

Alisaundra seemed to struggle with her thoughts, unnerving Moth with her silence.

"You're staring," he pointed out. "You told me not to stare, remember?"

She glided closer, her brow ridged in troubled thought. Moth shifted uncomfortably in his bath, glad for the cloudy water. He thought of calling out for Esculor or jumping up to get his clothes, but Alis wasn't really frightening him. She came to the very edge of the pool, squatting down next to him and threading her clawed fingers through the water.

"Listen," said Moth, trying to distract her. "I never thanked you for saving me the other day. From Artaios, I mean. I got a little mad when he started talking about Fiona. I shouldn't have done that. So thanks. Okay?"

Alis went from squatting to kneeling. She tapped a long fingernail against her blonde head. "In here. I see pictures. Old things."

"Pictures? You mean memories?"

"I remember," she said, "because of you."

Moth wasn't sure if she was happy or just accusing him. He kept his voice low and said, "Because you've been around humans again, right? You've been mucking around in my head. But this is good, Alis. You see? You *are* human."

"I am a Redeemer," Alis insisted. "I serve the Skylords."

"Yeah, all right. Tell me about your memories. What do you see?"

"They scream at me. They want to come out! I can't let them."

"Who? Who's screaming at you?"

Alis put her claws to her face, driving her nails into her scaly cheeks. "Family."

Moth stayed very still. "Tell me," he whispered.

"I remember . . ." Alis hesitated. "Remember . . ." Her reptilian eyes glazed over. "Sitting. My father's lap."

"Go on," said Moth. "You remember sitting in your father's lap . . ."

"He smelled like earth. I remember being afraid."

"Why?" Moth rolled onto his side, intrigued. "Why were you afraid of him?"

"Not of him," said Alis. Her eyes sparkled as the memory took hold. "Afraid to move. Afraid to make him uncomfortable. Afraid he would tell me to get off his lap." She made a little noise of happiness. "That was the best place. On Father."

Her fanged mouth smiled. Her black wings shrouded her body. But she was human, and Moth saw it.

"I would sit with him for hours," Alis continued. "And he would touch my hair." She pulled at a tangled blonde tendril, horrified by it. "Not this hair. Real hair. He would sit and I would sing, and he would stroke my hair."

Then she started humming to herself, her voice softly echoing through the cavernous baths. She no longer looked at Moth; her vision turned inward instead.

"Alis?" said Moth. "Look away."

"Why?" asked the Redeemer.

"I want to get dressed. Close your eyes or something."

Alis obeyed, letting Moth climb out of the pool and grab up his clothing. He didn't bother drying off, just slipped on his breeches.

"Alis, you can't talk like this to anyone," said Moth as he

pulled his shirt over his head. "If Artaios knows about your memories he'll punish you. You shouldn't even be telling me about them."

Alis stood up. "Do not trust Artaios," she warned.

"Huh?"

"He gives you the cloud horse. He gives you a room, servants. Do you wonder why?"

"Yes," admitted Moth. He felt ashamed suddenly. "I guess I do."

"Soon he will ask you questions," whispered Alis. "About Calio. The airships. Things no one else can tell him. About how strong humans are."

"You mean he's bribing me? But why? Why does he want to know—"

Before Moth could finish he heard Esculor returning, heading for the bath chamber in a flutter of wings. Moth turned back to Alis.

"Why, Alis?"

Alis flashed her pointed teeth and hissed, "To end the human dream."

She said nothing more, bowing to Esculor as the young Skylord entered the chamber, then left quietly, disappearing through the steam.

"Hideous creatures," said Esculor. He turned his perfect smile toward Moth. A hair comb flashed in his hand, ready to pamper his human charge. "Finished?"

"Yes," nodded Moth. "I think I am."

He stood, frozen, letting Esculor's jeweled comb sweep through his wet hair, trying to imagine Alisaundra as a girl.

HIGHER

THE *AVATAR* HOVERED at fifteen thousand feet, the last mark on her vacuum-powered altimeter. For nearly an hour she had been at that height, time for her crew to acclimate to the cold and thin air as they prepared for their ascent. Each man had left behind every bit of extra weight possible, shedding every knickknack and memento brought from home. Canisters and barrels had been tossed overboard, weapons were stripped of their heavy safety shields, and even the furniture in Rendor's quarters had been discarded, all to make the airship light enough for the climb.

Rendor peered through the rectangle of netting sewn into the tarp stretched across the ship's damaged bridge. His nose burned from the cold, but he did not shiver as he looked at the sheer wall of rock facing them. Snow and mist obscured the mountaintops. His breath froze on his lips. Already a headache from altitude sickness throbbed in his skull. On the other side of the mountain waited Pandera, warm and thick with breathable air. Rendor blew into his gloved hands. Behind him, Lieutenant Stringfellow sat at the engine console, taking deep, rapid breaths the way Rendor had shown him. Rendor counted ten breaths, then twelve as Stringfellow kept going.

"That's enough," barked Rendor. "A dozen breaths, no more." He looked at the others on the bridge. "If your hands and feet start tingling you've done too many," he warned. "Ten to twelve deep breaths every five minutes. Don't do it unless you have to."

Donnar nodded as he paced the bridge, seemingly immune to the dwindling air pressure. Bottling, on the other hand, had already vomited twice. He kept a bucket next to him as he watched a bank of gauges, his eyes the only part of his face visible behind a woolen scarf. Four additional crewmen manned the bridge as well, a pair of them assigned to consoles, the other two ready with tools to mend steam pipes or tears in the tarp. The entire crew had dressed in layers and drunk gallons of water to prepare their bodies for the moisture-sucking atmosphere. They were all well-trained and hand-picked, but none of them had ever flown as high as they would today.

Through the netting, the world was a swirl of clouds and jagged rock. Rendor felt the thrumming of the engines under his feet, felt the way the wind rattled the airship like a baby's toy, and knew the time had come.

"Commander Donnar," he said, "get ready to climb."

Donnar strapped himself in his captain's chair, pulling a stout leather belt across his lap. Bottling turned his covered face toward the Commander, waiting for the order. His right hand, fitted with a fingerless glove, hovered over a silver lever.

"Slow climb, Mister Bottling," said Donnar. "Stringfellow, listen for the watch."

Bottling eased the lever forward. The *Avatar* shuddered as hidrenium swelled her envelope. Rendor peered through his viewport as the airship slowly rose. The wind off the peaks swayed her back and forth. Stringfellow manned the engine deck, listening for Rendor's orders.

"Steady on the watch," said Rendor.

He ignored his growing fatigue and the pounding in his forehead, wrapping his arms around himself for warmth as the *Avatar* floated upward. Unlike the other airships he'd designed, the *Avatar*'s flatter shape made climbing easier, relying not just on hidrenium but also the force of the atmosphere to push her skyward. But it was the job of the engines to move her laterally, and unless he held a steady watch, one stray wind might send them crashing into the face of the mountain.

Rendor scanned the peaks, trying to spot the zenith. Broken clouds obscured his view. Behind him, Bottling was breathing hard to keep from blacking out. He tapped the glass of his many gauges, worried. Donnar sat with steely calm, scanning his nervous crew. When a sudden gust rocked the *Avatar,* he barely flinched.

"Report the watch," he called.

Rendor squinted hard, trying to squeeze back his nausea. Outside he saw the rocks rising still above them. "Higher."

Minutes passed. Bottling shivered over his bucket. Stringfellow gulped down nervous breaths . . . four, five, six. Even Donnar had turned blue. Rendor felt his hands and face starting to swell.

"Higher," he gasped.

He swayed on his feet, fighting for balance. He saw a picture of Fiona in his mind, still alive. Still beautiful, like his daughter. In his frock coat ticked his pocket watch, the only keepsake he hadn't thrown overboard. He fixed on it, imagining its perfect movement, concentrating on its steadiness.

He tried to speak but couldn't. He clawed at the net to support his wobbly legs. Behind him he heard someone fall from his chair. Donnar shouted for a report.

Higher, thought Rendor desperately. *Just a little higher . . .*

His eyes turned skyward, staring at the sun. The wind blew hard and the clouds slowly parted, and a glimpse of the mountaintop appeared. Rendor stuck his frozen face against the net in disbelief, blinking through its crisscrossed ropes. Past the mist and ice-covered rocks, far below the churning clouds, he saw a flash of green.

"Ahead," he gasped, clinging to the tarp. "Stringfellow . . ."

Before he could finish, Rendor fainted.

JORIAN'S LIGHTNING

EACH MORNING FIONA AWOKE in Pandera, she fought to stay asleep just a little bit longer. The comfortable bed of straw and the peace of the valley gave her a happiness she hadn't known since her parents were alive, and her dreams were sweet with images of meadows and tall, protective mountains. Under Nessa's care she had healed quickly, her bumps and bruises soothed by the unhurried days. As the wife of a Chieftain, Nessa's responsibilities were many, but she always found time to involve Fiona, teaching her to hay the beds and mend cloth and to make the traditional bread each dawn.

Fiona, who was accustomed to having servants cook her food, found an undiscovered talent for bread-making. She loved the way flour powdered her hands and the way the dough felt as it rose, like the soft belly of a baby. Mostly, though, she loved the closeness she felt to Nessa. To Fiona, Nessa wasn't just a centaur. She was also a strikingly beautiful woman, the kind Fiona had always wished to be. The kind her mother had been. Even covered in flour, Nessa was beautiful.

This morning, as Fiona struggled to open her eyes, she reminded herself of her bread-baking duty. Nessa would be expecting her. She dressed quickly, washed in a basin, and proceeded outside to the cooking hearth where Nessa was already kneading dough. A handful of others had gathered to help, mostly young males and females. Fiona knew them all by name now.

They greeted her excitedly, still amused about having a human in their village.

"Sorry I'm late," said Fiona as she sidled up to Nessa. "I overslept again."

Nessa, who never got angry, merely grinned. "Don't get your hands dirty," she said. "You won't be helping us this morning."

"Huh?"

A shadow fell over Fiona's shoulder. She turned to see Jorian towering over her.

"Today you're coming with me," the chieftain announced.

Fiona looked up, confused. "I am?"

"Don't be afraid of him," laughed Nessa. "It's time."

"Time for what?" asked Fiona.

"For you to learn how to defend yourself," said Jorian. His dark, humorless face didn't even crack a smile. He reached into a leather sack hanging from his torso. "I made you this."

The young centaurs gasped when they saw Jorian's gift—a bow, roughly half Fiona's size, made of shiny, knotty wood. A string of sinew stretched between its ends, giving it a taut bend. Fiona took the bow, surprised by the present.

"Thank you," she said, "but I don't know how to shoot a bow."

"You didn't know how to bake bread, either," Nessa reminded her.

"I will teach you," said Jorian. He patted his own bow, a much longer weapon looped over his shoulder. "Come."

Jorian led Fiona to the outskirts of the village, then beyond the shallow wall surrounding it. Fiona followed a few paces behind, confused but trusting. They climbed a gentle hill where the wildflowers rose to Fiona's knees. Jorian looked about, satisfied with the place. The sunlight shadowed his muscular arms. Fiona caught herself staring. The bow felt wobbly in her hand.

"You see the eagle?" said Jorian suddenly, his face turned skyward. Fiona snapped out of her daydream.

"What?"

Jorian pointed into the sun. "An eagle—do you see?"

Fiona squinted, catching a glimpse of the great bird wheeling high above the valley. "I do!" she exclaimed. "I haven't seen any birds flying so high here. Merceron says they're afraid to fly. He says the Skylords have forbidden it."

"Birds are safe here," said Jorian. His smile was proud, almost arrogant. "I rule Pandera, not the Skylords." He looked down at Fiona. "Raise your bow."

Fiona hesitated. "Jorian, I really appreciate you making this for me, but—"

"Listen to me, Little Queen—the birds know they can fly here. They know that I will fight for them. And I will fight for you if the Skylords come, and you will fight with me. Female or male, it doesn't matter. All centaurs know how to use a bow. Now, raise your weapon."

Fiona nodded, shaken by his words. She raised the bow up as she imagined she should, stretching out her arm. "Like this?"

Jorian crouched behind her, sizing up her stance. "Be comfortable. Keep your back straight but not stiff. I strung your bow lightly, but it will still kick back at you." He wrapped his arms around her, gently manipulating her. "That tree is your target," he told her, choosing the closest pine. "Stand in line with it, both feet."

Fiona did as he directed, trying to find a comfortable stance. "Back straight," she repeated. "All right."

"Now your draw arm," said Jorian. "Elbow up. Everything in line with the target."

This was a bit more awkward. Fiona imagined drawing back the string, keeping all her gangly limbs as straight as possible. She closed one eye and targeted the tree. "Now an arrow?"

Jorian dipped into the quiver at his side. Instead of pulling out one of the long arrows for his own bow, he chose a smaller one. "You should always nock an arrow at the same spot on your string every time," he said. "Lay the arrow in the rest . . ."

Fiona set the arrow onto the little bump in the bow. "Okay."

"Now nock it in the string."

"Okay."

She started drawing back. Jorian stopped her, adjusting her fingers with his own, then told her to continue. Fiona slowly pulled back the arrow, trying to keep form.

"Push with your bow arm and pull with your draw arm," said Jorian. "That's it . . . good and straight."

Fiona felt the tautness of the bow, the arrow's eagerness to fly.

"Aim . . ."

The tree was only a few yards away. Fiona lined up perfectly. "I got it."

"Relax your fingers," Jorian coached, "then let go."

Fiona held her breath and loosed the arrow. The bowstring twanged and the recoil pushed her into Jorian's arms. "Whoa!"

She hurried toward the tree, expecting to see the arrow dead center in its trunk. Instead she saw a gash mark along its left side. And no arrow at all.

"I missed," she groaned. "Where'd it go?"

"We'll find it," Jorian assured her. He rose up, looking pleased despite her failure. "Practice. You'll get better fast. You have an excellent teacher."

Fiona smiled but didn't laugh. "Jorian?"

Jorian was already pulling another arrow from his quiver. "Yes?"

"If the Skylords come, you'll have to give me up," said Fiona. "No one can beat them. The dragons couldn't beat them . . ."

"Centaurs are not dragons," boasted Jorian. "Have I not told you I would defend you?"

"Merceron told us all about the Skylords," Fiona argued. "They hate humans. They're not going to let you keep me here." She shook her head. "They'll kill you if you try."

Jorian handed her the arrow. "Take it," he said, then unlooped his own bow from his shoulders. "I want to show you something."

He retrieved another arrow, this one long enough for his own weapon. He set it into his bowstring, holding it all with one hand.

"I have no fear of the Skylords," he said. "The Skylords fear *me*. Ready your arrow the way I told you. Aim into the sky."

"All right," agreed Fiona, not knowing why. She nocked the arrow, got herself back into her shooting stance, and pointed the shaft skyward, waiting for instructions.

"Good," said Jorian. "Now watch."

He nocked his own arrow, tilted his bow skyward like Fiona, and began to pull back. As he did his draw hand started to glow, first a faint yellow, then a burning orange encasing his entire fist. Fiona watched in shock as the fire ran from his hand into the arrow, setting it alight, turning its wood into something else, something more like lightning.

Jorian closed his eyes. "Shoot your arrow."

Fiona pulled back her bowstring, aimed for the sky, and fired. The arrow whistled into the air, higher and higher against the blue sky.

"Watch it," said Jorian. "Don't lose it." He waited, waited, then he let his own shaft fly, not opening his eyes until the lightning shot from his bow.

It moved impossibly fast, catching up to Fiona's arrow, hunting it down like a hawk to a sparrow. High over the valley the two collided in a burst of fire. Little flaming bits of wood showered down, then disappeared.

"What was *that*?" Fiona shrieked.

"That," said Jorian, "is why the Skylords fear me."

The Skylords called it "Jorian's Lightning," a term that delighted Jorian. He explained the gift as a magic his father and grandfather had held before him, an ability of his bloodline to call down the fire of heaven. There was nothing an arrow shot from Jorian's hand could not hit, he told Fiona, and no living thing that could withstand it. Fiona imagined the Skylords swooping down on Pandera and how easily Jorian could pick them off—one, two, three bolts of fire, all with his eyes closed.

For the rest of the morning and into the afternoon she and Jorian practiced with her bow, sharing stories about their families and the places they called home. Gradually, Fiona got better with her bow. By the middle of the day she could hit a nearby tree every time. They walked deeper into Jorian's valley, he pointing out places he'd explored as a child, she enthralled by every word.

Finally, when the time came for them to return to the village, Fiona didn't want to go.

"It's a long way back," she said. She sighed dramatically. "A very long walk. I've been so sick lately . . ."

Jorian looked concerned. "You feel poorly?"

"Well, no, not really. It's just a very long walk."

She smiled, hoping he'd get her hint.

"You mean you want to ride me?" thundered Jorian.

"Can I? I rode horses a lot back home. I know I can do it."

"I am not a horse!"

"I've ridden dragons, too," countered Fiona. "Maybe me and Moth are the only people ever to ride a dragon."

"Ugh," scoffed Jorian. "What a disgusting idea. No wonder the dragons lost their war. You will walk, Little Queen. I'm not a donkey."

Fiona shrank back, sorry she'd asked. She wasn't really too tired to walk; she just wanted to climb upon such a noble beast, to really be a part of him. Like a real centaur.

"I won't ask again," she promised. "You're right, you're not a—"

She paused, sighting something over Jorian's shoulder, a small black mass coming toward them from the mountains. At first she thought it was a bird, or maybe a Redeemer come to find her. Then, a moment later, she realized it was something far worse.

"Oh, no . . ."

Jorian followed her gaze. "What is it?" he asked, spotting the object.

Fiona felt her old world crashing with her new. Any second now, they'd hear the two big engines.

"The *Avatar*," she said, barely able to get the word out. "My grandfather."

ONE MORE STEP

WITH ONE BLOW OF HIS HUNTING horn, Jorian called his centaurs to battle.

Out in the open, they could see the *Avatar* descending from the sky, like a great, black cloud obscuring the sun. They did not hide nor try to shield Fiona from what might come. Instead, they gathered in a meadow around their Chieftain, over two hundred strong, to defend their valley. Fiona stood at Jorian's side, nestled between him and Nessa. The *Avatar* had been badly damaged somehow, the front of its carriage covered with cloth, one engine whining louder than the other. The giant airship seemed to limp into Pandera, but Fiona warned Jorian not to be fooled.

"Remember the guns," she told him. "Once you hear 'em it's too late."

Surrounded by his fellow centaurs, his outsized bow clamped in his fist, Jorian watched in fascination as the airship floated earthward. He had promised to protect Fiona, but now she wasn't so sure.

"He wants the Starfinder," she told Jorian. "He must think I have it."

"Then they don't have the boy," Jorian surmised. "Your friend would have told them he gave the Starfinder to Merceron." He glanced at Fiona. "Right?"

"Yeah," said Fiona. "Or no. Moth's pretty stubborn sometimes."

"You're not making sense. If you're afraid, do not be. Never let your enemies see you afraid, Little Queen."

Fiona didn't know what she was feeling. Her feelings were a jumble. Part of her hoped Moth was safe on the *Avatar*, but another part hoped he'd escaped somehow. Maybe he'd eluded her grandfather that night she fell into the river. Maybe he was already with Merceron. Kyros, Jorian's friend and advisor, approached from the back ranks, muscling past young Tyrin to replace him at Jorian's side.

"The young ones are all inside," he announced. He'd galloped hard from the village and was short of breath.

Jorian pointed at the *Avatar*. "Look at that, Kyros," he said, unable to hide his awe. "How can such a thing fly?"

Kyros scoffed. "Dragons fly," he reminded his Chieftain. "What good did it do them?" He considered Fiona. "I should take you back to the village."

Jorian looked down at Fiona. "Is that what you want? You *would* be safer there."

"Everyone in the village is here," said Fiona. "So this is where I belong too."

"Little Queen," beamed Jorian. "Good. Then we shall face your grandfather together."

They watched as the *Avatar*'s engines slowed and the ponderous ship settled to the ground. Fiona wondered if her grandfather could see her, standing at the front of an army of centaurs. She wondered if he felt pride or fear, or anything at all. Kyros shouted for the centaurs to prepare themselves, sending them fanning out behind him. Without armor, with only bare flesh to protect them, Fiona knew the *Avatar*'s guns could cut them down like grass.

And yet they were fearless.

Fiona took Nessa's hand. Jorian was right—she was afraid. Nessa felt the coldness of her fingers and looked down with sympathy.

"It's all right," she whispered. "If you want to go to the village . . ."

Jorian overheard her and fixed her with an angry glare. "She's made her choice," he snapped. "This is her home now. Home is the one place where you don't run from anyone."

Embarrassed, Fiona straightened and tried to look tall, but she felt small surrounded by the centaurs. Small, like a little girl. She thought of what she would say to her grandfather when she saw him, how she might curse him or beg him to leave her alone, but when the door to the *Avatar*'s carriage dropped open, her whole brain went blank.

The centaurs fell silent as the first men appeared. Instead of swarming out like bees, they moved purposefully to flank the airship, rifles in hand. Jorian tensed. On top of the airship and along its catwalks other men appeared.

"He sees her," said Tyrin. "They won't shoot."

"No girl, no Starfinder," agreed Kyros. The old centaur let his hand hover over his quiver, itching to draw.

"Stand with me," said Nessa softly, gathering Fiona close. But Fiona pulled away. Another figure started down the gangway, portly, unsteady on his feet, a long dark coat sweeping behind him. Despite his familiar face, Fiona almost didn't recognize him.

"Grandfather?"

Fiona peered at him, confused. He stepped away from his wall of men, swaying as he walked, his skin pale and face wretched. A soldier hurried out to help him, but he waved the man back.

"Is that him?" Jorian asked incredulously.

"Something's wrong," said Fiona. "He looks sick."

"Battle," Kyros guessed. "Look at his ship."

Rendor struggled toward them, not stopping until he was halfway between the centaurs and his airship. Fiona could see him clearly now, his face grooved with exhaustion, his stance weary but determined. When his eyes met Fiona's, he reached out his hand.

"Fiona!"

Jorian galloped out a few yards, kicking up earth with his hooves. "I am Jorian, Chieftain of Pandera! This child's protector, Rendor!"

Rendor didn't flinch. "I came over those mountains to get her back, Centaur. If you think you can scare me, forget it."

The soldiers behind him brought up their rifles. Jorian laughed.

"You have trapped yourself, fool!"

"We've got guns," warned Rendor. "Ever see what a half-inch shell can do to a horse?"

"Stop!" screamed Fiona. She launched herself toward Jorian. "I don't want this! I don't want you fighting for me!"

Her grandfather took another step forward. "Fiona, you don't need him anymore. I'll take you home."

"You can't go home, human," spat Jorian. "Haven't you realized? The Skylords won't let you. You're trapped."

"Then we'll fight our way out," sneered Rendor. "But I won't leave without Fiona."

"But I don't have the Starfinder!" Fiona cried. "It's gone! We gave it to Merceron!"

"I already have the Starfinder, Fiona! I have it!"

"You have it? What . . . ?"

Her grandfather spread out his hands. "I came here for *you*!"

Jorian moved up, gently shoved Fiona aside, and raised up his bow. His hand was already glowing when he picked out an arrow.

"I'm vowed to her," he told Rendor. "That might not mean anything in the human world, but here it is gold."

"Jorian, no!" cried Fiona. "You'll kill him!"

She reached for him, pulling at his arm. Kyros shot forward and dragged her backward.

"Stop it!" she screamed. "Don't shoot him!"

Determined, Jorian nocked his arrow and drew back on his bow string. The arrow changed to sparkling light amid a cacophony of rifle bolts. Rendor put up his hand to stay his soldiers.

"If you shoot me," he told Jorian, "you'll be dead the next second."

Jorian aimed, ignoring Fiona's frenzied pleas. "One more step, human."

Fiona was crazed. She kicked at Kyros, even biting to break his grip, but the old centaur's arms coiled around her like a python.

"Nessa, stop him!" Fiona pleaded.

Nessa didn't move. Not a single centaur spoke to aid her. Astonished by their cruelty, Fiona cried out to her grandfather.

"Go back!" she hollered. "I'll find my way home! I will, I promise!"

Her grandfather held his ground. Staring down the flaming arrow, he took that last, forbidden step.

And Jorian let his arrow fly.

Horrified, Fiona watched it race toward Rendor, watched as her grandfather didn't flinch, then watched the arrow sail past his ear, up over his soldiers, and into the sky.

Fiona didn't know what happened. She looked at Jorian, who lowered his bow.

"Let her go," the Chieftain told Kyros.

Stunned, Fiona fell out of Kyros' arms. Across the field her grandfather dropped to his knees. Soldiers rushed forward to help him. Jorian held up a hand to keep his own fighters back.

"A brave man," said the Chieftain. "Like his granddaughter."

Fiona wanted to slap him. "A test?" she asked, choked by tears. She looked angrily at Nessa. "Even you?"

Jorian bowed down to face her. "He trapped himself here for you," he said, "but I needed to be certain. Go to him."

Fiona looked at her grandfather—out of breath and sick—on his knees in the grass. She hadn't run to him in years, not since she was a little girl. Now, though, Fiona ran.

UNBEARABLE PROPORTIONS

SKYHIGH PULLED HIS MESS KIT out from behind the seat of his dragonfly, hopefully opened its metal lid, then scowled with disappointment. His supplies had dwindled to a can of beans and two stale biscuits. Food in hand, he crawled out of his vessel and headed toward the cliff. After two full days of flying he was light-headed and famished, but his efforts were nothing compared to Merceron's. Somehow, the old dragon had carried him and his fuel-laden dragonfly to the very edge of the world, to a place where only a gigantic canyon separated them from the palace of the Skylords. Overhead the sky continued to darken, forcing Skyhigh to hurry. Once the moon came out, Merceron claimed, the Skylords' city would glow like fire.

Determined not to miss the show Skyhigh rushed toward the cliff, but paused as he emerged from the sheltering trees. At the very edge of the cliff lay Merceron, flat on his belly with Lady Esme on his head, his chin tucked upon his front claws. Together he and Esme stared longingly across the canyon. Behind the mountains the sun painted the sky a dazzling orange.

"Not much food left," said Skyhigh as he approached. He sat down beside the dragon on the smooth outcropping of rock, showing him the contents of the mess kit. "We could hunt if you want. Are you hungry? You must be hungry."

Merceron rolled a disinterested eye toward the biscuits and beans. "I don't know how you eat that anyway."

"You get used to it," said Skyhigh. He fished a can opener

out of the box and started working it around the rim of the can. Lady Esme spied the distant palace, entranced by the little specks flying around it—her fellow Skylords. "You're sure it's safe out here?" asked Skyhigh. "They might see us."

"They already know we're here," sighed Merceron.

"They do? Then why'd I bother hiding the dragonfly?"

Merceron shrugged. "I didn't tell you to."

Annoyed, Skyhigh pretended to turn his back. "Just for that you're not getting any beans. So, if they know we're here, why don't they come for us?"

"Because they have patience," snapped Merceron. "Every race has patience—except humans. Now would you mind shutting up?" He grumbled as he settled his long chin back onto his claws. "Fifty years, no flying. Then a boy comes along and suddenly I'm flying myself to exhaustion every day . . ."

"What are you muttering about?"

"Nothing. I'm tired. All right?"

Skyhigh offered him a biscuit. "Here . . ."

Merceron batted it away, right over the cliff.

"Hey! That was supper!"

"If you're hungry, eat," Merceron growled. "Please, put something in your mouth instead of your tongue."

Skyhigh stuck his spoon into the beans, silent for a moment as he watched the sinking sun. The moon appeared in the cloudless sky, its silver light beginning to tinge the far-off palace. Skyhigh set aside his tin.

"Merceron, we have to talk."

"Oh, no . . ."

"What's our plan? You haven't told me yet."

"No?"

"Listen," said Skyhigh crossly. "For two days you've done nothing but fly and keep quiet. I trusted you enough to come along, but the Skylords aren't going to just hand Moth over to us. I want to know why I'm here. What exactly do you want me to do?"

Finally, Merceron lifted his head. "Trust?"

Skyhigh nodded. "Yeah. I trust you. But I can't go further until you tell me your plan."

"That's not trust," harrumphed Merceron, and went back to staring at the palace.

His demeanor puzzled Skyhigh. "Why are you doing this?" he asked. "Why are you going after Moth?"

"Why are you?" the dragon countered.

"Because he's my friend. And I've known Moth a lot longer than you have, Merceron, so don't tell me it's because he's your friend, too." Skyhigh leaned back on his palms. "We've got all night, so you might as well start talking."

Lady Esme walked down to the tip of Merceron's nose. He snorted gently to move her back to his crown, then asked, "How much did Rendor tell you about me?"

"Not a lot," said Skyhigh honestly. "Moth, either. He said you were a wizard." An idea bubbled up. "Is that your plan to rescue Moth? Some sort of spell?"

"Only a human wouldn't know how ridiculous that sounds." Merceron closed his rheumy eyes. "Do you have children, Skyhigh?"

"Kids?" chortled Skyhigh. "No, thank heaven."

"A woman, then? Someone special?"

Skyhigh grinned. "I've got a lot of special women, but I don't think that's what you mean. Why?"

"Because I have a story to tell," said Merceron, "but I'm not sure you can understand it."

"We Skyknights are pretty smart, Merceron. Give it a try."

"All right, but remember you pushed me into this . . ."

"Go on."

Merceron kept his eyes shut. "Once there was a young dragon named Elaniel . . ."

Skyhigh laughed. "Sounds like a bedtime story."

"Are you going to listen?"

"Sorry."

The dragon started again. "Elaniel was the pride and joy of his parents. His father was a prominent dragon, a leader of his race. All the other dragons believed in him and trusted him, and Elaniel worshipped his father."

Skyhigh felt uncomfortable suddenly, not liking where the tale was heading. "Okay . . ."

"When the war with the Skylords started," Merceron went on, "all the dragons had to decide whether or not to fight. Elaniel's father wanted to fight, so Elaniel went with him. He thought nothing could happen to him. He trusted his father to protect him." Merceron opened his eyes, his gaze empty. "He *trusted*."

Skyhigh didn't need Merceron to finish the story. "Elaniel. He was your son."

"Yes," said Merceron softly. He searched Skyhigh for understanding. "What do you think it feels like to lose a child, Skyhigh? Can you imagine that feeling? Can you comprehend it at all?"

The answer came to Skyhigh easily. "I think," he said sadly, "that it's a tragedy of unbearable proportions."

The phrase made Merceron smile. "Unbearable proportions. You're a poet, Skyknight! Maybe now you understand. Elaniel trusted me and died. Lady Esme trusted me and got turned into a bird for it. Our friend Moth is just one of many. But this time I can do something about it. I can save him."

"I believe you," said Skyhigh. "But how?"

Merceron went back to gazing across the canyon. Skyhigh remained beside him, silent. It wasn't the palace Merceron was watching, Skyhigh realized, but the dying sunset.

PARTING

MOTH AND THE CLOUD HORSE spiraled up to the very top of the training chamber, the circle growing smaller and smaller with each revolution. Together they had performed the exercise a hundred times, so that now Moth could control the creature with only the smallest movements of his body. Above him, frets of sunlight poured down from the glass roof. Moth released the golden reins, reached up both hands, and touched the warm glass. Here in the Palace of the Moon, above even the clouds, the days were always perfect.

He pulled back his hands, took up the reins again, and slowly wheeled the cloud horse down again. Alisaundra sat with her back against the wall, her knees tucked up to her chest, watching curiously as Moth and the cloud horse glided to the ground. She had spent the morning watching him, no longer spying on him from the shadows or hiding when he called her. Now she was his constant companion. Moth wasn't sure, but it looked like she'd even brushed her hair.

"You fly like me now!" she called to him. "Only not so well."

"Soon," Moth promised, and turned the creature up again in a flaring pirouette. "Once Artaios lets me outside with her, I'll show you what she can do."

Alis' expression soured. "Do not ask him for favors," she warned. "Remember?"

Moth remembered, but couldn't help himself. The lure of the cloud horse was everything Artaios hoped it would be, and too much for Moth to resist. With so little to occupy his time, the cloud horse was the one bright spot in his captivity. He trained with the creature every day, spending hours in the glass-roofed chamber, sometimes with Artaios himself. While the Skylord plied Moth with questions—just as Alis had predicted—Moth learned what he could from Artaios, getting to know and love the cloud horse the way Skyknights loved their dragonflies. He had even given the creature a name—Comet, because of its long, glowing tail.

"Don't tell him I've been riding without hands," said Moth as he steered the cloud horse through the chamber. "I'm trusting you, okay?"

Alis raised a scaly eyebrow. "I cannot lie to my Master."

"No, but do you have to tell him everything?" Moth brought the creature up alongside her. "Listen," he whispered, "we're friends now, right? That's what friends do. They keep secrets for each other. If you want to be human again that's part of it."

Alis nodded. "I understand. I remember."

Moth smiled, noting her hair again. "You look nice today." He hesitated. "Pretty."

Her scaly face seemed to blush. "I . . . am trying." Her tone grew confessional. "I remember more things now. Family things. I will tell you later."

"Yeah, better wait," agreed Moth. Artaios always arrived for Moth's lesson promptly, but today the Skylord was already late, and Moth knew he'd come soon. "You should stand up now, too."

Alis took his suggestion, standing tall and instantly affecting a scowl. A second later, Artaios flew into the chamber, making even Comet jump.

"Egg!" bellowed Artaios as he hit the ground. "It's time."

Moth followed Artaios toward the Hall of Convocation. Confused, frightened, he walked behind the Skylord, followed closely by Alisaundra. Korace was already seated on his throne. Moth could see the decrepit ruler across the corridor. Around him, the galleries were crowded with Skylords.

"What's this?" Moth asked, alarmed.

Artaios paused at the end of the corridor and peered into the arena.

"Egg," he directed. "Look."

Moth had to force himself forward. Part of him expected to see a gallows or a headsman. Artaios put an arm around his shoulder, coaxing him out into the arena. In the center of the hall stood Merceron, head held high, smoke curling from his nostrils. Lady Esme rested on his shoulder. Next to him stood Skyhigh, small but ramrod straight, his face defiant.

"Skyhigh!" Moth called. "Merceron!"

The two turned toward Moth without a word. Before Moth could go to them, Artaios grabbed his shoulder.

"Stay."

"Artaios, let me go!"

"They've come to bargain for you, Egg," said Artaios darkly. "Hold him," he ordered Alisaundra, then strode out toward the throne. The crowd cheered at his appearance. Alis bent her lips to Moth's ear.

"Careful," she whispered. "Mind what you say."

Atop his massive silver throne, Korace put out a trembling hand for his son. Artaios stooped to kiss it. Together they glared at Merceron. Slowly, the clamor subsided. Skyhigh gave Moth a reassuring nod as Alisaundra led him out.

"Moth, don't worry," Skyhigh called. "We'll get you out of here."

"Out of here?" Moth looked at Merceron, realizing what was happening. "No! You can't give up the Starfinder!"

Artaios laughed. "You see, Egg? I told you he would come for you. The one noble thing about dragons is that they keep their word." He grinned at Merceron, pleased with himself. "But you don't have the Starfinder, do you dragon?"

"Merceron?" queried Moth. "What's he saying?"

"It's true, Moth," Merceron admitted. "I don't have the Starfinder."

A strange sound came from Korace, a wicked, cackling laugh. The creaky Skylord pulled himself up with his cane. "Rendor!"

At first Moth didn't understand. His eyes bounced from Korace to Artaios, then to the sad-faced Merceron. "Oh, no," he groaned. "Merceron, tell me you didn't!"

Merceron looked pleadingly at Moth. "You've seen what they are, boy, what they're like. The Starfinder is safe now. Rendor's taken it home."

"Rendor is trapped!" laughed Korace. "Like you!"

"Dragon, you've doomed yourself," added Artaios. "The humans are in Pandera. Rendor has the Starfinder, but he's betrayed you. They *are* trapped."

Merceron lost his arrogant air. The color left Skyhigh's face. Even Lady Esme seemed to understand their peril. She drew back on Merceron's shoulder, madly fluttering her wings.

"Esme," called Korace. "You're home now. Will you come to us?"

He held out his trembling hand, the very hand Moth suspected had transformed her in the first place. But Esme shunned it, klee-klee-kleeing angrily at Korace. Merceron smiled with a look of resignation.

"You don't have the Starfinder yet," he told the Skylords. "If it's in Pandera, then it's under Jorian's protection." He returned Korace's wicked gaze. "Why don't you go and get it?"

"Oh, we will," promised Artaios. "The noose is already closing around Pandera. Rendor won't escape it. But first . . ." He gestured toward Moth. "We have business."

Moth fought his iron grip. "Don't bargain for me, Merceron! Skyhigh . . ."

Skyhigh shook his head. "Moth, you're coming with me. I have a dragonfly ready to fly us both home."

"Us?" Moth looked at Merceron. "What about you? What about Esme?"

"Esme's already home, Moth," said Merceron. His old, reptilian eyes filled with softness. "This is as far as I go."

"What's that mean?" asked Moth desperately.

"They want me, Moth," Merceron explained. "They want me almost as much as they want the Starfinder. That's why you're going home with Skyhigh. And Lady Esme's staying here, where she belongs." He glared at Korace. "That's my bargain, Skylord.

Let the boy go and free Esme from your spell. Do that and I'll end our fight."

"No!" Moth shrieked. He dashed for Merceron, but Artaios quickly snagged his collar. Moth clawed at Artaios, scratching at him before Alis jerked him back. "Let me go! Alis, please!"

"Hold him!" roared Artaios. He loomed over the struggling Moth, his face thunderous. "He gives himself for you, boy. A lowly human! Do not spit on his sacrifice by wailing."

"Artaios, please! He's old. He can't harm you any more . . ."

"No, Moth," Merceron rumbled. "No begging. Not for me." He shuffled closer. "I *am* old. I've already lived a hundred human lifetimes. You haven't even lived once."

"But Merceron, they'll kill you!"

Merceron lifted Esme onto his hand. "They will use me," he said. "Blood for blood and life for life. I told you, Moth—I owe Esme for what she did. Let me do this for her . . .and for you."

"Merceron . . ."

"Say good-bye to me, boy."

Moth couldn't stop his tears. "I *can't*."

"Go with Skyhigh," Merceron insisted. "Don't believe what these beasts say. You're not trapped. Fight your way home!"

Moth wiped his running nose, trying to control himself. With Artaios and all the Skylords watching, he said, "We'll fight them, Merceron. I swear we will!"

Skyhigh stepped toward the throne. "Let me take him. Let me fly him out of here."

Korace waved him away as he sat back on his throne, much more interested in Merceron than another human. Artaios stooped down to face Moth, his wings enfolding them both like a blanket.

"You'll be safe, Egg," he said. His voice was surprisingly sad. "Alisaundra will take you both to the flying machine." He turned to Skyhigh, adding, "Protect him, human. Take him through the Reach. If you don't, you'll face me in Pandera."

Skyhigh smiled mockingly. "Then we'll see each other again."

He took Moth's hand. Alisaundra bowed to her Masters, then urged Moth and Skyhigh out of the chamber. Moth lingered, unable to leave.

"Merceron," he gasped. "I'm sorry . . ."

Skyhigh urged him toward the exit. "We have to go."

"I'm sorry!" cried Moth.

Alis took his arm. "Hurry, hurry. . . ."

Merceron gave Moth one last wink. "I'm not afraid, Moth. Fiona's trick, remember?"

For a second Moth paused, bewildered. Then he remembered, and with a touch of comfort, he nodded.

"Good-bye, Merceron," he choked. "My friend."

ALLIES

MOTH MOVED IN A FOG, following Alisaundra and Skyhigh to the place where the dragonfly waited, a huge platform jutting out from the cliff of Korace's tower. True to Artaios' word, no one had followed or tried to stop them. The platform was eerily quiet, as if all the Skylords in the city had gathered to watch Merceron's death. The dragonfly stood poised at the edge, ready to take flight. Skyhigh hurried to the craft, running his hands over the wings, inspecting it with his critical eye.

"She looks okay," he said, as though he'd expected some sort of sabotage. He popped the canopy and inspected the inside, too. Alisaundra waited, rocking impatiently on her clawed feet. Skyhigh was still talking, but Moth was a million miles away, his thoughts all on Merceron.

They'd left him to die. After Merceron had come all this way to save him, Moth had run away. He realized he was shaking. He hadn't stopped crying, either. He wiped at his cheeks, unable to make sense of things.

"What did he mean?" he asked. "Blood for blood and all that. What did he mean?"

Alisaundra said, "A sacrifice. It takes life to work the changing magic."

"What?" exclaimed Moth. "You mean someone died to change you into what you are?"

"I died," said Alis. "But to change me back would take another life."

"Merceron's life, you mean," said Moth. "For Esme. Skyhigh, did you know this?"

Skyhigh pushed him toward the dragonfly. "Moth, we don't have time. Merceron made his choice. Hurry up. . . ."

"Wait." Alisaundra spun Moth around. "I will come with you."

"Alis?"

"I can help you," said the Redeemer eagerly. "I know the way to Pandera. We can make it quickly."

"Alis, why?" asked Moth. "You're sworn to Artaios."

"Because . . ." Alis searched for an answer. "You need me."

"No way!" Skyhigh jumped in. "I don't even have room for her!"

"Skyhigh, she's right. She can help us," said Moth.

"Are you crazy? She's the one who kidnapped you! Now you want to take this thing with us?"

"She's not a thing, she's a person," argued Moth. He looked at Alis, sure of himself. "She's human."

Skyhigh gave a miserable curse. "Fine," he snapped, "but she needs to keep up with us. We're going full throttle, and there's no room in the dragonfly."

"I can fly faster than your machine," said Alis. "Have you forgotten?"

"Alis, you can come," Moth decided. "But we can't leave yet. Skyhigh, get the dragonfly going. Alis, come with me."

Moth bolted from the platform, back toward the tower. Skyhigh called after him.

"Moth! Where you going?"

Moth shouted back, "Get in the air and wait for us! I'm going back for Comet!"

INTO THE SUN

HIGH ABOVE MERCERON, the Skylords of the palace looked down from the ancient trees and galleries, waiting for his death. The young ones blinked in wonderment, while the veterans of the dragon wars watched, quietly satisfied. Merceron looked back silently at their luminous faces. The sun burned brightly in the sky, warming him. Weary, he succumbed to it.

At last, he would sleep.

He'd done everything right. He tried to remember some regrets, but he had none suddenly, and his clear conscience surprised him. True, Dreojen blamed him, but he no longer blamed himself. And though the Skylords might yet win the Starfinder, Merceron had at least saved Moth.

"Now it's your turn," he told Esme softly. He ran a finger lightly over her feathered back, hoping for one last glimpse of her the way she'd been. In his mind he'd held a picture of her all these years, the most beautiful Skylord he had ever seen. "Soon you'll be whole again, my friend. You'll forgive me for doing this."

Esme's eyes glowed with understanding.

"Dragon," said Artaios. "You give your life for a Skylord. Be proud. Not every dragon is so noble."

"I give my life for a friend," said Merceron, "and not for any of your kind."

Korace reached out from his throne, touching the sword at Artaios' belt. As his fingers brushed the strange metal, the sword began to sing, its vibrations sending an odd light across the floor.

"If you have words, speak them," Artaios told Merceron. He freed the sword from his belt "Be heard now. When I'm done, there will be nothing left of you."

Merceron studied Artaios, then his wizened father, then the arena packed with beautiful, vengeful faces. Did he have words? Should he curse them?

"Just this, then," said Merceron. He raised his voice so that all could hear him. "The sky belongs to everyone. It belongs to the dragons like it does to the clouds. It belongs to any race that can reach it. Even humans."

Korace gave a hiss of contempt. The galleries filled with shouts.

"Clip their wings, but they'll grow back!" Merceron went on. "And if you keep the sky from them—as you've kept it from my own race—they will destroy you for it!"

The hall erupted. Merceron basked in their anger. Artaios slowly raised his sword, his face joyless.

"No pain," he promised. "Close your eyes."

"No," defied Merceron. "I want to see."

With Esme in his upturned palm, he raised her above his head, remembering Fiona's trick . . .

His fear vanished in an instant, replaced by a memory of Elaniel. Once, he had raised Elaniel over his head as well, when his son was just a wyrmling. The thought played like a dream in Merceron's mind.

Fly Elaniel!

And Elaniel had flown.

Artaios touched the sword to Merceron's belly. Along the blade danced the dragon's life force.

A bird she had been, unable to speak with words or to think an entire, complex thought.

Small she had been, for nearly fifty years.

In her tiny, hollow bones, Esme felt the burning. A dazzling, blinding light engulfed her. She felt herself stretching skyward, felt Merceron collapsing. Her wings struggled madly for air. In a maelstrom of fire, an unseen force pulled her apart, raking her flesh. She was unable to fly, and the floor rose up to meet her. Instinctively she stretched her talons as she hit the ground.

Instead, her fingers scratched the stones. All around her swirled the mist, searing her skin. Weak, she lifted her head, about to scream. Her white wings draped her naked body. As the storm subsided, she remembered what she'd been.

And what she was again.

Next to her lay Merceron, lifeless on the floor. All around her stared her people. Esme trembled as she tried to push herself upright with her unused limbs. Her huge, snowy wings were moving with newborn life. She tried to speak but made no sound.

Artaios towered before her. She remembered him and his feeble father. The sword dangled in his hand. He bent to look at her, his eyes wide at what he'd done.

"Can you hear me?"

His voice was like an echo, gradually reaching her foggy mind.

"You're home now," he said. "You are welcome here, *if* you have learned from your punishment."

Past him sat Korace on his silver throne, watching her, waiting for her answer. All that had happened in fifty years came flooding into Esme's mind, giving her a bitter strength. With one mighty effort, she lifted herself.

"Speak," Artaios commanded. "Has your penance made you wiser?"

Esme tilted her face toward the sun. Its kiss fortified her. She stretched her wings, letting the warmth caress her feathers.

"Esme," Artaios warned, "if you leave here, you can never come back."

Esme wasted none of her strength, not even to answer him. Confident, she leaped for the sky, letting her wings beat the air.

"You'll be an outcast forever!" cried Artaios. "Forever, do you hear?"

Esme climbed ever higher, wrapped by the sun's yellow arms. Below her, her people watched in silence. For fifty years she hadn't spoken, her voice magically imprisoned. Now, in a great, exalting song, she released her unbound cry.

CLOSER

FIONA BENT LOW OVER HER grandfather's toolbox, careful not to bang her head in the small control room. A bank of levers covered the nearest wall, webbed with wires and steam conduits. Metal struts hung low across the ceiling—the airship's exposed, riveted skeleton. Fiona rummaged through the wooden box, shunting aside spools of string and discarded hardware.

"Is this it?" she asked, pulling out a small, box-headed wrench. She placed the wrench in Rendor's hand, who knew it instantly by touch.

"That's it," he replied, and the wrench disappeared beneath the console. With only his legs and torso exposed, he began tightening the newly repaired speaking tube.

Fiona sat back, eager to give the tube a try. She had worked on it with her grandfather the entire morning, first removing it, then hammering it back into shape, and now trying to maneuver it back into position. The metal tube rose up from under the console like a hooded cobra, its bendable joints shining and newly oiled. A tulip-shaped mouthpiece covered its other end. Underneath the console, Fiona could hear her grandfather tightening bolts. There wasn't much she understood about the *Avatar*, but she was learning quickly.

"Ready?" she asked.

"Not yet."

Fiona stifled a sigh. If she sounded bored, even a little, he might send her away. There were others who could better help her grandfather. Since recovering from his altitude sickness, he had spent nearly every waking hour with her. They ate together, made inspections of the *Avatar*, sat with the centaurs around their fires at night, and—on brief occasions—even talked.

Mostly, though, they made ready for war. Each day, scouts like Tyrin returned from the mountains with tales of fiery chariots and Redeemers hung with silver chains, of monsters called cloud horses and other, balloonlike beings the centaurs called "ogilorns." These huge, bulbous jellyfish things were as big as the *Avatar*, Jorian claimed, and when he sketched one in the dirt for them, Fiona nearly fainted.

"Purple they are," Jorian had said. "With hanging tentacles twice as long as the rest of them."

Ogilorns were rare, Jorian had told them, from a part of the world no centaur had ever seen. No one knew why they did the Skylords' bidding either, though the Chieftain took a guess.

"Slaves now," he concluded. "Conquered like the dragons."

Fiona thought hard about this as her grandfather finished with the speaking tube.

"Grandfather?"

"Yeah?"

"If an ogilorn is like a jellyfish, then a gun should be able to kill it, right? Like popping a balloon, right?"

"Hope so. Hang on now. Almost done . . ."

"What happens if the *Avatar* gets hit like that? Will it pop like a balloon?"

"You know what happens if an airship gets a hole in it?"

"What?"

"Not much. That's why the envelope's kept at low pressure. Slow leaks only. And the lifting gas is stored in different places. That's all those bladders you see tucked between the stringers. When we're done here I'll show you."

Fiona noticed the way her grandfather's voice changed whenever he spoke about airships. She still didn't have much interest in them—not like Moth, at least—but she loved how excited her grandfather sounded, like a little kid.

"What made you invent the airships?" she asked. "Why'd you want to fly so bad?"

He laughed. "What?"

"Was it your brother and the wings?"

Rendor pushed himself out from beneath the console. He sat up, frowning. "Did I tell you that story?"

"My mom did," Fiona answered.

"Huh. I told that story to Moth before he was captured. Funny you should bring it up."

"Whatever happened to Uncle Conrad?"

Her grandfather smiled sadly. "He died a long time ago, before your mother was born. Bastard never did make me those wings!"

Fiona tried to laugh. She wanted more from her grandfather, about her uncle, about everything, but every time she pushed, the old man made a joke. She flicked a fingernail against the speaking tube.

"Ready now?"

Rendor wiped his oily hands on his pants. "Run down to the bridge. Give it a try."

Fiona crawled out of the control room, then hurried through the narrow corridor toward the bridge, squeezing past others on the way. The *Avatar* was a maze to her, but she managed to find the bridge simply by pointing her nose in the right direction. The space was empty, except for Commander Donnar, who busied himself with a bank of gauges and a note pad. The tarp that covered the broken bridge had been temporarily pulled away, revealing the sun-splashed village and its centaurs, most going about their daily routines, others gathered around Jorian, training for the coming battle. Donnar gave Fiona a cursory nod as she headed for the speaking tube near the navigation deck.

"Hello?" she said, putting her lips to the mouthpiece. "Can you hear me?"

After a moment came her grandfather's reply.

"It works! I can hear you perfectly, Fiona! How do I sound?"

"Fine," said Fiona. "A little echoey."

"That's normal. Keep talking. Tell me what you see."

"Uhm . . ." Fiona looked out the open space where the glass windshield once had been. "I see the village. Jorian's outside with his warriors. They're charging each other, training for the fight."

"Okay. That's good, Fiona."

"Oh, and I see young ones too," Fiona noted. She smiled as she watched a team of little centaurs running along the field beside the older ones. "They're kicking a ball. Huh."

"What?"

"They're just having a good time, is all." Fiona couldn't pull her eyes away. "It's like they don't even know about the trouble coming."

There was a long pause at the other end of the tube. Fiona tapped the mouthpiece.

"Can you still hear me?"

"Yes." The voice was softer now, cautious. "Are you alone on the bridge?"

Fiona glanced at Donnar. The grizzled commander overheard Rendor's question. He nodded at Fiona, okaying her lie.

"Yes," she told her grandfather.

"Move closer to the tube."

Fiona put her face very close. "I am."

Another pause, this one longer than the first. Fiona waited, saying nothing.

"I'm sorry you're stuck here," he said suddenly. "You shouldn't be. I shouldn't have taken you to Calio." He took a shaking breath. "I'm sorry, Fiona. All right?"

Fiona swallowed. "Yes," she answered. She put her ear against the tube and closed her eyes.

"When your mother died . . . you think I didn't want you, but that's not true. I just wanted to be Governor more. My ambition . . ." Rendor struggled with his words. "I was right about the Skylords though. You see that now, don't you, Fiona?"

Fiona nodded. "I do."

He answered with a sigh. Fiona looked at Donnar. The old commander tinkered with his gauges, pretending not to hear.

"Why are you telling me all this?" asked Fiona into the mouthpiece. "Why now?"

"Because you need to know it. You've always needed to know it. Now because . . ." He stopped himself. "Fiona, before, when you asked about the *Avatar* . . ."

"Uh-huh?"

"It wasn't all true. If we pump the envelope too full . . ."

Donnar turned from his work, looking grimly at Fiona.

"Hidrenium changes when its over-pressured," continued Rendor. "If it's shocked by a charge, it explodes."

"Huh?"

"It could make the *Avatar* a flying bomb."

Fiona understood perfectly. "That's crazy! You can't—"

"Skyhigh can get you out of here in his dragonfly, Fiona. The Starfinder too. If it comes to that . . . I'll do what I have to do."

"Skyhigh's gone! And what about you? What about the crew?" Fiona turned to Donnar, who was suddenly rushing toward the broken window. Outside she heard a commotion. "Hold on," she told her grandfather.

All around the village the centaurs were staring skyward. Fiona went to Donnar's side and leaned out over the bridge. A small winged creature hovered high over the village.

"A Redeemer!"

But before Fiona could rush back to the speaking tube, she heard another sound rushing forward, a loud, familiar clanging sound. She turned toward it, stunned to see a dragonfly. Out on the field, Jorian tilted his bow skyward.

"Wait!" cried Fiona. "That's Skyhigh!"

Jorian heard her shout and held his glowing arrow. The Redeemer turned toward the speeding dragonfly. Rendor crashed onto the bridge.

"What's happening?" he asked as he maneuvered for a look.

Fiona couldn't answer. Jorian and his centaurs watched, astounded as Skyhigh's dragonfly screamed overhead. Rendor pointed toward the mountains, toward another object, slower than the dragonfly but much, much larger.

"That's a cloud horse," said Donnar.

Fiona squinted for a better look. Something was riding the creature, barely visible through the sparkling mists. She knew the rider in an instant.

"Unbelievable . . ."

THE BATTLE OF RHOON FALLS

"MERCERON IS GONE."

Fiona could still hear Moth's voice in her head, telling her the news. She would remember the sound of it forever, how he struggled to speak the words, and how a tear dropped from his cheek right onto his shirt. In that moment, all the amazement about his cloud horse evaporated. Even Fiona's grandfather staggered.

Maybe she had known he would die. Maybe she just didn't want to admit it. Without the Starfinder, the old dragon had nothing else to trade, but Fiona had never let herself wonder about that, pretending instead to believe in miracles, stupidly sure that not only Moth and Skyhigh would return, but Merceron with them.

Only he didn't. Just like her parents, Merceron had gone away for good.

To Fiona, there didn't seem much reason to remain with the others. Rendor and Jorian and Skyhigh all had so much to discuss. Even Moth had the cloud horse to tell them about. After endless hours of debate and arguing, Fiona had simply left their "war council," as Jorian called it. Stealing a pen and sheets of paper from Donnar's notepad, she found herself a quiet place away from the heated, pointless talk of battle, deep enough in the woods not to be seen from the village.

Fiona looked up through the trees and saw the moon, anxiously appearing in the dusky sky. Soon, Jorian or Moth or someone else would start to worry and come looking for her.

She shook the pen to start the ink running, and began to write.

"There," whispered Alis, pointing through the trees.

Moth hunched down so Fiona wouldn't see him. Her back was turned against the village as she leaned against a giant, half-dead trunk. Moth hesitated. Fiona had excused herself from the meeting and never come back, but Alis had easily sniffed her out.

"Okay," said Moth softly, "I'll talk to her. Go back to the others, Alis."

The Redeemer looked disappointed. "Let me talk, too. She is afraid of me, perhaps. That is why she hides."

"I don't think so. It's Merceron." Moth gave a wan smile. So far, no one really trusted Alis but him. "Go back to the meeting. They need you. Just tell them we found Fiona and that we'll come soon."

Alisaundra hooked her claws into the silver chain around her waist, thinking. "Merceron offered his life blood for his friend. Within Mistress Esme, Merceron lives on. You should explain that to Fiona."

"Yeah," sighed Moth, himself still stinging from Merceron's death. "It's just . . . that's not how things are where we come from, Alis. Don't you remember? It's hard for humans to believe in magic."

Alis struggled with the notion. "When I am all human again, then I will remember," she said. "I'll remember everything soon."

"You will," Moth promised. "I'll help you. But right now . . ."

Alis put up her hand. "I know. No more talking."

She turned and headed quietly back to the village. Moth considered the distance between him and Fiona. Strewn with dead leaves, there was no way for him to sneak up on her.

"Well?" Fiona called suddenly. "You coming or what?"

She barely raised her head as she spoke, even as Moth approached through the trees. When he reached her, he saw a wrinkled sheet of paper in her lap and a pen moving in her hand.

"Fiona?" He loomed over her. "We were expecting you back. What happened? What are you doing out here?"

"Writing a letter," Fiona replied.

Moth knelt down next to her, realizing why she hid her face. Her usually white cheeks were speckled with red blotches, her eyes puffy from crying. He reached out and touched her shoulder.

"Hey . . ."

Fiona tensed. "I just couldn't stay back there, Moth. All that talk about fighting and death. All those things out there waiting for us. Ogilorns! Whoever heard of a flying jellyfish?"

Moth tried to be gentle. "Fiona, we have to get ready. We can't run and hide." He looked at her. "You know that, right?"

"You mean my castle?" scoffed Fiona. "Yeah, some castle! All I did was bring the centaurs trouble by coming here. That's all any of us did, Moth—we just made trouble for everyone. If we had stayed in Calio . . ."

Her voice trailed off as she looked down at her paper, but Moth knew what she meant.

"Merceron would still be alive."

Fiona swallowed hard. "Yeah."

Moth sat down next to Fiona, getting close as he shared her tree trunk. "Merceron did what he wanted to do, you know. He gave Esme back her life. She's back with her own people now. And Alis says he's still alive in a way, because his life is part of Esme's now."

"She's a Redeemer, Moth. I still can't believe you brought her back here with you."

"She can help us. She knows more about the Skylords than any of us, and she's strong as a dragon! She's the one that put that hole in the *Avatar*."

"And the cloud horse?" asked Fiona. "What are you gonna do with that thing?"

Moth flushed. "Yeah, that was kind of stupid," he admitted. Comet, despite having taken Moth to Pandera, had already disappeared into the mountains. "Maybe she's gone to back to the Skylords. I was hoping she'd stay with me, but that was dumb."

"You could have ridden her out of here, Moth," said Fiona. "You *should* have ridden her out of here, gotten home while you had the chance."

"I am going to get home, Fiona," Moth insisted, "and so are you and Skyhigh and your grandfather—"

"No," said Fiona, shaking her head. "Not my grandfather." Again she couldn't look at him. "He didn't talk about this in the meeting, but he's got a plan, Moth. If we can't beat the Skylords on our own, he's gonna blow up the *Avatar*."

"Yeah, I know," said Moth. "That's what they were talking about when I left."

"Just when I thought I had a family again!" Fiona raised her face to the moon. "Now he's gonna kill himself."

Moth wasn't sure how to comfort her. "An explosion that big . . . it might destroy the Starfinder too. That's what he said, Fiona. He doesn't want the Skylords to get it."

"Crazy! Everyone on the *Avatar* will be dead!"

"He's doing it to save everyone, Fiona. To save *you*."

"I don't want him to!" cried Fiona. "I want him to be alive!"

She thrust down her pen and let the paper tumble from her lap. Moth picked up the letter she'd been writing and read the first few lines.

"What's this?"

Fiona snatched it back. "I told you, it's a letter."

"To whom?"

"To my family."

"Uhm, you don't have a family, Fiona."

Fiona looked exasperated. "Just pretend then, okay? Jorian said we're soldiers now. It's what soldiers do before battle; they write to their families."

Moth didn't understand, but didn't want to embarrass her either. "Who will you send it to when you're done?"

"No one," said Fiona. She picked up her pen again. "Maybe someone will find it someday after this is all over."

"You mean when you're dead?"

"Yeah," said Fiona. "When we're both dead."

Suddenly, Moth remembered something Rendor had told him. "You have no faith, Fiona," he said. "You don't believe in anything, and if you don't believe, we've got no chance at all."

"That's right, Moth, we have no chance," Fiona snorted. "You were at the meeting. Weren't you listening? The Skylords are coming, and all we have is a broken down ship to try and stop them."

"Really?" snapped Moth. "What about Jorian? What about Skyhigh and Alis, even? You don't have faith in any of them!"

Fiona sighed as if talking to a child. "Moth, we're going to die here, just like Merceron. That's why I have to write this letter, to tell people so they know what happened to us."

"Oh," said Moth scornfully. "You think that's what your family would want to hear? That you're scared? That you're about to die? That's *not* what soldiers write in their letters, Fiona. I know, because Leroux told me stories about them."

"Leroux told a lot of stories."

Moth took the pen from Fiona. "This is a story about an Eldrin Knight at the battle of Rhoon Falls."

"Everyone died at Rhoon Falls."

"Right," said Moth, "but there was this one Eldrin Knight that wrote a letter to his mother right before the battle. He told her not to worry, because they had so many men and weapons that their enemies would be crazy to attack them. He told her about the good friends he had in the company, and how he was safe. His mother got the letter a whole day before she found out he'd been killed."

Fiona went blank. "So?"

"Don't you see? His mother had a whole day of happiness. It was like a gift!"

"Moth, he *died*."

"Yeah, but he didn't tell his mother that! He could have written her a letter saying how scared he was, but he didn't. He didn't want her to worry. That's the kind of letter soldiers really write home, Fiona. If you weren't just pretending—if you really had a family to write to—that's the kind of letter you'd write, I bet." Moth handed Fiona back her pen. "I have to get back now," he said. "Don't stay here too long, okay?"

When Moth was finally out of sight, Fiona took her letter and tore it into tiny bits, showering the ground with them. Then, on a second piece of paper, she began again. She wrote for nearly an hour, pausing when her hand cramped, telling her mother and father not to be afraid for her. She wasn't alone, she told them, because she had friends to help her fight. She had a magical centaur named Jorian who could shoot an arrow clear to heaven, and a boy named Moth who wasn't afraid of anything.

Grandfather's here too, she wrote. *He told me he misses you, Mom. I know he won't let anything happen to me.*

When Fiona was finished, she folded the letter neatly one time and placed it under a rock near the tree for anyone to find. Then she stood up, brushed the dirt and grass from her backside, and headed for the village.

SEVEN SOULS

THE TWO-HUNDRED-FOOT OGILORN guarding Mount Oronor blinked its fifty eyes when it spotted Artaios' chariot. Engulfed in the mists crowning the mountain, the monster floated like a massive pink orb before the fortress, its barbed tentacles twisting in the cold air. Six keepers tended the beast—five Redeemers and a single, youthful Skylord. On the far side of Mount Oronor, Artaios could see another ogilorn on guard, it too surrounded by tenders. Culled from the darkest corner of the known world, the ogilorns had come at the order of Artaios himself, joining his thousand-strong army.

Artaios slowly guided his chariot past the massive ogilorn, disturbed by the way its many eyes tracked him through the sky. Ogilorns were violent, unpredictable beasts, known mostly for the way they hunted breeching whales with their blood-sucking tentacles. Artaios' father had used ogilorns, too. Artaios could still remember seeing one peel the skin from a dead dragon.

He arced his fiery chariot wide around the beast, toward its young, flying keeper. The Skylord pointed toward the fortress.

"Great Artaios," he greeted, shouting above the wind. "Rakuiss awaits you!"

Below, the ancient fortress was a hive of activity, with Skylords and Redeemers moving through the avenues, training with weapons and corralling the hordes of cloud horses. Fires belched smoke into the air and tiny, sparkling fairies darted through the foul air. The coming battle had brought the long-dead fortress back to life.

Over his shoulder, Artaios spotted Pandera, defiant behind its wall of mountains. Jorian's own army was on the march. Redeemer spies had been keeping watch over the valley. Rendor and his airship remained in Pandera, and the Starfinder with him. Artaios cast a cool glance toward the valley as his chariot descended. Despite his hopes, Moth was still in Pandera, too.

The chariot settled into a clearing near the main keep. Towers jutted up like teeth from the mountain, spiked with ragged stones. Skylords fluttered around the chariot instantly, each one greeting Artaios. Then, out of the mist another figure approached, his sandaled feet crunching the pebbly ground. He paused near the chariot, crossing an arm over his bent knee as he bowed.

"Magnificence," he greeted. "We are ready."

They were the only words Artaios wanted to hear. He let the reins drop from his hands, and with a flutter of wings vaulted from the chariot to land before his subject, stooping to put a hand on his shoulder.

"Rise, old friend," said Artaios. "Your lord is pleased."

Rakuiss rose, his left eye covered with an eye patch, his right wing bent awkwardly against his back. A veteran of the dragon wars, he was nearly as old as Korace himself, but had managed to stave off time's ravages. His experience and loyalty made him the perfect choice to lead Artaios' army.

"How fares your father?" asked Rakuiss. It was the same question the old warrior always posed, always with genuine concern. If Korace had ever truly had a friend, Rakuiss was it.

"Not well," confessed Artaios. "There aren't many days left for him, my friend. This matter of the Starfinder . . ." Artaios sighed. "It breaks his heart to see the realm at war again."

Rakuiss' good eye twitched. "To be so troubled, after all he has done. We will make Jorian and his abominations pay for this, Artaios. The humans too."

Artaios sagged, offering only a nod.

"What saddens you, Magnificence?" asked Rakuiss. "I promise you, the centaurs have no chance at all. Soon you'll have the Starfinder, I swear it."

Artaios smiled. His troubles had nothing to do with the Starfinder. "Everything you've done here pleases me, Rakuiss."

"What then? You are distressed, my friend, I can tell."

"No," Artaios lied. "Just anxious to have this over."

"Tell me to and I will end it," said Rakuiss. "All we await is your order."

Suddenly it seemed like all the Skylords and Redeemers stopped what they were doing. Artaios glanced around, impressed by the fortress, sure that Rendor and the Starfinder couldn't escape. Oddly, the notion saddened him.

"Soon," he told Rakuiss. "Now, though, let me go and speak with Ivokor."

Artaios picked his way through the giant, filthy cavern, his eyes tearing as he approached Ivokor's workshop. The sound of hammers and chains rattled his skull as he passed bare-chested gargoyles sweating over anvils and urns of liquid metal. Tiny, soot-covered fairies darted through the sulfurous air, their tattered wings barely able to sustain them. Through the haze of smoke Artaios spotted Ivokor across the foundry, hunched over his giant workbench. Pincers and clamps hung from pegs driven into the rock wall. Flecks of metal covered his hairy arms and sparkled in his mane. Dirty-faced fairies fluttered around him, handing off tiny tools. Ivokor growled as he ordered them about, barely missing them with swipes of his meaty paw.

"Ivokor," bellowed Artaios. As he approached, he kept his wings tucked carefully against his back, afraid to brush or damage them against anything. Ivokor raised his feline head in surprise, letting a jeweler's loupe drop from his eye.

"Artaios," he said, wiping his grimy paws against his heavy apron. "Why didn't anyone tell me you were here?" he griped, batting at the fairies.

"You're getting old, Ivokor," said Artaios. "You should have been able to smell me."

"Who can smell anything down here?" Ivokor tossed aside his tiny hammer and waved Artaios closer. "Come. It is done."

The fairies scattered as Artaios approached. Ivokor stooped and pulled a large metal chest from beneath his workbench, squatting down beside it, his tail swaying excitedly. Ivokor had the head of a lion and the strength of one too. His golden arms bulged with muscles, the same arms that had hammered out Artaios' magic sword.

"I finished it just last night," he said proudly. He waited until Artaios was hovering over the chest. "This time, I know I got it right."

"Open it," said Artaios impatiently.

A flick of Ivokor's fingernail snapped the latch. Slowly, he opened the lid, revealing its dazzling contents. Artaios drew back, his eyes stabbed by escaping light. A golden glow poured from the chest, bathing Ivokor's feline face.

"Seven souls," he said, his voice crackling with pride. "Seven lives, just for you."

Artaios beheld the golden armor, his fingers reaching for it through the shimmering. The breastplate pulsed with life. He could feel its soft heat, like breath against his hand. As his fingers touched the enchanted metal, the seven souls encased within it called out to him, singing in his mind.

"I feel them," he whispered. He closed his eyes as he listened to the ghostly chorus. "So strong . . ."

"They will protect you, Artaios," said Ivokor. "Seven times. That's all. Seven shots from Jorian's bow is all you can withstand."

Artaios held the breastplate up to his face, studying himself in its polished surface. The metal swirled with golden hues, the very essence of the sacrificed Redeemers. They were loyal, he realized, and none of them had been forced to give their lives for him. They had done so willingly.

Loyal, thought Artaios. *Not like Alisaundra.*

"Seven souls," he said softly. "Seven shots."

"That's right, and not a single one more," said Ivokor. "Let the others do the fighting for you, Artaios. Stay as far away from Jorian as you can."

"What?" Artaios glared at Ivokor. "Perhaps I should just go home to the palace. Would that be cowardly enough for you?"

"I'm serious," grumbled the smith. "Seven shots is all this armor can take. On the eighth you'll be dead."

Artaios gently placed the breastplate back into the chest.

"You forget who you're speaking to, Ivokor. Jorian will be the one laying dead, long before he fires seven arrows." He closed the lid of the chest with a sigh.

"Artaios?" probed Ivokor. His cat-eyes narrowed. "You're not happy?"

"Yes, yes, I'm happy, Ivokor," Artaios snapped. "I'm thrilled beyond words. I'm so happy I could dance!"

"My lord . . ."

"No, enough." Artaios stopped himself, feeling foolish. "The armor is fine. Better than fine. It's just . . ." He hesitated. "The humans, Ivokor."

Ivokor looked puzzled. "What about them?"

"I'm to kill them. All of them." The confession made Artaios wilt. "It's my father's will."

"I'm confused," said Ivokor. He leaned against his grimy workbench. "Isn't that why we're all here? To kill the humans, get back the Starfinder?"

"There are children, Ivokor." Artaios toyed with a box of rivets on the bench, twirling his finger through them. "One of them . . ."

Again he paused. Why was he so bothered about Moth?

"What?" pressed Ivokor. "One of them what?"

"Never mind." Artaios mustered a smile. "Thank you, Ivokor. You've done a magnificent job."

Ivokor regarded him strangely. "Just remember what I told you, all right? Seven shots."

"I can count," said Artaios crossly. "Have the armor brought up to my tower." He shook out his wings, disgusted by the sooty air. "I have to go. This place sickens me."

THE MOON IS HIGH

LIKE A FAINT, SHIMMERING STAR, Moth could see Mount Oronor from his place in the grass, aglow with fire. Next to him sat Fiona, cross-legged on the ground, and next to her sat her grandfather. Behind Rendor sat the entire crew of the *Avatar*, surrounded by the centaurs of Pandera, every one of them entranced by the image of Jorian framed against the night. The moon was high over Jorian's head, bathing his painted face and braided hair. Across his naked chest was strung his magic bow, throbbing with preternatural light. Mount Oronor loomed ominously over his shoulder, but Jorian was unafraid. In his hand he held a pot of crimson pigment.

All day long centaurs had waited for the moon to rise, to call them out to the grassy plain and hear the words of their Chieftain. They watched Mount Oronor, the fortress of their enemies, jeering at it, casting curses. They lit their own fires and beat their drums and danced their strange centaur dances. And now they were ready for war.

The drums were now silent; Moth could hear the wind rustling in the grass as he awaited Jorian's call. Tonight, he and Fiona would be warriors. Skyhigh and Rendor, too. He glanced at his friends, saw their grave faces, and remembered Leroux. Alisaundra crouched nearby, fascinated by the spectacle. She had watched the dances, asking questions of the centaurs like a curious child, and when she saw Moth looking at her, she smiled a big-sister smile.

"Tomorrow," Jorian boomed, "our enemies will fly against us. They are many, but we too are many. They are strong, but we are stronger!"

His voice carried over the crowd, chilling Moth with its power. His wife Nessa stood apart from Jorian, nodding proudly.

"We fight to defend what is ours," declared Jorian. "The Skylords fight only to take. They have slaves, but we have friends." His gaze fell upon Moth and his fellow humans. The crowd cheered approvingly. "Now we invite our friends to join us, to share our blood and sacrifice." He held up the little pot, the same red paint he'd used to stripe his own fierce face. "Are you ready?"

Fiona was first on her feet, setting aside the bow Jorian had made her. "I'm ready," she said, loud enough so all could hear her.

In a strange, ancient tongue, Jorian spoke. Though Moth didn't understand the words, they'd already been explained to him.

"Come forth this way toward me, to the place where I stand. Come forth this way toward me. Come straight toward me."

The ritual words were the ones every centaur heard once they were old enough to fight. As Fiona stepped forward, Rendor stood to watch her, his expression unreadable. To Moth he looked like an Eldrin Knight suddenly. Moth and Skyhigh stood as well, waiting their turn. Alisaundra shuffled closer to stand beside them. No one made a sound.

"Fiona, granddaughter of Rendor, friend to the centaurs of Pandera," said Jorian, "do you declare yourself a warrior?"

Fiona lifted her white face, catching the moonlight. "I do."

Jorian looked into her face, at the pattern the moon made on her, searching for the essence inside her. It might be a wolf, Nessa had told them, or it might be a river. It could be a tree, a butterfly, a flower, or a storm. The moon would reveal it. Fiona waited, never taking her eyes off Jorian, until at last the Chieftain saw the invisible spirit within her. He dipped his already stained finger into the pot, then traced it over Fiona's face.

"I see wisdom in you," he said as he drew. "A great fire of knowledge. I see bigness. I see nobility."

When he was done he looked at his work. Satisfied, he turned Fiona toward the gathering. Moth looked closely, eager to see the thing Jorian had drawn. Two batlike wings framed her face, and over her eyes were another pair, cool and reptilian. Moth had seen eyes like them before.

"A dragon," he whispered, almost incredulous. He beamed at Fiona, who seemed as shocked as he was by what Jorian had seen.

Now it was Moth's turn. He went to Jorian and turned his face toward the moon, just as he'd seen Fiona do. When the Chieftain asked for his oath, he gave it proudly. He felt the moonlight on his face, the strange sensation of Jorian's eyes boring deep into his soul. This wasn't just a guessing game, he realized. Jorian had real magic, and would find whatever was inside him.

"I see," Jorian said, squinting as he studied Moth's face. "I see . . ."

What? Moth wanted to shout. *What do you see?*

Jorian dipped his finger into the pot. As he raised it a horrible screech pealed overhead. Moth turned to see a large, misshapen bird fluttering above the crowd, its storm-grey wings beating the air. A shockingly human head bobbed out of its feathered collar. Part vulture, part woman, the thing gave a cackling laugh as it descended, hovering just out of reach.

"Harpy!" spat Jorian.

The centaurs rose, drawing weapons. Alisaundra sprung to her feet, and Rendor pulled his pistol. Old Kyros quickly drew a bead on the creature with his bow.

"Dead you are!" laughed the creature. "Dead on the morrow!"

Alisaundra was almost in the air, claws bared, when Jorian called out, "No!" He waved his arms to calm them. "This monster brings a message!"

The harpy laughed. "The mercy of Artaios! That is what I bring!"

Moth had never seen a thing so ugly. Huge, bulbous claws hung down from its mottled body. A hint of breasts rose beneath its feathers. Saliva threaded from its female lips as it spoke, mimicking a human voice. The head was nearly bald, hairy in spots, vulture pink in others.

"Traitor!" it said, leering mockingly at Alisaundra. "Artaios has his vengeance planned for you. Unending suffering!"

Alisaundra's fangs sprang out. "Speak your message," she hissed, "then die."

Her anger delighted the harpy. It fluttered higher, right over Moth and Fiona. Rendor aimed his pistol, ready to fire. "Jorian . . ."

"No, she won't harm them," said Jorian. He glared up at the creature. "You're nothing but an errand girl. Skylords send the foulest muck to speak for them."

The harpy flew closer to Rendor, taunting him with its talons. "You are the law breaker," it said. "Human. Spreader of plagues. No mercy for you."

Rendor's finger trembled on the trigger. "I know all about Skylord mercy, miscreant. Want to see mine?"

Skyhigh rushed forward. "Rendor, don't!"

The harpy bubbled, "Bring him the Starfinder! Artaios is kind. Give him what is his, and only the humans will die."

"Not only humans," retorted Jorian. He patted the bow at his chest in warning. "Tomorrow, Skylords will fall."

"Spare yourselves this misery!" called the harpy. She hovered toward Jorian. "Give Artaios the Starfinder, and he will spare these children both! He gives his word on this, centaur. Surrender the Starfinder. For that you get your lives, and the lives of these worthless pups."

Moth saw a flash of weakness in Rendor's eyes. Slowly he lowered his pistol.

"No!" cried Moth. "If Artaios wants us, tell him to come and get us!"

"Right," Fiona echoed. She pointed at her painted face. "You see this? I'm a warrior of Pandera now. I'm like a dragon! Tell the Skylords the dragons aren't finished yet. They aren't beaten. Tell them Merceron is still alive . . . in me!"

Rendor stepped toward her. "Fiona . . ."

"She has spoken," thundered Jorian. "Rendor, we are not slaves, any of us." He looked up at the harpy, and with a snort of disgust said, "Go and tell your master Pandera is for free people. Tell him we are warriors. If he wants the Starfinder so badly, tell him to come and die for it."

The harpy beat its wings in frustration. "Tomorrow, then," it spat. "Be ready for blood."

From the corner of his eye Moth saw Alisaundra spring skyward. Both hands shot out, grabbing the harpy by the neck.

"You are done, messenger!" she growled.

In a frenzy of wings she bore the harpy higher, throttling it until feathers fell like rain. The harpy screamed, bones popped, and the creature fell limp in Alis' claws.

"Alis!" Moth called, but it was too late. She was already flying off, carrying her victim with her.

"Where's she going?" asked Fiona.

Rendor stuffed his pistol back beneath his coat. "To deliver a message of her own, probably."

Stunned, Moth watch her disappear into the darkness, winging her way toward Mount Oronor. He didn't move until Jorian touched his shoulder. He held up his paint pot.

"Say it again, boy. Do you declare yourself a warrior of Pandera?"

Moth stiffened with resolve. "I do!"

As the gathering watched, Jorian traced his cool finger over Moth's face. Purposefully, quickly, the centaur drew, as if Moth's essence was perfectly clear to him now. Moth didn't move, not even to blink. He felt the presence of something inside him, rising up like a . . .

Like a bird!

Jorian stepped back. Fiona looked at Moth and smiled. Skyhigh grinned with a knowing nod.

"What is it?" asked Moth. "It's a bird, right?"

"It is a bird," said Rendor. He came in for a closer look. "Yes, absolutely."

"Ha! I knew it! What is it? An eagle? A hawk?"

"I know that bird," said Skyhigh.

"Yeah?" Moth looked at each of them, puzzled. "Well? What is it?"

Fiona took his hand. Her painted face glowed with warmth. "It's a kestrel, Moth," she said. "Just like Lady Esme."

BEAUTIFUL

ARTAIOS PASSED THE TWO REDEEMERS on guard outside the prison cave, peering inside. Moonlight flooded through the entrance, seeping through the bars at the other side of the small chamber. As Artaios' eyes adjusted to the darkness, he caught a glimpse of Alisaundra balled up in the corner of her cell, head buried in her knees, wings wrapped like a blanket around her body.

Her return had shocked Artaios. So had the "gift" she'd dropped at Rakuiss' feet. Rakuiss stood behind Artaios now, muttering in contempt.

"Look at her. Still just human garbage."

The old General had begged for the honor to execute her. Artaios took a step into the prison cave, standing imperiously before the cell, his hand resting on the pommel of his sword. Alisaundra had been driven mad by her closeness to Moth. Artaios understood that, even blamed himself a little. He wondered what it was like for her, caged in such an ugly body.

"Alisaundra," he called softly.

He waited for her to lift her head. She did so shyly, her eyes peeking out from her arms.

"You murdered my messenger," said Artaios. "Why?"

Her voice quavered. "Because—"

"Stand up!" barked Rakuiss. "You're talking to the Prince of the Sky!"

Alisaundra rose shakily. She hooked her claws onto the silver chain around her waist, lowering her eyes to the filthy floor.

"Answer me," said Artaios. "Why did you kill the harpy? Why did you betray me?"

"The boy maddened me, Great One. My head filled with human thoughts!" Alis put her claws to her temples. "So many voices! But I came to my senses. When I saw the harpy . . ." She raised her eyes pleadingly, looking only at Artaios. "My lord should never have such a filthy beast speak for him. I am your messenger! Seeing the harpy broke the human spell. I belong to you, sweet Artaios."

Rakuiss snorted, unimpressed. "She betrayed you, Artaios. She has to die."

Alis didn't flinch. "If that is your wish I will do it myself. Give me a dagger and I will slice open my guts for you!"

"Lies," hissed Rakuiss. "Kill her and be done with it, Artaios. We have work to do."

Artaios thought a moment, considering Alisaundra's pitiful face, the depth of her words. For years he had favored her, the brightest of all his Redeemers. Despite her crimes, he was glad she had returned.

"Do you wish to serve me, Alisaundra?" he asked. "Truly, is that the fondest dream of your heart?"

"Oh yes, my lord," sighed Alisaundra. "It is all I wish!"

"My lord, please! Don't fall for this!"

"Wait," counseled Artaios, smiling at his friend. "Wait." He stepped closer to the cell, looking at Alisaundra through the bars. "There is a breastplate of armor, made for me by Ivokor himself. Within its metal is held the souls of seven Redeemers. All true servants, Alisaundra. My best, most beloved slaves. If you are truly repentent . . ."

"I will join them gladly, Master!" Alisaundra floated toward the bars. "Let me prove myself. Let me be your most devoted one!"

"You'll give yourself freely? To live forever in a prison of metal?"

"Yes!"

"Swear it, Alisaundra."

"I swear it, my lord!" Alisaundra grabbed hold of her chain again. "By this chain I swear it!"

"On your knees," Artaios commanded.

Alisaundra dropped before the bars, bowing her head. "Tell me what I must do," she begged. "Tell me how to please you forever."

Her golden hair caught Artaios' notice. She had brushed it clean of dirt, probably to seem more human.

"I am merciful," he told her. "I can end your pain. All you must do is give me your soul."

Alisaundra began to weep. "My lord is gracious. My beautiful lord . . ."

Artaios reached between the bars, gently kneading her hair. Her whole body shook with sobs. "Dear Alisaundra," he sighed. "Soon this torment will be over."

"Yes," she groaned, raising her tear-stained face. She took his hand and kissed it, rubbing his palm on her wet cheek. "Soon . . ."

Artaios felt his arm wrenched from its socket. His face collided with the bars. Pain shot through his skull and shoulder. Rakuiss was screaming. With his eyes bulging, Artaios saw Alisaundra's rising, hissing face.

"I remember everything!" she rasped.

Artaios fought to free himself. Alisaundra's claws dug into his flesh, pinning him to the bars, forcing him through them. He screamed for help, his wings shooting out in panic.

"Look at what you did to me!" she commanded. "Look! I was human once! I was beautiful and I had everything!"

Her raging face filled Artaios' vision. Pain overwhelmed him, his screams bouncing wildly through the chamber. Rakuiss was cursing, pulling hard on his waist to free him. The Redeemers on guard bounded forward.

"I had a daughter!" seethed Alisaundra. "She came with me into the Reach! What did you do with her? What did you do!"

Artaios tried to talk but couldn't. With a broken jaw, he could only scream. Half his shoulder was already in the cell, squeezed through the bars. Furiously he beat his wings, fighting to save himself.

"I was beautiful," she said again. Finally, she extended one claw. "Now it's your turn to be ugly!"

Like a razor she drew her claw down his face, down his eye, his cheek, and his chin. The skin opened up, gushing blood. With a great laugh she released him, falling away from the bars as the others pulled him to safety. Artaios crumpled, covering his face. Through his bloody fingers he saw Alisaundra through the bars, pleased with what she'd done.

"For my daughter," she spat at him. "For all of us!"

The Redeemers flung open the gate, grabbing hold of her. Alisaundra didn't fight them. As Rakuiss stalked toward her, she grinned.

"Stop!"

Through pain and blindness, Artaios struggled to his feet. His face burned, the open wound sluicing blood across his neck and white garments. He pulled his sword, staring hatefully at Alisaundra. The Redeemers pinned her arms, holding her, but she didn't resist. Instead, her expression was serene.

"Kill me," she jeered. "You only send me to my daughter."

With one touch of his gleaming sword, Artaios granted her wish.

ONE WAY OR ANOTHER

IN THE PREDAWN DARKNESS outside the village, Moth, Fiona, and a thousand centaurs watched the airship *Avatar* start its noisy engines. The centaurs had worked throughout the night, moving their children and supplies out of the village, into the distant hills where they'd be safe from the invasion. Nessa, Jorian's wife, would be in charge of them now, promising the Skylords a "death of thousand cuts" if they followed the young ones into the hills. Jorian said a proud good-bye to his wife as he watched Nessa and a handful of warriors disappear with the children, but Moth could tell he was worried. The Chieftain's painted face lost all its tenderness as he turned to Rendor.

"When you are high enough, we will follow," said Jorian.

Fiona stood beside him, watching her grandfather with wide, troubled eyes. "I can come with you," she said. "I'm not afraid."

Rendor stooped down, taking her hand. The wash from the *Avatar*'s engines stirred his silver hair. "Remember what Merceron did for Moth?" he said. "He lived a good life and no one needed to cry for him. That's what I want, Fiona—no tears."

"I'm smart," said Fiona, "and I'm tougher than you think. I can help you up there."

"Your mother died in an airship, Fiona." Rendor struggled with his words. "I've already lost a daughter. If I lost a granddaughter too . . ." He shook his head. "You can't follow me, Fiona. Not where I'm going." He pointed toward the mountains.

"Right into their heart," he declared, so everyone could hear. "We'll punch a hole right through them. One way or another."

They all knew what he meant. No one dared a single word, except for Fiona.

"You'll come back," she said. "I know you will."

Old Rendor frowned. "To promise you that would be an insult, Fiona. A lie. Don't make me say that."

Fiona looked up at him. "Promise to try, at least?"

Rendor bent to kiss her forehead. Moth watched as Fiona's face twisted, forcing herself not to cry. Skyhigh waited anxiously beside Moth, eager to get airborne. This time, at last, Moth would join him in the air.

"There'll be plenty for you to do up there," Skyhigh had told him. "I'm gonna need help once the shooting starts."

Like Fiona, Moth didn't hesitate in joining the battle. With the image of the kestrel still splashed across his face, he was as eager as the rest of them to take on the Skylords. The centaurs had gathered and the *Avatar* was ready to fly. Artaios and his airborne army had yet to appear over the mountain, but dawn was coming quickly now. The centaurs stood in the tall grass, waiting for their Chieftain Jorian to lead their bloody charge. Over the mountains hung the Skylords and their countless slaves—Redeemers and dark fairies and the unspeakable ogilorns.

And there stood the *Avatar*, damaged but graceful, her committed crew ready to blow themselves to bits, and the Starfinder with them. Moth felt a lump settle in his throat, vowing never to forget the feeling and the way it made his skin tingle.

"Skyhigh," said Rendor. He dug into his coat and pulled out his pistol, handing it over.

"What this for?" Skyhigh asked.

"Take it," Rendor urged. "If you get shot down, you'll need more than your knife to fend them off."

Skyhigh nodded, understanding. "Thanks," he said, tucking the pistol into his belt. He turned to Moth. "You ready?"

Moth nodded quickly. Skyknights never said good-bye when they took off, so he didn't. He simply followed Skyhigh to their dragonfly, cracking his knuckles and trying hard to keep from turning around and seeing Fiona's heartbroken face.

* * *

At three thousand feet the *Avatar* leveled off above Pandera, just as the sun clawed over the mountains. Rendor strapped himself into his chair and stared out the open bridge, now stripped of its useless tarp. The dark world greeted him with a chilly wind and the ominous sight of Mount Oronor. Just behind Rendor sat Donnar with the rest of the bridge crew, busily checking gauges and delivering orders into a speaking tube. Tinny voices replied from every section of the ship. Bottling sat at his engine console, a single, steady hand lingering over the hidrenium lever. Lieutenants Stringfellow and Gann worked the *Avatar*'s flight controls.

The Starfinder rested in a lockbox near Rendor's feet. After all his years of coveting it, Rendor could barely look at it now. Once it had been beautiful to him. Now it was just an ugly reminder of all the troubles he'd brought his family. He realized he was full of regrets, but there wasn't time to explore any of them. And at least there was one thing he'd done perfectly—building the *Avatar*.

She was bristling with weapons, stripped of everything but guns and ammunition. Riflemen waited in her nose and viewing platforms, on the catwalks flanking her envelope and in the vents near her tailfins. She was no longer a ship of ambition and exploration. Now she was a warship. Her metal skin could take blow after blow and still she would fly. Even with one damaged engine, she would sail like a dagger into the black heart of the Skylords.

One way or another, thought Rendor as he gazed at Mount Oronor.

Finally, he turned away from the mountains and regarded his crew. Hand-picked, they had all known the odds the moment they'd come on board.

"Airmen," he said, "we're going straight at 'em. And if our guns don't take them out, we've got a nasty surprise for them. We won't be heroes and we won't be martyrs. Unless and until it's hopeless, we fight on."

Old Donnar nodded. Young Stringfellow did the same. Bottling's face turned hard like cement, and Gann held his breath.

Rendor knew they were ready. Now, at last, he'd find out what a bullet could do to a Skylord.

"Commander Donnar," he said, "make your speed fifteen knots."

As she looked up at her distant grandfather, Fiona felt like she was stuck at the bottom of the world. For the first time *ever*, she wanted to be with him. Around her the centaurs formed their marching hordes, each one fifty strong and shaped like an arrowhead. Jorian himself stood in the middle of his warriors. Bow in hand, flanked by Kyros and Tyrin, he observed his brothers and sisters with a prideful gaze. Around his neck hung a horn of carved ivory. Seeing the *Avatar* depart, he put the horn to his lips and blew a loud and forceful call. The thousand centaurs clapped their hooves to the ground.

"Centaurs!" cried Jorian, raising both fists like a wrestler. "Pull our enemies from the sky! From this day on, let it be known that the Skylords are mortal!"

The cheers from the centaurs shredded the air. Fiona clutched the bow Jorian had made her, the one she had practiced with for days.

"I'm ready," she declared. "Tell me where to go and I'll follow."

Jorian reached down, offering his powerful hand. "You ride with me, Little Queen."

She looked at him, stunned. "You mean *on* you?"

He opened his palm insistently. Fiona grabbed hold, and Jorian tossed her onto his back. He shook his black mane, squaring his shoulders at the sensation of Fiona's weight. Tyrin smiled but did not laugh. Old Kyros snorted. Fiona quickly pulled her bow over her shoulder, then wrapped her arms around Jorian's torso. In all the world, Fiona knew, there was no safer place than on the mighty centaur's back.

"Thank you, Jorian," she whispered in his ear, then squeezed him with a little hug. The affection made the Chieftain bridle.

"Hold on to me tightly," he warned. "When a centaur charges, even the mountains cower."

* * *

From a tower on Mount Oronor, Artaios looked upon the rising sun, his heart filled with melancholy. The human airship was aloft now, the tiniest of dots on the horizon. Around him flew his army, culled from every corner of the Realm. Three enormous, hideous ogilorns floated out beyond the mountains, their soft, bloated bodies a sickening shade of pink. Skylords and Redeemers perched on the balconies and ridges of the fortress, and dark fairies fluttered like starlings across the dawn, released from their prison in the foundry, their tiny, needlelike swords swishing in their dainty fists.

Artaios gazed through the eyeslits in his helmet. The sun rose with the color of blood.

Ivokor's armor wrapped his torso like a steel cage, holding together his fractured bones. Beneath his helmet his face burned with the scar Alisaundra had given him, and his eye stung with the damage, swollen and drooping. His right shoulder, dislocated, could barely wield his sword, and his right wing was fractured too, almost enough to keep him grounded. He was, he knew, lucky to be alive, and if Alisaundra had wanted to kill him she could have done so easily. But she did not. She had wanted to maim him, to destroy that part of him that was uniquely Skylord.

A figure dropped from the air behind him. General Rakuiss waited a moment before speaking. Artaios did not turn around. Even with the helmet to hide him, Artaios found facing anyone difficult.

"My lord? The airship . . ."

"I see it," Artaios sighed. His gaze shifted toward the ship as it floated ever closer. Artaios rested his hand on his sword. "I haven't the stomach for this, Rakuiss," he confessed. "Centaurs aren't dragons. This will be a slaughter. And the humans . . ."

"The humans have the Starfinder, my lord." Rakuiss came closer, putting his lips to Artaios' ear. "It's your father's wish, remember. End it here, before they come again."

"It won't end here, Rakuiss. Even if we kill them all, there will be others. They'll keep on coming through the Reach, or we'll go to their world to destroy them. And it will go on endlessly. Forever."

Rakuiss put a hand a hand upon his wounded shoulder. "You are the Sword of Korace," he reminded.

Artaios smiled. "Of course. And like a sword I will cut them down. I'll make my father proud today, Rakuiss. After all, that's what matters, right? My father's pride?"

Rakuiss looked suspicious. "Yes, my lord. We must all remember that."

"Rakuiss, how could I ever forget?"

He turned away from his general, took one last look at the rising sun, then lifted himself into the sky, his wounded wing and shoulder on fire with pain. One way or another, he would lead his army to victory. First, though, he would find the one called Skyhigh Coralin. That one, he decided, would be the first to die.

BATTLE

RENDOR WATCHED THROUGH the open bridge as a wave of feathers and scales rushed at them. He hunched over his chair, pulled a speaking tube to his lips, and waited for their chance to fire. One gigantic ogilorn had been unleashed against them, floating toward them and surrounded by Skylords and Redeemers. The small fairies with the tiny swords flocked like birds behind the ogilorn, urging it forward. A mass of tentacles reached across the sky, ready to grab the *Avatar*. The riflemen stationed on the bridge brought up their guns, choosing their marks.

"One good shot is all we're going to get before they swarm us," said Rendor into the tube. "Hold for my order."

His voice echoed through the airship. In the nose and on the platforms, airmen trained their weapons on the monster. Past its many, outstretched arms, Rendor saw the creature's toothy beak.

"Not yet . . ."

The *Avatar* continued forward, its engines whining. Rendor remembered the stories Merceron had told him, how the ogilorns were vicious but stupid. The thing came mindlessly toward them, proving Merceron's theory.

"Hold . . ."

The sky ahead filled with flailing arms. The Skylords veered away, knowing what was coming.

"Fire!"

All at once a hundred fingers squeezed their triggers. The

Avatar shook as the sky filled with lead and tracers. The ogilorn instantly drew back, screeching, its tentacles recoiling, sieved with bloody holes. On the bridge the crouching riflemen pulled their smoking bolts, loaded up new rounds, and fired again.

"Keep firing!" Rendor cried into the tube. He swiveled his chair toward Bottling. "All ahead! Keep after it!"

Bottling pushed the throttles and the *Avatar* lurched forward, hunting the wounded ogilorn. Skylords and Redeemers wheeled, arcing away from the deadly bullets.

Beneath the *Avatar*, the centaurs tilted a thousand arrows skyward. Sitting astride Jorian's back, Fiona drew hard on her own bowstring, aiming toward the center of the swirling mass of Skylords. She had watched the *Avatar* open fire on the ogilorn, sending the creature retreating in a hail of gunfire. The Skylords and Redeemers spread out across the sky, massing to decend upon the valley. Fiery chariots wheeled high above the fray, drawn by cloud horses and carrying the Skylord generals.

Jorian searched the sky for Artaios, a magic arrow sparkling in his fist. Next to him, Kyros took control of their horde, ordering the centaurs to hold their fire.

"Wait!" cried the old centaur. "Not until you can put one in their hearts!"

Fiona didn't know how long she could hold back her bowstring. The fingers of her hand ached as she pulled back, determined to send the arrow as high as it could go. Somewhere in the sky a trumpet sounded. The Skylords broke formation, screaming down from heaven like a flock of deadly angels. Fiona closed one eye, focused on a single mass of streaking feathers, and waited for Kyros' order. Jorian held still beneath her, choosing his own, unlucky target.

"I'm ready," said Fiona desperately. "I can't hold it . . ."

"Now!" cried Kyros.

Arrows rocketed up from the valley. Fiona loosed her bowstring.

Moth kept watch through the dragonfly's canopy, holding tight as the craft nosedived after the Skylords. An eruption of arrows rose up, whistling past their delicate glass wings. Over Skyhigh's shoulder, Moth could see the Skylords and Redeemers starting to fall, tumbling earthward. The ground was quickly rising to meet them, filled with shouting centaurs. Moth swiveled about, looking out for anything that had broken away to attack them.

"You're clear!" he shouted.

Skyhigh had his finger on the trigger. About to fire, he hesitated.

"What are you doing?" Moth pressed. "Shoot!"

"Moth, listen. You're gonna see some stuff you're not going to like. It's not like Leroux told you. There's gonna be blood . . ."

"Skyhigh, you're telling me this *now*? C'mon, shoot 'em!"

Almost in a full dive, Skyhigh caught a flock of Skylords in his gunsights. "Guess you'll just have to see for yourself." He pulled the trigger, and the Skylords exploded. Blood and feathers struck the canopy as the dragonfly corkscrewed away. Above Moth's head, a crimson smear stained the canopy. He stared at it, stricken.

"Do I have your attention now?"

"Oh, god, I'm gonna be sick!"

"You're a kid, Moth," said Skyhigh. "I wish you didn't have to see any of this. Now keep a lookout, will ya? Or we'll be the ones in pieces."

Artaios circled high above the battlefield, safe from the arrows and bullets, searching the ground for Jorian. Even with his spectacular vision, it was hard for him to make out the Chieftain from so far away. The centaurs had spread across the field like berserkers, pumping the sky with arrows and leaping up to snatch low-flying Redeemers. The airship drove madly toward Mount Oronor, ripping holes in the soft flesh of the ogilorn. In all his years and all his battles, Artaios had never seen such carnage. He'd expected the airship to be no more difficult to stop than a dragon.

He knew now he was wrong.

Too stupid to understand its impending death, the ogilorn stopped retreating, absorbing the airship's onslaught. To the south and east, the remaining ogilorns decended toward the centaurs. Without the airship and its weapons, Artaios knew the centaurs had no chance at all. As he wheeled above the fray, his eyes searched frantically for Jorian. Below, the thing Moth called a dragonfly chased his fellow Skylords, slaughtering them with its guns.

Artaios' cracked ribs throbbed inside his bewitched armor. His eyes tracked the dragonfly over the battlefield, careful not to drop too low and be sighted by Jorian. Wind pulled the golden hair under his helmet. The rush of air against his wings reminded him he was a god.

"I am the Sword of Korace," he told himself. "I am not afraid of anything."

Like a hunting raptor, he tucked his wings and dove for the dragonfly.

Fiona held tight to Jorian's mane as the centaur galloped out to clearer ground. Overhead the sky buzzed with dirty-faced fairies, swooping down upon the centaurs with their icicle-like swords. Tyrin ran furiously alongside his Chieftain. The young warrior had cast aside his bow and shield, slicing up the air with a pair of curved swords, cutting fairies in half as they tried to reach Fiona. Old Kyros followed close behind, covering their run with arrows. Fiona watched as a brown-cloaked Redeemer plunged toward them. From the corner of her eye she saw another centaur gallop forward, spring like a jack rabbit into the air, and smash the Redeemer unconcious with his shield.

"Jorian, where are we going?" Fiona shouted. "Don't take me away! I'm not afraid!"

Jorian laughed. "You fear nothing, Little Queen, I know! Look at the sky! Do you see?"

Fiona searched the battle above. She saw Skyhigh's dragonfly arcing through the sky, spurts of gunfire cutting down Skylords. And then another object caught her eye, making a meteoric dive toward the dragonfly. Before Fiona could ask what it was, Jorian pulled an arrow from his quiver. He nocked the bolt and drew back, turning it to lightning.

"Watch, Fiona," he crowed. "The fall of Artaios!"

* * *

Artaios passed Rakuiss' chariot, plummeting through a flock of fairies and the mist of cloud horses as he headed toward the dragonfly. Closer, closer he came, falling from the sky, homing in on the craft and unsheathing his flaming sword. Today, there was only one thing Artaios wanted, and it wasn't the Starfinder.

"Coralin!"

Coralin, Moth's hero. Coralin, who'd refused to take Moth home to safety. Without remorse, Artaios steeled himself for the killing blow. The human had been warned.

Then from the ground rose a sudden burst of light. Artaios veered quickly, glimpsed the thing as it screamed toward him.

Nowhere to hide . . .

He closed his eyes, hanging in the air, bracing for Jorian's arrow. It slammed into his breastplate with a shower of hot sparks. Artaios tumbled, nearly dropping his sword. The agonized wail of a Redeemer's soul tore from his armor.

One gone!

Artaios fanned his wings to right himself. One gone, but he was still alive. Astonished, he ran his hands over his breastplate. Except for the impact, there'd been no pain at all.

"I live!" he crowed. He flew a boastful somersault, then pointed his flaming sword toward the earth. "See me, Jorian! I live!"

Somewhere down below, the centaur Cheiftain was staring skyward in disbelief—Artaios could almost feel it. With newfound confidence, he spied the dragonfly again and dove for it.

Rendor unstrapped himself from his command chair and hurried toward the riflemen on the bridge. A crewman tossed him a rifle and Rendor snatched it from the air, kneeling beside the others as they trained their weapons on the swarming tentacles. The *Avatar*'s nose guns chewed through the squirming, pink flesh, splashing blood across the sky. A pack of sooty-faced fairies charged toward the open bridge, deftly avoiding the ogilorn's arms as they fought their way inside. Rendor drew a bead on the nearest one as it clawed against the *Avatar*, pulling its way through the gap. The blast from Rendor's muzzle blew the tiny creature into oblivion.

But Rendor knew they couldn't hold off the onslaught for long. Beyond the massive ogilorn flew Skylords and Redeemers, waiting for their own chance to board the *Avatar*. Rendor's gunners filled the sky with tracers, cutting down their enemies like weeds. Yet wave after wave they came anew.

"Governor!" cried Bottling. He had his hand on the hidrenium lever, ready to swell the envelope. "Should I?"

Rendor's eyes danced around the bridge, then back out at the ogilorn. They could still beat the thing. Maybe.

"Hold off!" he called back to Bottling. "This ugly beast can't live forever!"

Fiona blinked up at the sky, as stunned as Jorian by what she saw. Through the melee of bodies and bullets she saw the gleaming Artaios again, streaking toward the unsuspecting dragonfly. The Skylord had taken Jorian's arrow, shaking it off like rain.

"Still alive," said the bewildered Jorian. He glanced down at his bow, almost oblivious to the battle raging around him.

"What happened?" asked Fiona.

Another Redeemer came screaming out of the sky. Jorian twisted and galloped away just as Tyrin leaped for it. Two flashing blades cut the creature down. Young Tyrin swiveled back toward Jorian. Behind him, Kyros was pumping the air full of arrows.

"Too many!" called Tyrin. Blood streaked his gasping chest. "Jorian, the girl . . ."

"Don't worry about me!" said Fiona. She wrapped her arms around Jorian's chest. "I'm okay!"

Jorian bolted toward clearer ground, then nocked another arrow to his bow. Once more he spied Artaios. "Let's see how many he can take!"

Nausea sloshed over Moth as the dragonfly spiraled toward the ogilorn. The *Avatar*'s starboard guns halted as the crew spotted them approaching, streaking to their aid. Up ahead, Moth could see the bulbous eyes of the monster tracking them across the sky. He braced himself to crash, then heard the rat-a-tat of guns as Skyhigh squeezed the trigger. Bloody pinholes pocked the ogilorn. Tentacles flailed madly toward them. Skyhigh banked left, then right, then straight up high as a suckered arm whipped beneath them.

"Making another pass," Skyhigh shouted. "We clear?"

Moth fought to stay concious as blood drained from his brain. His wobbly eyes searched the sky as the dragonfly leveled out. Skylords and Redeemers still beseiged the *Avatar*. The tenacious ogilorn—half its limbs shredded or limp—continued after the airship.

"I think so," Moth replied.

"You think? C'mon, Moth, look!"

Skyhigh turned the craft hard, slamming Moth sideways. Moth peered through the filthy canopy for enemies. Something caught his bleary eyes.

"Wait . . ."

Coming at them from the left was a Skylord. Unlike the others, this one had broken free from the pack, homing in on them, an outstretched sword dripping fire as he flew.

"That's Artaios!" Moth gasped. He twisted for a better look. Artaios' sword was unmistakable, but now the Skylord wore a golden helmet and armor too. "He's coming after us!"

Skyhigh throttled the engines and the dragonfly sprinted forward. "He'll have to catch us, then," he said, and slammed the craft into a steep dive, right through the storm of arrows.

"Why?" Moth wondered. He clutched his seat with white-knuckled hands. "Does he know I'm in here?"

"Keep a lookout!" ordered Skyhigh. "Where is he?"

Moth could barely turn his neck to see. Artaios and his burning sword were gaining like a meteor.

"He's right on top of us!" he shrieked.

Skyhigh cursed and pulled up in a tight loop. For one quick second they glimpsed Artaios through the top—now bottom—of the canopy, changing course in a fluid arc and coming at them once more. Head to head, Skyhigh only had a moment. He lined up his guns and squeezed the trigger, spraying a fusillade of lead. Undeterred, Artaios kept on coming. He weaved through the bullets, raised his sword like a jousting lance, and put it through the dragonfly's nose.

Metal screamed. Moth cried out. "Hold on!" Skyhigh shouted. "I got it!"

But he didn't have it. They were going down.

Artois watched, stunned, as the dragonfly plummeted. For the briefest second he had seen something inside the craft, something he hadn't expected.

Moth . . .

He hovered helplessly as the dragonfly went down, not even seeing the bolt until it struck him. Jorian's glowing arrow slammed into his back, sending him tumbling through the sky. Artaios flexed his wings, shook off the shock, and spiraled down after Moth. Below him, another lightning bolt appeared.

Rendor tumbled, sliding across the floor as the ogilorn took hold of the *Avatar*. Men were firing their guns and shouting. A sliver of daylight shined through the open bridge as the ogilorn's pink flesh pressed against the ship. Rendor kept hold of his rifle, managing to roll himself onto his belly. He fired off another shot, as ineffectual as all his others. The *Avatar* shook as the tentacles closed around her, the eerie noise of rubbery suckers pulling at her sheathing. Donnar stumbled across the deck, dropping down near Rendor.

"Order the swell!" he barked. "Now!"

Rendor looked at his friend, unable to speak. They stared at each other. Rendor nodded.

"Bottling, do it!" Donnar ordered.

Still at his station, Bottling steadily pushed the lever forward. A faint hissing noise filled the bridge as the *Avatar*'s envelope swelled with volatile hidrenium.

Jorian and Fiona had nowhere to run.

Overhead, the sky turned black with Redeemers. Fairies and cloud horses blotted out the sun, and the Skylords circled like buzzards over the battlefield. Jorian and Kyros bounded over bodies. Protected by Tyrin's double blades, they fired endlessly into the sky. Around them, their fellow centaurs fought on, snatching Redeemers out of the air and crushing them beneath their hooves. But Fiona knew their cause was lost. The Skylords were just too many.

"Where's Artaios?" raged Jorian, searching the sky for him. He had launched five bolts against Artaios, all of them magically on target. Yet somehow the Skylord prince had persisted, flying on when even a single shot should have felled him. Fiona hugged her arms around Jorian. Unafraid for herself, she wanted only to save him.

"Jorian, go," she pleaded. "Go back to Nessa. I'll stay!"

Jorian glanced at her over his shoulder. "A centaur never runs, Little Queen. Remember what I told you? If they want you, they come through me!"

Fiona wanted to tell him it was hopeless; that he couldn't win no matter what. But she couldn't, and she didn't apologize either. She looked up in the sky, saw the swirling hordes, and cast aside her bow. Forget arrows. What she really needed was a big stick to bash some Skylord brains.

"Let me down!" she ordered Jorian. "I want to fight!"

"Don't you move!" Jorian thundered.

"Down! Let me—"

Fiona didn't see the Redeemer until too late. Like a battering ram it came at them, slamming into Jorian and spilling Fiona to the ground. She landed hard, knocking the breath out of her lungs and rattling her skull. She clawed to her knees just as a trio of Redeemers fell upon Jorian. Kyros and Tyrin galloped toward him. More of the creatures descended to stop them.

Fiona didn't cry or scream. She dug a rock out of the ground with her fingernails, gripped it like a hammer, and raced toward the Redeemers. She had almost reached them when another figure swooped down on her. Ivory arms swept around her waist. Suddenly she was flying, pulled aloft by snow white wings.

A Skylord!

Fiona hefted her rock. Twisting, she saw the Skylord's beautiful face, then realized the creature was smiling. Long, golden hair fanned out over her naked shoulders. She bore no weapons, wearing only an ill-fitting wrap of fabric. Fiona looked into the Skylord's mysterious eyes and knew her.

"Esme!"

Lady Esme carried Fiona away rapidly. But she hadn't come alone. Behind her came three enormous dragons, spitting flames and winging easily through the Skylords and their minions. Down below, a giant, feathered female dragon dropped to the battlefield. She reared her muscled neck, let out a furious roar, then cut a burning swath through the Redeemers.

Jorian and his centaurs broke from their attackers. The centaur Cheiftain stared up at the dragon. For the very first time, Fiona saw an expression she'd never seen him wear before.

Awe.

Up in the *Avatar,* Rendor cluched the Starfinder, ready to order the explosion. He had taken the artifact out of its lockbox, cradling it in his lap as he calmly counted the seconds, waiting for the ship's envelope to swell with just enough hidrenium to make the stuff unstable. Around him his crew continued the fight, each man picking up a rifle and firing hopelessly at the ogilorn, its oozing flesh still bulging into the bridge.

Rendor didn't pray or feel afraid. He was ready to die. All he really wanted was a big enough explosion to blow the Starfinder to bits. Beside him stood Donnar, pistol in hand. Instead of aiming his weapon at the ogilorn, Donnar trained it on the roof. One bullet there, and the envelope would blow. One bullet, and the *Avatar* would die.

Rendor heard the hissing stop. He could feel the pressure of the airship around him, filled to bursting now with hidrenium. Donnar closed his eyes.

"Wait!" screamed Gann.

The *Avatar* lurched starboard. Outside, something roared. Gann pointed toward the opening in the bridge. There, the sliver of sunlight started to grow. Rendor leaped up and grabbed Donnar's arm, pulling down the pistol before he could fire. He didn't know how or why, but the ogilorn was letting go.

"Vent the envelope!" Rendor screamed.

Bottling stumbled back toward his console, madly pulling levers as he reached it.

"Stop firing!" Donnar shouted. He hurried toward a speaking tube and screamed the order to the rest of the crew. “Hold fire! Hold! Hold!”

Rendor inched toward the opening in the bridge as the *Avatar* righted herself. The ogilorn’s tentacles were dropping away. He peered past the wounded monster, straining to see. A red blast of flames burst against the ogilorn, slicing through it like a sword.

“Donnar, bring us about!” Rendor cried. “Bottling, vent to nominal!” He clutched the Starfinder, raising it up like a trophy as he watched the dragons streak across the sky. “Stringfellow, get us back in the hunt.”

FALLEN ANGEL

"MOTH?"

In the dark, bleary world of his mind, Moth barely heard his name.

"Moth?"

He recognized the voice. Moth forced open his eyes. In front of him sat Skyhigh, still strapped inside the dragonfly. But they weren't moving. Slowly, Moth remembered what had happened.

"Moth, answer me . . ."

Skyhigh's voice was breathless, shaky from the crash. Moth glanced through the shattered cockpit. Covered in earth, the dragonfly had ditched in the grass. The engine had stopped. Moth could hear his heartbeat pounding in his skull and the distant sounds of battle. He checked himself, flexing his fingers, counting them.

"I'm okay," he answered.

For a long time Skyhigh didn't move. He breathed out hard, then ran a hand over his forehead.

"Skyhigh?"

"I'm bleeding," said Skyhigh, checking his palm. "We have to get outta here."

Moth fumbled with his straps. Skyhigh fought to open the jammed canopy. Moth reached up to help him, and together they managed to pry away the mangled metal. As the canopy opened overhead, Moth peered toward the battlefield. The centaurs were charging into one enormous mass. Above them, the Skylords and their army swirled in disarray. As he climbed out of the dragonfly, Moth saw the distant *Avatar* turning back toward the valley. This time, though, the airship wasn't alone.

"Dragons . . ."

Skyhigh turned to see. "What?"

"Look," pointed Moth. "Dragons!"

They had crashed far from the battlefield, but the sight of the dragons was unmistakable. Jets of fire spat from their throats as they spiraled after their enemies, burning them from the sky. Jorian's centaurs pressed toward the mountains as the *Avatar*'s guns opened a broadside. Moth and Skyhigh stared, dazed by the sight. Then, from the corner of his eye, Moth noticed a ruffle of white feathers.

There stood Artaios, mere yards from their dragonfly. He sheathed his flaming sword and took the golden helmet off his head, casting it aside. A shocking crimson scar ran down his beautiful face. His right shoulder and right wing drooped as though broken. He looked mournfully at Moth, then at Skyhigh.

"You see, Moth?" he said. "Only I can teach you to fly."

"Artaios . . ." Moth stepped forward. "What happened?"

"Your beloved Alisaundra did this to me," he said. His tone was calm but contemptuous. "I gave her wings. I gave her life meaning. She has ruined me."

Skyhigh went to Moth's side. "Where is she?" he demanded.

"She couldn't kill me," spat Artaios. "I am the Sword of Korace. Even Jorian's lightning cannot kill me now, human."

"Artaios, where is she?" Moth asked fearfully. "Did you . . . ?"

"I gave her a chance to serve me! Just as I gave you a chance to fly." Artaios glared at Skyhigh. "You—did I not tell you to flee? Did I not warn you to take the boy from here, to spare him this?"

Skyhigh reached into his belt and pulled out Rendor's pistol. Artaios scowled at the threat.

"I wear the armor of Ivokor," he said. "If you had any learning at all, you would know what that means. There is no way you can harm me."

Skyhigh aimed the gun right at his chest. "Let's see about that," he said, and cocked the hammer.

"I can't let you leave now," said Artaios. He moved closer. "I tried to spare you."

"Not another step!" warned Skyhigh.

"Artaios, go!" cried Moth.

Artaios didn't flinch. "Do it!" he ordered.

So Skyhigh squeezed the trigger.

Moth jumped back at the noise, then saw Artaios stagger. A look of utter shock came over him as he glanced down at his chest. A small hole in his golden armor started oozing scarlet blood. Artaios blinked as if he'd never seen such a thing before, as if the impossible had happened. He wavered a moment, then buckled to his knees.

"I am shot . . ."

Skyhigh lowered the pistol as Moth hurried toward Artaios. The Skylord looked up helplessly as Moth put his arms around his shoulders, seeking a way to remove the breastplate.

"Moth, leave him," said Skyhigh. "We have to get out of here."

"Get me something to make a bandage," cried Moth. "Please!"

Artaios fell back against the grass. "Ivokor . . ."

"It wasn't magic, Artaios," Moth explained. He found the latches on the side of the breastplate. "Just a bullet."

Artaios grimaced, understanding. Skyhigh came to stand over him. He hesitated, then helped Moth remove the armor. They rolled Artaios over to pull it off, then opened the white garment covering his chest, now soaked with blood. Beneath the garment was a perfectly plain bullet hole, just inches beneath the Skylord's heart.

"Skyhigh, what do we do?"

Skyhigh studied the wound. "Stop the bleeding. Somehow."

Moth pulled off his shirt, packing the wound with it and pressing down to stem the blood. A shadow settled over them as they knelt beside Artaios. Looking up, they saw a chariot pulled by cloud horses hovering a hundred feet above them. A Skylord leaped from it, sailing quickly toward them. Behind him, others darted down from the sky.

"Uh-oh," said Skyhigh. "Company."

Artaios was quickly losing consciousness. Skyhigh stood as the Skylord from the chariot fell like a falcon before them. Moth glanced up, recognizing his eye patch and battle-scarred face.

"Rakuiss. You need to get Artaios out of here," said Moth. He didn't bother greeting the Skylord or explaining what had happened. "You have to hurry or he'll die."

General Rakuiss looked down in shock at his wounded prince. Skyhigh once more pulled out his pistol.

"I got five more shots just like the one I put in Artaios," he warned. "Get him out of here and let us go. Otherwise you'll both be a couple of dead flying chickens."

The other Skylords dropped from the air. The general held them back. He knelt down over Artaios, stroking his golden hair.

"My prince, can you hear me?"

Artaios opened his glazed eyes, nodding.

"You're hurt," said Rakuiss. "The humans. But I'm going to save you. I'm going to get you out of here. You must hold on."

Artaios lifted his head and saw Moth over him, pressing down on his chest, hands coated in blood. He grabbed Rakuiss' wrist, and with the little strength he could muster said, "Humans . . . saved me."

Rakuiss reared back. "No, my lord. The humans did this to you."

"No!" railed Artaios. "They go!"

Rakuiss relented, pushing Moth aside. "All right, my lord," he said. "Yes."

He scooped Artaios gently into his arms, then winged skyward toward his waiting chariot. Without a word, his fellow Skylords followed.

THE VIEW FROM THE HILL

LADY ESME CARRIED FIONA far from the fighting, setting her down on a hillside overlooking the battlefield. The flight left Fiona breathless as she tumbled into the dandelions, then watched Esme drop soundlessly to the ground. The beautiful Skylord said nothing as she observed the unfolding battle. She sat down among the flowers like a child, wrapping her arms around her knees and her delicate wings around her shoulders. Fiona approached her carefully, wondering why she didn't speak.

"Esme?"

The Skylord tilted her golden head. Her brilliant eyes flicked toward Fiona, then back to the battle. The strangeness of her unnerved Fiona.

"You know who I am, don't you?" asked Fiona.

Esme smiled. "You are Fiona."

"That's right." Fiona knelt down beside her in the dandelions and buttercups. "You saved me. You brought the dragons to help us, didn't you?"

Esme's gaze tracked upward, toward the dragons burning up the sky. Out on the field, the centaurs had regrouped. Fiona heard the keen of Jorian's horn, but could not make him out among the throng. The remaining Skylords flew in confused circles, some of them abandoning the fight. Her uncle's airship pursued them, joining the dragons in the hunt.

"Who are they?" Fiona asked, gesturing toward the dragons. "Are they Merceron's friends?"

Esme looked unhappy. Frail, too. The garments she wore were haphazard, obviously thrown together just for modesty. But she really was beautiful, and Fiona had no trouble understanding why Leroux had loved her.

"Dreojen?"

Esme pointed toward one of the distant dragons. Fiona smiled. Merceron's mate was smaller than the others, but still a powerful, magnificent sight. Suddenly she remembered the mask Jorian had drawn on her face.

"Esme, you have to take me back," she said. "I can't stay here. I belong with the others."

Esme grimaced as she watched her fellow Skylords tumbling from the sky. "You will stay here," she said. "Safe."

Fiona couldn't understand. "Hey, you brought them here," she said. "What did you think would happen? You should be down there fighting with the dragons. We both should."

"I am a Skylord," said Esme. "I could never harm another."

"After what they did to you? Huh. I'd be glad to fight them if they did that to me."

Esme had no answer for her, or if she did she didn't speak it. For Esme, speaking came with effort. Fiona supposed it was from being a bird for so long.

"Okay," said Fiona, standing. "You can sit here and watch if you want, but I have to go."

Esme reached up and seized her hand. "No."

Fiona pulled free. "Esme, I have to! I promised I'd fight with them. I can't just run away."

"The battle is done," said Esme. "You will stay here. Stay safe." Her eyes fixed on Fiona, determined. "I will protect you."

With a sigh Fiona collapsed back into the flowers. If she tried to flee, she was sure Esme would just scoop her up again.

"Moth's out there too, you know," she said. "Why don't you go and find him?"

"Moth is safe."

"How do you know?"

"He is special to Artaios. He will not be harmed."

Puzzled, Fiona tried to locate Moth on the field, but they were too far away to see much of anything. Up in the sky she saw the *Avatar*, but no dragonfly, and wondered if Moth and Skyhigh were dead.

"What will happen now?" she asked. "What will you do, Esme?"

The lady lowered her chin to her knees. "I do not know."

"Can't you go back to the other Skylords?"

"I am an outcast now. Artaios proclaimed me so."

"Then you can stay here, with the centaurs," said Fiona. "I'm sure they'll take you, just like they did me. You'll be a hero, Esme."

"Hero?" Esme's expression darkened. "I am a traitor, child. If I am ever remembered for anything, it will be that."

A FRIENDLY FACE

BY THE TIME MOTH AND SKYHIGH had trudged back to the battlefield, the fighting was done. The dragons had chased off the two remaining ogilorns with the help of the *Avatar*, and Artaios' leaderless army scattered like birds after a gunshot. Moth stopped at the edge of the field, horror-stricken by the sight. Centaurs and Skylords lay dead atop each other, frozen in combat, their bent limbs intertwined. Redeemers and fairies lay among them, wings twitching as they tried to reach the sky. Lost feathers tumbled across the grass.

Overhead, he watched the Skylords flocking back to Mount Oronor. The dragons broke off from the ogilorns. The trio circled high above the battlefield but did not descend.

"Why don't they come down?" Moth wondered.

Skyhigh watched them with a shrug. "Dragons and centaurs don't like each other much," he said. He gestured out toward the middle of the field. "Look."

Amid the carnage stood Jorian. He too stared up at the dragons. But he did not wave at them or call to them or blow his horn in thanks, and that baffled Moth. Jorian merely watched them, looking bemused. Finally, the dragons made one more circuit over the valley, then headed off the way they'd come.

"Oh . . ."

Moth felt himself deflate. He wanted to cry out to them, to beg them to come back.

"We should help," said Skyhigh. He gazed exhaustedly at the bloody field. Moth straightened, determined not to be sick. He was a man now, surely. Facing so much misery, there was no way he could ever be a kid again.

Throughout the day Moth worked with the centaurs, bringing water to the thirsty and dragging the wounded away from the dead. Moth went where Jorian directed him, even offering aid to the Redeemers and fairies, all of whom rejected him. Those that could manage it pulled themselves from the field, beginning the long walk home to the Skylords, while others simply closed their eyes and died. Their sick devotion frightened Moth, because he knew the Skylords had abandoned them.

The *Avatar* limped back toward the village and did not return. As for Fiona, there were rumors that Lady Esme had returned, and that she had taken Fiona to safety. Moth worried about her but did not stop working, determined to remain on the field. He worked through the afternoon without a break, then into nightfall. Then, when he could barely stand any longer, he went to Jorian again. The Chieftain stood at the edge of the field. Moonlight blanketed the numerous dead.

"What else?" asked Moth as he slumped toward Jorian. His eyes were heavy, his back aching.

Jorian studied him. His stern face nodded. "On to me."

"Huh?"

"We're going," said Jorian. "You have done a centaur's work today, boy."

He reached down his hand. Reluctantly, Moth took it and let Jorian pull him onto his back. As the Chieftain headed back toward the village, the rocking of his gait lulled Moth to sleep.

It might have been an hour or two or a day or two—Moth couldn't say how long he'd slept. He awoke with the kind of heaviness that comes after being very ill, or very, very tired. He remembered riding on Jorian's back. He remembered the battlefield and dreaming about all the dead. He dreamed about Artaios, too, but when he opened his eyes, the dream disappeared.

He was in a bed of straw and realized at once it was Jorain's house. A wave of ease washed over him. He made a contented mewing sound. Fiona appeared from a corner of the room.

"Finally! You know how long you've been sleeping? I wanted to wake you but they said not to."

She was smiling, kneeling down beside him on the straw.

"You washed your face," noticed Moth.

"Huh? Oh, yeah . . ." Fiona touched her face where Jorian had drawn the dragon. "Nessa washed yours off, too."

Moth brushed his cheeks. He'd mostly forgotten his kestrel markings. "Esme?"

Fiona shook her head. "No."

Moth sat up. "What happened?"

"She's gone, Moth." Fiona put her hand on his shoulder. "She didn't speak to anyone, just me. She carried me to a hill away from the fighting. When it was over she took me back to the village. Then she flew away."

"What?" Moth tried to make sense of it. "She's gone? But she didn't even see me! When did she go? How long?"

"Yesterday. You've been asleep since then."

"I should have come back here!" Moth gasped. "If I hadn't stayed on the field . . ."

"No," said Fiona, shaking her head. "I told you—she just dropped me here and left. She said she knew you'd be safe. That didn't make much sense to me, but . . ." She smiled at Moth. "Hey, we're all still alive! My grandfather, Skyhigh . . . we made it, Moth."

"Not everyone made it," sighed Moth. He slipped back into the straw, despairing as he stared at the ceiling. He wondered how long it would take him to forget what he'd seen. "I can't believe I missed Esme. Why? Why'd she just fly away?"

Fiona flicked a strand of hair out of her face. "I could tell she was sad about bringing the dragons here. She saw them killing other Skylords. I guess she blamed herself. She said she was an outcast now. A traitor."

"But she saved us!"

"Yeah." Fiona nodded. "She knows. I just don't think it made her feel much better."

Moth closed his eyes. "After all this. All we went through, and I didn't even get a chance to see her."

"Hey," said Fiona. She gave him a sharp nudge. "Get up. There's someone you should meet."

SOMEDAY

THEY LEFT THE VILLAGE BEHIND, following a light glowing in the field and using the moon to guide them through the grass. Fiona held Moth's hand, moving excitedly through the night but somehow managing to keep her surprise a secret. Moth peered far ahead, at a giant outline lit by firelight. His fingers tightened around Fiona's.

The thing in the field looked like Merceron, but of course it wasn't. It was certainly a dragon, though.

"But she left," whispered Moth. "With the others. I saw them leave."

"She came back, Moth," said Fiona. "When you were sleeping. She came back to see you."

"Me?" Moth stared at the silent, star-gazing dragon, suddenly afraid. "She knows about Merceron. She must."

"Esme told her everything. Esme was the one who brought them here."

"Maybe she blames me," worried Moth. "For what happened to him. You think?"

"No . . ."

"Why's she here, then? What'd she say?"

"She came and spoke to Jorian. She asked permission to stay here till you woke up." Fiona took another step, waving for Moth to follow. "Don't be afraid. I'm not, and you remember how I felt about dragons!"

But Moth wasn't afraid for himself. Dreojen wouldn't harm

him. It was her expression he feared, the pain he knew he'd see in her eyes. He followed Fiona deeper into the field, leaving the village far behind until the noise from the centaurs died away completely, and only the sound of the wind and the crackling of Dreojen's fire could be heard. They stopped several yards from the dragon, who barely stirred.

"Dreojen?" called Fiona. She gently nudged Moth forward. "This is Moth."

The dragon finally looked away from the stars. Her horned head turned on her sinewy neck. A bit of flame sparkled in her mouth. Moth looked into her golden eyes, amazed by her. Her bronze scales shined like gemstones, reflecting the firelight, and a mane of colorful feathers flowed like water down her neck. A regal velvet cape blanketed her wings. She pulled at it with her claws to cover herself from the breeze. She lowered herself over Moth for a closer look, her expression curious.

"I was on my way home," she said at last, "when I realized I had to see you. I had to know what you looked like so I could remember Merceron properly."

Moth tilted up his face so she could get a good look at him. "I'm really just a kid," he said awkwardly. "Nothing special. Merceron was special." He had to swallow to keep from choking up. "He gave his life for me and Esme. I know that's why you're here . . ."

Dreojen brought her head even lower. "Do you know why he did that?"

"No," Moth answered honestly. "I don't. He hardly even knew me." He shrugged. "Like I said, I'm nothing special."

Dreojen crinkled her heavy brow, as if she knew a secret. She almost decided to speak it, then stopped herself. Her red lips curved in a smile. "Merceron must have thought you were worth it."

"The Skylords wanted the Starfinder," Moth explained. "But Merceron wouldn't give it to them. All he had was himself. Did Lady Esme tell you that?"

"Esme found us in our lair in the White Cliffs," said Dreojen. "She told me that you were a special child, and she told me how Merceron died. If you're afraid I am angry, do not be. I am more proud of my mate than I have ever been in my life. And dragons live a very long time!"

She laughed, and her ease made Moth laugh, too. Fiona came closer, and Dreojen looked up at the stars again. Moth finally realized she was looking at the constellation of Merceron.

"I forgot about the stars," he confessed. Without the Starfinder to bring them to life, they were nothing special, either. "It doesn't look like him."

"It never did," said Dreojen. "At least not to us. Just to the Skylords."

"Who'll replace him up there now?" asked Fiona. "In the Starfinder, I mean."

Dreojen sighed contentedly. "No one. Not as long as your grandfather keeps the Starfinder away from here. The Skylords have no dominion without it." She glanced down at Fiona. "He will take it home, won't he?"

"As soon as the *Avatar*'s able to leave," said Fiona. "Maybe a week or two. She took a real beating."

"What about you?" Moth asked Dreojen. "Where will you go?"

"Back to the White Cliffs," replied the dragon. "There's a library there. It's small, but it's our job to protect it. Merceron never had the chance to tell you about it, Moth. It's all left of our culture."

Moth moved closer to her. "Dreojen, can you take me there?" he asked. "I'd love to see that, just for a little while. The *Avatar* won't be ready to go for days. If you could take me there . . ."

"No," said Dreojen gently. "You belong here with Jorian and the others. The centaurs will keep you safe until you're ready to leave." Her golden eyes filled with sympathy. "But . . . maybe someday."

"Yeah," agreed Moth. "I'll be back. I know I will. I'm going to see you again, Dreojen. The other dragons too. Someday."

THE WAY HOME

THREE WEEKS AFTER THE WAR with the Skylords, the *Avatar* headed for home.

With the help of the centaurs, Fiona's grandfather and his crew had patched the holes in the airship's hull and constructed a new fabric covering for her bridge, one much sturdier than the tarp she'd been using. While Bottling worked to straighten the bent blades of her engines, Donnar and the others tested and retested the *Avatar*'s systems and made ready for her second trip over Pandera's treacherous mountains.

Dreojen had left the valley the same night she introduced herself to Moth, and Lady Esme had never returned. Moth supposed she was in hiding from the other Skylords, much the same as Merceron had been for all those lonely years. He thought about Esme often during those weeks in Pandera, and now he thought of her again as the *Avatar* passed over the river from the sunken forest, the very river Raphael Ciroyan had used to ferry them to safety. Just like Esme, they had never seen Ciroyan again either.

"I bet he's down there somewhere," said Moth as he leaned out over the observation deck. The water of the river churned slowly below them, reminding him of their first happy days in this world.

"Who?" asked Fiona. Lost in her own thoughts, her eyes had hardly left the direction of Pandera.

"Raphael," Moth whispered. "I bet he's looking up at us right now."

"I bet he's getting a massage from some mermaid," quipped Fiona. But she no longer seemed jealous. Her eyes shone with a pride that hadn't been there when they'd left Calio, before she'd become Jorian's "Little Queen." The wind on the platform stirred her orange hair. Fiona let it blow across her face.

"Maybe we'll see him again someday. Maybe one day he'll come back to Calio."

"I don't think so, Moth," said Fiona. "Too cold there for him. And too dangerous."

Moth was about to speak when he noticed Fiona's grandfather coming up behind them. The old man was digging into his frock coat for his pocket watch.

"Who are you talking about?" he asked, only half interested. He popped open the watch and studied its face. Moth and Fiona looked at each other with a secretive grin.

"No one," Fiona answered. She turned from the railing. "Grandfather, do you think there are other humans here?"

Rendor snapped his watch shut. "Others? Not likely. You saw how many Redeemers the Skylords have made." He stepped up to the railing. "The Skylords know everything here. No human can hide from them for long."

"Yeah," nodded Fiona. "I guess you're right."

"What about the Skylords?" asked Moth. "Do you think they'll come after us?"

"Not us," said Rendor. "The Starfinder." He put his arms around them both, gathering them close. Together they gazed out over the beautiful, magical landscape. "The Skylords won't stop," he sighed. "Even if Artaios is dead. All we did is bloody their noses and make them mad. They'll be back."

Moth stood tall, reassured by Rendor's embrace. "And we'll be ready for them."